Praise for
If Tomorrow Never Comes

"*If Tomorrow Never Comes* is a touching story of hope through surrender. Marlo Schalesky weaves a poignant story with a unique twist, touching the heart of those who struggle with unfulfilled dreams, reminding us things are not always as they seem."
— RACHEL HAUCK, best-selling, award-winning author of
Sweet Caroline and *Love Starts with Elle*

"*If Tomorrow Never Comes* is another beautiful, outside-the-box story from Marlo Schalesky. At turns painful and joyful, it was inspiring to see God work in the lives of two people who are so in love and yet so broken by infertility and the shadows of the past. Highly recommended!"
— TAMARA LEIGH, author of *Faking Grace* and *Splitting Harriet*

"Marlo Schalesky is one of my favorite authors. Within just a few pages of *If Tomorrow Never Comes* I was drawn into a world that is hauntingly beautiful and yet real-life all the same. I was swept away in this enchanting story about a mysterious locket, and as with all Schalesky's books, I wasn't disappointed. What a heart-filled, powerful, and well-told story!"
— TRICIA GOYER, author of ACFW Book of the Year winners
Night Song and *Dawn of a Thousand Nights*

"*If Tomorrow Never Comes* is a beautiful and bittersweet story of dreams crushed, but not destroyed. Of first love dying, but not yet dead. And of a merciful God who holds all our fates in his hands. Marlo Schalesky has woven a magical tale you'll have to read twice: once quickly because you have to know what happens next, and once slowly so you can savor the evocative poetry of her writing."

—RICK ACKER, author of *Blood Brothers* and *Dead Man's Rule*

"Kinna's mom had always led her to believe that fulfillment in womanhood is achieved most fully through motherhood. But when Kinna's can-do determination collides with the devastating desperation of infertility, her heart and life feel as barren as her womb. Through surprising plot twists reminiscent of Angela Hunt's style, Marlo Schalesky keeps readers guessing as she offers a challenging new perspective on God's possibilities."

—JENNIFER SAAKE, author of *Hannah's Hope: Seeking God's Heart in the Midst of Infertility, Miscarriage, and Adoption Loss*

"This story gripped my heart from the first page right through to the triumphant conclusion and beyond. Marlo Schalesky has penned a masterful tale about wrestling with both God and shadows from the past, with glimpses of the miraculous woven through. You won't be able to put this one down!"

—JANELLE CLARE SCHNEIDER, author

Other Books by Marlo Schalesky

Fiction
Beyond the Night
Cry Freedom
Freedom's Shadow
Only the Wind Remembers
Veil of Fire

Nonfiction
Empty Womb, Aching Heart

IF TOMORROW NEVER Comes

A NOVEL

MARLO SCHALESKY

MULTNOMAH
BOOKS

IF TOMORROW NEVER COMES
PUBLISHED BY MULTNOMAH BOOKS
12265 Oracle Boulevard, Suite 200
Colorado Springs, Colorado 80921

Scripture quotations are taken from the Holy Bible, New International Version®.
NIV®. Copyright © 1973, 1978, 1984 by International Bible Society. Used by permission of Zondervan Publishing House. All rights reserved. Some Scripture quotations are taken from the New American Standard Bible®. © Copyright The
Lockman Foundation 1960, 1962, 1963, 1968, 1971, 1972, 1973, 1975, 1977,
1995. Used by permission. (www.Lockman.org). Some Scripture quotations are taken
from the King James Version.

The characters and events in this book are fictional, and any resemblance to actual
persons or events is coincidental.

ISBN: 978-1-60142-024-4

Published in association with The Steve Laube Agency, LLC, 5501 North Seventh
Avenue #502, Phoenix, AZ 85013

Library of Congress Cataloging-in-Publication Data
Schalesky, Marlo M., 1967–
    If tomorrow never comes : a novel / Marlo Schalesky. — 1st ed.
        p. cm.
    ISBN: 978-1-60142-024-4
    1. Childlessness—Fiction. 2. Infertility—Fiction. I. Title.
    PS3569.C472813 2009
    813'.54—dc22
                                                        2008044281

Printed in the United States of America
2009—First Edition

10 9 8 7 6 5 4 3 2 1

To my girls:

Bethany…be thankful

Joelle…be truthful

Jayna…be good

Bria…be nice

But with God all things are possible.

MATTHEW 19:26

1

Only the fog is real. Only the sand. Only the crashing of the sea upon the restless shore. The rest is a dream. It has to be. I say it again and again until I believe it, because I cannot be here. Not now. Not with mist dusting my eyelashes, sand tickling my toes, salt bitter on my lips. Not when the whole world has narrowed to a strip of beach, a puff of fog, and a single gull crying in an invisible sky.

This is crazy. Impossible. And I'm too old for crazy. I won't be some loony old woman with a house full of cats. I refuse to be.

Besides, I prefer dogs.

I touch my neck, and my breath stops. The chain is gone. My locket.

My mother's voice teases me. "Not impossible, hon. Improbable. Because with God all things are possible." Her words, spoken in that ancient, quavering tone, hide a laugh turned wheezy with age. I hear her again. "Someday you'll lose that locket, Thea Jean. You just wait." Her grin turns the sides of her eyes into folds of old parchment. "And that's when the adventure will really begin."

But I don't want any adventure. All I want is a comfortable chair, a good book, the sounds of my grandchildren playing tag under the California sun, and my boxer at my feet.

I want to go home.

I glance out over the ripples of Monterey Bay. White-capped waves. Dark water. And then I know. That's what I need to wake me up, get me home. I need a cold slap in the face. Something to shake me from this crazy-old-cat-lady delusion.

I stride forward until the surf kisses my feet, the waves swirl around my ankles, knees, waist, arms. Cold. Icy. Welcome.

The water engulfs me. And suddenly it doesn't feel like a dream.

———

Fog closed in around Kinna Henley as she fell to her knees and pawed in the sand. The grains bit into her hands, filled her fingernails like black soot. And still she dug. Deep into the oozing wetness. Deep enough to bury her sin. Or at least the evidence of it.

No, not sin. She wouldn't call it that. Desperation, maybe. Determination. But not sin. God wouldn't bless that, and He had to bless today. He just had to. She was betting everything on it.

Kinna glanced over her shoulder. Somewhere, a gull cried. Once. Only once. Somewhere, water broke along rocks and sand. Somewhere, the sun rose over the horizon.

But not here.

Here, there was nothing but the fog and the shore and the sand beneath her fingers. Alone.

Barren.

She hated that word.

With a deep breath, Kinna reached into the pocket of her nurse's smock and pulled out six empty prescription vials that didn't bear her name. She held them in her palm. Minute bits of liquid shimmered in the bottoms, reflecting only gray, all that was left of the medication that held her hope, flowed through her veins, and ended in her ovaries. Expensive medication she couldn't afford on her own. But she needed it. She'd tried too long, prayed too long, believed too long…for nothing.

This medication, this Perganol, would change all that. It had to. She closed her fist.

What's done is done. I had to take it, God. Don't You see? I had to.

She turned her hand over, opened it, and dropped the vials into the hole. Then she covered them and pushed a fat, heavy rock over the top. Gone. Buried.

She wouldn't think of how those vials had been accidentally sent to the hospital. Of how they were supposed to be returned. Of how she said they had been. Or how she slipped them into the pocket of her smock instead. She'd told herself it didn't matter, no one would know, no one would care, no one would be hurt. She made herself believe this was the only way. And it was. Nothing else had worked. Not charting her temperature, not a million tests, not herbal remedies, not two failed attempts at adoption. Not even prayer.

A dozen long years of it all had taught her that. God promised happily ever after, but so far, all she'd gotten was month after month of disappointment, pain, and the fear that nothing may ever change.

But now, change would come. The medication was gone, the vials hidden, her ovaries full to bursting.

Finally.

A sound came. A shout, maybe. Kinna leaped up and turned, but no one was there. No one walking down the beach. No one swimming in the surf. No one making sandcastles along the shore.

She wouldn't think of that now. She would not remember the first time she had knelt in this sand, dug in it, made castles at the edge of the water. She wouldn't remember the boy who made her believe fairy tales could come true. Or what happened between them after that.

That was gone. Past. All that remained was the promise that had flowed out of those stolen vials and into her blood. That was all that mattered.

Today, everything would change.

Kinna picked up her bag and strode down the silent beach, her elbows bent, her arms swinging. Fast, determined. Five minutes up, five minutes back, turn and go again. Twice more, and she'd check exercise off her list for the day. Once, she exercised for fun. Now, it was a means to an end, a way to prepare her body, to convince herself that she was doing everything she could, everything she should. That's what life had become.

She sighed and quickened her pace. She missed the old Kinna, the one who laughed easily, who teased, who jogged along the beach just to feel the breeze in her hair and to smell the salty scent of the sea. The Kinna who still believed in fairy tales.

But soon she would believe again. She would laugh, tease, but not jog. Not for nine months, anyway. Because now her dreams would come true and the pain would end. God would finally do for her what she'd asked, begged, and pleaded for so many years.

Once, she'd been so sure that God would answer. So sure of her faith. God would not disappoint her, would not let her down. But the years eroded that faith, washing it away, bit by bit, as surely as the sea washed out the sand on the shore.

Until today.

Now she had faith again. She would stop being that woman filled with pain and doubt. She would be filled with faith…and more.

Right, God? She slowed. *Doctor's orders. Or at least, nurse's orders.*

God didn't answer.

But it didn't matter. She'd waited long enough. Tried, prayed, hoped. And finally, she'd happened upon those vials as if they were meant for her. As though it didn't matter if she just slipped them into her pocket. A simple act. Easy. So why did she still have to bury them in the sand?

She knew the signs of guilt. Growing up as a pastor's daughter taught her that. She knew a lot about guilt.

I did what I had to do. That's all. I can't live like this anymore. It's got to change.

She'd done what she never would have believed. Kinna Henley had become a thief.

She gripped her bag until it creased in her hand, pressing into the flesh of her fingers. Once, she'd wept and stormed, screamed and threatened. She'd sobbed into too many pillows, curled in too many corners, slammed too many doors.

Until now.

A chill slipped under her nurse's smock and twirled around the short hairs near her neck. It was so cold here, so lonely. Not even the call of a gull or the chatter of a sea lion kept her company. Nothing but endless waves and the eerie silence of the mist.

And God, just as silent.

This time, God, don't let me down. Please… Not again.

This time she'd made plans, acted on them. This time, she'd sold her soul. *No, it's not that bad. It's not!*

What if...? What if I fail again?

But it wouldn't come to that. It couldn't.

God would listen. God would relent.

Kinna didn't want fame or fortune, shoes, clothes, or the latest Prada handbag. She didn't want a new car, a new house, or even a new job. All she wanted was a child, a baby of her own. What she'd always wanted, as long as she could remember. A husband, a baby, and happily ever after.

Didn't God say that to His faithful? Didn't He say that all she had to do was pray? How could it be too much to ask for only what every other woman in the world seemed to have? Just a baby. To be a mother. Nothing more. It seemed so simple, so normal, so impossible.

This was her last chance. At least that's what the doctor said. _"One more cycle, Kinna."_ Cycles, not months. Everything was measured in cycles now. _"And then you need to consider in vitro fertilization."_

But she couldn't afford IVF. She couldn't even afford Perganol. The credit cards were maxed, the house mortgaged and mortgaged again. And Jimmy had said no more debt.

She closed her eyes. She'd done everything right. Perfect. She'd taken her prenatal vitamins, eaten her vegetables, not allowed a drop of caffeine to touch her lips, walked each afternoon. She'd charted her basal body temperature for a week, logged the dates, bought not one but two ovulation predictor kits with seven sticks each. She'd tested every day, twice a day, from day eleven to day fifteen. And this day, the time was finally right—the perfect time to conceive.

And, of course, there were the vials.

Around her, the fog swirled and thickened. The ocean murmured words of doubt. She wouldn't listen to that. Not anymore.

She kicked a bit of sand at her feet. A string of dried kelp slid between her toes and sandals. She flicked it away, then reached into her bag and took out the ovulation predictor stick she'd put there. Two lines, both thick, equal. She squeezed it in her hand and then pulled a picture from her bag, a funny photo of a laughing baby with tulips scattered around her. The perfect baby.

Her thumb brushed the baby's face. She blinked.

Stop it, Kinna. God wouldn't let you find that picture if He didn't intend to answer your prayers. She glanced up. *Don't forget, God. I have faith.*

Kinna reached the end of the beach and turned. Then she saw a glimmer in the sand. Silver buried in the tan-and-white blanket of a million tiny grains. She stooped and picked up the long chain, the dull necklace. She turned it over. An oval locket, old and worn. She grimaced. She had one just like it, except hers was new. A gift from Jimmy, who claimed it was an original. How like him to get a cheap knockoff and pretend it was something more.

She ran her finger over the intricate double-tulip design on the locket's surface. She opened it, and a bit of sand fell onto her fingers. She brushed it away.

Inside were two photos—an old man and an old woman, their faces wrinkled but still unfaded by time, clear enough that she could see their smiles, could tell they were happy.

Happy faces, content faces, his half hidden behind thick glasses, hers yellowed by the years. Faces that made her ache. Once, she thought she would look happy like that when she grew old. She and Jimmy. And they would. Just as soon as God answered her prayers.

Kinna closed the locket, dropped it into her bag, and listened as the chain rattled against the ovulation stick.

And then someone screamed.

Someone get me a cat, because I think I really have lost my mind. What was I thinking? This isn't a dream. The water is real. Too real. God is making fun of me, sending me here like this.

But it's not His fault I'm in these waves. I shouldn't blame Him. I've done this stupid thing. Batty old lady. That much, at least, seems true. I'd laugh, except my mouth would fill with salt water. It claws at me with freezing fingers. Reaches, grabs, forces my head under its black surface. And then I feel the first tendrils of fear. Of real, honest-to-goodness terror.

What have I done?

I fight and scream. My arms flail, my hands wave in air too gray, too heavy. The waves pull at me, drag me farther from the shore. My eyes go blind in the salty surf.

One wave. Another. I shout again.

My throat burns and I can no longer scream. Stupid. Crazy. Nuts.

The water grows colder. Arms of ice, embracing, drawing me down. Pulling me to the land of many cats.

Maybe I should have known. Should have seen the truth the moment I knew the locket was gone. Maybe...

But this is crazy.

This is real.

This...

What happens if you die in your dreams?

Kinna whirled toward the sound of the scream.

It came again, a shriek like a blade across her nerves. She faced the water. The sound echoed off the waves.

A cry. A shout. A scream for help.

She heard frantic splashing, a final, desperate cry. She threw her bag onto the sand and raced to the edge of the sea.

There! She could see the figure now, a black shadow on the water's surface.

A wave crested and the figure vanished. No other sound came.

Kinna kicked off her shoes and dove into the water. Cold surrounded her. Waves plunged against her, stinging her eyes, lifting her higher, crashing her down.

For an instant she glimpsed the figure in the water. A woman, older than Kinna, her arms thrashing, her head dipping beneath the waves. Sounds came again. Words and shouts that she could no longer distinguish.

The woman went under.

Kinna put her head down and swam. Hard. Fast. Fighting against the surf and current. Water silenced any further sounds, filled her ears with only the roar of the tide. Stroke, stroke, breathe. Water in her mouth. Salt and bitterness. She paused, glanced up. She couldn't see the woman.

Oh no. God, help…

A flash. An arm. *Was that…?* Then, nothing.

She swam toward the spot. Hoping, praying. Though God had never answered her before, still she prayed, believing, driving herself into the undulating waves.

And then she was there. A froth of white on the surface of the sea. Floundering limbs. Gulping mouth. A final stroke and she was beside the woman, then behind her.

"It's okay. I've got—" A wave silenced her words, drowning them in a salty onslaught.

The woman thrashed. Her arm slammed against Kinna's temple. The world turned black, then gray and green again. Kinna blinked, gasped for air.

The woman twisted and reached out, shouting words Kinna couldn't hear, couldn't understand. She started to climb, thin feet kicking into Kinna's legs. Weak hands, suddenly strong, shoved Kinna's shoulders deeper into the roiling waves.

Water closed over Kinna's head. She shoved the woman away, fought back to the surface. Air stung her lungs, water blinded her eyes.

The woman grabbed for her, but this time, Kinna was ready. She grasped the woman beneath the arms, turning her by force. A foot impacted her stomach. A hand scratched her face.

She shouted in the woman's ear. "Relax! I've got you."

The woman shuddered.

"Don't fight me."

Stiff arms stopped clawing. Kicking legs slowed.

"That's it. Stay loose now."

Kinna secured her grip, turned on her side, and swam one-armed toward the shore. After six strokes the woman grew limp.

"Stay with me."

The woman's breath rasped in Kinna's ear. She would be all right. They would make it safely to the shore.

A wave broke over them and still she swam, the woman pliable but breathing. A gasp. A cough. The waves came quicker, pushing them. Short, choppy, breaking in rolls of froth.

Then Kinna's toes found the bottom. She fought against the last of the surf, the final stretch of the sea. Her feet pressed into soggy sand, her body rose from the water. And then they were free.

Kinna dragged the woman onto the beach and fell to her knees beside her. She spat out a mouthful of water, then leaned, trembling, over the woman's pale face.

The woman's eyes fluttered open and fixed on Kinna. "You?" A single word, barely spoken. Then her eyes fell closed.

"No!" Kinna grabbed the woman's shoulders, pulling her upright and shaking her.

The woman's eyes opened again, staring. Her mouth moved, muttering words Kinna could not hear.

She leaned closer.

"The faces. Not crazy. Not." The words were slurred. "Not a dream." The woman's head tilted, her breath ragged and unsure.

"Shhh. We'll get you to a doctor. You'll be all right."

A hand gripped Kinna's arm. The woman's fingers tightened and pulled her closer. Her mouth moved again, and this time, the words were clear.

"You're Kinna Henley."

Kinna shivered. "How do you know me?"

The woman gave another shuddering breath, then fell back.

And breathed no more.

2

The world stood still. The ocean stopped swaying, the fog froze in place.

Kinna's hand shot beneath the stranger's neck. She angled the woman's head back, bent forward, and blew her own breath into the woman's mouth.

She sucked in a breath and blew it again into the woman.

Again.

Again.

The world started spinning once more. The ocean rumbled. The fog swirled in patches of dark shadow.

Faster. More. Another breath. She'd lost count.

The woman coughed, choked, and breathed on her own. A short breath. Then another, deeper, longer.

Kinna rocked back on her heels.

The woman turned her head. Her hair slipped back, and Kinna noticed a small, red birthmark behind her left ear. A mark shaped like a tiny seashell.

The woman sat up and touched the spot behind her ear. Then she pressed her hand into her chest.

Kinna put her arm around the woman's back, supporting her. She could feel breathing, steady and sure, beneath her arm. Steadier than she would have thought possible after what had just happened.

The woman blinked and focused on Kinna. "You're…"

"Scared out of my socks? Yeah, I'd say so."

"But…"

Kinna shivered again. "But I'm a nurse, so I'll get over it. Lucky for you." She gave the woman a crooked smile.

"A nurse. Of course." The woman glanced at her out of the corner of her eye. "You have bad breath."

Kinna stiffened. Her voice turned flat. "You're kidding me." Her teeth started to chatter. It was cold. So, so cold.

The woman's eyes slid closed. Then she laughed, an awkward, gurgling sound that made her chest ripple like the surface of the sea.

Kinna rubbed the woman's back. She seemed warm, too warm for someone who had just been pulled out of a freezing bay. "Next time I'll stop for a breath mint before saving you, okay?"

The woman peeked at her through one eye. "Take two."

Tread gently, Kinna. Just like at work. Her tone softened into her hospital voice. "Well, how 'bout you tell me your name, and then we'll go from there. All right, honey?"

A smile brushed the woman's lips. "Honey, is it? Name's Thea. Only my mother calls me honey, and only when something's wrong."

Kinna sniffed. "I call all my patients that." Still, Thea was right. *Honey* sounded strange out here on the beach with the water pounding along the shore and the fog still twisting over the sand. It was a word she only used at the hospital, and usually with patients she expected to die. A chill raced over her. Surely Thea wouldn't die now. She sounded too strong and too ornery. "Sit up straight and be still for a few minutes. Then tell me how you're feeling. Do you have any pain?"

"Pain?"

"You know, that thing you feel right before you say 'ow'?"

"Yeah, pain." She touched her chest.

"Describe the intensity, please."

"Um."

"On a scale of one to ten." Kinna envisioned the little strips at the hospital that showed simply drawn faces with various expressions for every level of pain. "One is like this." She stared with a straight mouth. "Ten is this." She screwed up her face and stuck out her tongue.

Thea laughed, this time a pure, clean sound. "Stop. That makes it hurt worse."

Kinna smiled and rubbed her hands over her arms. "If you can laugh like that, it's a good sign. Now, describe your pain."

"Three."

The fog thinned and split, allowing a few bright rays of sunlight to trickle along the beach. Warmth sprinkled over Kinna's back and arms. Blessed, beautiful warmth. She tipped up her face. "Well, you'll be all right, then. But you'd better go see a doctor anyway. Wouldn't want your insurance company to lose a chance to deny you coverage, right?"

"I don't suppose I have insurance. Not now." Her voice was still not quite right.

"Good thing you know people in high places then."

Thea closed her eyes then smiled. "Yeah, I know God."

Kinna snorted. "I was talking about me. But believe me, it takes an act of God to get into Emergency this time of day. So"—she stood and held her hand out to the woman—"I'll see what I can do. A nurse has connections, you know."

Thea shook her head. "I'm fine. Don't need a doctor."

Kinna sighed and dropped her hand. "Ah, you're one of those, are you?"

"One of what?"

"The"—she made her voice deep—"I-strong-cavewoman type. No-medicine-man-for-me."

Thea chuckled.

Then the voices came, shooting through the final wisps of fog and mixing with the growing sunlight. Children. Shrieking, laughing, screaming from the far end of the beach beyond where she could see. A girl and boy, young and free.

"Get back." The boy's voice shot over the sand.

"You can't throw it that far."

"Just watch me."

A yellow Frisbee spun through the mist. For a moment, it was visible before plunging into the water.

A splash. Another laugh. Then the voices grew more distant.

Kinna shuddered. Kids. She would not feel that pain. It would be a three on the hospital's scale. She wouldn't notice it at all.

Thea's voice interrupted her thoughts. "Don't you like to hear the children? Everyone likes children."

Of course I do. But… But it wasn't just the children, the reminder of years of pain and disappointment. That was only one edge of the hurt. The other cut deeper. Too deep to turn away. As kids, she and Jimmy ran barefoot on this same beach, darting in and out of the waves, laughing as the Frisbee splashed into the water. They had been too young to guess what would come. Too young to know that fairy tales had to be worked for, planned for. And for that edge, the only remedy lay buried back there in the sand.

Kinna cleared her throat and forced her gaze back to Thea. "All right, let's go. You need to see a doctor. A D-O-C-T-O-R. Right away."

The woman leaned back to lie in the sand "No. And you don't need to spell it."

"Honey."

Thea waved at Kinna. "You know, that really did sound just like my mother." She grinned. "I'll bet you ten bucks you're paler than me."

"Am not." A tiny smile pulled at Kinna's lips. *Crazy woman.* She studied Thea's legs stretched in the sand, her skin loose and full of liver spots, her hands tucked behind her head, supporting her. When Thea stood, she'd probably be a good four inches taller than Kinna and slender, athletic for her age. She wore a beat-up windbreaker that once was red, old sweats, and brand new Nikes. All soaked now and making a shallow puddle in the sand. Not at all the type of clothes one would expect on a woman just fished from the sea. "So, you always go swimming in your jogging outfit?"

Thea glanced down. "Just this time. It was supposed to be a reality check." She looked back at Kinna, meeting her eyes. One eyebrow shot up. "Strange, isn't it, that you pulled me out right at this spot on the beach? They say there's something magical about it, you know. At least, that's what my mother always says. A little piece of heaven on earth hidden behind the big stone on the beach."

This spot? Now she knew the woman was crazy. "I'll take you to the hospital where I work."

Thea blinked. "All business, aren't you? Focused on the goal." She chuckled. "My mom likes to say that you have to tip your head up sometimes and take a look around you. Because you never know what you'll see. So, go ahead. Have a look. Isn't this the most beautiful spot on the beach?"

Kinna barely spared a glance around her. *So what?* A big rock, a stretch of sand, a— *Oh no.* Her heart plummeted into her gut. Not here. She couldn't possibly have swum out of the water here. Of all the places on the beach where the water could have pushed them, why would it bring them to this little cove? Was it fate? Or God? Or guilt? She could not be here, on this tiny stretch of sand hidden behind a strange rock that had stood in this spot forever…or at least for thirty years.

This spot was magical, all right. It was right here that she had first met Jimmy Henley.

Kinna's gaze pulled back to just beside the fat rock, where he sat that day.

God, are You playing a joke on me? Or is this some kind of sign?

"On clear days you can see all the way to Santa Cruz from here." The woman's voice was quiet now, as misty as the thinning fog.

"But not today." The words came as a stunted whisper from Kinna's lips.

"No." Thea sat up again, all signs of trauma gone. She held still. Only those eyes moved, catching hers, looking deep, too deep, as if she could see the secrets Kinna hid there. As if she could read the memory that had come so powerfully to Kinna's mind. A memory she didn't want to see, didn't want to acknowledge.

Kinna jumped to her feet.

Thea didn't move. "What are you so afraid of?"

Kinna straightened her shoulders. "That you'll catch pneumonia. P-N-E-U-M-O-N-I-A." Her voice quivered. That swim must have taken more out of her than she thought.

The woman lifted her hand. "Good spelling. Now, shhh." She closed her eyes.

Kinna's brows drew together.

Thea's lips lifted into a half-smile. "You may glare at me all you want, but I am not going to the hospital with you. You did a fine job of rescuing me. I feel perfectly fit."

"You're welcome. And you can thank me by doing what I want."

For a full minute the woman didn't answer. She didn't get up either. Then she shook her head. "Sometimes not getting what we want is the best thing for us." Her eyes narrowed. "My mother taught me that too."

Kinna bristled. "Well, I'm sure your mother would say to listen to me."

The woman's laughter grew louder, deeper. "I'm sure she would. But I'd like to stay here. For a while more. Will you stay with me? Just to make sure I don't have a relapse or anything."

Kinna sat back down on the sand. *Infuriating woman.* But she liked her. She was quirky, teasing, and fun, like Kinna used to be, before…before…

She shot a glance at the huge rock shaped like a whale's back, at the bits of mussel shells in the sand beneath it. Some things never changed. Some things changed forever. But back then, she hadn't known the difference. She couldn't have.

That day she'd found what she wanted and didn't know it. Today she would find it again, but this time she knew it all too well. Funny she should come back to this very spot. Uncanny, really.

And it was all this crazy woman's fault.

She sat back down and dug her hands into the sand. It was cool still, slightly damp. Just like it had been that day so many years ago.

The first time she saw Jimmy Henley, he had been sitting in this same sand, with dried snot in his nose and a Frisbee turned up before him. Except the Frisbee was green—ugly, booger green. He scooped sand into it with his hands.

She had watched him, hair the color of brown kelp sticking straight up from a buzz cut, bony knees poking from torn swim trunks, his brows drawn in concentration. She walked up to him and stood there, her old doll tucked under one arm, her feet sprinkled with sand.

He didn't look up.

She flicked her foot and sent a few grains flying in his direction.

Still, he ignored her.

That simply wouldn't do. Nobody ignored Kinna Hollis, daughter of the famous Reverend Kenneth Hollis, author, speaker, and pastor of the largest church in the whole state of California. At least that's what Daddy's business card said. All but that last part. And it still said it after they had moved up from LA and the new church wasn't quite as big and Daddy didn't seem quite as famous. Still…

Kinna straightened her shoulders and glared at the boy. "What's wrong with you? Don't you see I'm standing here?"

The boy dumped another fistful of sand into his Frisbee. "I see you." He still didn't look.

She raised her chin. "Well?"

He picked up the Frisbee and shifted the sand until it was smooth. "Well, if you move a little that way"—he motioned with his head to the right—"you'll block the sun better. It's getting in my eyes."

She jammed her fists into her sides. "Who do you think you are, young man?" She used the same voice her mother used on her, or at least a fair imitation of it.

He grinned, set down the Frisbee, and continued scooping sand into it. "I think I'm a John Deere 310 backhoe with a new front-end loader and a bright yellow paint job. Who do you think you are?"

"Are not."

"Nice ta meecha, R-Knot."

Kinna huffed. "That's not my name."

He didn't answer.

She plopped down on the sand beside him and placed her doll on her lap. Strange creature, this boy, but he seemed safe enough. And interesting. She was bored.

"My name is Kinna Ann Hollis. K-I-N-N-A."

"That's a funny name."

She crossed her arms. "It was my grandma's name."

He answered with the "brrrm-brrmm-squeal" sounds of a tractor shifting gears.

"How old are you?"

"Almost nine."

Kinna scowled. He had her by a whole year. "What's your name?"

Finally, he glanced up.

Kinna caught her breath. His eyes were a brilliant blue, deep and shining. Like the fat sapphire earrings her mom wore only on the most specialest of occasions.

"Jimmy Henley."

Jimmy. The name didn't match the eyes. He ought to be called something more fancy, more exotic. "You from around here?"

"Yup."

"Where?"

He poked his finger behind him. "Down the road."

Ah, maybe he didn't deserve a fancier name after all. "I live up it." Even after being here only a few months, Kinna knew the difference between up the road and down it. Up was fine—big homes, big names, important people, "upstanding citizens," Mom called them. Down the road was run-down apartments, liquor stores, the "riffraff." That's what she'd heard. But now she didn't know if she believed it. No one who had sapphires for eyes could be riffraff. That she was sure of.

"So, Kinna Ann Hollis, you gonna stand up and block the sun, or you wanna play?"

"Fine. But I'm not going to sit in the dirty ol' sand and call myself a 3-F-10 thingie."

Jimmy shook the sand from the Frisbee and handed it to her. "Okay. You pretend it's a silver platter with a glass shoe on it. You know that story?"

"It's not a platter."

"Pretend."

She stuck out her chin. "I don't believe in make believe."

He snickered. "Then what's that in your lap?"

She looked down. "My doll. Her name's Sally."

He raised his eyebrows.

She jammed her fists into her hips. "Sally is not pretend. She is for practice. P-R-A-K-T-I-S. Practice."

"You can't just play? You gotta practice at it first?"

Kinna huffed. "No, silly. This isn't play. I practice for when I grow up. My mom says the day I was born was the most beautiful day of her life. She says there's nothing in the world more wonderful than having a child of your very own. So I'm practicing."

Jimmy shook his head. "Girls."

She dropped her arms back to her sides. "What?"

"Girls are dumb. And you may be the dumbest girl I ever met."

Kinna bristled. No one had ever called her dumb. Not ever.

"But I still like you. So, come on. You can bring that doll." He grinned. "Just for practice, of course." He reached for her hand.

She let him take it. His skin was gritty, dirty, but warm. Comfortable against hers. He glanced at her with those jewel-like eyes.

She looked away. "You know how to throw that thing?" She pointed at the Frisbee.

"Sure."

She snorted. Why would he scoop sand into it if he knew how to use it properly? "Show me." She raised her chin, just a little.

He stood and pulled her up with him. Sally fell into the sand. Jimmy shook the remaining grains out of the green disc, turned it, and flicked it toward the water.

Her mouth fell open as it sailed out over the waves. Eventually, it came to rest on the water's surface, too far beyond the wave's crest for her to see it clearly.

He grinned. "Told you."

"Aren't you gonna go get it?"

"No."

"But—"

"It'll come back in. We just gotta wait. Besides, now we can play."

"I thought we were supposed to play Frisbee."

"Do *you* know how?"

She glanced out over the waves and saw a flash of green. Her face warmed. "No."

He chuckled. "Then you be the princess Aurora. You know that story?" His voice grew soft. "It was my mom's favorite. Before…"

"Before what?"

"Nothing." He cleared his throat. "You're Aurora, and I'm Prince Phillip. He's the best prince because he gets to fight dragons with a big sword."

"I thought boys liked GI Joes and stuff. Not princes like this Phillip."

"That's 'cause they don't know about the dragon. What's cooler than killing the dragon and saving the kingdom?"

She folded her arms over her chest. "There's no such thing as dragons."

Jimmy huffed. "Call it practice, then. I don't care. You're Aurora. Your hair's about the right color for Aurora's. It's all pretty dark goldish."

Kinna swished her foot over the sand. "Thanks."

"And I'm Phillip. All we need now is a good piece of driftwood for a sword." He looked around.

Kinna unfolded her arms. She was a princess, huh? She liked that. But it was make believe, and make believe was for babies. "I told you I don't—"

He locked those incredible eyes on her, and suddenly she didn't remember what she'd been about to say. Maybe she was a princess. And maybe he was a prince. And perhaps there would be a happily ever after.

Or not.

But at least she tried. For him. She pricked her finger on a spindle, even though she had no idea what a spindle was. She fell into the sand, her eyes closed, her breathing heavy. She watched, peeking through the slit in one eye, as he battled the ferocious dragon at the water's edge. She held her breath, waiting, as he leaned over her, close, so close, with the dragon defeated and the enchantment about to be broken.

And then a shout shattered the dream. The vision vanished.

Jimmy drew back.

Kinna's eyes flew fully open.

A man staggered toward them, almost running with a weird, half-stiff, half-wobbling gait. A bottle swayed in his hand. "Jimmy!" The man's voice slurred as he slowed. "Get over here."

Jimmy sighed.

Kinna shifted up on her elbows. "Who's that icky man?"

Jimmy smiled, but there was no happiness in it. Just an awful kind of sadness. It pierced her, left her shaking. "Not much of a king, is he? More like the dragon."

"What?"

"My dad. He's not very good at pretending either."

The man stopped shouting, spun, and flopped onto the sand. He took a long drink from the bottle.

Kinna blinked. "What's wrong with him?"

"I've gotta go."

"Your Frisbee."

"You keep it." He turned and walked toward the strange man. "See ya around, Kinna Hollis." He called the words over his shoulder.

She picked up her doll and clutched it to her chest. "See ya, Prince Phillip."

He turned back, and a grin lit his face.

In that moment, Kinna knew her life had changed because Jimmy Henley had come into it, with his fairy tale games and sapphire eyes filled with hope and sorrow.

She sighed and rubbed her face with her hands. That was a long time ago. There were a lot of years, a lot of lost dreams, broken promises, and failed hopes between that day on the beach and now. But still, the truth was, she really did want the fairy tale. Just like she'd practiced.

And yet there was no little-boy Jimmy anymore. Only Jimmy Carlton Henley, a name too big for a simple construction worker, even if he was the foreman.

And there wasn't a little-girl Kinna to be wooed by deep blue eyes and the vision of a kingdom. She was a woman, and that fairy tale had died long ago.

She would never be Aurora again.

And she didn't want to be.

All she wanted was to be Mom. Finally. Because how could she continue to believe in a God who would withhold the one thing she longed for? How could she believe in His love if He never answered her prayers? How could her faith survive if God turned His back again?

And if He did, how could she live without Him?

J immy hated tulips. He hadn't always hated them, but he did now, as he stood like some kind of fool and stared at the white buckets that lined the sidewalk. Cheap buckets, filled with water and cheap bouquets. Cheap roses, cheap carnations, cheap tulips under a cheap canvas umbrella beside a rusty van. Crummy little flowers sold from the sidewalk on a too-hot day in April.

He reached into his back pocket and pulled out his wallet. Tacky blue and faded with time and ground-in dirt until the color had turned a dull gray. He preferred it that way. He turned the wallet over in his hand and opened it, revealing a receipt from Burger King, a frequent buyer card from the hair cutting joint down the street, and behind that, a five and two ones. All he had to his name—seven bucks. Almost nothing.

But it was enough for tulips. Cheap ones, anyway, from a cheap bucket on a hot sidewalk.

Because he loved Kinna. Still.

He pulled out the bills and coughed. Dust swirled through the air from the job site behind him. A car honked, drowning the tinny whine of a radio, the woman's voice singing in Spanish. He could smell sweet, pungent smoke drifting from behind the porta-potty. Alan was at it again. Someone probably ought to do something about that, but it wouldn't be Jimmy. He knew how to mind his own business. The guys appreciated that. He'd learned long ago to keep his head down, his mouth shut. Just run the job like he was told. That's it. No more.

He scratched his head and returned his attention to the tulips and the cash in his wallet.

The woman's singing stopped. A moment later, a short man sauntered from behind the van. "You buy, *hombre?* Or you just stand there blocking view for my customers?" He waved his hand toward the empty road.

Jimmy squinted at the man and moved to the right. "Hiya, Pedro." A few seagulls squawked overhead, headed for the bay.

Pedro grinned. *"Hola, gringo."*

Jimmy smiled. Pedro was twenty-five going on fifty and Mexican. Not Hispanic, not Latino, but Mexican. Jimmy had learned that the first time they met two months ago when Pedro set up shop on the sidewalk beside Jimmy's construction site. On his break, Jimmy had come to look at the flowers and made the mistake of calling Pedro Hispanic. Trying to be culturally sensitive and all. He should have known better.

He remembered how Pedro had crossed his skinny arms over his chest and snorted. "Hispanic? Who Hispanic?"

Jimmy didn't answer.

Pedro glared at him. "My sister Hispanic. My cousin, he Latino. I, Mexican. And proud of it. You remember that, gringo."

After that, he and Pedro had been *amigos,* friends.

Now, Pedro glowered at him much as he had done that day, but Jimmy saw the twinkle behind the scowl. Pedro jabbed a finger at the tulips. "Tulip day today? *Dos meses, sí?* Two months. About time."

Jimmy sighed. He never should have told Pedro he would buy tulips in April, just as he did every year. Now that the day was here, he didn't want to. Not because he didn't want to spend his last seven bucks, not because he didn't like Pedro, but because it wouldn't matter. It never really had. At least, not to Kinna.

Still, every year he'd looked forward to buying them. Red ones, yellow, that funny purple color that she liked best. It had been one of his favorite days of the year. Not anymore.

After twenty years, this was the first time he resented the fat little flowers. Hated the way they curved up, expectant. Hated their simplicity, their plainness. What if he didn't buy them at all?

He snorted. She probably wouldn't even notice. She hadn't remembered in all these years what the tulips meant, hadn't figured it out. But he always bought them for her anyway. Eight tulips on every anniversary of the first time they met. The *real* first time, not the one she remembered.

Every year she thought he got them for her "just because." And every year he planned to tell her the truth. Every year he chickened out. But this year…this year would be different.

Because maybe there would be no tulips.

He glanced down at his wallet. Faded faces looked back at him from a photo marred by a slight coffee stain in one corner. Happy faces, smiling. Kinna's and his, with him standing behind her, his arms around her, half covering the I Lost My Shirt in Las Vegas T-shirt he'd gotten her the day before. A picture from their honeymoon. They'd stayed in a cheap motel, caught the free shows, ate at $2.99 buffets, and were happy. She would have preferred Hawaii, but back then, being together was all that mattered. It was enough.

He frowned. Maybe it was only enough because back then she believed someday there'd be more.

But someday never came. Never would. He still couldn't afford more than a few lousy tulips from a street vendor. No wonder she looked at him like she did. The deadness in her eyes, the coldness, the utter loathing, like he was something she scraped off the bottom of her chintzy, knockoff purse, when all her friends were carrying something called Prada.

Jimmy rifled through the bills again and pulled out the five. Enough for a beer, but he didn't drink. Some days he wished he did. Today more than ever.

Kinna's words came back to him, echoing through his mind. She should have shouted them, screamed at him, shook her fist and burst into tears. She used to do that. Instead, she just stood there, with the cold eyes of a stranger, and looked right through him.

"I can't do this anymore."

"Do what?" he'd asked.

She shook her head. "Maybe if we'd tried IVF last year. Maybe if we were able to have a baby…" Her voice trailed away and died.

He clenched his jaw. IVF. In vitro fertilization. It ought to be IDF, in debt fertilization. He'd told her that before, told her they couldn't afford it, but Kinna was determined.

That was one thing that never changed. She'd bulldoze right ahead, her eyes on the goal. Didn't matter what was true, or real, or reasonable. She'd just push on.

That wasn't fair. Kinna was never cruel; she was just focused. So focused that she often didn't see. Not him or the mess their marriage had become.

Of course, it wasn't all her fault. He'd failed. He wasn't the fairy tale prince, and she wasn't a princess. That was it. End of story.

He wouldn't dream anymore. Kinna despised him for that too—for his hopes, his dreaming. "Stop dreaming and do something," she'd mutter. But dreams were safe. They always had been.

Until now.

The grinding of gears caught his attention. The sound stopped and a voice rose over the rumble of an engine. "Hey, Jimmy, get back to work."

Jimmy glanced up at the man sitting in the Caterpillar. *His* Cat. "My break. And get off my machine."

"Gotta move some dirt. Phase two can't wait." Bill shifted gears and the Cat lurched forward.

Jimmy pulled off his hard hat and rubbed his hand over his forehead. He ought to get back to work. They were behind. Phase one of the parking structure was only half built, phase two barely started, and if they lost money on this job…

Well, he didn't want to think about that. Not as foreman. Not after assuring George they'd make a profit this time. Enough corners were being cut already. So many times he'd had to turn his head and pretend not to see. But the big boss, George, didn't care. As long as the dirt *looked* compacted, that was good enough. As long as things seemed level, they'd better just keep on. If the concrete appeared cured, it didn't matter if the specs required more time. It wasn't right, but what could Jimmy do about it? Foreman or no, he had to do things George's way. It was better to just shut up and do his job. Better to work the Cat, watch the men, and act like nothing was wrong.

Better to get back to work. But he didn't move. He stared at the cheap tulips in the little sidewalk tent manned by Pedro.

"You buy, hombre? Eight tulips? Sí?"

Jimmy sighed. Their yard at home was full of tulips. Some years he'd bought her tulips in a pot, ones that could be replanted. Some years, he picked up flowers from one of the dozens of stands that dotted the street corners. The ones she replanted bloomed each spring, markers of the years, reminders of everything that had gone right, and too much that had gone wrong.

He'd always wanted to tell her the story, tell her why he bought tulips on April 8 every year. But he wouldn't now, even though he'd practiced it a hundred times.

He held the five dollar bill out to Pedro. "Here. You take it. No tulips."

"You pay for nothing?"

"You need it more than me."

"No, amigo."

Jimmy turned away. He didn't want to see the flowers, didn't want to acknowledge what they meant. *Don't think about it. Don't remember. Not today.*

But he remembered anyway. He knew just what he'd say if he ever told her. "Once upon a time, there was a princess of a land not so far away. And into her castle came a peasant boy…"

Of course, it hadn't been exactly like that. But close enough.

It was April 8 when his father had stumbled into the big rich man's church on the corner. It was Jimmy's fault. He'd told his dad he wanted to go to church. Begged him, and been cursed for it. It was Easter, after all, Jesus's resurrection. A day for new beginnings. Hope.

And a bottle of whiskey.

Jimmy should have known better than to ask about church, but his dad did take him in the end. Half-drunk, angry, and late. They sat in the back pew.

And made it three quarters through the service before his dad stood up and cussed.

They made it until the preacher started talking about how God loved everybody, enough to die for them. Dad couldn't stomach the idea of Easter proving God's love. He leaped to his feet as fast as a striking rattler and called the pastor's words the same thing that came out of a bull's hind end. Shouted it out so that every single person looked back and glared. Three ladies gasped.

The preacher, though, he just kept on talking. Didn't miss a beat as Jimmy slipped from the pew and snuck out the back door. He'd hidden in the bushes alongside the church. He remembered the smell of dusty earth and juniper, the way the branches had stuck into his back and made him itchy. He remembered the feel of his Tuffskins and the tightness of sleeves that had grown too short. He remembered how cold it seemed with a huge oak towering above, blocking the sun, and the crackle of a few old, dry leaves beneath him as he shifted his weight. Leaves from that giant oak, dropped last autumn and still waiting here to gossip about his shame. He curled there, mostly hidden, and promised himself, with a lot of sniffing and blinking, that he wouldn't cry. Told himself he didn't care. Pretended he wasn't a no-good nothing, wasn't some old garbage, even with a dad like that.

But he didn't believe it.

Until Kinna came. A girl with a bright yellow dress and hair the color of caramel. Oh, how he loved her hair. She peeked around the bushes and stared at him before sitting right down beside him, not caring that her perfect dress would get smudged with dirt.

He turned his face away, letting his mat of hair fall forward and hide his eyes. His hair was long then, curling over his ears, falling past his eyebrows. He'd gotten it cut the next day. For now, though, he was glad it hid him. He sniffed again and lowered his chin.

Then he saw the tulips, bright splashes of color against a gray background. They lined the walkway in front of him, blocked mostly by the wide juniper he sat behind.

The girl cleared her throat.

Jimmy winced. She would say something about his dad, but he wouldn't cry. He wouldn't. He wouldn't. He wouldn't. Why couldn't this stupid girl see that he wanted to be left alone?

"You like tulips? They're real pretty, aren't they?"

He snuck a glance at her. She smelled good. Clean. And she wore fancy white gloves.

"They're my very favorite. I planted those. Daddy says tulips are the cups from which we drink God's grace. G-R-A-C-E." Her voice turned sing-songish, then went back to normal. "Isn't that so nice?"

Jimmy made a sound in the back of his throat.

"You came in with that icky, loud man, didn't you?"

He hunched his shoulders and turned his head away from her. He knew what was coming next. The scorn, the derision. Or worse, the pity.

"That's okay. God doesn't mind. That man your daddy?"

Jimmy nodded and kept his face hidden.

"Mom says God is our Daddy in heaven. And He loves us just perfect, even when our daddy on earth don't."

Jimmy snorted. God didn't care about him. Why would He? He wasn't anybody. Just the son of a drunk.

It hadn't always been this way, not when Mom was alive. Maybe God had loved him back then. But things went bad after Mom died. They'd turned into this.

Just pretend. Make believe…

Maybe he could dream that God cared. In his dreams, everything was all right again. Nothing bad happened there.

"You okay?"

He drew his knees tighter to his chest. "You heard what my dad said about God's love."

She didn't answer for a moment. He heard the leaves rustle as she rocked forward and snaked her hand between the bushes. She drew her hand back and held a red tulip. She twirled it in her fingers. "You know 'bout the kingdom of God?"

Kingdom? He almost looked up. Now she was talking his language. He loved kingdoms, with princes and kings and scary dragons to be vanquished.

"The Bible says the kingdom of God is like a guy who finds this real beautiful pearl. He sells everything he's got and buys that pretty pearl for his very own."

Jimmy grunted. Great. The kingdom was a pearl. He rested his cheek against a worn spot on his pants. "Then I'll never be able to afford it."

The girl giggled. "No, silly. Don't you see?" She tapped the tulip on his arm, then stuck it into his hand. "You're the pearl."

Jimmy clutched the flower.

The girl sprung up and dusted off her dress. Then she leaned over and her fingers brushed his wrist. "That's what Easter's all about. My daddy said so. And the Bible says so too." Her voice grew as soft as her touch. "God gave everything to buy you." She stepped back.

He lifted his head, but she was gone. He saw a flash of yellow on the sidewalk, heard the faint click of a low-heeled shoe. He brushed the hair from his eyes and stared at the tulip in his hand. In his mind, he heard her words again and hoped they were true. Even if they weren't, it was the nicest thing anyone had ever said to him. He never forgot it. In time, it had changed his life, or at least he'd always believed so.

"Hey, gringo, you in trance or something? Wake up!"

Jimmy blinked.

Pedro stood in front of him. He pushed a small bouquet into Jimmy's chest and handed him back the five dollar bill. "Eight tulips. No charge."

Jimmy backed away and shook his head. "No. No, Pedro. *Gracias.*" He turned.

Metal screeched. Someone shouted. And then a thud shook the earth.

Jimmy's breath stopped.

Shouts erupted from the job site.

"It's Alan!"

"What happened?"

"The earth mover."

"Where's Jimmy?"

Jimmy sprinted up the short hill to the job site. A cloud of dirt filled the air at the back of the site. Men darted out of the rising parking structure and ran toward the raw earth of phase two. Dust settled.

Behind a pad of partially compacted dirt, at the bottom of an incline, the huge earth mover lay on its side, its belly facing the air.

He raced toward it. Alan was on the mover today, but he'd been smoking. And now…

Jimmy clenched his fists. Two men had reached the mover. He could hear them shouting.

"He's under there. I see him."

"He's moving."

"We're coming, Alan. Hang on!"

They were pointing now, one squatting, the other looking back, searching. For what? For who? Him? *Oh no.*

The squeal of gears sounded behind him. He glanced back.

Bill sat in the Cat, his face grim, his gaze bouncing from Jimmy to the fallen mover. The Cat stopped. Bill leaned out. "You'd better do this, Jim. You're better than me."

Cold sweat broke out on Jimmy's forehead. Him? No. What if…? He couldn't.

"This Cat's the only thing that's gonna lift that mover."

For a moment, his heart stopped. Dust filled his mouth. Words stuck in his throat, clogging his breathing. He forced them out in a breathless rush. "You're already up there, Bill. You'd better take it. Hurry."

Bill's eyes met his. Something flickered there. Then Bill slammed the Cat into gear and rumbled forward.

Jimmy sprinted toward the mover. Pete and Mike knelt beside it. Their knuckles whitened as they gripped the mover's door. It didn't budge. He slipped up beside them. He saw Alan's arm first, gray and splayed with dirt. Alan's face was pale behind the mover's cracked window, his eyes wide, his mouth gasping. Dirt plastered his forehead, his hard hat flung free of the wreckage. Then Alan's body, twisted, the gear shaft pressed into his ribs.

Jimmy tilted forward. If Bill didn't pull that mover up just right, those ribs would break.

Alan's eyes closed. His chest heaved with each breath. Then his eyes fluttered open, and his gaze caught Jimmy's. Fear and questioning, and a stab of disbelief.

"It'll be all right, man," Jimmy called to Alan, praying his voice would be steady, that his own doubts and fears wouldn't show. "Just hang on."

Alan's Adam's apple bopped twice as he blinked his acknowledgment.

The Cat rolled up, stopped. Its great claw reached toward the mover.

"His leg's pinned," Mike hollered up to Bill. "Careful. I don't think it's broken yet."

Jimmy's gaze darted up to Bill. *Easy now, not too fast.* The claw came closer, hooked around the mover's frame.

Pull. Easy.

The mover tilted up, just a bit.

Bring it back now. Back! Slow. No! Not like that!

The claw shifted. The mover shuddered.

And then came Alan's rending shriek.

4

I hold out my hand and wiggle my fingers just a bit. I want to draw her back. Toward me. Toward today. Toward what I think must happen next.

Because I've lost my locket, just like Mom said. And the adventure has begun.

Because cats or no, there's no turning back now.

Because I know this spot on the beach too. I know what it means. It means that God is up to something, and I have to play my part.

I'm starting to fear that maybe I'm not crazy, I'm only old. Old enough to know that wisdom sometimes looks like madness, and only faith can tell the difference. Mom taught me that.

What if there's a chance, just a chance, that this is real?

A chance that I am not a dream.

That tomorrow depends on today. And today upon yesterday.

A chance that I can reach back and touch what will come.

I've got to take that chance. Crazy as it may be. Today. Yesterday. Tomorrow.

Mom always says, "Chances are the doors God walks through." And now it's time to open the door.

Then they can send me to the cats.

Kinna stared as the woman held out her hand, wiggled her fingers, and chewed her lower lip.

Thea's eyes turned round and wide, like sand dollars washed in with the waves. "Oh, I get it. Isn't that just like God?" She smiled, her tone soft, thoughtful. "You have it, don't you?" Her laugh rang out over the beach. "Of course you do. How funny."

Kinna frowned. "What are you talking about?"

"My locket. I lost it, and I'll bet three bags of kitty litter you found it."

"Why?"

Thea chuckled again. "Because it's my dream, isn't it? Or maybe it's God's. Either way, you found the locket. With a double tulip design."

Kinna glanced at her satchel, still lying at the water's edge.

Thea nodded and muttered something under her breath about getting the locket, ending an adventure, and getting back to a chair and a boxer. Then she pulled herself to her feet and trudged toward the satchel.

Her legs didn't wobble, her breath didn't shudder. Her skin didn't rise with a million tiny goose bumps. If Kinna hadn't dragged her out of the water herself and watched her breathing stop, she'd never have believed this woman had nearly drowned less than ten minutes ago.

But stranger things had happened. She'd worked in the hospital long enough to know that. People hung onto life and bounced back from death's door. Others dropped away just when everyone thought all was well. It was part of the mystery of life and time, and Thea was just another brushstroke on the canvas of that mystery.

Kinna rose and followed Thea's footsteps toward the water. She jogged to catch up. The children were far away now, splashes of color against the backdrop of deep green sea. Their voices had faded, leaving only the rush of water and the determined footsteps of the woman in front of her.

"Wait."

Thea didn't slow.

Lord, this woman is so not part of my plans today. Kinna quickened her pace and raised her voice. "So, rifling through my bag is going to be the reward I get for pulling you out of the water?"

Thea knelt beside Kinna's bag. "I won't rifle. It'll be more of a peer-and-pluck."

Kinna sighed and moved closer, until she stood just beside the satchel. "Here, let me look."

Thea didn't glance up. "The locket was my mother's. A family heirloom."

The expression on Kinna's face froze. *Heirloom?* Hardly. But as brash as she might be, there was no way she could she tell a woman she'd just pulled out of the bay that her cherished locket was a cheap trinket, probably from Wal-Mart. Jimmy always shopped at Wal-Mart.

"Oh, um, so where did your mom get it?" Kinna knew the woman wasn't going to say Wal-Mart, even if that was the right answer.

"Dad had it made for my mom at some specialty shop in Carmel. But you know that, don't you?"

A chill ran down Kinna's spine. That's where Jimmy said he'd gotten hers. Maybe it hadn't come from Wal-Mart. But there was no way

Jimmy would pay specialty shop prices. She'd believe babies came from storks before she'd believe that. Besides, he probably didn't even know the way to Carmel. Sand City maybe, with its huge box stores and discount outlets. But Carmel? Never.

Kinna snaked her arm around Thea and grabbed her bag from the sand. She reached inside and fished around for the locket, her hand moving across the ovulation stick she'd placed there.

Thea paused beside her. "It's in there, isn't it?"

"Somewhere."

Thea nodded, then plopped down on the beach. She pulled her legs toward her chest, wrapped her arms around them, and waited.

And waited.

Kinna couldn't find the chain. She cleared her throat and opened the bag wider. "I hope you don't mind, but I opened it. There was a little sand inside, but the pictures were fine."

"Figures." Thea's words were quiet.

Kinna's gaze bounced up.

The woman turned her head, her eyes probing Kinna's. "So what did you think of them? The people in the locket, I mean."

Kinna sucked in a breath and saw the faces again in her mind. Smiling faces that glowed with happiness. Or was it hope? Faces that made her long for something more, something better. But she was being silly. They were just faces. Ordinary people in an ordinary locket with ordinary lives.

Her fingers grasped a bit of metal. A pen. Where was that locket? "Who are they?"

The woman turned back and stared at Kinna before answering. "My parents."

"They looked so, I don't know, content, I guess. Happy."

The woman's eyes stayed fixed on hers as she forced out words, slow and steady. "They were. They are." She smiled and again looked out to sea. "Those pictures were taken the day their first great-grandchild was born."

Kinna's hand stopped moving in the bag. Children. Grandchildren. Great-grandchildren. No wonder they were happy. The Bible called children a heritage from the Lord, a reward. Her throat closed. She should know. She'd skipped over that Scripture passage often enough in her Bible.

The woman's tone softened. "We had better pictures of them, but Mom insisted we use those two. Dad in his glasses, her with only a hint of a smile."

Kinna's fingers rummaged around the bottom of her bag, but the locket eluded her. She sat down and dumped out the bag's contents— a cell phone, lipstick, keys, sunblock, her hospital badge, and a half-empty package of chewing gum. And beneath them, the plastic ovulation stick.

Kinna pushed the phone to one side and found the open locket. She picked it up. Faces and bits of sand. Faces that made her want to know more, believe more. She wanted to keep them, study them, unlock the secret of joy in their eyes. Instead, she held them out to the woman.

But Thea wasn't looking at the locket. She stared at the ovulation stick that had fallen from Kinna's bag. Thea glanced up, and Kinna thought she read pity in her gaze. Then the look vanished.

"Ah, you found it." Thea reached out, waiting for Kinna to place the locket in her hand.

She did.

"Thank you." Thea snapped it shut and clutched it to her chest. Her eyes closed and her breath came in a ragged spurt. Then she coughed, deep and disturbing to Kinna's ears.

"We should get you to that doctor."

Thea smiled. "On one condition."

"What's that?"

"Tell me a story."

"About what?"

"Tell me the story of when you first fell in love."

Kinna gripped the steering wheel and stared out over the road. Three miles to the hospital. Not enough time to tell a story, especially not a story about love.

Thank goodness.

She peeked over at Thea in the passenger seat of the minivan. As expected, the woman was watching her, waiting. Kinna could almost hear the words that shot from her glance. *Come on, you promised me…*

Thea raised her hand to her forehead and drew in a long breath. "Well?"

"What?"

"My mother always used to tell me stories when I got hurt. I'd close my eyes and listen, then I'd feel better. So, tell me my story."

You are *crazy.* "And that will help how?"

The woman chuckled, then coughed again. "It will. Pretend I'm one of your patients. Would you tell them a story if you'd promised?"

Kinna pursed her lips.

Thea sighed. "How 'bout you start by telling me about your husband?"

Kinna shook her head. She didn't want to talk about Jimmy. It was too personal, too painful. But she had to say something. She shrugged. "What's there to tell? Jimmy's a construction worker." Another grimace twisted her lips. "Who's too cheap to buy anything in Carmel."

Thea pressed back into her seat. "Can't you tell me something good?" Her tone gained strength. "How old were you when you met?"

Kinna flinched and flexed her fingers around the steering wheel. "All right. We were young. Kids. And we met on the very beach where I pulled you out of the water."

The woman nodded, glanced out the window, then closed her eyes. "See, now that's interesting. Tell me more."

A sigh escaped Kinna. She didn't want to remember, especially now. She didn't want to talk about the past. Didn't want to bring back memories of when things were different, better, before she knew what they would become.

"You met there?"

But why not tell it? This woman didn't know her or Jimmy. She couldn't judge, couldn't condemn. To her, it was just another story about strangers. Just a tale to pass the time.

"Are you going to tell me about it or not?"

Kinna rubbed her hand over her face. "The second time we met, we were playing pirates when Jimmy fell. Cut his foot. I bandaged it." With her brand new T-shirt. Even now she could remember the feel of his skin beneath hers as she wound the cloth carefully around his arch and tied it at the top. And she remembered too what he'd said that day.

"I was wrong about you. About what I said the other day." He paused and licked his lips. "You aren't dumb. You're the nicest girl I've ever met."

Thea's voice reached out and drew her back. "I bet he appreciated that."

Kinna allowed a small smile to touch her lips. "That's the day I knew I wanted to be a nurse. I wanted to care for people, help make them better, help make them happy again." And it was also the day she first fell in love with the boy with sapphire eyes. But she didn't say that. She couldn't, promise or no. So much had been lost since that day.

"We'd gone up to the rocks just before that. Someone hollered for us to get down, but we didn't pay any attention. Jimmy just led me higher and higher, through the steep places and to the other side. We couldn't see the beach anymore. Only the wide ocean, with its pirate ship broken in the water and the cargo spread out before us. I was the captured princess flung onto the shore. He was the valiant pirate-turned-rescuer who saved me." She paused. "And then it turned cold, and we went home."

The woman sat up. "That's it?"

"Yep." But it wasn't. That's not how it ended at all.

Instead, they heard another shout. She yanked on Jimmy's sleeve. "We'd better go home now. It's getting cold."

Jimmy pulled her down beside him. "Not yet. Not till I show you something. It's a secret, so you can't tell."

"No more make believe. I've gotta go."

"This isn't pretend. Not this time." He grabbed her hand and stood. "Come on."

She couldn't resist. She never could resist when he looked at her like that. She followed him until they came to a flat place in the rocks.

"Look." He knelt beside a nest of mottled eggs. "Aren't they beautiful?"

She squatted beside them, her brow furrowed, her breath coming in quick spurts. "What are they?"

He frowned. "Eggs, silly. You spell that E-G-G-S."

She punched him in the arm. "I know how to spell *eggs*. But what kind are they?"

"I don't know, but I'm going to watch them every day until they hatch. Then I'm gonna find out." He ran his finger gently, lovingly, over the surface of one egg. His gaze turned soft.

And then something awful happened. Something that turned her stomach, even now, after all these years. Jimmy's father appeared from around the rocks.

Thea touched Kinna's arm, and she jolted back to the present.

"That's not all that happened, is it?" Thea's gaze wasn't teasing now, and her voice had turned oh-so-gentle.

Kinna sniffed. "How do you know?"

"Tell me what happened."

She wrinkled her nose. She didn't want to tell. It would make it more terrible, more real. Or maybe, telling it would make the memories fade, once and for all.

She would tell, and then it would be done. Gone. Past. She cleared her throat. "We found some bird eggs out in the rocks, but Jimmy's dad came and stepped on them."

"On purpose?"

"I don't know. It's not something I like to remember."

Thea tightened her fingers in a gesture of sympathy. "It was a long time ago."

Kinna nodded. "Twenty-nine years. An eternity."

The woman drew in a long breath, this one steady, calm. "So what's a few more months?"

Kinna swallowed as the minivan turned the final corner to the hospital. "What do you mean?"

The woman glanced up at the tall building before them.

Kinna pressed her lips together. "You don't understand. Sometimes a person has waited long enough. Sometimes her heart can't take any more." *Or her faith*.

The woman opened her fingers. The locket gleamed against her skin. The silver caught a ray of light and flung it across the woman's hand. Dull silver, with beckoning faces inside.

"Then promise something else."

"Promise what?"

"That someday you'll be as happy as the faces in my locket."

"Of course." It was an easy promise. She would be happy in exactly two weeks, when the pregnancy test came back positive. Then she'd be as happy as could be. No more doubts. No more hurting. No more failure. Only the kind, good-natured Kinna who she'd once been. She pulled into the hospital parking lot, found a spot, and parked.

Before the engine shut off, Thea reached out and dangled the locket between them. "Be careful, Kinna." She shifted in her seat and flicked a bit of sand from her still-damp clothes.

"Why?"

"Don't step on the eggs." With that, she snapped the locket closed, turned, and opened the door.

5

Shame. Like a flock of seagulls chattering in his soul. Noisy. Incessant. And all too familiar.

Jimmy stomped up the steps of the portable office. A plastic sign swung on the door. Skytop Construction. It could have been his. Well, at least fifteen percent his, the cut that George had offered him when he'd started. A percentage of ownership and lower wages. That had been the deal. Jimmy had chosen salary, to be just an employee. Steady, reliable, no risk. That's all he'd wanted out of life. But somehow, even that was turning out to be beyond his grasp.

Shame.

Bill was already on the Cat. It was better that way.

Shame.

I couldn't have done any better.

A lie. He could have done it, should have.

Alan will be fine.

Only a broken leg, they said. And a couple busted ribs. But Jimmy could've gotten the mover off without breaking Alan's leg or ribs. He should have. But he didn't.

Shame.

He pushed open the door of the small, three-room office and poked his head inside. "Karly? George?"

No one answered. He stepped inside. A set of plans lay unrolled on a far table. A stack of papers sat on the desk. Plastic flowers that were actually pens, a clock in the shape of a schnauzer, a beat-up calendar, an old radio playing country music. He hated this stuffy little office. Hated the thin walls and cheap paneling, the whir of the fan and the smell of dirt mixed with sweat. And hated more the reason he was here—to fill out a report on the accident. To tell George what happened. To hide as much of the truth as he could.

Shame.

"Hey, Jimmy."

He turned and saw her. Sultry black hair, impractical heels, a skirt much too short for a job in construction. Karly would never learn.

She waggled her fingers at him. "Hey, cutie. I told the boss you'd be in." She tilted her head and gave him a look that said more than he wanted to hear. Full of promise and innuendo. Admiration.

More than he deserved. Especially after today.

Then she smiled. The same smile she always gave, just for him. The same one he'd resisted, ignored, and denied. At least, until now.

God, help me.

He shifted his weight and stared out the dusty window. "Alan broke three ribs and his leg."

Karly nodded. "Boss won't be happy about another workers' comp claim. Not on this job. We've lost a bundle already."

Jimmy shrugged. It wasn't his fault. He couldn't have helped. Not really.

Liar.

Karly sauntered toward him. "Was he high?"

Jimmy winced and scuffed his boot over the low carpet.

She pulled a flower pen from the bucket on her desk, then picked up a form and attached it to a clipboard. She handed it to him, tipping forward until her blouse gaped at the neckline. "I guess I couldn't expect a guy like you to rat out a friend." She smiled again, suggestive and promising.

His heart thudded in his chest. He needed that look right now, full of trust and invitation. Without questions or doubts or accusations. Karly made him feel better, just like she always did.

Kinna used to look at him like that. Gaze at him as he ran his fingers through her burnished gold hair. Her hair wasn't dark gold anymore. It was more of a medium brown with strands of gray, but he loved it anyway. Thick and soft in his hands, curling gently over his fingers. It had been too long since he'd felt her hair against his skin. He missed it almost as much as he missed seeing in her eyes the look Karly gave him now.

These days, no one but Karly saw him that way. No one but her bothered. Most days, he ignored it. Most days, he just went about his business, did his job.

But most days weren't today.

Today, Jimmy met her eyes. Today, he took the pen from her hand and let their fingers brush. Today, he looked her full in the face and wondered why a girl like her showed interest in a guy like him. "Alan's a good guy."

"You always say that."

Jimmy returned Karly's smile, hers flirty, his cautious. But he smiled all the same.

Shame.

The pen clicked. He swallowed and averted his eyes from her plunging neckline.

"I've filled it out for you, so just sign there."

He grunted.

"And then the big boss wants to see you." She leaned in.

He glanced over the form, then signed his name.

She took the pen. "Thanks, Jimmy."

He handed back the clipboard. This time, their fingers missed. He took a step back, willed his voice steady. "So, what's George want? I don't know any more than what's on that form." He pointed to the clipboard in her hand.

"Well—"

The door flew open and Skinny Mike stepped inside. He leered at Karly. "Hey, baby, you two-timin' me?" His glance skittered to Jimmy.

Karly flinched. "You know I ain't never dating the likes of you, Mike Greenly. So you can just shut your mouth."

Jimmy turned toward Mike.

Skinny Mike leaned against a file cabinet, his arms folded across his chest. Three years operating the skip loader and the man still didn't have a single muscle to show for it. His face wrinkled in a nasty grin. "Why don't you come on over and talk to a real man?" He whistled. "That's some fine—"

"Mike!" Jimmy choked out the man's name. He turned away and muttered to the floor, "Guy needs a cold shower."

Mike scowled. "You say something there, Jimmy?"

Jimmy shrugged.

"Good thing I like ya. Besides, I was just complimenting a fine derrière."

Jimmy shook his head. "Drop it, all right? Anything new on Alan?"

Mike sucked his teeth, then dug a toothpick from his pocket and stuck it in the side of his mouth. "Naw. Guy was so high he didn't feel a thing."

"Shhh," Jimmy hissed at Mike, then shot a glance at Karly.

She turned away, pretending not to hear.

"Should have been you up there, Jimbo. Thought Bill was gonna drop that thing right back on ol' Alan's head."

"Bill was already on the machine."

"Yeah? Well, you can explain that to Alan once he wakes up. Anyway"—he pulled a bunch of stapled papers from under his arm—"here's the new schedule, like you asked for. Tell George this'll set us back at least two weeks. Machine's broke. Alan's broke. Suppose he'll want to lay off some guys till we get 'em fixed."

Karly sighed and took the papers from Mike. "George knows. That's why—" She stopped and glanced at Jimmy. Her face flushed. "Well, thanks, Mike. I'll be sure he gets the new schedule."

Jimmy glanced at the papers and frowned. Even from a glimpse, he could see the schedule was impossible. And that would mean more shortcuts, more things left half-done, undone, and covered up. More things for him to pretend not to see.

Mike slapped his hands on his thighs and headed for the door. When he got there, he looked back at Karly. "Offer's still open. A night with a real man. Ya can't lose."

Karly chuckled as Mike left the office and slammed the door behind him.

Jimmy turned back toward Karly. "Sorry about that. Mike doesn't know how to treat a lady."

At first, she didn't say anything, just looked at him, her eyes soft and thoughtful, her smile gone. "Why do you do that?"

"What?"

"You don't want me to go out with him, do you?"

"Of course not."

"Why do you care?"

Because my dad wouldn't. Jimmy shrugged. "I dunno. You don't need some idiot drooling all over you like that." Idiot. He might have called Mike something else, something off-color, but he didn't use that kind of language.

Karly licked her lips. "Well, I guess it's nice. Thanks."

Something strange fluttered in Jimmy's gut. He crossed his arms and forced the feeling away. "So, where's George?

"Big office."

His breath caught. "Downtown? Oh no, not…"

She nodded. "He's making cuts. Thought you should know."

Jimmy shoved down the panic. "But I can't…not now. I need this job."

Karly put her hand on his arm. She was close. Too close. He could smell her perfume, sweet and heady, like a watermelon Jolly Rancher left out in the sun. His breath quickened.

So did hers. "Don't worry, I reminded him you're the best operator we've got. The very best. So even if he assigns a new foreman…"

"Thanks, Karly. I owe you."

Her smile returned, the sultry one that teased. "Yes, you do." The words bubbled up, half-laugh, half-suggestion. "So, how 'bout a drink after work?" Her fingers played over his arm, then reached up to touch her collar. "After all, you ruined my chances with Mike."

His gaze dropped to the hint of lace peeking from the lowest spot on her neckline. It was pink. He shouldn't notice things like that. He averted his eyes. "You know I don't drink."

"Never?" Her voice lowered.

Never.

A memory came to him, clear and ugly. Broken egg shells, splattered yolks. A sharp breeze winging in from the bay. And Kinna's eyes, wide with unspoken horror. He remembered the stale smell of booze on his father's clothes, the red, bleary eyes, the mouth twisted in a sick grin.

"What you doin' up here, boy?" his father slurred. He didn't even notice the broken eggs under his shoe, or if he did, he didn't care. "Shirkin' your work again. Playin' stupid baby games, I'm bettin'." He swung out his hand. "Get outta here. Get to work." He waved his arm toward the path. As he did, his eyes slid toward Kinna. He stopped and leered.

Jimmy shivered.

His dad tipped forward. His eyes narrowed. "Ain't you that stuck-up preacher's girl?" He laughed, a horrible sound that ended in a snort. "What you doin' out here alone with a brat like him?" His arm swung back toward Jimmy, though his eyes never left Kinna's face. His voice turned sharper, clearer. "Tell me, preacher girl, what kinda game are you playin' with no-account trash like him?"

Kinna's face turned pale. Before Jimmy could stop her, she balled up her fist and slammed it, hard, into his father's belly. It wasn't much, a puny fist into a gut hard with liquor, but it was enough.

His father stumbled backward.

Jimmy grabbed Kinna's hand. "Come on. Hurry."

Together, they bolted down the path, back toward the beach. His father's voice chased them. Crude words, a string of cussing, then threats, unblurred by the effects of alcohol. Jimmy glanced over his shoulder to see his dad following at a strange, lumbering run. Only his dad ran like that.

"I'll get you, boy! You're gonna pay for this!"

And pay he did. Again and again in the months and years to come. Paid so badly he wished she'd never done it. Paid until it had driven him to a single moment. A single outburst. A single event that changed everything.

Jimmy blinked and focused on Karly before him. He shook his head. "No. Never." He would never be like that stinking, disgusting man he had to call Dad.

Never again, anyway.

Karly's fingernails tapped the clipboard. Her lips came together in a pout. "Okay, coffee then. They opened that new little place inside the bookstore."

Coffee. That was innocent enough. They were friends, after all. And what was a little latte between friends? But he knew better. Coffee was just a beginning. And after that...

He closed his eyes. *I can't do this.* He opened his eyes and tried on a little smile. "Raincheck. All right?"

She sighed and shook her head. "All right, Jimmy. Raincheck." She touched his chest with one of her pink manicured nails. "But you still owe me. And I plan to collect."

He held his breath. With one simple word, he was caught. He'd said "raincheck" when he knew all along that the right answer was no.

Jimmy swallowed and stepped into the big glass elevator. He pushed number four, and the floor rose. The buildings outside shrunk until he could see a glimmer of sunlight on the bay. The brass handrailing gleamed in front of him. The windows shone. He shifted on his feet, his gaze dropping to the stains on his old jeans, the dirt crusted along the sleeves of his T-shirt. He wiped his hand over his face. He didn't belong here.

The elevator dinged and the doors opened. Jimmy didn't move. Then he let out his breath and slithered out of the wide doors. Down the hall and to the right was George's office. It wasn't large, but it was plush. A place to meet with clients and architects. A place to display artistic drawings of projects won and buildings built. A place to smile, and compliment, and tell men they no longer had jobs.

Oh God...please don't let it happen to me.

He trudged down the long hallway and glanced through the glass door. He could see through the main room and into George's back office. The man sat at his fine cherry wood desk, with his fine silver pen set, his perfectly framed photo of his wife and two kids, and a flawless model of the boat he now had docked in the bay.

Jimmy opened the door.

George looked up. "Come on back, Jim."

Jimmy rubbed his palms on his legs, then walked into George's office.

"Shut the door."

Jimmy did.

George rose and shook Jimmy's hand in a grip that nearly crushed his knuckles. "Thanks for coming." He sat back down, but somehow was no less intimidating seated. "I suppose you know why you're here?"

Jimmy didn't answer. He didn't know. Didn't want to know. Didn't want to even guess.

"Sit down. We need to talk."

That couldn't be good. Those words were never good. He lowered himself to the edge of a small chair. Upholstered in fine leather, but still too short.

"Things have been bad on the Petersen job. Lost a boatload of money already."

Jimmy nodded. The leather beneath him squeaked.

"Then, after today…" George's voice trailed off. He pierced Jimmy with a look. "You should have been on that Cat, Jim. I wish to God you were. Might have made a difference. Might have saved a job."

"They say Alan will be all right."

George slapped his desk. His voice boomed. "Alan? I'm not talking about Alan."

Jimmy froze.

George leaned forward. "Truth is, I can't afford you anymore. Not after today. You're a great operator, a decent foreman, but we need more than that."

"But…"

"We need a leader out there."

A leader. He was doomed.

George narrowed his eyes and nodded. "You understand." He reached for some papers on the edge of his desk. "I'm sorry."

No.

"I'm letting you go."

You can't.

"Good luck."

Blood drained from Jimmy's face. Then he stood and walked away.

6

Kinna didn't know why she was at Wal-Mart of all places. She hated it, with its too-small aisles and too-large families crammed into them. She had enough crazy in her life, she didn't need to come here to get more. But after a quick shower at home and a change of clothes, she'd come here anyway. It was the locket's fault. Jimmy's fault.

She had to see if they sold those lockets here.

It would only take a minute. To the jewelry counter, have a look, get out. A simple plan. Except… She stopped, her path blocked.

A huge diaper display towered in the middle of the aisle. On one side sat two empty carts, on the other, a woman with her own cart and her own family wedged into the space alongside the display.

Kinna turned her head. *I won't look. I'll just squeeze by. Stupid narrow aisles. No wonder I can't stand this place.*

She glanced up. Too late. There, staring at her from the sides of the diaper boxes were dozens of fat-cheeked babies. All smiling. All chubby and healthy and happy. Her hands turned clammy.

She swallowed and took a deep breath. *Come on, God. This just isn't fair.* Her eyes strayed again to the faces grinning at her from the boxes. *He has my color hair.* The thought came unbidden, unwanted. *But not Jimmy's eyes.*

She straightened. *Okay, God, I'm taking this as a sign. You won't let*

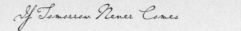

me down this time. Not after what I've sacrificed. You'll give me a baby. You'll save my faith. You won't let me be tested more than I can bear, and I can't bear being childless anymore.

She pressed her hand against her right side over her ovary. Both sides were swollen, tender, enlarged. Just as they should be. Just as she'd planned. Hyperstimulation had hopefully released a half dozen or more viable eggs. One of them would take. One would become the baby she'd always dreamed of.

Kinna grabbed a diaper box from the top of the stack, then dropped it into one of the empty carts and gripped the handle. *See, God, that's faith. And didn't you say we just needed to have faith to move the mountains? Well, get out the backhoe 'cause I've got two mountains right here,* she tapped her sides again, *that need to turn into one big one right in the middle.* She patted her belly, turned away, and nearly stepped on the woman reaching for her second box of diapers. "Oops, sorry."

"Está bien." The woman tossed the diapers into her cart before reaching for another package. A little girl with big, dark eyes peeked out from the far side of the cart. A boy, probably four years old, stared at Kinna, his nose running and a finger stuck in his mouth. Propped at the top of the cart was a worn car seat with a pink blanket lolling out the side.

The baby. Another sign that soon it would be her pushing a cart like that. Her with the baby in the car seat.

But what if…?

Kinna gripped her new cart and maneuvered down the aisle. She had to find the jewelry counter. Watches were safe. Pendants, earrings. Lockets.

A minute later, she found the counter. A saleswoman sauntered over and put on a forced smiled. "Can I help you?"

Kinna swallowed. "Where are the lockets?"

The woman motioned to a countertop display, then let the smile drop as she wandered back to the far side of the counter.

Kinna moved closer to the spinning display and turned it until she found the lockets. There was a silver heart that read "Mom," a piece in Black Hills gold that had a rose etched into the cover, another silver heart, a plain locket, and one that looked like it had a picture of a hummingbird on it. But no tulips. She spun the display. Birthstone pendants hung on the rest of the sides. She spun it again. No more lockets.

"Is this all you have?"

"Yes, ma'am, that's it."

She hated being called *ma'am*. It reminded her she was getting old.

"Have you ever sold lockets with tulips?"

The woman paused. "No, ma'am. Not in the five years I've worked this counter."

No tulips. Maybe he got it at Target.

A burst of rapid Spanish grabbed her attention. She turned. There again was the woman and her children, her cart now filled with more than just diapers. Her hand gripped her son's wrist as she berated him in Spanish. Kinna could understand most of it. Something about how they don't steal. How they pay for what they want. The woman grabbed a DVD from the cart and waved it under her son's nose.

"Mal. Muy mal." It was a bad movie. And no, they weren't getting it. She didn't want to stain even her cart with such filth. She raised her eyes toward heaven and muttered something Kinna didn't understand. Then she shoved the DVD into her son's hand and jabbed her finger at a far bin.

The boy stared at his feet as he slumped back to the bin and dropped the DVD into it.

Kinna watched the rounding of his shoulders, the way his dark hair fell over his eyes as he shuffled back down the aisle. It reminded her of another time, another place. It reminded her of Jimmy.

This remembering—it was that woman's fault. That woman from the sea. Something about her rekindled memories that had lain dormant for years, memories best hidden. But that crazy woman made the memories come to life, even now, when Kinna was far from the beach, and Thea was gone.

Still, she remembered. Jimmy and his dad. Only Jimmy's father hadn't been half so kind as this woman here. And the problem hadn't been a DVD.

Back in those days, there was no Wal-Mart. Kmart ruled the retail world. It was a time of blue-light specials and rows of discount shoes in shallow bins. Kinna's mom rarely shopped at Kmart, but they were there to buy some flowers for a women's event at church, a mother-daughter tea. Because that's what life with God was all about—happy families, children dressed in ties or dresses, wiggling in the pews, events for moms and children, station wagons, and mothers with hands clasping small fingers, their bellies round with promise. Kinna had always believed that life would be hers too someday. She would have the round belly, the mother-daughter teas. Happily ever after. Just like the Bible said. Didn't it?

She thought so then, anyway, that day at Kmart with her mother, shopping for flowers.

Jimmy and his dad were there for an entirely different reason. They were buying flowers too, but she didn't find out until later that they were for Jimmy's mother's grave.

She turned up the flower aisle and spied Jimmy and his dad. She waved and pointed to her doll, Sally, tucked in the crook of her arm.

Her mother touched her shoulder. "Right here, Kinna. We'll just pick up a few of these." She motioned to a bunch of bright yellow sunflowers, but her eyes were focused elsewhere. She had seen Jimmy and his dad too.

Kinna started to say something then stopped as her mother's grip tightened.

"I think about thirty will do. Help me count." She pulled a handful of sunflowers from the bunch and began to count them.

Kinna set Sally on the shelf and joined in. "One, two, three." And then she felt a touch on her arm, softer than her mother's touch, more tentative.

Jimmy stood next to her with a quiet smile and sparkle in those dark blue eyes. He took a step back and withdrew his other hand from behind his back. He held a bright orange tulip, plastic and a little bent, but she didn't notice that at the time. All she saw was the flower and Jimmy's grin behind it.

"For you."

"Tulips are my favorite."

"I know."

She reached out, but her fingers never touched the stem.

Jimmy's father grabbed the flower. "What do you think you're doing, boy?" He shoved the flower at Jimmy. "We ain't got the money for this. And I sure as"—his gaze darted up, toward Kinna's mom— "sure as God made little green apples ain't raising no thief." He cleared his throat. "You hear me, boy?"

Kinna grabbed Sally just as her mom touched Kinna's shoulders and drew her back behind her. "It's okay, Mr. Henley. He was just showing her the flower."

"I know my own boy."

"No harm done." She put on her church smile and locked eyes with Mr. Henley.

He grunted, then glared at Jimmy with his lips pressed in a hard line. *I'll deal with you later.* He didn't say the words, but Kinna read them with cruel clarity in those hard, angry eyes.

Kinna's mom turned and hustled Kinna back down the aisle. "We hope to see you at church again, Mr. Henley." The words sounded hurried, stilted, even to Kinna's ears.

They rushed around the corner. And then the sound came. A hand against bare skin. A slap so loud that it echoed all the way to her heart.

Her mother tensed, but they didn't slow. Didn't turn back. They just hurried down that aisle, pretending not to hear, not to know.

But Kinna heard. She knew. And she never forgot it.

After all these years, she could still hear the sound of that slap.

———

Jimmy pushed the door open quietly in case Kinna was home. In case she wasn't on a shift at the hospital. He used to keep track of her schedule. He used to do a lot of things.

He sighed and looked at his empty hands. No tulips. And no job. But he wouldn't tell her that. He couldn't. Once he would have come home and told her everything, but not anymore.

So much had changed in these last years. It was probably his fault, but it was hers too. Obsessed, that's what she was. And critical, cruel. He didn't understand it.

But she was still his wife. Even if she didn't believe in him anymore.

He stepped through the door and allowed it to click closed behind him. He smelled vanilla and a bit of spice. Candles. She was home.

He slipped out of his light coat.

"Jimmy, is that you?"

He tossed the coat onto the back of a chair. "Yep, I'm home." He poked his head through the kitchen doorway and his breath stopped. "What…" The word choked and sputtered to a halt.

Kinna stepped away from the table, one hand lingering on the petal of a bright orange tulip. She had a whole vase of them, multicolored, perfectly shaped, and not from him.

"Nice, huh?" A smile touched her lips.

Fury touched his. How could she? He was the one who bought her flowers. No one else. His eyes narrowed. "Who, who got…" He shoved the words out from beneath the tightness in his chest.

She frowned. "What's wrong with you? You look like you're about to have a seizure."

His hands shook. He crossed his arms over his chest to steady them. "Where'd you get those?"

"Wal-Mart."

She was lying. Kinna hated Wal-Mart. What kind of game was she playing with him now?

"They're silk. They make all the fake flowers from silk these days. Not plastic anymore. They're a lot nicer."

What was she talking about? Then he understood. She *had* remembered. She knew this was the day he usually brought her tulips, so she'd bought her own to upstage him. To reject him. Again. Today, of all days.

He couldn't take it anymore. His face heated. "So you just happened to be in Wal-Mart and got some flowers? I'm supposed to believe that?"

She glanced up at him. Her eyes flashed. "Of course you are. Why wouldn't you? I thought they'd be nice. That you'd…we'd…"

His lips felt dry. He licked them. "Maybe they're from that doctor friend of yours. What's his name? Jeff?" He didn't know why he said it. He didn't really believe it, but the words came out anyway. And with them came the blinding fear that maybe they were true.

Kinna slammed her fists onto her hips and whirled toward him. "Stop it, Jimmy. Don't you dare ruin everything."

His jaw stiffened.

Her voice rose as she continued. "If you must know, I was there seeing if that locket you got me was from Wal-Mart, or if it really was an original like you said. Then I saw the flowers."

The locket? What did that locket have to do with anything? She was grasping now, reaching for anything she might use to hurt him. Stupid locket. He should have known not to have bothered with it. "Oh, now you doubt that too?"

She didn't answer. She just looked at him, and he read in her eyes, in the moisture gathering there, the hundred little ways he'd let her down. The days when he'd made promises and failed to live up to them, the times when he was almost telling the truth, but she called it a lie anyway. The slow erosion of trust. Perhaps he deserved it. But he hadn't lied about that locket.

The locket hadn't been pretend.

She turned her face away and stared at the flowers. "It doesn't matter anyway."

"Yeah, right."

"Let's just drop it, okay? D-R-O-P it." She stomped away.

Drop it? He was all for that. He didn't want to argue about everything. Why couldn't she just believe in him like she used to? He turned his mind from that question. He knew the answer, knew it too well. But there had been a time when she stood by him, a time when he could do no wrong. A time when she cared about him—him, not just some baby that didn't exist.

They had run along the beach, Kinna just a step in front of him. Their feet flashed together in the sand, kicking up a fine cloud as they sprinted down to the water's edge.

He let out a fierce laugh. Then he fell. Pain lanced up his foot. A sharp cry burst from his mouth. He grabbed his ankle and rolled in the sand. Sunlight spat in his face, drying the grains of sand stuck there.

Kinna stopped, turned back. "You okay?"

"My foot." He looked down and saw a green shard of glass sticking from his heel. Dark red blood oozed from the edges of the cut. His stomach turned. He hadn't been careful. His dad always said he had to be careful, he couldn't get cut. Bruises were fine. A dozen deep, horrible bruises. His dad didn't care about those. But a cut? That was different. He couldn't lose blood. He didn't dare. His blood was too rare, like his mom's. "Funny blood" his dad called it.

Kinna jogged back and knelt beside him.

A seagull squawked overhead. A similar sound grunted from his throat as he continued to squeeze his ankle.

"Hold still. Let me see."

Jimmy drew in a shuddering breath and stopped himself from rocking.

She moved closer and examined the glass. "Looks like the dragon got you after all."

He tried a smile and failed. "It's just a scratch." Isn't that what all brave knights said?

Her brows furrowed. "Don't move." She gripped the glass and plucked it from his foot.

Blood welled in the wound, then dripped out over his skin. He groaned and tried to keep himself from shaking. It was just a little cut, just a little blood. He'd be fine. "It's okay…isn't it?"

Kinna chewed her lip, then helped him hobble to the water to wash the cut. The salt water hurt, but it did the job. After that, she took off the T-shirt she wore over her swimsuit.

Jimmy blinked. "W-what are you doing?"

She shook out the shirt, then used the sleeve to wipe away the water from around his cut. Next, she placed his foot in her lap and gently bound it with her shirt. "There, that should keep the sand out and the blood in."

His eyes widened. "Your shirt? Won't you get in trouble for that? What will you tell your mom?"

Kinna looked into his eyes. "The truth, of course."

The truth. He shivered. For her, maybe the truth was cheap. For him…he shuddered.

Kinna waved her hand at him. "Does it hurt?"

"Not anymore."

"Now, when you get home, you wash that out and get a nice big Band-Aid on it. You gotta keep it clean. Maybe use a little perry-oxide or something. I don't know how to spell that. Do you have any?"

He shrugged. He didn't care about perry-anything. All that mattered was that Kinna had given him her shirt to make his foot better, to stop his bleeding. And she'd decided to face the truth to do it, no matter the consequences. No one had ever done anything like that for him before. He touched her arm. "Thanks."

She smiled. "It wasn't nothing."

"You really are a princess, aren't you?"

She sat back on her heels and wrapped her arms around her knees. "And this is what all fair princesses do for handsome princes."

He flushed. "I ain't no handsome prince."

She stared at him. "You are to me."

The memory faded. Jimmy closed his eyes, wishing he was back in that time, when she still trusted him, when he was still her hero. But things changed.

Kinna walked back into the room, her pace slow now, defeated. "I'll put them away, if you want. You don't have to see them."

Jimmy opened his eyes and forced himself back to the present. There was no use remembering what had been, and what had been lost. "No, it's not that."

Kinna cleared her throat. "I just wanted to get them, that's all. They reminded me of something."

Jimmy grimaced. *Something bad about me, right?* "Let me guess, another time when I've disappointed you?" *Like I did today. If only you knew…*

She regarded him as intently as she'd done on the beach all those years ago. But her look was completely different than it was then, totally opposite. And then all expression dropped from her face. Her voice wasn't hard, or cold, or biting. It was nothing. It was simply dead. "Of course you wouldn't understand."

You never do. She didn't speak the words, but he heard them anyway. Just as he had a hundred times.

He wanted to answer. Wanted to say something that communicated all his hurt, all his frustration. She was the one who didn't understand. She was the one who had done this to them. What had happened to the little girl on the beach?

Same thing that happened to the boy.

We grew up.

7

My mother always says God's plans are crazy-wild. I used to think she was irreverent for saying so. Now I suspect she's right.

What else do you call it when you toss yourself into the sea, only to be fished out again? When you lose a locket, only to snatch it back? When you see a life crumbling and can only ask for a memory?

What is a memory? What is the past?

A promise? A challenge? A place where we bury hope like a treasure that now needs a map to be found?

Crazy.

But if I know one thing, it's that happiness can't be found by grabbing at our dreams. It's found when the sea comes in, the sands shift, and the fog is so thick that you can't see tomorrow, but you hope anyway. You trust. You believe the dawn will come.

It's found when there's nothing left to cling to except the One who brings that dawn. The One hidden in the fog. It is found in faces in a locket, washed by sand, wrinkled with time. I've seen it in their eyes. Heard it in their laughter. They taught me that, but Kinna doesn't know it. And I wonder how she ever will.

I pull my locket from my pocket and look into the faces I see there. But the faces are fading. The pictures grow lighter, even as I watch them.

The faintness scares me...scares me more than a roomful of felines.

Somehow I know I can't let them fade away.

———

Kinna shoved the tulips into the cupboard and slammed the glass door shut. The afternoon sun reflected off the surface and sent splinters of light into her eyes. She squinted and turned back to Jimmy. "There, they're gone, all right?"

Jimmy crossed his arms over his chest and scowled deeper. "Fine."

"Fine."

"Good."

"Good." She moved away and glanced at her bag on the table. The bag that held the ovulation stick. The bag that held her hope.

She rubbed her temples and took a long breath. This wasn't going at all as she had planned. She mustn't forget, mustn't lose sight of what this day meant, what it had to mean.

After all, today was the day. Even if it didn't feel like it, even if the sight of tulips made Jimmy fly into a rage. Why would he pick a fight today? Why couldn't things just go as planned? When he got home, she was supposed to have nice silk flowers on the dinner table, takeout pizza ordered, sparkling cider in long-stemmed glasses, and all the credit card bills hidden away in a drawer. It would have been perfect.

Except he'd ruined it, just like always.

Kinna sighed. This wasn't the first time things had gone wrong between her and Jimmy. She should be used to it. After all, they argued most of the time and were silent the rest. She thought it was just the stress of trying to have a baby. Of infertility.

She sucked in her breath. No. She wouldn't use that word. Not aloud. They were trying, they weren't infertile. Even after all these years…

Barren.

The word whispered through her, taunting and ugly.

Infertile.

Just as ugly, just as taunting.

Jimmy had used that word once, and she hated him for it. It was a horrible word. And another thing for them to fight about.

She pressed her hand against the closed cupboard door, then turned toward Jimmy again. "I've got an hour and a half before I need to leave for work."

"So?"

She swallowed. "So…um, clean up and maybe we can…"

He sighed. "Clean up? That's all you've got to say?"

She clenched her jaw. "Yeah."

"Fine." He spun on his heel and strode down the hall toward their bedroom.

What was wrong with him? Couldn't he just be happy, cooperative? After all, they were in this together, weren't they? A vision of tiny vials in the sand sped through her mind. Well, maybe not together in everything.

She followed him down the hall and into their bedroom. He was already in the bathroom, the door shut. It would be okay soon. She needed everything to be okay. She could do without tulips, pizza, and long-stemmed glasses, but she couldn't do without him.

All right, God, here we go. Give me a baby. Save my faith. I'm ready for my happily ever after.

The sound of the shower rumbled through the room. His clothes were thrown over the chair. She stopped beside them, touched them with just the tips of her fingers. Dirt, grease, and a little blood. Someone must have gotten a cut. It happened all the time on the job site. As long as it wasn't Jimmy's blood.

She took the clothes, stepped toward the bathroom door, and dropped them into the hamper. Then she pulled off her pants and shirt and folded them neatly across the chair. She peeled back her socks and placed them on top. Next she stepped up to her dresser and squirted a little perfume behind her ears and at the base of her neck. Pure Seduction by Victoria's Secret. Well, she'd soon see if the scent lived up to the label's claims. She sat on the edge of the bed, wearing nothing but her bra and panties. She perched there, and waited.

The shower turned off.

She swallowed.

Now or never. Her sides ached, a sign of ovulation. A sign the Perganol had done its work. A good sign.

Jimmy came out of the bathroom. His gaze turned toward her. His eyes narrowed. "What are you doing?"

Kinna shifted on the bed. "Today's the right day, Jimmy. For…er, you know." She patted the covers. It seemed silly to do it, childish, but she couldn't stop herself.

"You're kidding, right?"

Her brows drew together in a frown. She never kidded about this. "I tested. Remember? I've been testing every day."

Jimmy sighed and headed into the closet.

"Jimmy?" Her heart beat faster. "Where are you going?"

He didn't answer.

"Jimmy?"

He poked his head out the door.

She sucked in a breath. He was wearing jeans now, and a clean T-shirt with the words Stupid Is as Stupid Does plastered across the front. Dressed. It didn't make sense. It couldn't mean… Words stuck in her throat. Questions. Fear. And then, the first wisps of fury.

Jimmy's jaw tightened. "I can't do this anymore, Kinna. Not like this."

She clenched her fists, fought to control her tone. Calm. Gentle. Reasonable. "But, you know…today. It has to be today." *The vials. You don't know about the vials.*

He turned back into the closet and spoke a single word. "No."

She could hear the pain in that word, the regret. And still she didn't believe it. She couldn't. A chill dribbled down her spine. "What do you mean?" The question came out low, whispered. Afraid.

He came back out and stopped, his feet spread, his legs locked. He shook his head and zipped his pants. "I know what you're saying. And the answer is no. I can't do this. I told you." He didn't meet her eyes as he said it. He just stared at his feet, at the carpet, at the edge of the skirt around the bed.

"No?" Something cold and heavy lodged in Kinna's gut. Her hands shook. She clenched them together. "But we have to."

"No. We don't. Not like this." He turned and yanked some socks out of his drawer. Above him hung a photo from their wedding. Two people making silly faces into the camera. Her hair in some crazy eight-ies style. Him with a wispy mustache. Happy people. Laughing and in love. So long ago, too long.

This isn't happening. He wouldn't dare. Not this month, this cycle. God?

No answer.

Her gaze fixed on the picture again. Goofy smiles, a future of nothing but joy, his hands strong around her, his knuckles still slightly scarred from an incident he refused to talk about. And still they had hope. That day was all about hope.

This day was too.

"Please, Jimmy. Don't be silly."

"Silly? That's how you see me, is it?" He turned his back and leaned over to put on his socks. "I knew it."

This was a dream. A very bad dream. In a moment he would turn around and everything would be okay. She cleared her throat. "Jimmy? Let's be reasonable."

He stood, turned, and pierced her with his gaze. "You want to talk reasonable?" His voice rose, just below a shout. He mastered it, his tone changing, chilling. "How reasonable is it to march in here, announce that today's the day, and expect me to jump like some trained monkey? I'm sick of this, Kinna. I've had it. I'm not your sperm bank."

She shivered and stood. Her fists tightened into tense balls. "What's wrong with you? Don't you want a baby? It has to be today. This cycle. Right now. Don't you get it?"

"I understand just fine. I'm not stupid. And there's nothing wrong with me, but there's plenty wrong with us. I'm not gonna just leap up and perform whenever Clearblue Easy snaps its fingers. I've had it with that."

"You've got to!"

"I do not!"

"Take off those jeans!"

He grabbed his wallet from the dresser and stuffed it into his pocket. "You don't have a clue. You…you…and then you expect me to…I won't. Not anymore." He stalked to the far side of the room.

Her tone sharpened. "We're supposed to be in this together."

"Together?" He laughed, a bitter sound that filled the room and scraped along nerves already raw. "Together? You've got to be kidding me. You come in with flowers and these plans. You don't even ask, you don't even care—" He clamped his jaw shut and turned away, as if he couldn't bear to look at her, to see her.

"Look at me! You promised. You said—"

He whirled and stabbed his finger at her. "How do you know what I said? When do you ever stop to listen to what I say? All you care about is having a baby. That's it. You're obsessed." He slapped his palms together. "Together, huh? You know how you spell together? G-I-V-E-M-E. That's right. Give me. Perform. Do what I want when I want. That's not 'together.' That's not love. And I'm not going to be a part of that anymore. I'm done."

Kinna trembled. It didn't make sense. He couldn't be saying what he was saying. He couldn't mean it. "We can talk about this later. After. But for now…" She motioned toward the bed.

Jimmy threw his hands up in the air. "You are unbelievable." He dropped his hands and started toward the bathroom.

Kinna took a step toward him. "You, you can't—"

He turned. "That's right. I can't. And I won't. W-O-N-T."

"But, but…"

Jimmy grabbed the doorknob.

"No, Jimmy, don't walk away from me."

He let out a loud sigh. Then he stepped into the bathroom and slammed the door.

She stood in the middle of the room, not believing, not accepting. Ovulation sticks for a week, and she finally got a positive. This was the day. *The* day. Tomorrow would be too late.

Tick tock. She heard the biological clock again. Too late.

How dare he?

Kinna flew to the bathroom door and pounded her fists on the white planks. "You get out here right now, Jimmy. You know how much this means to me. I won't let you—" A sob cut off her words. She tried to swallow it, tried to shout past it, but failed.

She backed up and dropped onto the bed.

The bathroom door swooshed open. Jimmy looked at her, his hair combed, his shirt tucked. "Forget it, Kinna. The answer's no. If you want me, it'll have to be for more than DNA."

"But it's got to be today."

He paused. "Why, Kinna? Why today?"

She sniffed. "Because…because I took drugs. Perganol."

"How much?"

"Enough."

"That's expensive. You didn't put it on credit again, did you?"

She swallowed. "No."

"Our insurance doesn't pay for anything related to infertility."

"No."

His eyes widened. "You didn't…Kinna, you're a nurse!"

She clenched her jaw and glared at him. "That's right, I'm a nurse. And it's about time it paid off."

He stared at her. "Who are you?" He backed away. "I don't even know you anymore." He shook his head, then pushed past her, out the bedroom door.

"Jimmy, you come back here. Jimmy!" She leaped up and ran down the hall.

A moment later the front door slammed. Her voice softened to a plea. "Jimmy?"

He didn't answer. He didn't come back. All that reached her was the sound of his work boots on the wooden porch.

Then, even that was gone.

8

Jimmy heard her calling him, heard her feet racing down the hall, but he didn't slow. He didn't dare this time. Instead, he flung the front door open and strode out.

He couldn't do it again. Couldn't be there with her, as husband and wife, as she focused not on him but on the goal of an elusive child. All she cared about was the cycle, the day, conception. Cared so much that she'd done the unthinkable. She'd stolen drugs. How could she not know how dangerous that was? And how had she gotten those needles injected without help?

He'd always known she was strong and determined, but he'd have never dreamed that determination would lead them here. Somewhere in all the trying, in all the hopes and disappointments, in all the weeks and years of charts and drugs, sticks and tests, he had lost her.

Lost the girl he'd loved, lost the friend he'd counted on. Lost everything.

And still she didn't see it. Didn't see him. Not anymore.

Today had been the final offense. He'd had the chance to be a hero, and he'd failed. He'd lost a friend, lost his job, and lost his self-respect. But she didn't care. Didn't even bother to find out.

His hands balled into fists.

Who—no, *what* did she think he was? A means to an end. That's it. Nothing more. He wouldn't be part of something that had gone this far from what was right.

"Jimmy?" Kinna's voice came from the house behind him.

But it wasn't Kinna. Not the Kinna he had fallen in love with. Not the Kinna who used to love him, laugh with him. Not the girl who once leaned over a sandcastle and told him that maybe fairy tales did come true.

This was someone he didn't know. Didn't recognize.

A stranger who had stolen the only woman he had ever loved.

———

Kinna stood at the window, shaking. She watched Jimmy storm to the car, get in, and slam the door. Watched him and did not cry. The hurt was too deep.

How could he?

Easily. He'd done it a hundred times before. Just left, refused to resolve anything. Refused to face the truth. Refused to fight for their marriage, for her dreams.

But this time it was worse. This time he had taken her dreams, her hopes, her prayers, and crushed them. He had destroyed her with a single word. *No.*

Kinna let the curtain drop into place and stared at her hands. They had stopped shaking and were still now. Numb. Unfeeling. She blinked. Outside, she heard the car pulling away from the driveway. Then the sound died away.

He was gone.

Completely, absolutely gone.

Jimmy had betrayed her, left her, and taken her last chance with him.

Oh, God. What am I going to do? How can I last another month, another cycle, another year? My faith won't last. God, it's now or never. God?

The thought of God hurt too. Everything hurt.

God, what are You thinking, letting him get away like that?

"For my thoughts are not your thoughts, neither are your ways my ways," declares the LORD.

Great, God was answering with a stupid Bible verse she'd learned in third grade Sunday school. But He was right. His ways weren't her ways. She'd have never thought up something as dumb, as horrible, as this.

She crossed her arms. *Don't say it. I won't listen to any "I work all things together for good" line. I'm not seeing anything good here. Not even one tiny glimmer. How could You have let me down?*

But maybe God didn't. Maybe this was all Jimmy's fault. Jimmy had disobeyed God. Jimmy had shattered her dreams, her plans.

Okay. If that's the way he wants it…

Kinna turned and strode back down the hall to their bedroom. *Her* bedroom. He'd lost the right.

She sniffed back her tears, put her clothes back on, then stomped to the closet. She grabbed his shirts and threw them onto the bed. His pants followed. Then his one tie, his shoes, the jeans he wore to work, until the bed was heaped high with Jimmy's clothing.

Next she moved to the dresser. Socks. T-shirts. Underwear. She emptied every drawer, separating his things from hers. The boxer shorts he hated, the old, holey undershirts, the dress socks he never wore. She left her things and took out his, throwing them onto the bed, not caring if they fell to the floor.

After all, this was what he wanted. What he drove her to. If he didn't want to be her husband… The thought stuck in her chest and twisted there. She swallowed and steeled herself against the emotions that ran raw.

He deserves it. I don't care.

A lie, but she forced herself to believe it anyway. To act on it. Because to do anything else would hurt even more.

She grabbed the last pair of socks in the drawer and gasped. Pain sliced through her finger. Something sharp and small. She pulled out her hand and saw a thin line of blood across her index finger. It smeared the toe of one white sock. She stuck her finger in her mouth, then poked her other hand back into the drawer, feeling for the offending item.

There—a cool, thin edge, ribbed on one side, smooth on the other. She scooped it into her hand and drew out a small orange shell, old but unbroken. She turned it over in her palm. Still perfect after all these years. Still that same delicate shade of orange, mixed with creamy white.

She frowned. She wouldn't think of what it meant now, what it used to mean. She wouldn't remember. She dropped the shell back into the drawer and buried it in a pile of her panties. Those days didn't matter anymore. All that mattered was what Jimmy had done to her. What he had not done.

The past was gone.

She began to close the drawer, but as she did, a glint of silver caught her eye.

The locket. The same one she'd found on the beach, only shinier, brighter, and empty. This one was hers. Without faces, without happiness, without joy.

Barren.

She picked it up and clutched it in her hand. It still looked new, unused. She'd planned to put pictures of her first child inside it. Jimmy had said it was for pictures of him and her, but she knew better. It was for the baby. Always for the baby. She thought he'd understood that.

She let the chain slither through her fingers as she dropped the locket into her other hand. The locket that had once meant he loved her. And now meant he did not.

The locket reminded her so strongly of another place, another time. Jimmy had never known how the sight of a locket both hurt and healed her, reminded her of her pain and gave her hope. It conjured an image etched in a single memory of her mother's smiling face. Her mother, not with her church smile, but a real one. Rare and wondrous.

A smile and a baby's soft coo. So long ago, but still as vivid in memory as the day Kinna lived it.

The sun had shone through the window of the parsonage that day as Annie Smith sat smiling on the bright, floral couch with a baby in her arms—a happy, pink-wrapped bundle that cooed and didn't cry. Annie was barely nineteen and newly married, but there were whispers about her. Whispers Kinna's mom didn't share.

Some old hymn played on the tape deck. Outside, her dad's voice rose and fell as he practiced his next sermon while washing the car. Water splashed. The tape turned to another hymn. Something by Fanny Crosby, Kinna thought.

The baby flailed a tiny arm. Then came a funny popping sound. Sucking, maybe.

Kinna snuck farther into the room. She could almost see the baby's face, the chubby cheeks, the wisps of dark hair against the fluffy blanket.

Her mom sat on the couch next to Annie. Light glinted off her auburn hair, making it seem even brighter than usual. "She's beautiful, Ann. Perfect."

Annie shifted on the couch. "Thank you, Mrs. Hollis." She grinned, her face alight with a look Kinna had never seen there: happiness. Or something more, something like the look Kinna imagined when her dad talked about God's joy. Folks never much looked that way when he talked about it, but Annie looked that way now. Aglow, like little bubbles of laughter might sneak out and pop along the sun-strewn path to the window.

Annie is happy. God-happy. Like the kind we sing about. That's what it looks like. The thought tickled the edges of Kinna's mind. Happiness. Joy. Despite all those long evenings when the girl had come to the parsonage to cry and complain. Despite how she ranted about not wanting that fool's kid. Despite her threats about abortion and how she wouldn't marry that no-good, no-account loser and wouldn't have his baby neither.

But she did have it. And now she sat on the couch and looked at that little baby as if she'd never seen anything so pretty.

Kinna's mom looked too, as if she'd burst with pride. "You're a woman now, Ann. Welcome to God's wonderful plan for your life. Aren't you glad?"

"Yes, I am." Annie leaned forward. The necklace around her neck swung out over the baby. It caught the rays of sunlight and tossed the light back into Kinna's eyes. A locket. Inside, she just knew there was a picture of that cute little baby. The baby that had made Annie a woman, made her happy, and made Kinna's mom smile like there was nothing better in all the world.

Kinna never forgot that moment. Never forgot the flash of silver and the glimmer of peace. Of wholeness. And she just knew that someday

God would give her that same peace and wholeness. Someday, she would smile like that too. Someday she would be filled with that same joy. Someday, she would wear a locket with the image of a tiny face. And she would be a woman too.

But someday never came. *Oh, Lord...*

A knock came at the front door. Kinna jumped and dropped the locket into her pocket. The knock came again.

Could it be? She rushed out of the room. Maybe Jimmy had come back. Changed his mind, become contrite enough to knock instead of just barging back in.

She smoothed her hair. Maybe she should put on a touch of lipstick, another spritz of perfume.

Another knock. There wasn't time.

She jogged to the door, grabbed the knob, then paused and practiced a forgiving smile. *Jimmy, I knew you would come back.*

She flung open the door. The pimply face of a pizza delivery boy grinned at her. "Your order, ma'am."

She stared at him, at his stupid red hat, his shirt stained with pizza sauce, the ridiculous earring in one ear.

He held the box out toward her. "Eighteen-eighty, please."

Eighteen-eighty. The cost to put the last nail in the coffin of hope.

She retreated to the kitchen, pulled a twenty out of her purse, and gave it to the boy. "Keep the change."

"Gee, thanks."

She ignored the sarcasm in his voice.

He stuffed the bill in his pocket, then trotted down the steps and away.

Kinna stood in the doorway, the pizza box in her hand, her heart thudding a dull, sickly beat. Three minutes later, she shut the door and returned to the kitchen. She dropped the box onto the table, opened the flap, and took out a slice of pizza. Then she pulled out a chair and stared down the hallway.

From here, she could see the little room she'd converted into a nursery. She could see the seafoam green of the walls, the edge of the light maple crib, and a corner of the box of diapers she'd bought at Wal-Mart. And just barely, she could see Sally, one eye missing and a tear in a dress that used to be turquoise blue. A doll sitting on a shelf, waiting, waiting, waiting for another little girl to play with her in the sand.

I'm sorry, Sally.

Kinna shifted her vision to the end of the hall, to the open door of her bedroom and the pile of Jimmy's clothes on the bed. It wouldn't take long to move them to the guest room. Just a few minutes, really. A couple hundred seconds to finish what Jimmy had started.

A couple hundred seconds to end what had taken a lifetime to build.

9

Kinna dropped the final bag onto the guest room floor and glanced at the clock. Three minutes after five. Early for her double shift at the hospital, but she couldn't stay here. Her gaze flitted over the room. His shoes piled near the closet, his brush on the dresser, his clothes flopped over the chair. Her throat closed.

Don't think about it. Just walk away.

Could she? She had to. She had to get away and forget.

The best place to do that was at Marnie's Books and Brew bookstore and coffee shop. She'd nibble a sandwich and drown her sorrows in mocha and whipped cream. That always helped.

She grabbed her purse and headed for her minivan. Ten minutes later, she pulled into the full parking lot at Marnie's and crept along, looking for an empty spot. A woman with a stroller sauntered out to a red SUV. The SUV's lights blinked as the woman drew closer.

Kinna slowed the van. Her eyes narrowed. *Great. That's the only spot.* Her foot jammed onto the accelerator as she moved on. There was no way she was going to wait and watch some woman with her baby. She'd go without mocha first.

Come on, God, a little help here.

A BMW backed from a spot in the next aisle. *That's more like it.* Kinna zipped around the corner and into the spot.

"Thank you, Lor—" She stopped. She wouldn't thank Him. Not for this. God could answer stupid parking lot prayers, but not prayers for a baby or a marriage? There was something wrong with that. *You're messing with me, aren't You, God? Well, I don't think it's very funny.*

She clenched her jaw and pushed the thought from her mind. She was here for coffee and a little peace. Nothing more. She put the van in park, opened the door, and jumped out.

Marnie's was a cute little place, with a bookstore on one side and a coffee bar on the other. All about were scattered odd tables with mismatched chairs. Kinna's favorite was the table fashioned from driftwood. Jimmy preferred the one made with auto parts. But there were others too. One made with old-fashioned bottle caps, another with flowers pressed beneath a glass top. One of tin foil, which Kinna hated, and a big, long one covered with bumper stickers from all around the world. Marnie claimed to have gathered all the stickers herself back in her wild days.

Kinna had never had any wild days. She'd never wished for any until now. Maybe if she'd had wild days, this mess she called her life wouldn't hurt so much. Maybe she could tell herself that she deserved it. But she'd always played the good Christian girl. Gone to church, read her Bible, prayed. Didn't stray, didn't cuss, didn't steal. Well, didn't used to steal, anyway.

He won't give you more than you can bear. She'd believed that, banked on it, but it wasn't true. This day was more than she could bear. Jimmy's refusal, his clothes moved out, her hopes in shambles, her heart shattered, their marriage broken.

How can I believe now? How can I really think there's a loving God? Lord, I told You this would happen. I told You my faith can't endure one more day of facing this pain. There has to be a way. I can't believe that I've come this far to hear "no" again. I won't believe it.

Somehow, I'll find another way. Now, I need a miracle. And somehow, I'm going to get one.

Kinna straightened her shoulders and pushed open the coffee shop door. The merry tinkle of a bell rang in her ears as she stepped inside and turned toward the glass counter. The shop was as full as the parking lot. Groups huddled around tables—mothers with children, couples, and lots of people in business suits, just getting off work.

She weaved through the tables to the counter. The heady aroma of coffee filled her senses, along with something else, something sweet. Cookies right from the oven.

The woman behind the register flicked back a bit of dyed black hair and spoke before Kinna could order. "Decaf double white mocha, whip, organic milk, three pumps. Coming right up." She smiled.

Kinna laughed. "You got it, Marnie. And add a turkey sandwich." She dug in her purse for her wallet, then paused. "Wait. Make that with caffeine."

Marnie stopped. One eyebrow lifted to her hairline. "The coffee or the sandwich?"

"Both."

Marnie scratched out something on the cup's paper sleeve, then handed it to the kid behind the espresso machine. "Taking a walk on the wild side, huh?"

Kinna lifted her chin. "Yeah, I guess I am."

Why not? She'd cut out caffeine when she and Jimmy had decided to try to get pregnant. She hadn't had regular coffee, tea, soda, or a steaming cup of hot cocoa in years. She'd cut out a lot of things. Sweeteners, tap water, even Clairol hair coloring to cover those ugly strands of gray. Despite all that, she wasn't pregnant. And she wouldn't be.

"You want a double?"

"Sure." Wait, that was stupid. Her patients at the hospital wouldn't appreciate her being jacked up on caffeine, and Mai would be certain to notice. "Well, actually, let's just go with a single, please."

"Good choice."

Kinna stepped back from the counter and made her way toward the little outcropping where her coffee would appear. A single would be fine. After all, she couldn't let Mai know anything was wrong. "You and big man have a fight again, yes?" she'd say in that quick Vietnamese accent. "And now you drink too much coffee. Bad. Very bad." And then Kinna would have to make some excuse.

Mai liked the "big man"—what she called Jimmy even though he was only five foot eleven, still taller than Mai's husband who stood five foot six, max. Ever since Jimmy had gone over to their house one Saturday and re-dug their septic lines, he could do no wrong. "He is a good man," Mai always said. "He digs fine, big holes for free." But Mai didn't know how hurtful Jimmy could be.

A voice called out her order from behind the counter. "Large mocha, organic milk, with caffeine."

Kinna grabbed the cup and the bag with her sandwich and turned. A bit of steaming coffee sloshed from the cup's lid and splashed over her hand. She sucked in a breath.

"Are you all right?" The voice behind her was rich, with a hint of laughter. Kinna turned.

It was the woman from the beach. The locket gleamed at her neck. "Oh, it's you."

Thea threw out her arms. "See, 100 percent healthy. You do a good job of rescuing. I've never felt better."

Kinna studied her. Her hair, dry now, was a soft, light gray, swept into a style Kinna had never seen before. She wore no lipstick, no blush, no mascara. She didn't seem to need it. And she was right, she looked great.

Thea studied her. "Can't say the same for you, though. You look terrible."

Kinna frowned. "Thanks."

"What happened?"

"Nothing."

"Gotta be something if it left you looking worse than a cold swim in the ocean." She touched the locket's silver surface and narrowed her eyes. "The faces. I wonder…But it's not too late."

Kinna sighed. Half the things Thea said didn't make sense. The problem was that the other half did. Too much. She shifted her coffee to her right hand. "Too late for what?"

"For a good cup of coffee, of course. And a little chat. Join me?"

The kid behind the counter called out another order. "Carmel latte. No whip."

Thea picked up the coffee, careful not to spill. She turned back to Kinna. "Well? You're not meeting other friends, are you?"

Other friends? Kinna took a sip of her coffee. She didn't have many other friends anymore. She used to, but somehow, they'd all drifted away, had kids. She'd gotten so she couldn't stand the baby showers and kids' birthdays, and pretty soon, she had a lot of acquaintances and not so many friends.

"I have to get to work." She lowered the cup. "So I'll just…"

Thea clucked her tongue. "Did you know that people often look down and to their left when they lie?"

"No."

"You got a spot on your shoe."

Kinna glanced at her left shoe.

"Ah. Caught you."

Kinna's gaze flew back to the woman.

Thea smiled. The gesture softened her features, making them almost pretty, almost young again. "I'm too old to fall for that 'got to rush off to work' line. Your shift doesn't start until six, right? Besides, you were there when I needed rescuing. And now…honey." She emphasized the last word.

Kinna's face turned hot. "I don't need to be rescued."

The woman's eyebrows lifted and she chuckled, a rolling, rich sound that coaxed the smallest smile to Kinna's lips.

She stiffened her shoulders, willing herself to be firm, stern. "I don't."

Just because you saved a woman from drowning didn't mean she had the right to butt into your life. *Rescue me. Crazy woman. I'm fine.*

Except, of course, she wasn't. But still, she didn't want the whole world to know it. She should just walk out. Eat her sandwich and drink her coffee in the car. Alone. Like always.

Kinna tucked her sandwich bag beneath her arm, turned, and strode toward a table near the back wall. The driftwood table, her favorite. She maneuvered around a fake ficus and resisted the urge to look over her shoulder to see if Thea followed. She pulled out a chair and sat at the tiny table.

A moment later, Thea sat across from her. Another slow smile spread across her face. "This is my favorite table too. Hope you don't mind."

Did she? Maybe. At least she wouldn't have to sit here alone, staring at the woman with the stroller, or the other with the twin girls, or the giggling high schoolers who were someone's daughters too. She lifted the cup to her lips and took another sip. "How did you know this was my favorite?"

"Lucky guess." Thea set her cup on the table, set a paper bag next to it, and opened the bag. Three of Marnie's fresh cookies peeked from inside. Thea pushed the bag closer to Kinna. "Have a cookie."

Kinna scooted back in her chair. "No, thanks."

The woman pushed the cookies closer. "Don't tell me you're watching your weight."

"Well, no."

"Then have yourself a cookie. You deserve it. Anyone who fishes an old woman out of the water, lies about having to hurry to work, and has to talk to a not-crazy old lady over coffee deserves a cookie." She grinned.

Kinna took a cookie and bit into it: White chocolate macadamia nut, her favorite. "So, Thea…is that short for Dorthea?"

Thea studied her, then relaxed. "Aletheia. Means 'truth' in Greek."

Aletheia. A strange name, too young for a woman who looked sixty. "I've never heard that name before."

Thea twisted the sleeve on her coffee cup. "Named after a friend of my mother's."

"Must have been quite a friend."

"She was. Or so I've heard." Thea flicked her fingers in the air then settled them around her coffee cup. "But my friends just call me Thea."

"Okay, Thea."

Thea looked into Kinna's eyes. "So, this means we're friends?"

Kinna licked her lips, then took another sip of coffee. Friends. Hardly. But what else do you call it when you save someone's life?

There was something different about Aletheia. Something that reminded Kinna of something, or someone. And she wasn't sure she liked it.

Thea took a swig of her coffee, but the gesture didn't hide the flash of her smile.

Kinna liked the woman's smile, even if she wasn't sure she liked the woman herself. It made her eyes sparkle and wrinkle a little at the corners, just like Jimmy's used to do, back when they were happy, like those people in the locket. There was a safe topic. She set down her cup. "Tell me about your parents. Were they always happy together?"

Thea laughed. "Hardly. They've had tough times just like anyone else."

"But they love each other. Stayed together."

"Seventy-plus years and counting."

"Wow. And they never doubted? That they belonged together, I mean."

For a while, Thea didn't answer. Then she licked her lips. "Of course, they doubted. No one lives a fairy tale."

Kinna picked at the seam of her cup. Once she'd wished for a fairy tale. Once she thought she'd found it. Happily ever after, forever. "How many children did they have?"

The woman smiled. "Just me. They called me their miracle child."

"Well, one child is better than none at all. It's enough." Kinna stared at her half-empty coffee cup.

"Enough? Really?

"How many children did you have?"

"Five, and now I'm the grandmother of six more."

"No wonder they're so happy." She tried to keep the bitterness from her voice and failed.

Thea's eyes narrowed. "They're happy because they chose to be. They chose to love."

Pain lanced through Kinna's chest. "Sometimes love isn't enough."

"How do you spell love, Kinna?"

Kinna straightened. "What did you say?"

"I said that love *is* enough, if it's the right kind of love."

Kinna's voice lowered to a whisper. "And what kind of love is that?"

"God's. From God. G-O-D." She glanced away. "That's how I spell love."

Kinna swallowed. Thea was a Christian, and now she'd hear some useless tripe about how God could heal anything, how she just had to believe, how everything would turn out all right. All the things Kinna once believed, once built her faith on. But it was no good anymore. Thea didn't understand. No one did.

"I'm a Christian too." It came out short, defensive. She'd been a Christian as long as she could remember. Before she could remember. She knew all the phrases, all the buzz words, all the clichés. She believed in God. God just didn't believe in her.

I'm not blaming God, am I? I'm blaming Jimmy. It was all Jimmy's fault. But she didn't feel like letting God off the hook completely.

Thea brushed a crumb from the table and looked into Kinna's eyes. "I know."

"You seem to know a lot."

Thea took a sip of her latte. "I could tell you're a Christian. No offense, of course."

Kinna forced herself to relax. She was too touchy these days, too sensitive. Hadn't Jimmy been saying the same thing?

Well, he was wrong.

Are you sure?

Yes.

Thea leaned back and smiled that warm smile that reached all the way to her eyes.

Relax, Kinna. God knows you need a friend. Especially now. And especially one who didn't know Jimmy, or at least one who wouldn't go running to him with everything she said. Or judge her, or tell her she was really to blame.

"My mother said there was a time before I was born when they almost divorced. Said she'd given up hope, and Daddy had too."

"You're kidding. What happened? To keep them together, I mean. What changed?"

"They remembered."

"Remembered what?"

"Everything."

Kinna frowned.

"So, what happened today?" Thea's voice deepened as she spoke.

"What do you mean?" Kinna blinked and shifted in her chair.

Thea pointed at her. "A woman doesn't wear that look for nothing. Something's changed."

Kinna swallowed. "All right. I moved my husband's clothes to the guest room." She gripped her cup in tight hands and stared at Thea, expecting condemnation, surprise, or disapproval.

Instead, Thea just looked at her, her expression unwavering. "How will he take it?"

Kinna's throat tightened. "Maybe he'll finally sit up and take notice."

Thea scowled. "Don't you think he notices already?"

"If he did, he'd fight for our marriage. He wouldn't just walk away whenever I say something he doesn't like. Walk away when..." She couldn't say it, couldn't voice what he'd walked away from. Not just her, but everything that mattered to her. He'd walked away from it all and never bothered to look back.

"Men are like that."

A chill danced over Kinna's arms. She stared at her coffee, at the shimmering taupe surface, at the wisps of whipped cream. Stared and tried not to scream.

Thea's hand touched her arm. "It doesn't mean they don't care."

"It does for Jimmy." The words slipped from her, low and pained.

"Are you certain?"

Certain? Of course she was. How could it be any other way, when he...when he...*I just want to forget.*

But she couldn't forget. Not what happened at the house, and not what happened years ago. It was a little memory, one she hadn't recalled in a long, long time. Jimmy had hidden his feelings before. Said he didn't care, shouted it even, when he cared very much. She'd seen the truth, but he was young then, just past his eleventh birthday, and less skilled at walking away.

They were at the beach again—it seemed they were always at the beach—but it was cold that day. They wore puffy down jackets and looked like pink and green versions of the Michelin Man as they crouched behind an outcropping of rocks beneath the pier.

Kinna wrinkled her nose and moved closer to him. "Stick out your tongue."

"No."

"Come on. Let's see."

Jimmy stuck it out.

She giggled. "It's all blue."

"Let me see yours."

She put out her tongue, then crossed her eyes, trying to see its color. She couldn't make it out. "Well?" She garbled the word, her tongue still outstretched.

He grinned. "Red. Now I'll try a cherry one and see if my tongue turns purple. You get raspberry."

Kinna pulled two more Jolly Ranchers from her pocket and handed him the red one. "Okay, here's yours. Let me know when you're done."

"I bet we'll have the same color. Show me your shell collection."

They'd hunted shells for an hour and had them heaped in little piles before them. Hers were all black and ugly, mussel shells pried from concrete blocks beneath the pier. His were ugly too, except for one. It was orange and delicate and shiny. Perfect, except for a tiny chip in its side.

Jimmy tipped forward on his knees and poked a finger at her pile of shells. "We'll have to pretend they're different colors."

"Like candy?"

"That's a good idea. Let's use the rest of the Jolly Ranchers."

"They'll get all gross if they touch the water."

He scowled. "Guess you're right. We'll just use my orange shell." He cleaned it off in the water, then cradled it in his palm. "This used to be the bed of a tiny mermaid princess. It's shaped from a perfect pearl."

She leaned closer and touched it with one finger. "It's pretty enough, Jimmy. You don't have to pretend."

He pulled it away from her. "You're no fun."

"Can I have it?"

"No."

"Why not?"

"Because it reminds me of my mom. She had one just like it that she kept her rings in. She had an opal and a great big brown one she called 'tiger's eye.' I liked that one."

Kinna patted Jimmy's arm. She wouldn't take the shell now, not for anything. It was special.

"I gotta go. My dad's here." Jimmy pointed behind Kinna.

She looked back. Jimmy's father sat on a rock, waiting. Just waiting. His long hair blew in the breeze as he looked out over the bay toward Santa Cruz. He didn't seem drunk.

She pointed to the shell in Jimmy's hand. "Think your dad would like it? Maybe remind him of something happy?"

Jimmy didn't answer as he stood and stared at the shell. Slowly his fingers closed over it. He straightened his shoulders and strode toward his father.

Kinna followed a ways behind. She stopped as Jimmy held out the shell. "Look, Dad, it's just like the kind Mom used to have on her dresser."

For a moment, Kinna thought his father wouldn't even look, but he did. His gaze slipped down to the shell in Jimmy's hand. His jaw hardened. "That ain't nothing like it, boy." He stood and walked away.

Jimmy didn't move.

Kinna sidled closer. "Maybe he's just grumpy." She whispered the words so only Jimmy could hear.

"It doesn't matter." Jimmy's tone was flat, dead.

Kinna touched his arm. "Yes it does."

He batted her hand away. "No, it doesn't, Kinna. He was right. I was wrong. This isn't like Mom's shell. It's no good."

She stepped back. "It's still real pretty."

Jimmy opened his fingers and threw the shell into the sand. Then he followed his father.

"Jimmy!"

He looked back. "You keep it, Kinna. I don't care." He turned away. And then he shouted. Loud enough to send the seagulls flapping from the rocks. Loud enough to make tears jump to her eyes. "You hear me? I don't care! I don't care one bit!"

Funny how she could still remember all the details. Still hear how the waves sounded on the rocks, and the call of a seal way out in the water. Still smell the briny scent of seaweed and see the twisted vines of kelp on the shore. And still see that tiny shell and how it glistened in the sand.

She had kept it all these years, that same silly shell she'd found in her dresser today. Because she knew Jimmy cared. No matter what he did, no matter what he said, she knew the truth.

Kinna's gaze met Thea's across the table. "How can anyone be certain of anything?"

Thea nodded.

Kinna looked away, past the ficus and across the room.

And there she saw Jimmy, sitting at the bottle cap table, his coffee in front of him.

And beside him was another woman.

10

Jimmy twirled the stir stick between his fingers, then dropped it into his coffee. In the seat next to him, Karly jabbered about her sister's parakeet.

He tried to listen but failed.

He tugged at his collar. It was too warm in Marnie's today. Crowded. Normally, he'd love the action. People coming in and out, voices, laughter. Watching the door to see if he could spy a friend, calling out a hello. But today he sat with his back to the door, hoping no one would see him with this woman who wasn't his wife. But what did it matter? He wasn't doing anything wrong. Just coffee, that's all. He shouldn't feel so ashamed.

The only person he could see clearly was the man cleaning the table opposite him with quick, efficient strokes. The old guy had been working there for six months, but Jimmy still hadn't learned his name, still hadn't talked to him. And that just showed how much Kinna's attitude had changed him, made him into someone he didn't want to be. It was her fault.

Well, maybe not, but it made him feel better to blame her. Otherwise, this would be yet another thing he'd done wrong. *What's one more?*

As if reading his thoughts, the man glanced up and frowned. Then he bent over and snatched a stray napkin that had fallen beneath the table.

Jimmy allowed his gaze to wander. He could almost make out the edge of the coffee bar without moving his head. He could hear the hiss of steam as Marcus made another cappuccino. Good kid, Marcus. Always asking how he and Kinna were doing.

Kinna.

Jimmy forced his attention back to Karly. Her words came faster now, but her voice seemed too high, too screechy. What was wrong with him?

She wouldn't be here if she knew you lost your job.

And you shouldn't be here at all.

He squelched the thoughts. Lots of guys changed jobs, and lots of guys got coffee with women other than their wives. It didn't mean anything. It was good for him to expand his social circle, get out a little, enjoy the company of others.

Only he wasn't enjoying it. Not at all.

He glanced over Karly's shoulder. The cleaning man had moved to a narrow counter along the wall to straighten packets of artificial sugar and restock the straws. The man was older, with a head shiny-bald, and his shirt crisp and clean despite his work. He smiled as he waved to a little boy a few tables over. The gesture seemed familiar.

Jimmy watched as the man tucked his rag into his back pocket, then straightened a chair at the table made entirely from crayons. He picked up something else from the floor. A pacifier.

Jimmy swallowed.

The man moved right. And this time, Jimmy's gaze followed. He couldn't help it. The man handed the pacifier to a woman at the next table with a baby in her lap.

Jimmy shuddered. *If you'd told her the truth…*

I can't.

It's only a baby.

Only a baby. There was no such thing as only a baby. If Kinna had taught him anything, it was that. It was a good thing Karly sat next to him and not Kinna. Karly didn't even notice the kid. Her eyes were fixed squarely on him, the man with her at the table. Just as it should be.

He turned to her and smiled.

Karly leaned closer. "If you were there, Jimmy, you'd have been able to get that parakeet out of the downspout no problem."

Downspout? Jimmy blinked.

Karly tilted her head slightly, her fingers resting on the table between them.

"What?"

Karly lowered her gaze. "I've seen how you operate the machinery at the site. You would have gotten that engine's ladder up there in two seconds." Her smile filled with admiration, confidence, as she raised her eyes to capture his. "Just like Alan would have gotten out without all those broken ribs if that stupid Bill hadn't insisted on running the machine himself. I can't believe he didn't let you do it."

His pulse quickened. It had been too long since someone looked at him like that. Too long for him to tell her what really happened. "So the bird was all right in the end?"

Karly took the lid off her coffee cup and slowly stirred her drink.

Jimmy watched the movement of her hand, the swirl of the liquid. Why didn't it look like that when he stirred?

Karly licked her lips.

Jimmy grabbed his cup.

She moved closer.

He took a quick gulp of hot coffee and choked.

Karly jumped up and patted him on the back. "Are you okay?"

He sputtered and looked up. "Yeah, sure. Wrong pipe."

Her lips pursed. She was close, so close he could see the flecks of gold in her eyes. Too close.

He scooted back. "Thanks."

She didn't move. Not back to her seat, not to the other side of the table. He didn't know if he wanted her to.

"Jimmy." Her gaze fluttered down again. Her tone softened.

He knew what was coming, and he wanted her to say it. Wanted it, and didn't want it. He didn't know how to stop it, either way.

She touched her chest, her fingers near a neckline much too low to be this close to a married man.

Her mouth opened.

He caught the scent of her perfume.

"You know that I—ouch!"

Glass shattered. Shards flew. Bits of coffee splattered over Jimmy's chest and arms. He jerked back.

Karly screamed and tipped sideways.

The man who'd been cleaning tables stood behind her. "Sorry, miss." He reached out and righted her. On the floor beside them lay pieces of a broken mug. "You all right?"

Karly smoothed her hair with one hand and turned toward the man. "I'm fine." The softness in her voice had gone. "Just be more careful, okay? And clean up that glass."

The man rubbed his nose, and Jimmy noticed the terrible scar that marred his right cheek and ran all the way to one clouded eye. "Beg pardon, miss." The man's eyes narrowed, and for an instant, Jimmy saw something there. And it wasn't apology.

He stood.

The man took a step back. He rubbed his fingers alongside his mouth, then grimaced. A familiar move. Where had Jimmy seen it before?

"I'm sorry, miss, but I think I got some chocolate on the elbow of your blouse." He reached out and touched the spot. "Sure did. I hear chocolate stains real bad." He clucked his tongue. "If it don't come out, you go ahead and send me the dry cleaners bill."

Karly yanked at her sleeve, her eyebrows bunching as she saw the stain. "You can bet I will, old man."

The man pulled out his rag and twisted it in his hand. "They say if you soak it right away…"

Karly glanced at the man, then over at Jimmy. She sighed. "Next time, huh, Jim?"

He nodded.

She laid her hand on his chest and smiled up into his eyes. Then she grabbed her purse from the opposite chair. "You have my number. Give me a call." She turned, her shoes crunching broken glass.

Jimmy nodded again, then watched her sashay around the tables and out the door. The bell danced as the door swung shut behind her, but Jimmy couldn't hear it over the awkward thudding of his heart. He let out a long breath.

The man swept up the bits of glass with a minibroom that hung from his belt. He scooped them into a dust pan, emptied it into the trash, and strode back to Jimmy. "Well, I'd say that was a close call, son."

Jimmy plopped into his chair and ran his fingers through his hair. He stared at the man. The bald head, the terrible scar, the lines that wrinkled his forehead. None of it was familiar. And yet…

"Guess I should say I'm sorry I ran off your girl."

A pang jolted through Jimmy. "She's not my girl."

The man pulled out a chair and flipped his rag over his shoulder. "Appears she wants to be." He sat down.

"Do I know you?"

The man shook his head. "Do you? Name's Joe." He stuck out his hand.

Their eyes met. Something tightened in Jimmy's stomach. Tightened and twisted, until he fought the feeling down. He shook the man's hand. "Jimmy."

"So, you gonna make that flighty chick your girl?"

Jimmy frowned. "That's none of your business."

Joe clucked his tongue. His tone remained even, neutral. "Nope."

"I'm married."

"Yep."

A chill, cold and awful, slithered through Jimmy's gut. "How'd you know?"

"You got a ring. She don't."

Jimmy rubbed the gold surface of his ring with his thumb. A simple band, etched with a dove and a cross.

The man watched him, studied him, waiting. As if he expected something. As if he wanted something, yet was afraid of it too. He shook his head. "All right, then. Look, son. I know you don't need some fool old man meddling in your business."

"No, I don't."

The man grinned. "Then it's a good thing I ain't no fool old man."

Jimmy sat back. The man was still eyeing him with his one good eye, his arms crossed over his chest, the overhead lights shining off his bald pate.

The man's eyes slipped down, away. His voice lowered. "I seen you plenty of times in here. You seemed like a decent sort."

Ah, that explained it. The man had seen him in here with Kinna.

Joe sat forward and put his elbows on the table. "Look, son. It's just that I ain't always been like this." He waved a hand toward his face and chest. "I had a real nice family once. Wife. Kid."

Something tickled at the edge of Jimmy's mind. A memory, maybe, or a dream. A nightmare. "What happened?"

His voice turned bitter. "Threw it away. And now all I got is this dirty old rag." He took the rag from his shoulder and tossed it onto the table. "And a minimum wage job at someone else's coffee shop."

"Sorry." Jimmy looked at the old man and wondered what it had taken for him to lose everything. Had it just slipped away little by little? Or was there one big mistake that stole it all?

"Not that I ain't grateful for this job, mind you. And I'd sure appreciate it if you didn't say anything to Marnie about my little mishap. The broken mug's bad enough, but she don't need to know about the chocolate on the girlie's blouse."

Jimmy smiled. "I won't. But Marnie'd understand. Looks like you're doing a great job here."

Joe guffawed. "Except for that bit about knocking over your girl, breaking a bunch of glass, and putting stains on her shirt."

"Just an accident." He paused. "Wasn't it?"

Joe didn't answer.

"Well, they can always use cheap help over at the Petersen construction site if things don't work out for you here." Jimmy tried to keep the bitterness out of his voice. "They hire part-time too. You got any experience in construction?"

Joe looked away. "I spent the last twenty years in prison, son. I don't got experience in nothin' but mindin' my own business. And now I ain't even doin' that."

"You sound perfect for the Peterson job." Jimmy studied him. Prison. Strange that Marnie would hire an ex-con, but then, Marnie was always doing something unexpected. That's why everyone liked her. Ten to one Marnie had given the man a long lecture about God's mercy and second chances, then hired him just to prove her point.

"So, you gonna tell me why you're here with that other woman?"

"Don't you have work to do?"

"Break time."

"You always give Marnie's customers the third degree?"

"Only when they look like they need it."

"Well, I don't."

Joe lifted the eyebrow on his good side.

Jimmy grimaced. "All right, you got me."

"So what are you doing here with that two-bit—I mean, with that unattached young lady?"

"Just coffee as friends. Nothing more."

"And what would your wife say if she knew?"

Jimmy blew out a breath. "She doesn't know." He rubbed his forehead. "And even if she did, she wouldn't care. My wife only cares about two things: her job and having a baby. And since I can't help with either of those…" He waited for the man's quip, for some derogatory remark, for anything.

Nothing came.

Jimmy scooted back in his chair. "My dad always said she was too good for me. Said she'd figure out what I was eventually. And then, well…I guess he was right."

Joe tipped back until the front legs of his chair lifted from the ground. "You listen to your daddy, son? Even when he sounds like a doggone fool who don't know his backside from a gopher hole?"

Jimmy grunted. "Good thing he's not here to hear you say that."

"I suppose you think he'd take me out to the back forty and give me a good thrashing."

Jimmy sighed. "Something like that."

Joe leaned forward. "Listen, son. I've got something to—" He stopped and took a deep breath. "What would you say to that daddy of yours if he were sitting right here?"

Heat rose in Jimmy's chest, scalding, burning. His fists clenched beneath the table. "I wouldn't say a thing. I'd get up and walk out. I've got nothing to say to that man. Ever."

"Sounds mighty bitter. Don't the Good Book say something 'bout forgiveness?"

"I haven't seen my old man in over twenty years. Probably dead, for all I know. For all I care."

"Well, I suppose some guys got it comin' to 'em."

"Yeah?"

"Yeah." Joe pressed his palms against the table. "But then again, some guys don't get what they deserve."

"You sound like you know what you're talking about."

He nodded. "I do. And let me tell you, I've listened to enough fools in my life, and been a big enough one myself, to know stupid when I hear it. I got a PhD in stupid. So you listen up. You got a wife. You got a chance. And that's something to fight for."

"I am."

"You are, eh?" He scowled. "I wonder if that's what it looks like to her." He jabbed his finger toward the other side of the room.

Jimmy's eyes followed the gesture. Across the tables, over the counter, behind the ficus. To Kinna.

His eyes met hers. His stomach dropped to his shoes. How much had she seen?

Kinna didn't remember how she'd gotten out of the coffee shop, into her car, and all the way to the hospital. She just remembered sitting there, staring, as that pretty twentysomething hussy moved closer to her husband. And closer, until she could almost see the breath from those too-red lips fanning his cheek. Could almost hear the whispers. Could almost feel those perfectly manicured fingers reaching out to take everything Kinna had once held dear. But it hadn't happened. It was only a touch, then the woman was gone. The old man had chased her away. That blessed, blessed man. Maybe he was an angel.

She'd kept watching until that instant when Jimmy's guilt-ridden eyes had risen to capture hers. That moment when all the fear, all the regret, all the hurt of these past years exploded in a single burst of agony within her.

Then she understood. This was why he had refused her. This was why he had crushed her last hope. Another woman.

It all made sense. It changed everything.

And this time, it was she who'd fled.

She straightened her hospital nametag and rounded the corner toward the nurses' station. Mai sat behind a stack of manila folders, her fingers rhythmically tapping the keys of the computer on the desk. She paused and rustled through some papers.

Kinna slowed.

Mai glanced up. "You early. Double shift for you tonight, yes?"

Kinna nodded.

A man pushed an old woman in a wheelchair past her and down the long hallway. The chair creaked as they turned into a room. Behind her, the elevator beeped. Above, the intercom crackled. Familiar sounds, calming, but they did nothing for her nerves tonight.

Mai straightened a stack of papers and frowned. "You look sick."

Kinna let her gaze drop. Here it came. Mai would ask if she had a fight with the big man, and the lecture would ensue. Not tonight. She couldn't stand it tonight.

"Pale." Mai's brows knit together in a deeper scowl. "Are you pregnant?"

The question slammed into her gut like a fist. She caught her breath. "No. N-O."

Mai sighed. "Maybe next month? You keep trying. You and the big man."

Kinna shook her head. She wasn't going to have this conversation. Not after what she'd seen at the coffee shop.

It shouldn't have mattered. She shouldn't care. She was the one who moved Jimmy's clothes. She was the one who had thrown his shirts into the hall in one big heap, then kicked them along the carpet and into the guest room.

She shuddered. She'd thought Jimmy would be horrified by what she'd done, that he'd understand at last how much he'd hurt her by refusing her. But what if he just took his clothes and moved out altogether? What if he saw what she'd done and didn't say a word? What if he really didn't care after all?

Him and God. What if neither of them loved her? What if today proved it?

She caught her breath. "I'm going to check on Mrs. Tilden." She turned toward the room at the far end of the hall.

"Kinna?" Mai's voice called out behind her.

She ignored it. No more questions. No more frowning eyes. No more probing into things too tender to touch. She just had to be Nurse Kinna again. Care for her patients, pray for them, bring a little light into their hospital stay.

"Kinna."

No. Her patients needed her. Mrs. Tilden needed her. Mrs. Tilden was her favorite. There was something special about that woman. She adjusted the lanyard around her neck, reached for the door, and opened it.

The room was quiet. She stepped inside, pulled back the curtain, and saw the empty bed. Her throat closed. *Oh no.*

"I tried to tell you," Mai said softly behind her. "She passed away this morning."

Kinna's knees shook. Patients died. It was part of the job, and she'd known Mrs. Tilden was terminal. But why today? *Lord, why today?* She took a deep breath. "Did she wake up?"

Mai touched her shoulder. "Yes."

"And she knew?"

"Yes."

"I'll miss her." She put up a finger before Mai could comment. "And don't say anything about not getting attached. I know the drill."

Mai nodded. "Your shift not start for ten minutes. Maybe you take time to think?"

Or to fall apart. Kinna sighed. "Shut the door."

Mai did. The room seemed so empty now, so quiet. A different silence than when Mrs. Tilden lay here. Then there had been a strange sort of peace in this room. Now there was only emptiness.

Kinna moved to the side of the bed and ran her finger over the taut sheet. Yesterday a woman slept here. Today there was nothing. Sometimes life was like that. You had something, and then it was gone. Other times, you never had it at all. Pain, loss, disappointment. Maybe that's all life was. And then you died. Where was the hope in that?

Barren.

A bit of white caught Kinna's eye. She bent over and picked something up from under the chair. A single petal from a gardenia. She lifted it to her nose and inhaled a wisp of sweet scent, the last lingering smells of life and hope. She rubbed the petal between her fingers, then slipped it into her pocket.

She glanced at the clock. Just seven minutes to compose herself and find the cheery, efficient woman who was Nurse Kinna. Seven minutes to forget what she'd seen at the coffee shop, what she'd done at home, what she'd once hoped for—what she'd lost.

No, not lost. Somehow she'd figure out how to resurrect her dreams, her hopes. She wouldn't let them die. Kinna Henley wasn't a quitter. She could do anything she set her mind to. That's what Mom always said. And she had to believe it, especially now.

She sat in the chair, leaned back, and closed her eyes.

Outside, she could hear the low beep of the intercom, the muffled thud of thick-soled shoes, the squeak of a cart being pushed by. She rubbed her temples, willing herself to erase the images of Jimmy and that woman, of his face as he left her, of the brilliant color of his eyes, even after all these years. She tried to forget, but all she could do was remember. That face, those eyes. And superimposed over them, the image of the twelve-year-old boy he had once been.

"It's no use, Kinna." She could hear his voice across the years, could see the intense look he had given her as they squatted behind the first pew. "Won't do no good."

Kinna opened the big book in her lap and stabbed her finger at the words. "It says it right here. 'And whats-o-ever ye,' that's fancy-talk for 'you,' 'shall ask in my name, that will I do.' John 14:13. And that's God talking, so it's got to be true."

"Yeah? What's the rest of the verse say?" Light from the stained glass window slanted across his face in colors of red and blue.

She rolled her eyes. "It doesn't matter. I'm telling you, we just ask and God will fix it."

"We can ask till the fog comes in, but my dad won't all of a sudden let me go to summer camp."

"The Bible says so. The B-I-B-L-E, and that means something."

"I say it's Dad that's gotta do the asking."

"Well, he's not doing it, is he?"

Jimmy folded his arms across a chest just startling to thicken with muscle. "No."

Kinna stared up at the big cross at the front of the church. Her fingers picked at the olive green carpet. "Well then, I'm going to. And you can't stop me."

She did. And he didn't.

She prayed that Jimmy's dad would let him go to the camp that summer. She prayed he would stop his drinking and be a good dad to Jimmy. That he would go to church, read his Bible, and stop being mean. She prayed he would love God and be nice. She prayed everything would be good and happy and perfect always.

But Jimmy was right. It was no use. His dad kept drinking, he didn't read his Bible, and he sure didn't let Jimmy go to camp that summer. Even though she'd prayed.

Just like she prayed Mrs. Tilden wouldn't die.

But Mrs. Tilden died.

And that God would give her a baby.

But she was still barren.

And that somehow Jimmy would understand and help her.

Instead, all she got was some young hussy with too-red lips and a too-low blouse.

Why even pray, God?

Kinna opened her eyes and looked out the window on the far side of the room. In the distance, she could see the swaying of the cypress trees and the first licking of fog through the branches. The sky darkened. Voices drifted past the room from the hallway, grew loud, then faded to silence.

Kinna stood. She reached into her pocket and touched the smooth petal of the gardenia. Then she felt something else. Cold, round, etched metal. She drew the locket from her pocket and opened it.

And there was nothing inside. No faces. No smiles. No hope.

She dropped it back into her pocket. And then she prayed. Really prayed, even though it was no use. Even though God wouldn't answer her prayers. She prayed, anyway.

Then the intercom screeched.

11

The Harley screamed around the corner and headed for the cliffs. The last dribbles of sunlight skimmed across the ocean and trickled into Jimmy's eyes. Wind blew in his hair. He squeezed his hands, and the motorcycle spurted forward. Someone shouted. Pavement turned to gravel, gravel to packed sand. The rocks loomed before him. Faster. Farther. Nothing but wind and sky and endless ocean. Only the water before, and all his fears behind. Gone. Forgotten.

He crashed through the wooden fence. The ground fell away. And then he was free. Free as an osprey flying away from all his problems, all his past. Free.

The water rushed toward him. Its face sparkled, its mouth open wide.

He fell. Down, down. And never hit the water.

Jimmy opened his eyes. He stood at the edge of the beach. There was no motorcycle, no wild ride, no airborne flight, no leaving his fears behind. There were just the last trickles of sunlight, the waves of the bay, and a sandpiper hopping along the beach.

He sighed. He should have come up with a better fantasy. He couldn't afford a Harley, even in his dreams. The best he could do was one of those cheap scooters with the lawnmower engine they rented at the place down the road. He squeezed his eyes shut and adjusted the image, replacing the roar of the Harley with the shrill buzz of a scooter. The image became a lot less appealing.

He grimaced and plunked down on a rock. In front of him, the sandpiper stopped and pecked at a shell, long strands of kelp washed over mussel-ridden boulders, and the sun slipped behind the horizon.

He shook his head. His plan to drown spectacularly in the ocean wasn't going to work out, so he'd have to think of another way to avoid Kinna. To avoid explaining about the coffee shop, or how he let Alan down, or how he lost his job. It would be better if she never found out, never knew all the mistakes of this one day. Coffee with Karly was only one of them, a small one, and even that Kinna wouldn't forgive. She would just sputter and accuse and blame. And slip farther from him.

Why should he care? What did it matter? In his better moments, he thought they had a chance, but when the illusion slipped away, he knew better. There was no way he could make things right. No way he could ever make her happy. Not like before, not like when they were kids.

In those days, he'd made her an origami swan. It was a simple thing, but she had clutched it to her chest and told him how perfect it was, how beautiful. She said she'd keep it forever. And she probably would have, if he hadn't made it out of his dad's paycheck.

He messed that up too, just like he did everything else without even trying.

God, what's wrong with me? Why can't I do anything right? Help me. Fix this mess I've made.

Two more sandpipers hopped down the beach. A white gull joined them.

Jimmy pulled a bit of bread out of his pocket, broke it into chunks, and tossed it to the birds. He always kept a few crusts in his pocket.

The gull squawked at the other birds, then snatched up the biggest piece. The sandpipers settled for the crumbs.

He looked at them and frowned. "I know just how you feel, boys."

The sandpipers blinked at him, then hopped closer, looking for more bread.

He crumbled some more in his hand and held it out. They blinked again and hopped back.

"Come on." If he tossed it to them, the gull would get it. But if they'd just hop a little closer… Jimmy slipped down from the rock and dropped to one knee. He let a couple small pieces of bread fall to the ground.

The sandpipers looked at them but wouldn't come nearer.

Just take a chance. He willed them closer. *I've got something good here for you if you just come. Don't be afraid.*

They turned and hopped away.

Jimmy grunted and dropped the bread back in his pocket, then straightened and sat back on the rock. Silly birds. He'd given them bread before. Why couldn't they just trust him?

Why couldn't they—

A wild yowl shattered his thoughts.

The sound came again.

Jimmy pivoted on the rock. His eyes widened. On the path along the beach, a woman rollerbladed with her dog. One arm flailed like a windmill while the other stuck straight out in front of her as the dog pulled her along.

She sped closer, wind plastering her gray hair back from eyes as round as pennies and a mouth that matched. Yellow light flashed over her face as she rolled beneath a streetlight. Shadows embraced her, followed by another glow of light, until it seemed that Jimmy was watching her in the flickering of an old black-and-white movie. Then the dog— half mop, half monster—quickened its pace to a long lope.

The woman shouted again, and Jimmy leaped up. The dog bolted, and the woman plunged forward. She dropped the leash and both arms windmilled. The woman tottered then spun left.

The dog surged forward and jumped.

Jimmy saw nothing but fur and teeth and a hung pink tongue flying toward him. He gasped and fell backward as the dog hit his chest. Bits of rock dug into his back.

Sharp teeth. Hot breath. A soft, gooey tongue splashing all over his face. He pushed the dog back and forced his way up to a sitting position. The dog dropped its paws onto Jimmy's shoulders and panted in his face.

A voice shot from Jimmy's left. "Down, girl! Get off!"

He glanced through fur and a wagging tongue to see the woman, somehow still upright, rolling toward him.

She waved her arm. "Get down, Tulip!"

Jimmy froze at the name. He shook his head. It couldn't be. This had to be some kind of joke.

The woman hit the edge of the path, then quickstepped through the sand toward him.

The dog lowered its paws and laid its head in Jimmy's lap. He scratched it behind the ears as the woman stumbled up to him.

She let out a long breath and grinned. "Sorry about that." She took the dog's collar and tugged.

The dog didn't budge.

The woman pushed a wisp of hair off her flushed face. She lifted her foot and shook it at the ankle. "Just had to try these ridiculous things. I've wanted to forever. Had visions of sailing down the path like a windpiper."

"A what?"

She laughed and shook her head. "Never mind." She flopped down on the rock beside him. "I should have stuck to dreaming about it." She leaned back then held out her hand. "Name's Thea. I'm sorry you had to see all that. Not the way I typically like to meet new people."

He chuckled and shook her hand. "Jimmy. And this meeting isn't half as bad as the one I had a minute ago." He nodded toward the long-haired dog.

Thea grimaced. "She seems to have taken a liking to you. Glad you caught her for me."

Jimmy patted the dog's head and ran a hand down the shaggy fur. He loved dogs. Not that he'd ever owned one. But dogs meant happy boys with sticks over their shoulders, straw hats and fishing, lazy summer days, and someone who liked you just because you were you. Everyone ought to have a dog. Too bad Kinna hated the mess.

He handed Thea the leash. "Here's your dog."

"Oh, she's not mine."

"Don't tell me you're a professional dog walker."

"They have those?"

"Of course."

Her eyebrows flicked up. "You people are so innovative."

"You're dog-sitting then?"

"You sit on your dogs too?"

"What are you talking about?"

"What are *you* talking about?"

Jimmy frowned. "You taking care of someone else's dog." Though who would let this nutty lady tend their dog, he couldn't figure. The owner must have been desperate.

"Ah." Thea nodded. "I see. No, she's a stray. I found her wandering the beach this morning. Looks like she's been homeless for awhile now. My family's always been big dog lovers, so I couldn't just leave her there. I'm hunting for a new home for her." Her eyes narrowed, and she looked him up and down. "She likes you."

Silence.

"My dad always says every man needs a good dog." She gave him a quick wink.

The dog nuzzled into his ribs, then looked up at him with big brown eyes. He rubbed the mutt's ears.

Thea stood.

Jimmy glanced at her and noticed her necklace. A locket, with tulips engraved on the silver surface. It was similar to the one he'd had made for Kinna. Very similar. What was it with that locket lately? He moved forward. "Nice necklace."

The woman touched it. "Thank you, sir." She reached down, loosened the rollerblades, and knocked the sand from their wheels. "I need to take this a little more slowly. Join me? Walk the dog? I don't think I can handle any more of her."

Jimmy scowled. "I'm not taking this dog."

She patted his arm. "Just a little walk. Down the path."

"And that's it."

"Of course."

"All right, then." Why not? He could walk on the sandy side while she tried out the blades along the path. It wasn't like he had anything to rush home to. Especially since he couldn't get his hands on a good, fast Harley.

Thea rolled up her pantlegs. The skin underneath was spotted with age, but firm and strong, as if she did a lot of walking.

"Come on. We might spy a few otters, if we hurry." She wobbled back to the path, then started to roll slowly down it.

Jimmy pushed the dog off him, took the leash, and followed. The path wound along the beach and was almost empty tonight, most people having left hours before. They kept on. A bicyclist passed, going the other way. Then an old man and his wife, and then another older man, his hat pulled low and what looked like a scar over his face.

Jimmy slowed. The dog growled.

The man pulled his hat down further and hurried past without a glance.

Thea pointed out over the waves. "There they are. Look." She lost her balance, tipped, and righted herself again.

Jimmy jogged to catch up. The dog trotted beside him. After a few strides, he reached Thea's side. "You okay?"

She nodded and waved a hand toward the water. "Look at them, they're playing now. You can see the dark shapes in the water."

He squinted at the surface of the bay and saw a couple shadows dipping in and out of the surface. Otters. They were his favorite sea creature. He used to sit and watch them for hours, make up stories about their lives, pretend he was one of them. But that was when he was young.

He quickened his pace to match Thea's. "Ah, to be an otter, huh? A few waves, a little food, and they're happy."

The woman shot him a glance. "And a bit of make believe?"

Jimmy halted.

Thea didn't. Her voice raised and carried back to him. "But we aren't like them, are we? Takes a lot more to make us happy. And even then…" She looked back. "Are you coming?"

The dog pulled Jimmy forward until he caught up. The light from a streetlamp hit Thea's locket. He focused on it, glad for a change of subject, yet afraid to ask too much. He coughed. "So, tell me about that locket."

She reached behind her head and unfastened it. As she did, she brushed back her hair and Jimmy noticed a birthmark behind her ear. Thea's hand brushed the mark as she took off the locket. "It's very old. Look. My parents." She opened it and held it out to him, losing her balance in the process and jolting sideways.

Jimmy grabbed her elbow. "Easy there." He glanced at the faces in the locket. They seemed nice enough. Kind of plain, normal.

"They're both still alive. In their nineties now." She clipped the locket back around her neck.

"Wow." Jimmy tugged on the dog's leash to bring her closer. "What are they like?"

She grinned. "A lot like those otters. Playful, happy."

He grimaced. Some people were just lucky, he guessed. "Must be what kept them young. Were they always that way?"

She laughed and sped up. "Nope."

Jimmy trotted to keep up with her, the dog heeled at his side. "How did they do it? Stay together all those years? Go from not happy to happy?" He panted out the words.

A wry smile touched her lips. She stopped.

He stopped too.

She looked him in the eye. "Do you really want to know?"

"I do."

She leaned closer and whispered, "My dad got a dog." She whirled and zoomed back down the path in the opposite direction. And this time, she didn't totter, didn't waver. She just left him standing there with the dog's leash in his hand, his jaw dropped to his chest.

After about fifty yards, she waved and shouted over her shoulder. "Good luck. God bless!"

He blinked and watched her speed away like a pro. Then it hit him. She was leaving him with the dog, and she wasn't coming back.

You've got to be kidding me. He'd prayed for help, prayed for guidance, and instead, God gave him a dog. That settled it. God was taunting him.

God and that crazy old woman who zipped away down the path.

12

Kinna rushed down the hospital's hallway. The intercom had said room 335, at the end of the hall. She hadn't made out the rest of the announcement.

Mai darted from the nurses' station ahead of her.

"What happened? Who is it?" Kinna called to Mai's back.

Mai didn't turn as she answered. "Guy in 335. Cracked ribs and a fractured shin."

"And?"

"Convulsions. Fell out of bed, I think. Renee too puny to lift him."

Kinna caught up with Mai. "New patient?"

Mai nodded. "In today. From the Petersen job site."

Kinna sped up. That was Jimmy's job. Her heart beat faster. She remembered the look on his face as he'd come home that afternoon. She'd thought he was just mad, but maybe there'd been more. Had there been an accident on the job? Jimmy hadn't said a word. Had he almost been hurt? He could have been. But she wouldn't know. She hadn't listened to him, hadn't asked how his day had gone like she used to. Hadn't done a thing to let him know that he mattered.

She bit her lip. It had been a long time since she'd stopped long enough to ask about his day. Maybe it wasn't all Jimmy's fault.

Her face turned hot as she hurried into room 335.

Renee, fine-boned and standing just over five feet tall, sat on the floor beside a man. The man's eyes were closed, his head thrashing back and forth. The sheet on the bed was pulled to one side, and the sling that had held the man's leg hung limp.

"What happened?" Kinna rushed forward.

Renee didn't look up. "He just threw himself off."

"Why weren't the rails up?"

"I don't know."

The man started yammering in gibberish.

Renee smoothed back his hair and attempted to keep his head still. "Just be quiet, okay? You'll be all right." She looked up at Kinna and Mai. "I couldn't lift him back up."

The man's eyes shot open and he let out a wild shriek.

Renee cringed and stood.

Mai frowned and pushed past Kinna. She strode over to the man and grabbed him under the knees. "You hush." Her voice held a tone of fierce command. "No cry like little baby. You be fine. Hush."

Kinna stepped around Renee and positioned herself at the man's shoulders. She rubbed her hand along the man's arm. "You're going to be fine, honey. We're all here to help you." She looked a Mai. "Ready?"

Mai nodded.

"What's your name?" Kinna raised her voice over the man's shuddering moans.

He gulped. "A-a-alan."

"Well, Alan, we're going to pick you up and put you back in your bed. Okay?"

The man howled and flailed an arm in the air.

Kinna took it and pushed it back to his side. "You have to lie still. We're going to get you back into bed."

"I need drugs, man." Alan's voice wavered to a tinny whine. "Gimme morphine."

"Let's get you back into bed."

"Codeine. Anything."

Renee stepped closer. "He had his pain meds an hour ago."

Kinna sighed and tightened her grip under the man's shoulders, then nodded to Mai. Together, they lifted him and placed him back on the bed.

He shouted a curse as his head touched the pillow. "Gimme the drugs. I need the drugs!"

Kinna ignored him, lifted the rails, and placed Alan's leg back in the sling while Mai checked him for further injury.

"He's fine. Not hurt."

The man's eyes unfocused.

Kinna grimaced. "I'll stay. He needs someone here."

Renee blew out a long breathe. Then the two nurses left Kinna standing beside the man in the bed.

He blinked three times, then turned to face her. "You the drug lady?"

"Not today. I'm the nurse."

"Nurse, huh? What you got to dull the pain?" His words were slurred. His head flopped to one side of the pillow. He looked up at her through watery eyes. "Hey, you're kinda cute."

Kinna forced down a smile. "Where does it hurt?"

His hand rose and rested over his chest. "My heart, woman. It's breaking for you."

Kinna turned her laugh into a polite cough. She reached over and let her fingers hover over his leg. "Well, considering that you broke your shin and just these lower ribs here"—she wiggled her fingers over the left side of his chest—"I suspect that your heart, way up here"—she moved her hand again—"is going to be just fine."

He let out a deep sigh. "You wound me, beautiful lady. Perhaps just one more shot of morphine will dull my misery."

"Hmm." Kinna patted his arm. "I think you've had quite enough narcotics, don't you?"

He turned his head away. "Ah, the angel turns tormentor. Can't you see I'm a man in the throes of agony?"

"Well, you're certainly in the throes of something."

"Don't make me throw myself from the bed again. You know I can't take no more."

Can't take any more. Kinna winced. The words were familiar. Too familiar. She stared at the man now sweating in the bed. *Do I sound like that, God? Am I no different from this man wheedling for something to stop the pain? But he's been given what he needs, and now is not the right time for more.* She glanced at the ceiling. *God?* Her gaze fell back to the man.

Alan squinted at the nametag around her neck and blinked again. "So, what's your name, cruel angel?" His eyes opened wider. "Kinna Henley, RN. Hey, I know you."

"You just close your eyes, Alan. Get a little rest. The doctor will be here in a few minutes to make sure you're all right." She adjusted the sheet over him.

He pulled it away. "You don't look like no uptight witch. But maybe you are. Karly says…"

Kinna's stomach twisted. She thought she'd throw up. *He's just a poor man in pain. He didn't mean anything by it.* She almost snorted at that lie. "Who's Karly?"

"You don't know Karly?" A lazy smile oozed over his face. "Well, she ain't no angel. Not with them long, pink fingernails, and them big, ripe—well, you don't want to hear about those."

"No. I don't." *So her name is Karly.* Somehow it didn't help, knowing the name of the other woman, having a label to plaster over the image in her mind. Karly with her big, ripe…self, and Kinna with her empty, barren one. How could she compete with that? And why should she have to? Uptight witch, indeed! That horrible woman.

And Jimmy, how could Jimmy—?

"Well, Kinna Henley, I hope you're gonna make him pay."

"Pay?" Had this man read her mind? Did he see the thoughts that scampered behind her gaze?

"Pay for putting me here. His fault, you know. Coward." Alan groaned. "Gonna make him pay for what he did to me. Should have been him on the Cat, but he just stood by. Didn't do a doggone thing."

A coldness washed through Kinna's chest and settled in her stomach. That was her Jimmy, not doing a doggone thing. Walking away when he should have been there. Should have saved her. *Make him pay.* She shivered.

"Stupid Jimmy."

Kinna put her hand on Alan's forehead. It was damp and sticky. "You'd better rest now."

His head lolled to one side. "Just a few drops of morphine…all I need. Can't take no more, I said. Gimme drugs."

"Persistent, aren't you?" She shook her head. *"Perseverance is a virtue, Kinna Ann,"* her mom always said. *"There's no free lunch."* She'd learned that the hard way. No free lunch, no free dinner, no free breakfast. Nothing came easily.

She took a deep breath. She could use a little morphine too. No, not morphine—more Perganol. She'd just have to try harder, do more, figure out a way to get rid of Miss Long Nails and get Jimmy and herself back on the same page again—the baby-making page. But where in the world was she going to get the money for more treatments? *Can't take no more, God. Gimme drugs.*

She glanced at the man in the bed and suddenly had the urge to give him exactly what he wanted.

———

Well, it's done. Silly, foolish, but the only thing I could think to do. I can't see how a dog changes anything.

At least it wasn't a cat.

Dad still believes a dog will cure any ill. "When things go wrong, bring a dog along," he's said a hundred times. Then Mom adds, "But make sure it's a great big one." And every time, they laugh. I grimace. An inside joke I've never understood.

All I know is Dad never could abide small dogs. And Mom says no family's whole without a canine member.

But how can a dog save a family? Dad's always been a little crazy. Happy-crazy, bold and daring. Maybe that's where I get it from.

And I think that's what my mother loves about him.

Ninety-some years old, and he still putters around on that old motorcycle of his. Mom insists he wear a helmet. "Be careful lest you knock some sense into that addled head of yours," she calls after him.

"We could use the money," he hollers back.

"I said 'sense,' not 'cents.'" Then she chuckles.

They've been that way for as long as I can remember. Teasing, joking, laughing over some private joke.

But there was a time, back before I was born, when the jokes had all grown cold. That's what they told me. But things changed, Dad says. All things are possible.

And Mom smiles that small, secret smile of hers, takes my face in her hands, and touches the birthmark behind my ear. She's done it a thousand times. Then she kisses my cheek and tells me to go wash up. I'm an old grandmother now, and still she's telling me to wash up.

That's what I love about her. That's what I love about them both. The hope, the joy. The belief that anything is possible, if only you believe.

So how can I not want the same for this Kinna and Jimmy? How can I not hope, pray, that someday their faces will be like those in my locket? Someday, they'll be happy too.

Maybe that's why I'm here. Maybe I'm not just a loony old woman. Maybe I just need to help them see.

I open the locket and sigh. The faces seem dimmer now, less distinct. A few pieces of sand still cling to their images.

I shut the locket and press it to my chest. Beneath my fist my heart beats, and my breath comes in rattled bursts.

Time is running out.

———

Jimmy tossed the bag of dog food onto the table, then flipped through the mail. More credit card bills. He stacked them up and reached for a postcard with a baby rattle on the front. He turned it over and sighed.

Another baby shower invitation for Kinna, this one for someone at church. He folded it into a tiny square, walked across the kitchen, and placed it under an old banana peel in the trash. The last thing Kinna needed was to see that. Jimmy grimaced and looked at the stack of bills. He wouldn't open them. Better not to see, not to think about it.

The woman's words came back to him. *"A little make believe."*

Well, he wasn't the only one pretending. Kinna was doing it too, pretending that a baby would fix all their problems and everything would suddenly be all right. That was a fairy tale if he'd ever heard one. Except there was no happily ever after. Not anymore.

Jimmy opened a cupboard. Outside, he could hear the dog snuffling around the yard. He reached into the cupboard and took down a heavy crystal bowl, a wedding gift from one of Kinna's aunts. No, that would never do.

He put it back and pushed aside a huge plastic punch bowl, a stack of plastic cereal bowls, and a big contraption shaped like a sombrero. They'd used that once, maybe, for chips and salsa. He chose that one, then put water in the middle and food around the rim.

Jimmy glanced out the window. The dog ran past, then slid to a halt and yipped at the birch in the yard. It was a happy sound, free and full of joy. Jimmy smiled. He should have gotten a dog a long time ago. Why hadn't he? Kinna, maybe. Or maybe he just hadn't bothered, hadn't thought a dog would make him happy. And maybe it wouldn't, but he was keeping her anyway. He didn't care what Kinna said.

He turned from the window. The sound of scraping came from outside, followed by a muffled bark and paws thudding into the ground. He placed the bowl on the counter near the door, then went to search for a blanket the dog could sleep on. By the time Kinna got home, the dog would be all settled in.

And he would have gotten her a Tulip after all.

He shook his head and headed down the hall. It was about time he got a dog. He'd never had one, not even when he was a kid.

He paused. No, that wasn't quite true. He did have a dog. Once. For three glorious hours.

He'd found the pup behind the trash bin at the back of Kinna's church. He and Kinna had been kicking stones and talking about what it'd be like for him to be in high school next year.

"You'll still be my friend, won't you, Jimmy?" she'd said.

"Of course, you doof." He cuffed her on the shoulder.

"Things change when you go to high school. Mom told me that."

He scowled and crossed his arms. "Some things don't change. Ever." He looked down at her, at her upturned nose, the flush of her cheeks, the brightness of her eyes behind her glasses. And that beautiful, glorious hair. Darker now than it was when they were younger, but just as soft. He almost reached out and touched it, almost ran his fingers through its lushness. But he didn't. He just imagined it. Made believe.

He glanced away, before she read too much in his eyes. She was always looking at his eyes, and sometimes he was afraid she'd see too much there.

But this time, just this once, he wished he could tell her how beautiful she was. Other kids teased her about being the preacher's kid and carrying that Bible around with her all the time. They didn't take the time to look at her, to see what he saw.

He reached over and brushed her jaw with his thumb. "It'll only be a year, Kinna. Then you'll be in high school too. And it'll be great, I promise."

But he broke that promise. That, and too many others. No wonder they'd ended up like this.

On that day, though, she'd believed him. And believed in him. She smiled and turned her head toward his hand. Her lips brushed his palm. Accidentally, but he felt it all the same.

Then a sound came—high-pitched, strange, and sad—and the spell was broken. They were two awkward kids again, teetering at the edge of their teens, between cooties and crushes, and not knowing how to cross over to the other side.

He dropped his hand. "What was that?"

Kinna stopped. "What?"

The whine came again.

Jimmy pointed to the trash bin. "It's coming from back there."

Kinna shoved her smelly Bonne Bell lip gloss into her pocket and hurried toward the garbage bin. "Sounds like something's hurt."

"Come on." He ran to the big bin and glanced behind it. Wide, brown eyes met his gaze. "It's a dog."

Kinna peeked beside him. "I think it's a puppy. Way ugly, though."

Jimmy shoved the bin. It gave a loud squeak and moved a couple inches out from the wall. He squatted down and put out his hand. "Here, boy."

"Maybe it's a girl."

He wrinkled his forehead and glanced back at Kinna. "You always say, 'here boy' to dogs. Don't you know anything?"

"Yeah, you know that from all the dogs you've owned?"

He flushed. "Well, no."

She raised her eyebrows and put on her haughty, I'm-grown-up voice. "See."

"You don't have a dog either."

Her chin lifted into the air. "I'm allergic."

"To what? Being wrong?"

She stuck her tongue out at him, and suddenly she was just a kid again. "I'm always right, Jimmy Henley. And we'll get along much better as long as you remember that."

He laughed. So did she.

She stood on tiptoes to get a better look at the mutt behind the bin. "Kind of a scraggly thing. Looks like someone buried him and dug him up again."

Jimmy looked at the dog. She had a point. The pup was ugly, clumps of its brown hair dirty and matted. Its eyes were watery, and trails of goo ran down its muzzle. "I don't care." He clucked to the dog. "Come here, boy."

The dog didn't move.

"It's not a horse. You don't cluck to it."

"You got a better idea?"

"Yeah, I do." She flattened herself against the wall, then inched behind the trash bin. After a moment, she'd picked up the pup and squeezed back out again. "Here." She plopped the dog into Jimmy's arms. "It looks a lot like you did the first time we met." She wrinkled her nose and pointed to the mucus in the dog's eyes.

"I didn't have gunk coming out of my eyes."

A grin tipped one side of her mouth. "No, not your eyes." She tapped her nose, then sidled past him, back into the parking lot behind the church.

"Hey, that's not fair."

"I got you your dog, didn't I? You owe me."

Jimmy shifted the dog in his arms. Now it seemed more like a grown dog than a pup. Its torso was almost as big as Jimmy, but it was light. Thin. Way too thin underneath all that thick fur.

The dog whined again and butted Jimmy's chest. He sat down, crossed his legs, and lowered the dog to his lap. "Ah, just look at him, Kinna. Makes your girlie heart melt, doesn't it?"

"Oh, please." She stuck her fists into her hips and shook her head. "P. U. He's awful. And he looks sick. Maybe you'd better leave him here. I'll have my dad come and take care of him."

Jimmy clutched the dog closer to his chest. "No way. He's mine." He held the dog tight. "I'm going to name him…" He paused and thought. "Dragon. His name's Dragon."

Kinna squatted beside Jimmy. She put her hand on his arm, careful not to touch the dog. "Dragon, huh? Are you ever going to get over your thing for Prince Phillip? Talk about a girlie hero."

"Name another prince who fought a dragon and won."

"Whatever."

"I'm going to take my dragon home and clean him up." He struggled back to his feet, holding the dog against him. The pup was too big to hold like that, but Jimmy did it anyway. "And you can just stand around here kicking rocks all by yourself." He staggered a few steps, the dog still in his arms, its back legs trailing down and bumping him in the knees. "Besides, he just needs some food and water. He'll be fine. Won't you, Dragon?" He nuzzled his cheek against the dog's fur. It was something a little kid would do, rub his face on a dog that way, but Jimmy didn't care. It was his first dog, and he loved him.

Kinna shrugged. "All right, Phillip. But what's your dad going to say?"

Jimmy's face hardened. "I'm keeping him."

"Fine. Stay here." Kinna turned and strode toward the church.

Jimmy yelled after her. "You'd better not be getting your dad."

She didn't turn back. Instead, she marched into the church and reappeared a minute later with three foam cups in her hands. She walked up to Jimmy and held out the cups. "Here."

They were filled with water.

He set Dragon on the ground. Dragon sniffed at the cups, then carefully lapped water from one of them. Jimmy stroked his head and gazed down at the most wonderful creature God ever made.

He carried that dog all the way home that day. It took him an hour, but the time didn't matter. When he got to the apartment, he played with Dragon in the yard. He tried fetch and Frisbee, but that didn't work. So then he played pirate hideout in the old fort someone had made years ago in the front of the apartment complex. He huddled in the fort with the dog and made up wild stories of Caribbean adventures, just like he did when he was a kid, and Dragon perked up his ears and nestled closer.

As the sky grew dark, Jimmy took the dog into the apartment and to his room. There, they romped and laughed and chased one another until they rolled on the floor, exhausted. Here, Dragon seemed happier, more energetic.

Jimmy laid on the floor and stared up at the bumpy, white ceiling. Dragon laid his head on Jimmy's chest. He rubbed his hand over the dog's head. "See, boy, you just needed a good home."

Dragon licked his face, then stood and jumped on the bed. He wagged his tail and yipped at Jimmy.

A door slammed.

The grin fled from Jimmy's face. Dad was home.

Jimmy scuttled to the bed and put his arm around Dragon's shoulders. "Shhhh."

The dog yapped again. Jimmy shushed him.

Footsteps sounded down the hall. Heavy. Uneven.

He shuddered.

A voice boomed from just beyond the door. "What's that noise, boy?"

Jimmy swallowed, then jumped up and pushed Dragon toward the closet. He shoved the dog inside, then snuck in after him. Quietly, oh so quietly, he closed the closet door.

Then he waited.

Light drifted in through the slats of the closet door. He held his breath. The bedroom door opened.

Footsteps came. Closer. Heavier.

Jimmy held on to Dragon and pushed back farther into the closet until his spine hit the back wall. He could see his father through the cracks in the door. His dad paused and looked around the room.

The dog whined, sharp and low. Jimmy held him closer.

His dad turned.

Jimmy saw his face, flushed and coming nearer. He pressed into the folds of a pair of jeans, a worn-out coat.

The coat fell. Jimmy trembled.

His dad reached out. The door flung open.

Jimmy gasped. Their eyes met, and then his dad's gaze moved to Dragon, huddled behind Jimmy.

His dad's hand clamped Jimmy's shoulder and pushed him aside, then grabbed Dragon by the scruff on the neck. "What're you doing with this flea-bitten old mutt?" He yanked the dog out of the closet and strode toward the door.

Jimmy leapt from the closet. "No, Dad. He's mine!" He ran down the hall after them. Dragon whined again, a pitiful sound that struck

Jimmy's heart like a dart. He reached toward his dad. "Please, Dad, please. I want to keep him. Please, can I?" He grabbed his dad's shirt.

Dad pulled away. "No dogs allowed."

"Please, Dad."

His dad carried that dog by its scruff all the way to the front door and barged out. The screen door slammed.

Jimmy raced up to it.

"Stay there." His dad shouted the command over his shoulder.

Jimmy watched, with his nose pressed to the screen, as his dad threw the pup into the car, got in, and drove off.

He never saw that dog again, and he never had another. Until today.

Jimmy pulled an old blanket from the shelf and tucked it under his arm, then went back to the kitchen and grabbed the dog's food bowl. He pushed open the front door, flipped on the porch light, and stepped outside.

"No!" The blanket dropped from under his arm. The food almost followed. In the yard lay dozens of Kinna's tulips, uprooted, scattered, piled next to heaps of freshly turned earth.

The dog raised her head out of the tulip bed and looked back at Jimmy. Dirt covered her paws and nose.

Jimmy groaned.

Holes dotted every flower bed. Petals lay everywhere. The dog yipped and bounded over to him, then changed direction and headed for fresh earth.

"No! Stop! Bad dog." Jimmy set down the food bowl and rushed toward the dog. She turned her head toward him, her tongue lolling in what looked too much like a doggy grin.

Jimmy ran his hand through his hair. He should have known better than to get a dog. Should have known it would turn into a disaster. He looked up at the sky. "God, why are You doing this to me? Haven't I been through enough?"

Unfortunately, God didn't answer. He didn't make the tulips magically replant themselves either.

Jimmy groaned again and made his way over to the first flower bed. The dog trotted up beside him. He put his hand on her head. "Guess I know why they call you Tulip."

The dog laid down, then rolled over on her back. Her tail thumped on the ground. Jimmy shook his head and rubbed her tummy.

He leaned over and picked up a yellow tulip, bulb and all, then stuffed it back in the ground and pressed the dirt around it. He let go. It sagged to the left. He picked up another flower and shoved it in the dirt next to the first. It looked even worse. This was never going to work. Still, he'd better try. Maybe, in the dark, Kinna wouldn't notice. He shooed the dog toward the food sombrero, then knelt and began replanting tulips.

After ten minutes, the hair on his neck prickled. Someone was watching him. He glanced toward the dog. She lay on the porch, her head between her paws. He looked the other way, toward the front gate and saw a figure, dark despite the glare of the streetlight.

The man put his hand on the gate and moved closer, so that the light shone on his face.

Jimmy let out his breath. It was only the man from the coffee shop. He stood and wiped his hands on his pants. "Hey, Joe, what's up?"

The man raised one hand. "Howdy, son. Whatcha doing there?"

"Planting flowers. Or, at least, replanting them."

Joe pushed open the gate and came inside. "At night?"

Jimmy shrugged. "Gotta do it before the wife comes home."

Joe nodded. "Ah, I see. Need help?"

Jimmy shook his head. "Naw, you don't have to do that."

"Nope." He came closer and surveyed the damage. Then he knelt down and grabbed a tulip.

Jimmy squatted beside him. "You show up at the craziest times."

Joe grinned. "Seems so."

"God send you or something?"

The man guffawed. "You'd think God could do better than me. Would hope so, anyway."

Jimmy laughed too.

Then came the sound of thick toenails on wood. Jimmy turned. Tulip stood behind him, her stance wide, her teeth bared. She stared at Joe and growled deep in her throat.

Joe rose slowly and backed away. "You didn't tell me you got a dog."

Jimmy swallowed. He moved toward Tulip. Her eyes didn't move from Joe's face. "Easy, girl."

Tulip growled again. Lower. Deeper.

Joe shook. "Never could abide dogs."

Tulip crouched.

Joe sprinted toward the gate. He flung it open and bolted out. Tulip sprang after him. The gate slammed on her nose.

Jimmy rushed to the fence. "You all right, Joe?" he hollered, but Joe didn't turn. Never in his life had Jimmy seen a man that old run that fast. "Joe? Come on back." He paused, his hand on the gate, his eyes fixed on the figure retreating beneath the streetlights.

His heart thudded in his chest. There was something about how the man ran, something about the way his shoulders swung loose, at odds with his short, choppy stride. Something…and suddenly Jimmy saw not an old, bald man, but a younger one. Long, curly hair flowing down his back and a beer bottle in his hand.

His breath stopped. "Dad?"

13

Kinna stared at Alan snoring in bed 335-A. It was time to wake him and take his vitals. She hated waking patients when they slept like this. She'd rather keep the lights low, let him sleep, but the rules demanded he be checked at regular intervals.

She reached for the light switch and paused.

Alan let out a loud, snorting snore.

She grinned. *Crude, crazy man.* She ought to dislike him, but she didn't. When all was said and done, he was too much like her. *God, I asked for a baby, and instead I got this guy. Come on, You can't do better than that?*

Her hand dropped. She walked to the far side of the room and turned on the small light above the empty bed. It shed enough light for her to do her job. Just enough, and no more.

She grimaced. Life was like that. You walked around in a dark room, and when you got a light, it was only a flicker in the distance. Only enough to do what you had to do and no more. Sometimes she wished God would just turn on the big light overhead and let her see what was really going on. But all she got was the flicker. The tiny fluorescent bulb that blinked and hummed and spat tiny bits of illumination into ever deepening shadows. Perhaps it was God being kind, not wanting to scare her with the light, but she didn't like it.

She wrapped the blood pressure cuff gently around Alan's arm, placed the oxygen monitor on his finger, and started the machines. They beeped and flashed tiny lights.

Alan opened his eyes. "What? Hey!" He grabbed the cuff.

Kinna stopped his hand. "Shh. Go back to sleep. I'm just taking your blood pressure."

"Get it off me!" He squirmed and pulled at the cuff again.

Kinna gripped his hand and squeezed. "Hold still, honey. Now I have to do it again. It won't hurt."

Alan sniffed and peeked at her through the slit in one eye. "Think you can sweet talk me, huh? Calling me honey."

"The last person I called 'honey' was an old lady I had to resuscitate. So don't think you're special."

Alan opened both eyes. "All right, baby. Let's start that resuscitating." He puckered up both lips in an exaggerated kiss.

Kinna chuckled. "Keep dreaming, honey." She pulled off the cuff and rolled it up.

Alan laughed, then put a hand to his ribs. "Stop it. You're making it hurt. See, now I need morphine."

"Renee gave you another dose when you were asleep. You should feel fine."

"Oh, man." He scowled. "You mean I slept away some of my high?"

"I'm afraid so. Go back to sleep. Your blood pressure's normal."

"No drugs, no kiss. Just 'go back to sleep.' You sound like my ex-wife."

"Wise woman. Now stop jabbering and close your eyes."

Alan closed one eye. "You this bossy at home?"

She glanced at him, then gathered up the rolled cuff and oxygen monitor and placed them back on her cart. "That's none of your business."

"Bet you are." He let out a low laugh, not enough to jiggle his ribcage, then smiled at her.

She couldn't help it. She smiled back.

"Well, if I were Jim, I guess I wouldn't hold it against you."

She straightened his sheet. "Hold what?"

"Don't have no kids to boss, so you gotta boss us men. I understand." His last word slurred as his head slumped back into his pillow.

Something cold lodged in Kinna's gut. "That's not why…" She clamped her lips shut. Her hands trembled.

"We don't cry, Kinna Ann. Not in public." Her mother's words came back to her through the years. *"Someone might see. We stay strong, hide our tears. People won't want to believe in Jesus if we go around weepy, will they, sweetie? Smile and say God is good. Believe that God blesses those He loves."*

But that was all crumbling now, right here before this strange, rough man. She took a deep breath. *God is good.* The problem was that she didn't buy that line anymore. Not after today. Not after Jimmy…

Kinna turned away from the bed.

Belief. Trust. Faith. Love. Links in a chain that was breaking, shattering under the strain of too many years, too many tears, too many hopes dashed. Too many times she'd believed, truly believed, that this time God would answer her prayers, just like Mom said. And He hadn't.

"You okay, girlie?" Alan's question broke through her thoughts.

She turned back around and sniffed. *"We don't cry in public, Kinna Ann…"*

"Sorry I said that. Didn't mean nothing by it. Jim don't hold it against you. Never said nothing to me, anyway." His words drifted off, as did his gaze.

Kinna stiffened. "Of course Jimmy doesn't hold it against me." *Does he? Am I less of a woman? Less of a wife?*

Alan's voice rose again, quavering this time, wavering. "Me, though, I don't want no kids anyway. Come here, baby." He tried to pat the space on the bed next to him, but instead slapped his hand on the bedrail. "Ow. Where'd that come from?" He stared at the silver bedrail as if he'd never seen one before.

"It's always been there. And for your information, Jimmy loves me." The words sounded silly, like something she would have said in junior high. Not the words of a woman staring down the throat of forty. Not the words of a kind, competent nurse.

Alan gurgled. "Ah, what's love anyway, huh? Tell me that."

A good question. Kinna turned away. Love. L-O-V-E. Jimmy said she spelled love like *give me*. Maybe she did. Wasn't that part of love too? Didn't Jesus say to ask whatever you will in His name?

But that wasn't true. Asking didn't get you anywhere. She should have learned that by now.

So how was *love* spelled? Maybe it was spelled P-A-I-N, because that's all her prayers had gotten her so far. A lot of pain and disappointment, and a whole lot of doubts.

"Love is patient…Love is kind…not self-seeking…always hopes. Love never fails." The words came back to her, whispers from an age long past. Whispers from a time when she'd measured love like that, tested it against those very words from the Bible.

How can God love me and not give me a child? How can Jimmy love me when I can't give one to him?

Kinna shuddered. The doubts again. The crumbling of a faith that once seemed strong. And behind it, the sickening, sinking fear that God didn't love her, and neither did Jimmy. Maybe they never had.

He used to love me, didn't he?

He didn't today. The words came as a rustle through her mind. *He rejected you, destroyed your dreams, walked away. He crushed your hopes, let them die.*

She tried to ignore the whisper. Tried to shut it out.

He doesn't want you anymore.

"They say they love you, but it don't mean anything. Just pretty words, that's all." Alan snorted.

Kinna shook her head. "That's silly." Her voice fell.

"Yeah? Prove it."

Kinna frowned. "You can't prove love. You just…you just know, that's all."

Alan laughed. It wasn't a nice sound. "Ain't you a Christian? Jimmy said he was."

Kinna shuddered. "So?"

"So God proved it, didn't He? Ain't that what those crosses in your ears mean?"

Kinna touched one of her small gold earrings. It was almost funny, being preached at by this crude, drug-desiring man with blurry eyes and less-than-proper manners.

She turned her cross earring in her fingers. Was he right? Did the cross prove God's love? It was supposed to. A sacrifice like that shouldn't leave any questions at all. So, why did she still doubt? Why did she need more?

"Yes, that's what the cross means."

But God, if You really loved me, You'd give me the desire of my heart. Isn't that what the Bible says? "Love spelled G-I-V-E-M-E." Her stomach turned.

"So what's Jim done to prove it?"

Kinna didn't answer.

Alan grunted. "Thought so. He's the same coward at home as he is on the job, ain't he?"

"He's a good man."

"Yellow-bellied."

Kinna pursed her lips. "I don't want to talk about this."

"Girlie, I'm doing you the biggest favor of your life." Alan's voice gentled. "Telling you the truth, that's what I'm doing."

Truth. What was true? Did Jimmy love her? She didn't know. Did she love him? She closed her eyes. Yes. Except—*love always hopes, it never fails*—maybe she didn't know that either. She didn't know anything for certain, not since Jimmy rejected her. Or maybe it happened before that. Maybe she hadn't been certain in a long, long time.

"I don't know what's truth anymore."

"You'd better find out. And while you're doing that, get me some more morphine, would you? I'm dying here."

Kinna's mouth drew into a thin line. "You're not dying. You've had plenty of morphine. You don't need any more."

"You could use some, though. Loosen you up a bit. Get some for both of us."

"Go to sleep."

"All right, as soon as you tell me what you're gonna do to Jim."

"Is that what this is about? Getting back at Jimmy?"

"Maybe. Maybe not. But if I was you, I'd make that coward take a stand. I'd make him prove it." Alan yawned.

How was she supposed to do that? And yet, she needed to know if it was possible that he loved her still, even in her barrenness. Loved her despite all that had gone wrong. If he could prove it, then maybe she could silence the doubts about God too. Maybe she could hold her faith together for a little while longer. Maybe it would be enough to keep her fears at bay for one more cycle, one more try. If only Jimmy would prove his love. If only she could believe it. If only she could make him choose her over that too-young woman with the too-red lips. But how?

And then it came to her, like a flash of light in the midst of her fear. A way to know for certain. A way to force his hand.

"Divorce." She breathed the word aloud for the first time since she'd said, "I do." She'd promised that word would never pass her lips, that she would never dirty her mouth, or her mind, with such a thought, with such a word.

She said it again.

Alan rolled toward her. He opened his eyes. "Now you're talking. Get rid of the bum."

Kinna crossed her arms over her chest. "Maybe I'm the bum. The deficient one."

"That's a big word."

"Yeah, well—"

"Divorce is a big word too." Alan looked straight at her. He didn't seem sleepy anymore.

"I didn't say I'm getting a"—she drew a breath and straightened her shoulders—"a divorce. I'm only…"

He raised his eyebrows. "What? Pretending?"

She narrowed her eyes and stared out the window. A long moment passed. Pretending. That was it exactly.

It was so simple, really. She had to make Jimmy fight for her, make him afraid of losing her. Then he'd forget that long-nailed bimbo in the coffee shop and he'd see, he'd finally see, how much having a baby meant to her. He'd understand that he couldn't just refuse her and go on with life. Choices mattered.

She needed to scare him enough to choose her. The threat of divorce would do just that.

Unless…

No, she wouldn't think of that. Jimmy still loved her. He had to. He just had to.

God? Divorce?

It wouldn't be real, but if all went right, it would be enough. She turned toward the door.

Before she could reach it, she remembered the only bit of advice her dad had ever given her about marriage. *"Don't ever talk about divorce, Kinna. Don't even say the word. Not even in jest."*

She scowled. What did Dad know? He didn't understand. *"Don't push so hard, Kinna. Relax. God will move in His own time."* Dad had said those words too. Foolish, useless words. She didn't listen to them either.

Desperate times called for desperate measures, people always said. And she was plenty desperate. She licked her lips and glanced over her shoulder toward Alan. "What do you know about divorce?"

A tiny grin touched his lips. "Me? Why, I'm an expert." He tapped his chest. "I've been divorced four times."

She raised her eyebrows. No wonder he looked like he did. "Keeping the lawyers busy, are you?"

Alan rubbed his nose. "Me? Nah. Didn't use no lawyers. Got them papers online. Forty bucks. Couple clicks and…" He yawned again. "Well, you get the picture."

She stared at him. Divorce papers online. That had to be a sign she ought to do this crazy thing to make Jimmy prove he still loved her. Surely it wouldn't be so easy if it wasn't right.

Kinna shut the door to Alan's room, then hurried down the hall to the computer.

I sit on a rock at the edge of the bay. I sit and do not move.
I'm waiting. For what, I don't know. To wake up, I guess. To find
that this is all a dream, and I'm really snoozing in my chair at
home with the sun twinkling through the window and my dog
curled on the rug before me. Waiting for Mom to call for me from
the bed on the other side of the room. Waiting for Dad to come
in from puttering around the yard. Waiting for the grandkids to
tumble in the door demanding peanut butter and jelly. Waiting to
get on with our Easter weekend, just like it's supposed to be.
Waiting for Good Friday to give way to the Resurrection morning.
Waiting.

Because that's where I belong.

Instead I sit here and stare at the fading faces in my
locket. They're just contours now, shades of gray against a darker
background.

I can't make the colors come clear again, but I know the
faces matter. I mustn't lose them. I can't allow them to wash
to white.

But what can I do? I don't control time. I'm just one person.
Alone, feeble, old.

Lord?

The waves slap against the rocks. The sun rises to spit bits
of light against a black ocean. And I wait.

What does it mean to be faithful? What does it mean to do
right? When you try but fail? When you believe, yet everything
still goes wrong?

"In the failures, God shines most clearly," Mom often says.

"Look for Jesus in the old feeding trough, not in the cushioned crib. Look for Him on the dry, dusty road, not in palaces made by men. Look for Him with a crown of thorns, not a crown of gold and gems. Look for Him when all seems as it should not be.

"That's where Jesus is found."

So why can't I find Him?

I close my eyes and feel the ocean spray on my face. I breathe deeply of the salty coolness and think the impossible. Maybe Mom is wrong.

———

Kinna glanced over her shoulder, then adjusted her chair so her body blocked the computer screen from anyone walking by. She'd found the Web site, answered the questions, and paid the fee. Was it really this easy to tear asunder what God had put together? She clicked a button and the printer next to her hummed. Apparently it *was* this easy.

After her time with Alan, it had been a quiet night. No emergencies, no code blue, no cranky patients pushing the call button every two minutes. Nothing to distract her from the crazy plan that had congealed on the screen before her.

Too simple. Too easy.

It'll never work.

It has to.

Stupid idea.

It'll wake Jimmy up, at least. Show him I mean business. Show them both.

God knows the truth already.

Truth?

Once she thought she had a corner on truth, but it had become a fuzzy, nebulous thing.

Dad would never approve of what she was doing, of the chance she was taking. Dad always insisted she do right by Jimmy. Even when he told her to keep her distance from "that boy," he still wanted her to treat him right.

Just like that day so long ago in her front yard. She remembered the roses in bloom, the sprinklers clunk-clunking on the neighbor's grass, an old tabby licking her fur on the sidewalk before them. And the great, gnarled elm where Jimmy had secretly carved their names on the side next to the fence. They'd giggled over that.

Jimmy had climbed the tree and sat on the bottom branch. He swung his legs, still covered by brown Tuffskins when everyone else wore Lee jeans. It was embarrassing to still be in Tuffskins in junior high, but that day, Jimmy didn't care and she didn't mention it. She never did.

"Come up, Kinna. You can almost see the ocean from here."

"Dad says not to climb trees. It's not ladylike."

Strains of the theme song for *General Hospital* drifted from the open window behind her. Mom was watching her favorite soap again and wouldn't be out for ages.

"Hurry up." Jimmy stuck his hand down and wiggled his fingers at her. "It won't hurt. Here, I'll help you." His hand grabbed hers.

"Oh, all right." With his help, Kinna shimmied up beside him. The branch was rough beneath her legs, the bark catching the hem of her skirt. She loosened it and brushed bits of dirt from the hem. "It tore. Mom's going to kill me."

Jimmy made a face at her. "You could climb a lot better in pants."

She frowned. "I know."

He shrugged. "It doesn't matter. Look." He pointed north. "There's a big boat out there. You can see it if you look between those leaves."

She leaned forward.

His grip tightened on hers. "Hey, be careful."

She looked down and realized she hadn't let go of his hand. They sat side by side on the tree, and for a breath, their eyes met and held. She blushed. He smiled.

And everything was so…right.

Then a car door slammed. Her dad shouted.

Everything changed.

Later that night, her dad called her into his study. With his Bible laid out on the desk before him, his commentaries open, his sermon notes stacked neatly on the corner, he told her how disappointed he was. "You do right by that boy, Kinna Ann. Don't lie to him."

She crossed her arms. "I didn't."

"You lie every time you lead him to believe things that aren't true."

She never understood what her dad meant by that. But now, maybe, she did.

Beside her, the final page spat from the printer. She reached over and gathered the papers.

Just because it's not for real doesn't make it a lie.

Doesn't it? Dad would die if he knew.

All that matters is that this works. You have to make him fight for you. Stand up, be a man.

Love always…

She shoved the papers into her bag and closed the Internet program. A hand tapped her shoulder. She jumped.

Mai stood behind her.

"You startled me."

"You daydreaming." She sniffed. "Bad dream too, by the look on your face."

Kinna made her features relax. "It's nothing. What's up?"

"They want to see you in the administrative office. Right now."

Kinna swallowed. "What? Why?" Did this have something to do with that Alan? Or did they know she was doing private business at a hospital computer? How could they find out so fast? She trembled as she stood.

Mai patted her arm. "No worries. Just questions about some lost medication." She caught her breath. Her eyes widened. "Except…it is fertility medicine."

Something icy and terrible dropped into Kinna's stomach. They knew. Somehow they knew.

She turned and walked down the long, long hallway.

14

F *ired. Let go.* Words she'd never thought she'd hear. But words that had been hiding, unspoken, in the echoes of other words: *Leave of absence. Resignation. Final investigation.* They slammed into her with tidal force, because no matter what words were used, the result was the same. *Fired. Let go.*

Kinna jammed the key into the ignition and started her van. She glanced up at the beige hospital walls before her. *I loved being a nurse.*

But what else did she expect? At least, that's what the nurse administrator said.

It came back to her now, foggy, like a nightmare that pulsed in and out of focus. Standing before that desk, her throat dry, her mouth like cotton, with nothing to say. No excuses to make. No explanations. Just the silence and that awful whispering of shame.

Kinna knew she'd been wrong, knew she'd sinned, but then, as now, the desperation clamored louder. The cry of hopes dashed drowned the quiet voice of *shouldn't, don't, just believe…*

She'd gotten what she deserved.

She could see the woman again in her mind, white-faced, her eyes watery. Ugly fluorescent lights glinted off stacks of fat file folders, and Martha Rodgers rifled through papers, refusing to meet Kinna's gaze and muttering words like "inquiry," "years of service to this hospital," and "I can't believe it."

Kinna couldn't believe it either. But Martha had suspected her, suspected those vials might disappear. Normally, Kinna would have been fired after a long, in-depth investigation. Normally, she would have had time to better hide her tracks. But Martha was fast. She found the half-empty box in the mailroom and Kinna's signature on the check-out form, verifying she had checked it before sending it to be shipped back.

It was supposed to be simple. Take half the medication, leave the rest. Send the box back to the pharmaceutical company. By the time anyone noticed, it would be assumed there was a mistake. She would assure them the box had been full. They would claim it wasn't. Her word against theirs, and nothing to prove her guilt.

But Martha was not only fast, but thorough. It used to be what Kinna liked about the woman. Now, she had to wait and see if Martha would file a report to the state's board of nursing examiners. Today she'd only lost her job. She could still lose her license.

It didn't matter. The state board report would come in time.

Time.

It hadn't worked out at all like she'd planned. She was supposed to be pregnant by the time anyone started asking questions. She was supposed to be moving on with her life, happy, complete. Free.

But those plans had crumbled in taunting bits around her. She should have known they would.

Kinna blinked up at the building. Three floors up, that little slot of a window, was where Martha had said it, her eyes not angry or accusing. Just flat and red, as if she didn't see Kinna. As if she didn't want to.

Kinna didn't want to either. If she flipped down the visor mirror, what would she see? Sin? Yes. Regret? Probably. Defeat? No. She wouldn't admit to that. Not while she still had a final card to play. *The papers…I don't have anything else left.*

She sniffed, then shifted into reverse and pulled out of the parking place, the same one she'd parked in every workday for the last fifteen years. All the patients she'd attended to. Their smiles, their tears. Their whispered fears. Her prayers for them in the dark of night. Touching their hands, looking into their eyes. Telling them someone cared, they'd be all right. Was it all a lie?

Oh Lord…

All because she'd stolen those vials. What did it matter if other people's insurance paid for those medications and hers did not? She'd still thrown her life away for a single chance to change everything and gained nothing in return. Her job gone, her chance for a baby slipping away. Her husband…

She glanced at the papers in the seat next to her.

You're a fool, Kinna Henley. You're going to lose him too.

"Shut up!" She slammed her minivan into drive and sped from the hospital's parking lot. *The speed limit's thirty-five.*

"Great. Now I'm talking to myself." Her hands clenched the steering wheel harder.

It just wasn't fair. She'd been called to the administrator's office, Mai had been called to the maternity ward. Kinna had gotten fired, three other women had had babies. It really wasn't fair. Mai said they had a sixteen-year-old girl in there that night, along with a woman over forty and another having her sixth kid.

Women got pregnant all the time, including many who didn't want to. Teenagers, singles, women who aborted their babies. Bile rose in Kinna's throat.

Young kids got pregnant after one night in the back of a Chevy, and she and Jimmy had been trying for years. They'd even tried in the back of their car once, just to see if there was something about the backseat that helped with conception. It didn't work. Maybe because they owned a Honda.

So she schemed and tried and ran out of options. She only had one chance left. One chance to let Jimmy prove that he loved her after all. Despite it all. For better or for worse.

Kinna glanced down at her bag as the car swung around a corner. Something red tumbled out from beneath the seat. A single silk tulip. It must have come loose from the bunch she'd bought at Wal-Mart yesterday.

She turned onto Ocean View Boulevard. To her left, the bay shone like a black pearl. Sunlight peeked over the horizon and sent ribbons of gold shimmering over the dark surface, glittering and peaceful. Quiet whispers of morning across an ocean once black. A flock of gulls perched along the split rail fence bordering the road. They didn't move as her van passed.

She sighed and loosened her grip on the steering wheel. She loved this kind of day, when the sun came out early and sprinkled hope in golden rays over her world.

Hope. She needed a little of that to get her through this day. She reached down to pick up the tulip.

A horn squawked.

She looked up. A car raced toward her. Dim headlights. Bright blue hood.

She swerved right. Her tires banged into the curb, jumped it.

The other car zoomed by in a flash of electric blue. And in that flash, she saw a single image. One of those stupid yellow placards from the nineties, bobbing in the window. Baby on Board.

Kinna yanked the steering wheel back toward the road. The van spun, dipped, and spurted forward. She felt the thud of impact, the screech of bending metal. Her head jerked. The van slammed to a stop. Pain lanced over her forehead.

And then silence, except for her breathing and the wild thumping of her heart.

She steadied her breath and put her hand to her forehead. No blood, only bruising. It hurt, but she was okay. The world stopped spinning and her vision cleared.

"I'm okay. I'm fine." She opened the door and stepped out.

Her van sat halfway on the sidewalk, its front crumpled by a round trash can. *Jimmy is going to kill me.* She reached up to wipe her face with her other hand. Only then did she realize she still held the silk tulip.

She got back in the van and turned the key. To her surprise, it started. Carefully, she backed up and guided the car off the sidewalk. Her hands shook on the wheel. She gripped it tighter, but still they wouldn't steady. She parked in a spot alongside the road and shut off the ignition. There was no way she could drive home now, not like this.

How am I going to afford to fix this car? What I am going to say to Jimmy? Wasn't losing my job bad enough? I know I deserved what happened at the hospital, but how did I deserve this? It's just further proof that...

She remembered the yellow placard.

Kinna clenched the tulip in her hand, grabbed her bag, and headed across the road to the beach. A sandy path led to her favorite rock overlooking the water. The beach was empty this morning. She almost expected to see Thea, but no one was there. Only the birds, and the waves, and the shimmers of dawn.

And You, God, taunting me.

A shiver went up her arms. Her legs wobbled. She stumbled out onto the beach, not caring if the sand sprinkled into her shoes or if the sun shone in her eyes and made her squint. She gripped the tulip harder.

Are You out there, Lord?

Once, she and God had been on better terms. Once, she'd known she could pray and everything would be all right. But not today. Especially not today.

"You can do anything you set your mind to," her mom always said. *"Accomplish anything. Reach any dream."*

Mom had lied.

It didn't have to be this way. But it was, and God had done nothing to make it better. Daddy always said God loved her, but Daddy didn't have any answers for this.

Well, she had answers. Or at least, she was going to get some. She would make Mom right. Anything you set your mind to…well, her mind was set.

Kinna walked along the beach, one hand stuffed into her pocket, her head down. She listened to the water, the seagulls, the dull thudding of her heart. She touched her hand to her abdomen. Empty. Barren.

She hated it.

I don't know what I believe anymore, God. Are You good? I'm not so sure. Do You hear us? Sometimes I hope it's not so. Because if it is, why have You turned Your back on me? Why don't You love me like Daddy said You did? Why have You let my life turn into one big crash?

No answer came. Nothing but the lapping of the waves, the shriek of gulls, and the pounding of a broken heart.

Maybe if Jimmy had—

She stopped the thought. She ought to get home. Turn around, drive back to their house, and face another day, another loss. But today she dreaded it more than usual. Dreaded facing Jimmy.

Today she would play her last card, the very last card of all, and this time, he wouldn't turn away. This time, she would know. She would make him choose, once and for all.

If only he'd chosen out of love.

She reached into her bag, dropped the tulip, and pulled out the papers she'd printed at the hospital. These papers, ice cold in her hand, would either end all her dreams or begin them. They'd either force Jimmy to listen, or force him away forever.

She was betting on the former. Counting on it, enough to risk everything. It was worth the risk. She would do anything to know, to be certain like she once had been, that he loved her. Any risk was worth that, even this. Even papers that spoke of the ugliest word of all.

Divorce.

Surely he'd listen to her now, pull them back from this brink.

Divorce.

She saw Jimmy and Karly again in her mind, bright fingernails on suntanned skin. His skin. Her husband.

Kinna's stomach churned.

Gulls are even worse than cats. After four hours of sitting on this ridiculous rock, I've decided that. Ugly bird-vermin. It started with one, scolding me from the water's edge. Then a dozen more joined it. Then two dozen. Then three, until I couldn't have moved from this rock if I wanted to. I threw my arms up to scare them away, but they only flapped about and settled again, yapping to one another, squawking at me.

So here I've sat. Waiting.

And then I see her. She doesn't see me. She walks like a woman who can't see anything at all. Not the waves, not the gulls, not the hope in a new dawn. Or if she sees it, she will not take it in or accept it. Strange how some can see and yet are blind, and some are blind and yet see.

She comes closer, and the gulls fly away. Stupid birds. But I can rise now and watch as she turns toward an outcropping of rocks nearer the water's edge.

Lord, You have thrown me in her path for a reason, brought me here to this beach, at this time, because there is something I must do. But what? If this isn't a dream, then what is it? Why am I here as the pictures in the locket fade away?

I look up, my gaze following the gulls as they retreat across the bay. Maybe I'm here to make her see, make her understand. My fingers touch the locket around my neck. Maybe I need to make her see the faces, or at least the hope.

She kneels in the sand. I see a flash of red in her hand, and then it's gone. Buried.

Oh Lord, why can't I just go home?

15

Jimmy was dreaming. Except he knew he was dreaming, which meant it wasn't quite dreaming. It was a memory, really, haunting him in that bleary place between sleep and awake, darkness and light.

He didn't want to relive it, didn't want to feel what he felt then, hear what he said. He didn't want to remember the lies.

But it came anyway. And morning didn't chase it away.

Kinna's purse sat on the kitchen table. A dozen pamphlets sat beside it. Words stared up at him from the pages, words he didn't understand. Endometriosis, hysterosalpingogram, sonohysterography, myomectomy, intrauterine insemination, in vitro fertilization. And beside them, an alphabet soup of equally obscure acronyms: HSG, SHG, IUI, IVF, GIFT, ZIFT, FET. He gulped and shoved the pamphlets away.

"What's this all about?"

Kinna picked up the pamphlets, straightened them, and set them back in front of him. "This is what we're going to do next if this cycle fails."

His eyes widened. "All of it?"

"Whatever we have to."

He blinked. "Where are we going to get the money to pay for all this?"

"Insurance."

His face turned hot. "It doesn't pay for infertility stuff. Nothing to do with infertility, remember?"

A hardness came into her eyes then, and in that instant, he saw more than anger there. More than he ever wanted to see. She looked away. "You checked?"

His gaze slid away. "I said I did, didn't I?"

"Well, did you?"

Even in his dream, he felt the slap of those words. Of her disbelief, her lack of trust in him. "We can't afford it."

"I want to do IVF."

"Kinna, come on…"

"I don't care what it takes, Jimmy." She lifted the pamphlets and shook them in his face. "I want to have a baby! No matter what it takes. Nothing else matters. Not even you."

She hadn't said that last part, not in reality, but she said it in his half-dream, and it was just as real, just as ugly.

"A baby isn't everything. We can be happy, just you and I."

"Not without a baby, I can't. I want to be a family. A real family, Jimmy. How can you not understand that?"

He leaned forward. "I do understand." But he didn't. "I'll look at our insurance again." But he wouldn't. "You know I want a baby as much as you do." In truth, he was afraid. Of having a baby and losing Kinna. Of not having one and losing her just the same.

"This means everything to me."

Everything. As if all their years together didn't matter. As if everything they had was nothing but trash. Maybe his dad had been right.

It hadn't started that way. At first, there was just excitement, deciding to try for a baby, hoping to get pregnant. Plans and hopes and hours discussing what they'd name a baby, where they'd send a child to school, if they wanted a boy or girl, how many kids altogether, what they might look like. A baby rattle sent from her parents in Madagascar. A dozen trips to Babies "R" Us to pick out just the right crib set, just the right baskets, just the right Mozart CDs to make their baby brilliant. An afternoon painting the nursery. A stack of books from Borders on everything to know about pregnancy and babies and how to be the absolute perfect parents.

Kinna was so excited, and he was willing.

But months turned to years, excitement to fear, fear into bitter accusations. Into a hundred arguments just like the one he dreamed.

I don't want to remember it. I don't want to live it again. I don't want to live it at all. I just want to pretend everything's all right.

The memory changed, shifted.

He stood outside his father's bedroom, holding a drawing of the ocean at sunrise. A father and son walked along the shore together. He'd written "To Dad, From Jimmy" in the bottom corner and shaded it so carefully, not one mark too dark or too light. The ocean was the perfect mix of green and blue, the man's hair was long and brown, the sky a brilliant kaleidoscope of colors above them.

He peeked in the door. His dad sat on the bed, his back to Jimmy. He held a photo in his hand. A small, oval cameo. Jimmy's mother.

Jimmy paused, the door open only a crack before him.

"I can't do this, Jean," he heard his father say. "I ain't cut out to be a single dad. Thought it would get easier, but it hasn't. All these years, and it ain't one bit easier."

A snuffling sound came from the bedroom. "I told you we shouldn't have had him. We were plenty happy just the two of us, but you wanted a kid. And now I'm stuck with him and you're gone. Been gone for so, so long."

Jimmy's dad began to cry. It was an awful, horrible sound. Jimmy listened until he thought he would throw up, and still the sound came.

Jimmy crawled away from the door, back to his own room. An old poster of Prince Phillip met his gaze, a poster his mother had given him. One of the last things she'd bought him before...before... She was the only one who'd really understood why he loved the prince from *Sleeping Beauty.* The flashing sword, the fiery dragon, the happy prince who had no fear. Years had passed, but he still loved Phillip, still stared up at the noble face and wondered if his "happily ever after" would ever come true.

With a last glance toward the poster, he stumbled to the far side of the bed, pushed aside his skateboard and a Hacky Sack, and leaned back against his old Speed Racer bedspread. He spread his picture out in front of him and envisioned himself walking down that beach with a real father. The image failed, and he saw his father walking the beach alone. He was happy, not drunk, not sobbing.

It's all my fault.

Jimmy rubbed his thumb over the picture until the figures smeared and blurred, then he crumpled the paper and threw it toward the trash can in the corner. He ripped down the silly kid's poster and tore Speed Racer from his bed. He rolled up Prince Phillip and shoved him under the bed.

It was time to grow up and take responsibility. Time to realize he was to blame for everything that had happened to his dad.

And suddenly he was on the beach, shouting after a man who ran away from him. A man who ran with shoulders loose and legs stiff. A man who never turned around.

Dad? Dad! Dad...

Sunlight glared off the ocean's surface and flashed into his face, blinding him.

He opened his eyes and saw the curtains were open. Dawn was here and he still lay in bed. The guest bed, where Kinna had banished him, a guest in his own home. All because a baby meant more than he did. Maybe it always had.

He closed his eyes again, willing himself to return to that other place, back when Phillip still hung from the wall, before he knew there was no happily ever after.

Happily ever after...

The words rolled in his head. Why had he ever grown up?

From the garage, the dog howled.

Good grief, what am I supposed to say now? She sits on the rock, with sunlight in eyes too dry, bits of sand clinging to cheeks that should be damp and are not. I know she won't cry. Her soul is bleeding, but she won't let it show. Not yet. Not here. And not to me.

Stubborn.

I should have known.

Still, I would help Kinna if I could. I would paint the picture of a future filled with hope and laughter, promise and purity, but she wouldn't believe me. Not yet.

So I say nothing. Instead, I hand her the silk tulip that she buried in the sand, and I came behind and dug up again. I wonder if she has any idea what it means, this symbol of her past, of her hope. I doubt it.

Still, she takes it from me. At first, I think she will throw it out into the waves, but she doesn't. She just holds it, as if she can't decide to keep it or cast it from her. As if she can't decide if I'm friend or foe.

But that's okay. I'm not here to make her happy. I'm here to make her think. And perhaps to make her remember.

Kinna frowned at Thea as the woman handed her the tulip and sat on the rock beside her.

"I saw your van alongside the road."

Kinna cringed. "Looks bad, doesn't it?"

"Could be worse."

"Yeah, how?"

"You could be dead."

Kinna snorted. "Thanks for the encouragement."

Thea chuckled. "Seemed like you needed it."

"Gee, thanks."

Thea ignored the jab. "You're welcome."

"What are you doing here?"

Thea shifted on the rock. "Sitting by you." She rubbed her back. "But these old bones aren't as nimble as they used to be."

"You can get up. There's a bench back there a ways." Kinna motioned down the beach.

Thea grinned. "No, I like it right here. Don't you? It's a beautiful spot, with the sun coming up that way. Gives a person hope, don't you think?"

"Hope?" *Hardly.* "Why are you here, Thea?"

Silence stretched between them. Thea toyed with the locket at her neck. She opened it and looked down at the photos, then brushed her thumb across the image of her mother's face and sighed. "I'm not sure. Not yet, anyway. But I think I'm here for a reason."

"Don't tell me. You're here to save me." Kinna couldn't keep the bitterness from her voice. Bitterness that only intensified at the sight of those faces, faces that signified everything that should have been.

But "should have been's" died a long time ago, and no faces trimmed in silver could bring them back.

Kinna shifted and bumped her bag. It tipped, spilling lipstick, car keys, tissues, and the divorce papers. She really needed to get a zippered bag.

She reached for the papers, which lay unfolded and open, like the locket. But without the joy, the hope.

Thea's hand touched her arm.

Kinna looked up into a gaze that pierced her. The look—sorrow and fear—stole her breath. Then the look was gone, replaced with a quiet sternness. *What have you done?* The words flashed between them, unspoken, but as clear as if they'd been shouted in her ear.

Words rose up in Kinna in response, hot, furious, and just as unspoken.

You don't understand. No one does. I need to know that he loves me. I need to know that God loves me. After all these years of pain and sorrow, I've got to know. Even if it means dancing with divorce. He'll listen then. They'll both listen.

Thea sighed. "I'm not here to judge you. Just to listen. That's what friends do. And you told me we were friends, right?"

Kinna crossed her arms. The tirade quieted in her mind.

"So how about you put those papers away and start talking?" Thea pointed to Kinna's satchel.

Kinna slipped the papers and other items back into her bag, then looked down at the tulip. Sand was stuck in its crevices, one petal was bent, one edge frayed, but it was still a tulip, still intact.

"Tell me more about your husband."

Kinna shrugged. "He's a good guy. Great guy. Everybody likes him." *Except that Alan fellow.*

"So what went wrong?"

Kinna pressed her palms into her thighs and rubbed, as if she could rub away the question so she wouldn't have to face it. "What went wrong? Everything."

"But there must have been something you saw in him once. Something that made you love him."

Kinna stared out over the water. There had been something, and it started right here on this beach. They walked along the sand, side by side, her thinking of the three weeks to come, him dreaming of shapes in the clouds. The tide was going out and they sat on the edge of the water, where the sand still shimmered with wetness.

"We made a sandcastle once. Not too far from here." The words dropped between them.

Thea waited, silent, patient, until Kinna went on.

"Jimmy loved castles. He couldn't get enough of them. He was about to go into high school, and he was still making sandcastles. He could shape turrets with his bare hands, without a shovel or a cup." She made the motions with her hands, as if forming the sand between them. "And I loved to help him. Thirteen years old, and I was still up to my elbows in wet sand. Guess that should have told me something."

Thea nodded. "Mom always says that it's okay to dream, but it's better to believe."

Kinna shrugged. "Maybe. Maybe not. I don't know anymore."

"Then what?"

She settled back and continued the story. "We sat in the sand that day and made the biggest sandcastle you ever saw. It had fifteen turrets, three draw bridges, and a big, fat moat. We were so proud of that thing." And of one another. She'd never forget how Jimmy had looked at her over a dark turret and smiled into her eyes. How he reached over and touched her hair with his sandy fingers.

"You're beautiful. Did you know that?" His sapphire eyes sparkled.

She blushed and looked down. "You've got sand on your nose."

"Still can't take a compliment, can you?"

She made a face, then snuck a glance at him. He was grinning at her. There wasn't a speck of sand on his nose.

Thea sighed.

Kinna took a breath and continued, pushing the memory forward to a safer place. "Jimmy found these bits of driftwood and made them into the king's court. A big piece of kelp was the fiery dragon. There always had to be a dragon."

"And a princess?"

"I felt like one. I didn't know any better."

"A daughter of the great king."

Kinna looked up. "What?"

Thea smiled. "Sounds like fun."

She supposed it was. But it didn't stay that way. "Jimmy always knew how to make a good time. Until…"

"Until?"

"Some other kids came. Kids I knew from school. Rob and Mike, Marty and Pauline. They were in my grade, and they didn't like me much."

She paused again, remembering. They were brutal, those four, scorning her for carrying her Bible, for being Miss Goody Two-Shoes, for making castles in the sand with a boy. "They called me four-eyes and knocked over our castle. The turrets, the drawbridges. They even kicked in the moat."

"What did Jimmy do?"

Kinna's brows drew together as she remembered. "I thought he'd be mad about the castle, but he wasn't. He didn't even look at it. Instead, he picked up this big piece of driftwood and held it out in front of him. 'Don't you ever call her that,' he said. Then he swung that stick over his head and slammed it into Rob's shoulder.

"They ran away then, all of them, and Jimmy chased them and shouted that they were pansies and didn't know a beautiful girl when they saw one and he'd better not hear them say anything like that again. Then he came back and took my hand. He never once glanced at the ruined castle."

She smiled. "It was the first time I saw him stand up to anyone. He was my knight in shining armor."

Thea nodded. "He's still that boy, you know."

Kinna frowned.

"He still wants to be a hero."

Kinna shook her head. "It's too late now. There are no more bullies, no more sticks to turn into swords."

"There are still memories, your history, the past."

"It's not enough." It never had been. Jimmy had promised her something that day. After the bullies had gone, as the tide came in, he'd taken her hand, looked into her eyes, and promised he'd always be there for her.

Except he wasn't.

Not when she fell off her bike and broke her arm, not when her mother was diagnosed with skin cancer, not when her best girlfriend Molly moved away to Oregon.

And not when she came back from camp and found him gone. It would be two years before she saw him again. Two long years. So much for her knight in shining armor.

But that day she believed it. That day, she believed that they would be together forever.

"We have each other, Kinna," he'd said, "and that's what matters."

"But our castle's all kicked over."

"Is it?" He smiled.

She frowned. "Of course, it is. Look." She waved toward the pile of sand that had once been perfect turrets, a perfect drawbridge, and a perfect moat.

"It's still there, Kinna. You just can't see it as well."

She sighed. "Don't be dumb. It's gone."

He stepped closer and stood beside her, his voice quiet in her ear. "Look deeper. You can see it if you try."

She didn't try. She couldn't. To her, it was just a lump of sand.

Thea put her hand on Kinna's arm again. The touch was gentle. "You don't just have the past. You have the future too."

Kinna rose and turned away. "No. I don't like what I see when I look there."

Thea pulled herself up beside Kinna. A smile brushed her lips. "Believe me, you can't see everything. Not from where you're standing. You can't see anything at all." Thea stared out over the beach.

Kinna followed her gaze. She saw nothing but the sand and the water and the rocks. When she looked at the future, she only saw more pain, more disappointment, more darkness. More spinning off the road and crashing into cans. More castles smashed into the sand. And little hope for anything else.

There was no more make believe. She couldn't protect Jimmy anymore, and he wouldn't protect her. Reality had come at last. No more fairy tales. No more princes and princesses. They'd grown up, and the dragons had won.

There was nothing left but to go home and face him. To play her last card and hope that somehow it would be enough to make things change. That finally things would be different. Because of the threat of one word.

Divorce.

A word that proved the castle really was only a pile of sand.

16

Jimmy stepped into the shower just as her purse hit the table. He heard the thud of it down the long hallway, the same sound he'd heard for years. Only this time, he heard it from the guest bathroom.

Kinna was home. He didn't want to face her, didn't want her to explain or argue. Didn't want to talk about his move to the guest room or the torn tulips or the man who'd run away under the streetlight. And most of all, he didn't want to see the look she gave him so often now.

Maybe he deserved it. Maybe he deserved it all. The lost job, Karly, and a crazy dog. *Three strikes, you're out.* And then there was his refusal. She ought to understand why he'd done it, but she didn't. Wouldn't. His clothes thrown into the guest closet told him that.

He had tried to save them, to make her see what she was doing to the two of them, but instead of saving them, he had driven her away. Or made her drive him away. All the way to the guest bedroom. Next to the nursery. There was a bitter irony in that.

He shook his head and closed the shower door, then turned on the water. As long as she didn't think he'd heard her come in, she wouldn't come back here. She'd leave him alone.

Jimmy sighed. It was sad when a man hid from his wife by taking cover in the shower. Pathetic. But that was exactly what he was doing, and it wasn't the first time.

He closed his eyes and dipped his head under the water. If only he could go back to that first time. If only they could go back, but it was like another world then, and they were two other people. Young, in love, happy. Sharing one bedroom, one bathroom.

And thinking it would never change.

He'd come home from his first day at the new construction job. Dirt covered his stiff new jeans and had worked its way into his hair, his eyelashes, even his teeth. But that wasn't why he hurried to the shower.

He didn't want her to see.

"Jimmy, is that you?" she'd called.

He didn't answer. He just turned on the water and hopped in before it even got warm. If he could just get through the shower, get cleaned off with that orange gunk he'd grabbed from the garage, then maybe she wouldn't know, wouldn't notice.

"Jimmy?" He heard her open the bathroom door. "Remember we have that banquet tonight. You're supposed to introduce Dad before he speaks."

Of course he remembered. She'd been talking about it all week. Her dad was being honored for his work in the community, for getting alcoholics off the streets. How could he forget?

He willed her not to come in to the bathroom.

She did anyway.

Steam billowed out the door. She gripped the plastic curtain. "What's wrong with you?"

"Go away."

She pulled back the curtain.

He turned his back.

"What did you say?"

"I'll be out in a while."

"What's that on your ear?" She reached in and tugged on it. Then she touched his chin and turned his head toward her.

Her eyes watered. Her lips pursed.

He looked away. "I'm sorry. I know how important tonight is to you, but well, you see…" He snuck a glance at her, expecting to see her fury.

Instead, she was shaking. No, not shaking. Laughing.

She lifted a hand to her mouth. A snicker escaped through her fingers. "W-what happened to you?"

He ran a hand over his wet hair. "Dropped a wrench into a bucket of tar." He touched his cheek, feeling the black spatter that covered his skin.

"That was clumsy."

He scowled. "Wasn't me who dropped it. One of the guys. He said he was sorry."

"Was he?"

"No."

She swallowed her giggle, but her eyes watered more.

He grimaced. It had been a test, of sorts. Get tar all over the new guy, see how he reacts. See if he was a panties-in-a-bunch sissy or if he could be trusted. For Jimmy it had been easy. He'd had a lot worse done to him, so a little tar was simple to shrug off.

He squeezed some orange goo onto his hand, then rubbed it into his skin. "This stuff'll take it right off." He rinsed.

She chewed her lips, and he could see the corners still tipping up.

"What?"

"It didn't work."

"What do you mean?"

"Well, at least it will go great with your black suit. The color matches perfectly."

He groaned. "I'm gonna kill those guys."

She laughed out loud. "Good thing I married you for better or for worse."

"Thanks."

She leaned against the side of the shower. "You're welcome, freckles."

He splashed water at her, but she didn't back up. Instead, she stepped into the shower and kissed him all over his tar-spattered face. And that had led to more.

Jimmy grunted and returned his thoughts to the present. Somehow, he didn't think today would end in quite the same way. There was no tar, no banquet, and certainly no understanding wife on the other side of the door. What happened to "for better or worse"?

He washed his face then let the hot water run over his face and neck. They'd come a long, long way from that giddy couple, newly married. Back then he wanted nothing more than to be with her. Now, too often, he only wanted to get away.

And both then and now, he didn't get his wish.

A dog. Kinna couldn't believe her eyes. There was a dog in her garage. And by the looks of things, it had torn up three towels, one large blanket, and a box of laundry detergent.

She threw her purse onto the kitchen table, then returned to the garage door.

The dog was still there.

She blinked and rubbed her eyes.

The dog looked up at her from the pile of torn towels and thumped its tail.

She heard the sound, so it couldn't be a figment of her imagination. It had to be real.

Kinna shut the door and rested her back against it.

Jimmy had lost his mind. There was no other explanation. Because against all odds, against all reason, there was a dog in the garage. Absolutely. Positively. Impossible.

The dog barked.

Kinna closed her eyes. *Not again.* But she remembered it anyway— that day, so many years ago, when Jimmy came, white-faced, to her house, looking like he might barf all over his 49ers jacket. She asked what was wrong, but he wouldn't tell her. Eventually, she got the truth out of him. His dad had taken that mongrel dog away, just like Kinna knew he would. She'd tried to warn Jimmy, but he wouldn't listen. He just had to get attached to that mangy pup.

For a full week, he dragged himself around the beach, the church, the park. He refused to build sandcastles, saying he never wanted to see another dragon. All he did was talk about that dumb dog.

And then, after a week, he stopped talking about the dog. But he never forgot about that ugly, straggly mutt.

And he never knew what happened to it. How could she ever admit that his dad had brought that awful thing to her dad? They'd taken it to the vet, found out it was sick and couldn't be cured. They had to put that dog down. And there was no way, ever, that she'd tell Jimmy.

And now, after all this time, here was another dog, just as scraggly, just as ugly.

What was Jimmy thinking?

Kinna opened her eyes and returned to the kitchen table. There were too many memories lately, too much pain. At least they made her feel again, even if much of the feeling was regret, sorrow, or confusion.

Her purse fell over. She didn't bother to straighten it. Instead, she stared out the window and tried to imagine what would possess Jimmy to get a dog. Did he think a dog could replace a baby? Just get something to care for, and things would be all right? That would be just like him. Gloss over the pain and try to fix it with some ridiculous solution.

But a dog? A dog didn't fix anything.

She shook her head. *I just want to go back. Before all the fighting, before the arguments, before the confusion and the pain of trying to have a baby and failing again and again. I want to go back to when I still believed in hope.*

When God still cared.

When there were no dogs to wonder about.

When I still loved a boy named Jimmy Henley.

He couldn't stay in the shower forever, but he let the water run and run and run.

Once he got out, he would lose her. The coffee shop, the job, the refusal, and now the tulips. He was doomed.

But the water was getting cold.

I don't want to face her. I don't want to lose her. Not again.

He cranked the water knob all the way left, all the way hot. He turned and let the water roll over his back as he remembered another place, another time. He remembered the sound of a toilet flushing and the stench of soured Coors. He remembered being fourteen.

And he remembered his dad.

That day, he walked into the little apartment his dad had rented for them. It was a nasty place, with peeling wallpaper, a cracked kitchen sink, and an upstairs neighbor who played Van Halen day and night. "Runnin' With the Devil" was playing then. Jimmy could tell from the sound of a car horn booming through the ceiling. What kind of song used the sound of a car horn as part of the melody? Only Van Halen. He hated Van Halen.

He strode through the door and closed it firmly behind him, then took a deep breath. The toilet flushed. The water ran. Dad was home.

Above, the sound of the song's car horn changed to the screech of guitars. Jimmy straightened his shoulders and reviewed the paper in his hand one more time. He had his speech prepared and a list of ten absolutely-impossible-to-deny reasons he should be allowed to go to camp this year. It would be his final chance. He closed his eyes and saw the list in his mind. Kinna had written it up, so neat in her perfect print. First, he was supposed to thank his dad for all he'd done to feed and clothe Jimmy. He'd argued about that one, but Kinna insisted he had to start by saying something nice. Then he was to go on to all the reasons camp would be good not only for Jimmy, but also for his dad. And lastly, he would talk about where he'd get the money to go. How the church would help. His dad wouldn't like that part, but maybe by the time he'd gotten that far, his father would be softened.

Fat chance.

Jimmy pushed that thought from his mind and focused on his speech. He squeezed the paper tighter in his fist and headed for the kitchen.

Last night's dinner dishes were piled in the sink, bits of dried baked beans still stuck to the plates. A piece of dried up hot dog lay on the counter. Jimmy rubbed his hand against his leg and shoved the list into his pocket. Maybe if he washed the dishes and cleaned the counter, his dad would be in a better mood. Maybe if he shined the faucet and picked up those beer bottles from the floor, wiped up the spilled strawberry jam, and took out the overflowing trash. If he did all that, then maybe…

Jimmy spent the next fifty-three minutes cleaning until the kitchen's surfaces gleamed. Then he waited.

But his dad didn't come.

Jimmy reviewed his list one last time, then folded it and returned it to his pocket. He stepped into the hall. The sound of footsteps came from the bedroom at the hall's end. His bedroom. He frowned.

"Dad?"

He heard the creaking of a door, then a heavy thud.

Jimmy hurried down the hall and peeked in his bedroom door. His father stood at his bed, a suitcase open before him on the rumpled blankets. He caught his breath and pushed the door open wider.

His dad didn't turn. Instead, he grabbed Jimmy's few clothes from the closet and slapped them into the suitcase. He dumped out the drawer of socks and underwear. He grabbed up the blankets on the bed.

Jimmy shook as he watched. "W-what are you doing?" His voice cracked.

His dad didn't glance his way. He just closed the suitcase and latched it. "What does it look like?"

"I don't know."

His dad straightened. His face was pale, his eyes clear and unblurred. He wasn't drunk.

That scared Jimmy more than anything.

"We're going to your grandma's."

"But…"

"Right now." He tossed the suitcase at Jimmy's chest. It hit him and thumped onto the ground.

Jimmy staggered back. "But why?"

"All you need to know is that things are gonna get ugly if we stick around here. Pack up your stuff."

A horn beeped. Van Halen again?

His father's brow furrowed. "Taxi's here. Let's go."

Jimmy's gaze flew around the room. "My poster…" The one still shoved under the bed. The one he had never been able to throw away.

"Leave it. That's for babies, anyway."

Jimmy's throat closed. *This isn't happening. It can't be. I'm going to close my eyes and pretend—*

"Jimmy!"

Jimmy's eyes flew open.

"We've got to go. Now."

Above them, Van Halen cut off. In the eerie quiet, Jimmy could hear his heart thumping. His father's hand gripped his arm so tightly that his skin turned white beneath his dad's fingers. His dad pushed him toward the door, then let go.

Jimmy grabbed his suitcase and hurried out. His dad picked up an overstuffed duffle, swung it over his shoulder, and followed him out the door. Neither of them looked back. Not to the things they'd left behind, not to the bits of furniture and old photos, not to the sparkling clean kitchen where Jimmy had left his hopes.

The rest was a blur. The trip to the bus station, the long ride to Glendale in Southern California. The little pink house where his grandma lived, and where he would live for the next two years.

He learned a lot there. How to do an ollie on his skateboard. How to swim and solve for *x*. How to sit so still he was almost invisible.

But he never forgot Kinna, and he never forgot her God. Grandma believed, and at some point during the endless Sundays in that cramped and dusty little church on the corner, Jimmy found that he believed it too. Despite his father, despite everything, he knew God was real. He knew that God mattered, and he believed that someday, somehow, he would see Kinna again.

And he did, in just two years. No time at all, and an eternity. Because it was enough time for Kinna to forget she was his best girl. Enough for her to start high school and begin looking at other guys the way he wanted her to look only at him. Enough for her to change from the little girl he'd known to the first inklings of the woman she'd become. Enough for him to almost lose his chance with her. Almost.

But even then, he never dreamed they'd end up here, with her so unhappy and him hiding in the shower. He had never, ever believed it could come to this.

Oh God, how did this happen? How did we become these people, filled with bitterness and hate and hopelessness? I want the fairy tale back. I just want things to be like they were before. Please God, let us go back…

The floorboards creaked in the hall.

"Jimmy?"

Kinna. He shuddered. Too late. It was already too late.

He slapped the water from his face and turned off the shower. "I'll be right out." He dried off, then grabbed his underwear and jeans and threw them on.

"I'll be in the kitchen."

Nothing good ever happened in the kitchen. He stepped out of the bathroom, still drying his hair. He could see a glimpse of her green hospital scrubs in the kitchen beyond. This wasn't how he was hoping to face her, but it would have to do.

He tossed the towel over his shoulder, then walked down the hall and into the kitchen. Her bag sat tipped on the table as he expected, her keys next to it. Kinna stood by the sink, her back to him. She held something in her hands. She stared at it, then set it on the counter and turned toward him.

He waited.

Her eyes flickered over his bare chest, then back up to his face. Her face flushed, and he cleared his throat.

And still she didn't confront him.

He ran his fingers through his damp hair. "Look, about the coffee shop—"

She glanced away. "You don't have to explain."

But he did. They both knew it. "She's just a girl from work. Nothing's going on."

She nodded slowly. "And if there was?" Her tone was so low, so quiet, that he almost missed her words.

He wished he had. How could a man answer a question like that? How could he endure the utter despair in her voice? How could he stand that he'd caused it? "Please, Kinna."

She held up a hand and shook her head, then raised her eyes to his. He expected to see tears, but her eyes were dry.

She licked her lips. "It's time we faced the truth."

No.

"Jimmy."

He gripped the towel as tightly as he could. "I don't want to sleep there." He motioned toward the tiny guest room at the end of the hall. His voice rose. "You know that. I never said—"

Hers rose louder. "You chose. You said—"

"Let's not go there again."

"You never want to 'go there.' You just want to avoid—"

"Sure, let's drag it all out again. Everything you hate about me."

"I don't hate you."

"Really? Then why am I sleeping down the hall?" He was shouting now. Loud enough for the dog to start barking.

"You know why." Her gaze flicked to the garage. "And how could you get a dog?"

"Because I needed someone around here to care about me, who didn't think I'm a no-good, no-account loser." The words spewed out before he could stop them.

Kinna slammed her lips shut, and her face turned pale. She swallowed and blinked. He watched the emotions play over her face. Shock, fear, confusion, guilt. And sorrow.

"Oh, Jimmy." She stood there, almost trembling, almost vulnerable. She moved closer, and her voice softened, reached toward him, drew him with its innocence. "I never meant—"

"I know." He'd done it now. Made her feel sorry for him, made her want to protect him. Just like always.

She glanced away. "Do you remember that day on the beach when we were kids? When those bullies ruined our sandcastle that we'd worked so hard to build?"

"I remember."

"You chased them away with that piece of driftwood."

"That was a long time ago."

"I know."

"A lot changed that day."

"I know."

"What made you remember?"

She rubbed her nose like she used to do as a kid. It made him smile. It made his chest ache. She glanced up at him. "It made me feel safe."

Would the accusations come now, the deep, bitter questions about why he wasn't the man she thought he would be? Is that where this was going? Or was it guilt driving her, making her remember times when they'd been on the same side, when they'd fought the enemies together instead of turning on each other?

She took a step toward him, until she stood so close he could hear her breath. "Our castle's crumbling again, Jimmy."

He nodded and pulled the towel from his neck. "But this time we're the bullies, aren't we?"

A sad smile crossed her face. "And we don't have any swords."

"Can't we go back, Kinna? To the way things used to be? Can't we just pretend…?"

Her head tilted a bit to the side. Her eyes shone now, wet with tears. Her mouth parted, just a little. The scent of her surrounded him. Hospital antiseptic, fresh cotton, a bit of the sea. Uniquely Kinna. Uniquely his wife.

He reached out and touched her cheek, the softness of her skin. This couldn't be happening. This was make believe.

And yet she was here, looking at him with those eyes, leaning in enough for him to feel the tension between them. The yearning. The need. The heat that had been cool for too long.

She tipped her chin toward him. His gaze swept her face, longing for the look in her eyes he'd once seen there. The look that wanted him just for him. Only him.

But it wasn't like before. He knew that, and so did she.

And still…

His hand slipped behind her head, burying itself in the softness of her hair. He still loved her hair. He drew her closer.

Her fingers brushed his chest. "Oh, Jimmy."

He lowered his head and kissed her. Full, deep, and rich with all they had been, all he dreamed they would be.

They broke apart.

And then he saw the papers on the table.

17

Kinna sensed the change in him. The stiffness, the rejection. Did she repel him so much that he couldn't even stand her kiss?

His eyes swept up to meet hers, and her breath stopped at the look she saw there. Loathing. Fear. A terrible coldness.

Alan had been right. Jimmy didn't love her anymore. He couldn't, and look at her like that. She hadn't even given him the papers.

She backed away.

The dog began to whine as if it, too, sensed something. As if it knew something had changed forever, and there was no going back.

Kinna dropped her chin and her eyes filled with water. It would do no good to cry now. It was too late for tears. She'd schemed and hoped and tried, but what was the use? Her own husband couldn't bear to kiss her. Couldn't bear to be near her.

She turned away.

He didn't move behind her. Didn't speak.

They stood for the longest time, together, apart. And finally he whispered a single question into the silence that stood like a wall between them.

"What are you playing at, Kinna?" He spoke as if each word was a shard of glass tearing him, cutting them both.

She couldn't answer. Couldn't even meet his gaze.

How could she still love him, still want him, still desire his kiss after all the pain of these last years, these last days? She should have known it would come to this.

But it was only a simple kiss.

"Just go." It was all she could manage. Any more and she would cry. She didn't want him to see her cry. Not over him. Not like this.

His footsteps sounded behind her, quiet, sad. They traveled down the hall to the guest room, where she had moved his clothes. She'd meant it as a threat. He'd taken it as license.

He wants to be free of me.

Because she was less than a woman. Less than desirable. Less. Just less. And always would be.

She'd tried, though. She'd tried to be everything, to be everyone. Perfect wife, perfect mother, perfect nurse. She'd failed at them all. A husband who didn't want to touch her, a job that had been lost, a barren womb.

She'd wanted it all. She got nothing. Just a husband who preferred pretty young women in coffee shops to kissing his own wife. Of course, that other woman was young, fertile. And Kinna was…Kinna was not.

She could hear him moving around in the guest room. He was quiet, too quiet. No stomping, or throwing things, or banging doors. He moved in near silence, as if someone had died.

She turned and glanced down the hall. She could see him passing in front of the door. He paused and pulled a T-shirt over his head. His back rippled with muscles gained over years at the job site. He looked so different than he once did, back when they were young. He was thinner then, but the same height, with that little fuzz over his lip that would never become a proper mustache. Sixteen and trying to grow a mustache. She remembered the feel of it the first time they kissed.

He hadn't been repelled by her then, but maybe because it wasn't a real kiss. It was just a sample, an experiment. Even that first kiss was just pretend. Maybe everything had been.

But it had seemed so real.

After two years, he'd come back to her, like nothing had changed. But they were grown up now. She was fifteen, teetering on the very brink of womanhood and ready for her first date ever with Steve, the cool guy who sat in front of her in French class. The one her best friend Tracy thought was so "ooh la la."

She stood at the front window of her parents' home, wearing her brand new purple polo shirt, 501 jeans, and the prettiest purple leg warmers bunched over her calves. Leg warmers had gone out a year ago, but she wore them anyway because they matched. She'd teased her hair full, just like Jennifer Beals in *Flashdance,* put on way too much makeup, and even dabbed on a little Liz Claiborne perfume. Behind her, Soft Cell sang about tainted love from the boom box on the table.

As Marc Almond continued to sing, she began to wonder if he was right. She ought to run away, because the seconds ticked to minutes, and still Steve's slick red Camaro didn't come around the corner.

Surely he didn't forget. Not her first date. Her very, very first.

The whole cassette she'd taped off the radio played through as she waited. She could hear her parents and Jimmy and his dad in the kitchen. This was the first time he'd been over since the months he'd been back. And now they were all there talking about something important, from the sound of their voices. Something about rehab and the room over the garage. But Kinna wasn't paying much attention to that. Besides, it wouldn't matter anyway. Jimmy's dad wouldn't go to rehab for a whole other year.

What mattered now was that she was finally, finally going on her first date. It was just Burger King and some movie where Michael J. Fox went back in time, but it was her first. And with a guy two years older than her, a senior. She'd had to drop her pencil four times in French class, then hang around outside the basketball court for two weeks to get him to ask her. Daddy didn't approve, but it was still a date. Steve was cute and popular and had a cool car. What else mattered?

Except it was 7:30, and he was forty minutes late. The movie started at 7:20. Maybe he'd run out of gas.

Headlights swooped around the corner outside. Kinna grabbed her purse and moved toward the window. She held her breath.

The car turned into a Chevy Luv and sped past.

Three minutes later, an old Monte Carlo rumbled by. Then a hatchback. And still Steve didn't come.

Kinna dropped her purse back onto the sofa and folded her arms over her stomach. He was coming. He had to be. She played with the long, feathered earring dangling from her ear. Another five minutes went by.

He wasn't coming.

Stood up on her first date. Rejected. Left. Forgotten.

Oh God, please...

And then his arms surrounded her, warm and gentle. Jimmy drew her back toward him until her back pressed into his chest and she felt his heartbeat through her shirt. He held her there, without speaking, until she didn't have to fight the tears anymore.

"Steve's a jerk."

She sniffed and nodded.

"He would have been a lousy date anyway."

"First date."

"Oh, Kinna." He turned her toward him, put his finger under her chin, and lifted her face to his.

She gazed into his sapphire eyes and felt whole again.

He smiled. "Tell you what, I'll take you to that movie. And to the new Sizzler on the corner too. It'll be a way better first date than you'd have had with that stupid Steve."

"You know that doesn't count, Jimmy."

"Why not?"

"We're friends, that's why. This was supposed to be a date. A real date."

"I know you're bummed, but we can pretend, can't we?" He looked into her eyes, and she saw shadows of Prince Phillip shimmering in his. "Like we used to."

"I don't know. I turned fifteen and a half on Tuesday, and I'm supposed to be able to have a real date."

"Come on, Kinna. You deserve a great first date with someone who will treat you right. Not like Steve."

She crossed her arms. "And we'll go back to just being friends afterward?"

"Sure."

"Okay."

Kinna grabbed up her purse again and called into the kitchen. "Mom, Dad, Steve didn't show. I'm going to the movie with—"

Jimmy squeezed her arm and frowned. "No, not like that, Kinna. That's not how a first date is supposed to start. Stay here." He let go of her arm and walked into the kitchen.

Kinna peeked through the door. Jimmy stood before her father and…was he? He was! He was asking her dad permission for a date. He was crazy to the max.

Shortly, Jimmy rejoined her. "Come on. Your dad said we could stay out until eleven."

"Eleven? He told me ten."

Jimmy grinned. "That was with Steve."

He opened the front door and ushered her out, and they strolled out to his beat-up VW Rabbit. He opened the door for her, and she slid in. It was no red Camaro, but it was here and she was in it. Going on a date.

Jimmy jumped into the driver's side. He smiled at her. "Buckle up."

And they were off. He paid for dinner at Sizzler, paid for three games of Pac-Man in the restaurant's lobby, paid her way into the movie, and held her Members Only jacket.

And then he held her hand. Just as he'd done so many times before, except this was utterly and completely different, his fingers just curling around hers as Marty McFly blasted into the past in his DeLorean DMC-12. And Jimmy didn't let go. Not when Marty sang rock'n'roll to a school full of fifties teens, not when he saved his father, not even when lightning slammed into the clock tower and sparks lit the screen.

Afterward, they had a frozen yogurt and he took her home five minutes before curfew. They stood on the front porch, his hand still touching hers.

Kinna gazed up at him. "Thank you, Jimmy. It was an awesome first date. I know you couldn't afford—"

"Shhh." He put his finger on her lips. "It didn't cost a thing. It was all make believe, remember?"

"But—"

"The perfect date. I promised, didn't I?" He moved closer and whispered in her ear. "I don't recommend this for every first date, but…"

He turned his head. His lips met hers, and he kissed her. Sweetly, gently, giving instead of taking. As if he was sharing a bit of his soul with her.

Warmth flooded her, and she kissed him back, just a little.

Then he let go and his eyes searched hers. Deep, sparkling blue. They stole her breath. She stepped back.

He smiled, and the moment faded. "Don't worry, Kinna. It's just pretend, after all."

But it didn't feel like pretend. It felt like the most real thing that had ever happened in her life. The most real thing that would ever happen.

Jimmy watched her all the way into the house, until she closed the door and leaned against it, her eyes fluttering shut, her fingers touching the spot on her lips where it still tingled from his kiss.

Jimmy's kiss.

Twenty-four years later, Kinna again reached up and touched her mouth. But this time, it was cold, trembling, with no sweetness left behind.

Behind her she could hear Jimmy walking past, carrying something that squeaked. She stole a glance behind her.

He held his suitcase in his hand, the big black one he never used.

She turned her back. His footsteps went past. The front door slammed. He whistled for the dog.

Then they were both gone, and the silence was an ocean that drowned her.

She turned around at last, took a ragged breath, and gripped the table's edge with white hands.

And then she saw those cursed divorce papers, fallen from her bag and open on the table, bearing their names.

And finally, she understood. He'd seen the papers, seen what she had done. And he had still walked away.

18

Jimmy leaned against the bar and stared at the amber liquid in his glass. He should have known this day would come. He should have seen it in the way she looked at him, in the way she didn't look at him. Her eyes averted, sliding away, ashamed.

Before him, dim lights danced off the liquid's surface, mixing with the trickle of noon sunlight that drizzled through the windows. He ran his fingers down the mug's cool sides, leaving tracks along the frosted glass. Behind the bar, a man filled another mug with Heineken, then slid it down to the far end of the counter.

Jimmy stared at his beer as if he could spy within its depths a reflection of the very moment when everything had gone wrong.

Was it when she sat on the edge of the bed in her bra and panties, and he'd refused her? No, it had happened long before that. When he told her they couldn't afford IVF? When he missed the appointment at the fertility clinic? When their first try at adoption fell apart? Or was it that first month when they'd tried to get pregnant and failed?

Maybe it happened earlier yet. Maybe it happened in this very bar, in this very spot, all those years ago.

But back then, it was not him who sat here, but his dad. The stools weren't padded, and the air was heavy with Marlboro and Camel smoke. Hippie-haired men hung their bellies on the bar and called for

Jim Beam on the rocks as they watched the Dodgers win another play-off game.

He'd come looking for his dad in this old, seedy bar tucked between the motorcycle shop and what had now become a place that sold mobile phones. It wasn't so run-down then, and men flocked here after work to have a laugh with the boys before going home to their wives and children. Except his dad rarely came home. He just sat on this stool, calling for another drink, until Jimmy came and stood at the door. Moe would see him and nod, just once, and a moment later, the old bartender would tell his dad he'd run out of money on his tab.

Except for one day. That day, his dad didn't want to leave. That day, he swaggered over in those tight Wranglers, one thumb hooked through a belt loop, the other hand gripping a half-drunk scotch.

Jimmy stood just inside the door. "Come on home, Dad. Dinner's ready."

"Go home, boy. I ain't done yet."

"I can wait."

"Not in here, Jim." Moe flicked his rag toward Jimmy then pointed to the sign on the wall, No Onc Under 21 Allowed. "Go on, Henley. Booze'll be here tomorrow, just the same." He tucked the rag into his back pocket.

Jimmy's dad growled, then took another swig of his drink. "You know what today is, boy?" Blurry eyes locked on his, then blinked.

Jimmy shook his head.

"'Course not. Why should you care? Took her from me, that's what you did. Turned me into this." He stared down at the glass of scotch, then slowly twisted his wedding ring around his finger. "Would have been nineteen years."

The murmured words barely reached Jimmy's ears. Back then, he didn't understand them. He opened the bar door and urged his father to follow him out.

Dad took one step toward him. Scotch sloshed from the glass and splashed over Jimmy's arm. The sour smell washed over him as he jerked back.

Dad glowered. "Ashamed of me, are you, boy? Old man embarrasses you, does he?"

"No, Dad. Come on."

His dad slammed the glass onto a table by the door, took one step, two, and the door swung shut behind him with a quiet thump.

Bits of sunlight glinted off the sidewalk. Jimmy's dad squinted and glared at him, lank hair drizzling down his forehead and hiding his eyebrows. "I weren't done with my drink, boy."

"Come on, Dad. No one wants to see you like this."

Dad's voice grew louder, less distinct. "Your fault I'm like this. Your mother's fault too. Same blood. Same stupid, weird blood." He raised his fist, and Jimmy knew what was about to happen.

He ducked before his father's knuckles could smash him in the head, and stumbled backward.

"Mr. Henley!" A voice, strong, shocked, burst out behind him.

Jimmy caught his breath. He knew that voice. *Oh no, not here. Not now. I don't want him to see me like this.* Jimmy pressed his back against the bar's outer wall, then turned toward the voice. *He* stood there, and worse yet, *she* did too.

Oh Lord, help.

"Hello, Mr. Hollis. Kinna." He swallowed. "Uh, nice day, huh?"

Kinna's brows drew together as she glanced between him and his dad, and then she smiled. She didn't understand, didn't know what was happening right before her eyes.

Mr. Hollis stepped up. "Evening, Henley. Jimmy."

His dad grunted, then sniffed at the scotch that had spilled over his hand. He grinned. "Evening, Reverend." He motioned toward the bar's door. "Buy you a drink?"

Jimmy would never forget the look on Reverend Hollis's face as his eyes traveled from Jimmy's dad to the front of that bar. He'd never before seen that particular shade of gray on a person. He thought Mr. Hollis was going to be sick, but the moment passed.

Mr. Hollis straightened his shoulders. "No thanks, Henley. Me and my *daughter* were just going to pick up some tulips at the flower shop next door. Perhaps you'd like to join *us*."

Kinna stepped forward. "That would be great. Missy said they have purple tulips in today. Come on, Jimmy."

Jimmy didn't move. He stared at her, at that bright smile, those soft, kind eyes. So innocent and so genuinely glad to see him, to invite him to join her. As if she and her dad had happened upon just another parent-child outing, with no undertones, no problems, no sour scotch soaking his sleeve.

She touched his arm, her fingers gentle on his skin. "Coming?"

Heat rushed through him. A desperate hope, a wild longing to just go with her and forget. To lace his fingers through hers. To move closer, and—

His father burped.

Jimmy jumped.

Then it was Dad's hand on his arm, with a different kind of heat and without anything like gentleness. He pulled away.

His dad grunted. "We ain't coming. We got business to finish, don't we, boy?"

Kinna's smile faltered. She stepped back. "Business? What business?" She looked up at him.

Jimmy looked deep into her eyes. Words stopped and twisted halfway up his throat. He couldn't tell her the truth, couldn't stomach seeing the revulsion that was sure to come on her face when she realized why he was there with his drunk father, scotch trailing down his sleeve.

So he smiled and lied. "Just checking out the motorcycles." He gestured toward the shop on his right. "Gnarly, huh?"

She rolled her eyes and laughed. "Boys."

Her father dropped his arm over her shoulder and turned her, protecting her. "Better hurry and get those flowers, Kinna." He pulled her forward, past them.

Time slowed as Jimmy watched her moving away from him, satisfied with his lie.

"See you in a while, crocodile." She shot the words over her shoulder as she and her dad entered the flower shop. A bell tinkled over the door.

If you knew. If only you knew…

Shame, sharp and bitter, sour as the scotch staining his shirt, choked him, drowning him. She deserved better, but, oh, how he loved her.

Her hair swayed like Willy Wonka's chocolate river, a bit of it caught in the ruffles that stood up from her shoulders and ran down the front of her shirt. She glanced back at him one last time before the door shut. Her eyes twinkled, her nose turned up just a bit at the end. He remembered the dusting of freckles over that cute little nose, freckles that had faded over the years until he could no longer see them.

He loved her then, but not enough to tell her the truth. Never enough for that. Even now, after all these years, it wasn't enough.

Maybe things between them had gone wrong then, but what would she have done if he'd looked her in the eye and said, "Sorry, I can't see the tulips now because my dad's soused and I can't get him to come home"? Maybe that's what he should have said. Maybe he and Kinna were never meant to be.

Because now he was the one sitting in a mostly empty bar. He was the one with a drink in front of him, the one who didn't want to leave. He rubbed at the fingerprints on the bar's surface and stared at the liquid in his glass because he couldn't face the accusations in his own soul. The only friend he had left was the amber liquid that beckoned, danced with light, promised oblivion. And that was enough.

Maybe Dad had it right all along.

Except now there was no old Moe behind the bar, just some kid hired at minimum wage. There was no Dusty Baker in left field, no Ron Cey on third base, no Steve Yeager catching behind the plate. Those days were gone.

Except they weren't. They never really left at all. He should have realized that. You never get away from who you are. You're never free.

Oh God...

The door creaked open behind him. He didn't turn. It never used to creak like that. He sighed and stared deeper into the glass.

Oh God. Oh God, oh God, oh God.

He tried to pray. Tried to believe, like he once did, that somehow God would find a way, that it wouldn't end like this. But all these years of failure and disappointment had eroded his faith too. Had brought him here.

He deserved nothing else.

God was for better people, more faithful people, like Kinna's father and mother, now abroad as missionaries to Madagascar. Those were the people God listened to, not people like him who just tried to get along in life and messed up even that.

No, this is where he belonged, on this stool in this bar, with a frosted mug in front of him. Just like his dad had tried to tell him.

That day, as Kinna and her father disappeared into the flower shop, his dad shoved him out of the way and stormed back into the bar, shouting about high-and-mighty, good-for-nothing holier-than-thous judging him.

And Jimmy shouted back, as loud as he could. "They are not!"

His dad paused in the bar's doorway, turned back, and laughed. Just laughed, high and wild, until Jimmy understood. Dad was laughing at him.

The door swung open, and the crowd roared at another homerun hit by someone like Steve Garvey. And Jimmy stood, immobile, as his father disappeared into the bar. He could still hear that laugh.

Now there was no baseball on the television. Instead, it spat out news about the weather and another upheaval in Iraq. It showed the new great white shark at the aquarium and the latest bike race around Cannery Row.

But the sound of laughter still rang in Jimmy's ears as he sat at the bar, drink in front of him, the old jukebox playing something from Styx behind him. He sat and saw not the beer, but the divorce papers. Those awful, agonizing papers. Papers that were destined, perhaps, since that other day so long ago.

Maybe Dad had been right to laugh all those years ago.

The truth had caught up with him at last. He couldn't outrun it anymore. She'd finally seen him for what he was, had been seeing it for some time now. Pieces of the drunkard's son. Tears in Prince Charming's cape. Because none of it was real. He wasn't a prince. He was nothing. Nobody.

Jobless, gutless, wifeless. Worthless.

"Something wrong with your drink, dude?"

Jimmy looked up at the peach-fuzzed face of the bartender. "It's fine."

"You've been staring at it for half an hour. I got a new stout on tap. Or a pale ale, if you like that better."

Jimmy shook his head. "No. This one is great." If he wasn't careful, he might order a scotch. If he could bear the smell.

No, the beer was fine. All that mattered was that he sat where his dad once sat. Sat with nothing. No family, no job, no hope. Kinna would call it ironic. He didn't know what to call it. Predictable? Inescapable? Fitting? He couldn't make a good thing last either. He messed it up too. Always.

He'd tried, done his best, but it wasn't good enough. Never good enough. He should have known that someday he'd end up here.

Just like Dad.

Jimmy picked up the mug and drank down the beer in a single, long chug.

19

ilence. No snuffling dog, no spray of water from the shower, no voice from the other room. Nothing.

Just the barrenness. Not only within, but surrounding her, drowning her. Ugly, sickening silence.

Jimmy was gone. Not just left, but gone.

The house was empty. Of sound, of life, of hope.

Oh Lord, what have I done?

She squinted up at the ceiling. *Don't answer that! And don't say it's my fault. Don't even.* She knew it already.

Kinna clenched her fists and pressed them into her forehead. Divorce papers. What a stupid idea. This was all that Alan's fault.

Okay, God, now what am I supposed to do?

"*Love is not self-seeking. It is not easily angered. It keeps no record of wrongs.*"

Kinna grimaced. *You've got to be kidding.* She wasn't the one who needed to do the loving. It was Jimmy. He started all this by interfering with her perfectly perfect plans. He was the one who walked out, not once but twice. There was no way she'd go crawling back to him, making him think he was right.

"*Love does not delight in evil, but rejoices with the truth.*"

What was truth? The truth was she wanted a baby. She wanted to know that Jimmy loved her, that God loved her. And the truth was that Jimmy and God weren't cooperating. Or was the truth that she'd driven Jimmy away? That something had gone wrong, and there was no fixing it?

"Love always hopes, always perseveres."

Not this time.

She pulled her phone from her purse and flipped it open. It was a cheap thing, not even one of those neat, flat ones. Just the freebie she got for signing up for service. But the money she'd saved had paid for three cycles on clomiphene citrate pills. Not that they'd done any good.

Kinna stared at the phone's numbered buttons. She had to talk to someone, anyone, but there was no one to call. No friends who were close enough, no family. Her parents were halfway across the world.

Barren.

She pressed her fingers into her temples. *Stop it. Stop with that word.*

It's your own fault.

No, it wasn't. Infertility wasn't her fault. She'd done nothing to deserve that. *That one's in Your court, God. I know Who's the author of life. I know Who gives it and Who withholds. That's not me, God, that's You. And I'll never, ever understand why.*

Kinna slammed the phone closed and threw it back in her bag.

She flipped through the mail. Bills, ads, and a postcard of a big ball of string. She turned it over. The annual postcard from Tracy, her best friend from high school. She hadn't seen Tracy in eighteen years, but every spring she got a postcard from Tracy's latest vacation with her family. It would have been different if Tracy went somewhere exotic, but she never did. Last year, it was some crazy hot dog eating contest, and the year before that, a tour of old American outhouses. She got three postcards that year. One said, "We got great video. Let's get together someday and catch up!" with a lopsided smiley face and a big, loopy "T." Kinna hadn't answered. There was no way she wanted to reconnect with someone only to hear about how great her life was with her wonderful husband and four beautiful children. So she'd let it drop. Just like she'd let all her other relationships drop in these past years.

"Well, no regrets." The words seemed to echo in the air.

She and Tracy had been close once. They'd read forbidden romances with a flashlight under the sheets at her parents' house. They'd passed notes about cute boys at school. They'd both bleached their hair blond in one huge color disaster in the tenth grade. They'd promised to be friends forever. Forever lasted about three years after graduation.

I've made other promises about forever too. She turned her wedding ring around on her finger and sighed, then took the postcard and sat on a kitchen chair.

Tracy had been there that night, back in their junior year, when Kinna's heart throbbed and she knew that Jimmy Henley was absolutely, positively the most wonderful guy in the whole wide world.

It had been a year since their pretend first date, and Jimmy had finally come into his own at school. He found something he was good at, and it transformed him from a lanky kid to the star guard on the basketball team. And suddenly, Jimmy was popular.

He hung out with the cool kids, had a hundred friends, and scored twenty-plus points a game. He got his picture in the newspaper. He could have any girl he wanted.

But he went out with none of them more than once.

Then, there was Kinna. A serious junior, with books piled high in her arms as she hurried off to French class. Glasses, a Bible, and one too many pimples.

She hung out with Tracy, and maybe a couple others from the speech club. She scored ninety-seven on her geometry test. She had her picture in the yearbook, a group photo, way in the back on the band page, with a clarinet in her hand. She didn't have a boyfriend.

And she never went out with a guy more than once.

She hadn't wanted to. She had goals back then, plans. Dreams of nursing school and a career, of leading hundreds of people to Jesus. Plans of having a family, helping people, making people well. Maybe she'd even be a missionary for a while, somewhere in the jungles of Africa. She learned later that Africa didn't have jungles. Jungles were in South America, but she never was that great in geography.

But somehow, that night, all those dreams and plans seemed so far away. Distant, unimportant. What mattered was that Pacific Grove High was down by one point with seventeen seconds left on the clock. And Jimmy had the ball.

She and Tracy sat in the stands, in the fourth row. Cheerleaders in shiny nylons led the count down from twenty. Jimmy dribbled up the court.

Seventeen. Sixteen. Fifteen.

He beat his man and dribbled across half-court. Kinna held her breath.

Fourteen. Thirteen.

She let it out and grabbed Tracy's hand.

Twelve. Eleven.

They squeezed each other's fingers. Jimmy passed the ball.

Ten. Nine. Eight.

The center dribbled. Jimmy bolted left, away from his man.

Seven.

Sweaty bodies. Bright lights. Tube socks. Shimmering pom-poms. And the clock ticking.

Six.

She tipped forward on the bench. The center passed the ball back to Jimmy.

Five.

"Come on, Jimmy. You can do it!" The words burst from her in a shout.

Jimmy hesitated, but she knew he'd heard her. Then he surged between two opposing players. The ball flew up, bounced off the backboard. And…

Two.

In!

Kinna screamed and jumped to her feet. Tracy followed. The buzzer sounded. The crowd erupted in wild shouts and applause, then started chanting. "Jim-my! Jim-my! Jim-my!"

She watched him, his face alight, his back pummeled by slaps from teammates and friends. He turned to the crowd and searched it with his eyes, finding her. The thirty feet between them became nothing as he smiled a smile she knew was just for her. She smiled back.

Then she sat down, Tracy began chattering, and the moment was lost. Tucked away in her memory to be brought out now, in this lonely kitchen, by a silly postcard she wouldn't answer.

She tore the postcard in two and dropped it onto the table. Why remember? What good did it do? Those days were gone. That boy and girl had changed, turned into other people.

Life did that. It changed you, challenged you, made you hard and bitter. How she'd love to go back to that time when dreams were still fresh and full of hope, to when love was a simple thing and a dance could cure all her woes. She'd even put up with that pimple on her chin again, if only she could turn back the clock.

That night after the game, she and Tracy stood outside the auditorium and listened to Bonnie Tyler sing about her total eclipse of the heart. Tracy tugged down the sides of her neckline until her bare shoulders showed. She stuck her hand in her purse and pulled out a tube of lipstick. "Want some?"

Kinna shook her head.

Tracy applied the lipstick, rubbed her lips together, then pinched her cheeks. "Okay, ready? Let's go."

"I can't. Remember?"

A breeze picked up a few fall leaves and swirled them around their feet. The song changed to something by REO Speedwagon.

Tracy made a face. "Ugh. Gag me with a spoon. Your dad. No dances, no Rick Springfield concert with me next week, no all-nighter at the skating rink. Sometimes you being a pastor's kid just barfs me out."

Kinna shrugged. It didn't matter, really. She didn't want to be in there with sweaty boys and too-loud music. Who needed that?

Tracy stuck the lipstick away and huffed. "Look, I'll stay out here with you until your dad comes."

Kinna took her friend by the shoulders and pushed her toward the door. "No, you won't. Get in there and have fun. My dad won't be here for a while, and I don't want you missing anything. Tomorrow you can tell me all about it, okay?"

Kinna opened the door. Fast electric guitar music burst out. Kinna blinked into the swirl of light and color that splashed over the ceiling and the gyrating bodies inside. "Go on." Her words were lost in the blast of sound.

"You sure?" Tracy mouthed the question.

Kinna nodded and motioned for her friend to go.

Tracy plucked her student ID card from the pocket of her too-tight jeans and showed it to the teacher inside the door. Then, with one last glance back, she stepped inside, and the door swung shut.

The music dimmed and changed again. The sounds of a soulful guitar thudded through the air, followed by the squeal of a synthesizer. She didn't recognize the song. Something from some British band, she supposed.

She swallowed and leaned her back against the wall. She could feel the thrum of the music through the stucco, the beating of feet. She could sense the heat, smell the sweat. The stars shone bright above her, the silhouettes of trees swaying gently in the breeze. The air was cool. Somewhere to her right, a streetlight sputtered, a car rounded a corner and sped away, and a cat crossed the street and jumped over a wooden fence.

And behind her, Jimmy danced with someone else in a hot, steamy room filled with the urgent hum of the latest song on the top ten charts. Sometimes it was really, really hard to be the pastor's daughter.

Kinna slid down the wall and sat on the cold concrete, her knees pulled to her chest and her back still pressed into the cool stucco. She closed her eyes and tried to block out the beat of the music, the sound of voices, the ache in her heart.

Lord, I know it's wrong for me to want to be in there. Dad told me all about boys and dances. And I believe him, God, I really do. I'm going to do what's right, stay pure, marry someday, have a family. Someday I'll have a locket around my neck and a baby in my arms, just like Annie. And I'll be glad I didn't let some stupid boy touch my behind during a lame high school dance. I'll be glad then. But…but now…

She opened her eyes and stood. The leaves rustled above her, the streetlight winked and went out, but the music didn't stop. It called to her, beckoned her, accentuated the loneliness of standing outside in the cold when all her friends were inside, together.

She swayed, just a little, to the tune. A slow dance. She put up one hand, then the other, imagining…

Someone touched her shoulder.

She spun around.

And somehow, Jimmy was there, his blue Izod shirt crisp, his hair still damp from his after-game shower. He put out his hand. "Will you dance with me?"

Her gaze dropped. "I can't. You know that."

He lifted her chin with his finger. "Just once, Kinna. Come on. To celebrate."

His eyes sparkled. The streetlight sputtered on again. She stood, transfixed. "But my dad…"

He grinned at her. "Don't worry. I'll keep my hands where they belong."

She blinked. "Of course, you will. I didn't mean…"

He chuckled and held out his arms. "Well? Any more excuses?"

She moved into his arms just as Billy Ocean began to sing about life being a fairy tale. She smelled his Polo aftershave and the detergent he used on his shirts. He drew her closer, but not too close. She smiled as their feet shuffled in a slow circle.

Jimmy hummed gently in her ear. Then lyrics came, so quietly she almost didn't hear them. "I woke up, and suddenly…I'm in love."

Billy Ocean's words. Jimmy didn't mean them, but her heart hammered, and her breath came more quickly.

Suddenly...

Don't be silly, Kinna.

Suddenly...

It's just pretend.

She looked up. A smudge of blush marred his collar. *See? Just pretend.* She touched it. "What's this?"

He stopped singing and made a face. "Suzy Templer. Don't even ask."

"She likes you."

"Shhh..." His voice lowered. "I don't care. Just dance, Kinna."

She slipped her arms closer around his neck.

His hand left her waist and brushed the hair back from her cheek. His tone softened again to a whisper. "You're Aurora, remember? And I'm Prince Phillip. This is our dance, the royal ball. The dragon is dead, and Maleficent is defeated." His hand again trailed down her back, stopping at her waist. "So just dance, Aurora."

Kinna danced, gently swaying in a slow circle. As she did, she looked into those perfect eyes, smiled into them as the music spun around them, and felt his warmth near, so near. Jimmy, her Jimmy. Here, she was safe. Here, she was happy. Here, she was whole. She was a beautiful princess, and he was a handsome prince. All was good, right, perfect. As it should be.

Then a blaze of headlights slashed across Jimmy's face and flooded the sidewalk, washing away her dream. They jumped apart. A car door slammed. Someone shouted her name.

She turned and shielded her eyes. "Dad?"

He strode toward them. "What do you think you're doing?"

Her gaze shot to Jimmy's, but instead of meeting eyes wide with fear of her father, Jimmy smiled down at her. He moved closer and spoke so low that only she could hear him. "It was worth it, wasn't it?" He backed away. His voice raised. "See you later, Sleeping Beauty."

She watched him disappear into the shadows, then turned back toward her dad and winced at his fierce glare.

"Kinna Ann Hollis."

She swallowed.

"What did I tell you about dancing with boys?"

Her chin dropped to her chest. "It was just Jimmy." She barely muttered the words, but her dad heard them anyway.

"He's just like any other boy, Kinna." He opened the car's passenger door and held it wide. "And it's not appropriate—"

"I know." Kinna got into the car without another word.

The whole drive home, neither spoke. Her dad because he was probably praying. Kinna because she was reliving those golden moments in the moonlight and telling herself that Jimmy wasn't just like any other boy. Not at all.

The next day, she didn't tell Tracy a single thing about her dance under the stars. To talk of it would have ruined its almost-perfection.

But maybe, in the end, her dad had been right. She should have never danced with Jimmy. She should have never let herself fall in love.

She couldn't remember the last time she and Jimmy danced together. Maybe they never had. Maybe she'd imagined it all.

Kinna shook her head and brushed the pieces of the postcard into a pile, then picked up another envelope. What good was the past? What good did it do to remember? It was today's problems that mattered. Today's losses. Today's plans. And right now, she needed a new one.

She turned over the envelope in her hand and caught her breath. Emblazoned on its front were magic words straight from a fairy tale, 0% for Six Months. She ripped open the envelope.

"Need cash fast?" *Yes!* "Call now to apply. Approval in minutes." *Approval?* "Even if you've been denied before."

See, this was the God she expected, the one who performed miracles. Here, finally, was an answer from God. A real sign, as in sign here and get the money, get the procedure, get the baby. Perfect.

You're grasping at straws, the voice of reason whispered through her.

I know, but what else do I have? the voice of desperation muttered back.

Kinna picked up the phone and dialed the big eight hundred number plastered on the front of the application. What was one more bill? This, at least, could get her closer to her dream.

But what about the papers?

They backfired.

Maybe this will too.

She ignored the voice.

Five minutes later, as promised, she had a new credit card number and fifteen thousand dollars in credit. Finally, things were looking up.

Except, if she was going to use that fifteen grand for IVF, she'd need Jimmy. Which meant she'd have to find him.

She paused, considering. She could find him, or find a donor. Lots of women did it these days. Celebrities even. But still…

Jimmy's words came back to her, along with the look on his face as he said them. "Who are you? I don't even know you anymore."

Kinna glanced up and caught her reflection in the kitchen window. Mouth drawn tight. Eyebrows bunched. Jaw firm. Who was that woman in the glass?

And then another question came, whispering in her mind and throbbing with sorrow. *How far, Kinna? How far will you go for your dreams?*

She closed her eyes and shivered in the silence.

20

Jimmy's stomach twisted, then emptied itself on the sidewalk outside the bar. He stood, wiped his mouth, and shuddered. Did it count as drinking if you threw it all up minutes afterward? He tried to straighten and failed. How did people drink that stuff? How did his dad? Jimmy could barely keep it down for five minutes.

A siren sounded briefly, then shut off. That was all he needed today, to be arrested for public intoxication. He wasn't drunk, but he smelled like it. Probably looked like it too.

Footsteps came up behind him, heavy and solid. He turned. A police officer stood a few feet away, his arms crossed.

"You all right, buddy?"

Jimmy wiped the last of the vomit from his mouth, dropped his chin, and nodded. "Sorry, officer. Just got a little sick. I'll be moving on now."

The officer stepped closer. "Jim? Jimmy Henley? Is that you?"

Jimmy's gaze flew to the officer's face. "Bob?" Not just a police officer, but one of the elders from his church. He'd never live this down.

"You been drinking?"

Jimmy grimaced and motioned toward the soggy bit of concrete at his feet. "Not really."

"I'm gonna have to—"

"Officer!" A woman's voice burst from behind Jimmy. He glanced over his shoulder to see Thea, the woman who had given him the dog. He'd tied Tulip to the lamppost around the corner, but Thea must have untied her, because she had the dog again and strode toward him at a brisk pace. She stopped next to him and smiled up at Bob. Her brows furrowed. "Why, you're Bob Marley, aren't you?" She laughed. "Of course." Her gaze shot toward the sky. "Thanks."

Bob studied her face. "Do I know you, ma'am? You look familiar."

Jimmy inclined his head toward her. "This is Thea. She's a dog lover."

Tulip wagged her tail and yipped.

Thea smiled at the officer. "You wouldn't know me, Mr. Marley, but I know you as an honest man and a good one. Now"—she took hold of Jimmy's arm—"I'm going to take care of this young man here, so you just leave him to me."

Bob's gaze swept Jimmy, from his yellow-spattered shoes to his stinking shirt to his sweaty face. "Jim, are you all right?"

Jimmy nodded. "I'll be fine, Bob. I'm not drunk." He pushed a puff of air from his cheeks. "I couldn't manage it." A failure, even at that.

Thea's arm tightened on his. "Come on, let's get some coffee." She patted her leg. "Heel, Tulip."

Bob nodded. "See you Sunday, then, Jim. Remember, you need prayer, you just call the church and get on the prayer list."

Prayer list. Not a chance. *Hello, this is Jimmy Henley. I need prayer because I'm a loser. Lost my job, lost my wife, lost my lunch.* Like he was going to tell anyone that. Calling for prayer because a relative was sick was one thing, calling because your life was in shambles was another entirely. You don't trust people with stuff like that. His dad had taught him that and Kinna's had too. Not intentionally, maybe, but that didn't matter. Jimmy had learned to keep his mouth shut and his nose clean.

He touched his face. Well, maybe he'd not done so well on that last part. He coughed. Who knew that beer smelled so bad when it came out again? He waved at Bob. "Thanks, man. I'll see you at church."

Bob strolled away.

Thea let go of his arm and evaluated him. "You're a mess. You should know better than to try to drink."

"I know."

"You need coffee."

"I'm not drunk."

"I know you're not drunk. And besides, coffee doesn't help you stop being drunk."

"I wouldn't know."

"Well, you do now."

Yeah, he did. Strange, he knew lots of guys who'd have a beer now and again and be fine with it. They didn't throw up all over themselves at the first mug of alcohol. So why did he? "Can't believe I threw up."

Thea paused. "You don't know, do you?"

"What?"

She clucked her tongue. "Well, you see"—Thea turned and began walking down the street—"sometimes a smell or a taste is associated with such bad memories that your body rejects that thing. Like an allergic reaction." She stopped and motioned to him. "Well, are you coming?"

"Where?"

"For coffee, of course." She cocked her head. "A double, I think. On me."

"I can pay for it."

"It's still going to be on me."

"Stubborn women." He muttered under his breath.

She laughed. "I take after my mother."

Jimmy grinned. "All right. You have a car?"

"Nope. There's our ride." She motioned toward a four-seater bike surrey for tourists, complete with canvas top, steering wheels, and flashy red pedals. A sign proclaiming Rentals by the Sea with a phone number flapped from the surrey's top.

Jimmy blinked. "That?"

"Yep."

"We're going to pedal?"

"All the way to Marnie's. You need it."

He didn't need a bike ride; he needed some sanity. And this woman wasn't going to give him that.

She chuckled. "Come on, take a risk. What's there to lose?"

He glanced at her. Lose? Nothing. Not anymore. He stumbled toward the surrey.

Thea hiked up her jeans and climbed into the surrey, then whistled for the dog. Tulip jumped into the backseat, turned two tight circles, and lay down. Tongue lolling, she stared at Jimmy.

He scowled. "All right, all right. I'm coming." He climbed in the front seat and put his feet on the pedals. "Ready?"

They pedaled away from the curb. Cars zoomed past on the left, skinny tires crunched over rocks beneath them, and behind, the dog panted and yipped and finally laid her head over Jimmy's shoulder.

After ten minutes, without turning to look at him, Thea spoke. "So Jimmy, you wanna talk?"

"Nope."

She gave a curt nod. "Didn't think you would."

"So why'd you ask?"

The surrey shuddered as another car passed them.

"Just to be nice." She turned the wheel as the surrey lumbered around a corner. "You stink, by the way."

"I know."

"You going to pass it off as a new cologne? Eau de Pew?"

"I guess so."

"Stick with your old stuff."

"I would if I could."

She slowed her pedaling and glanced at him. "You can. If you dare."

"What do you mean?"

"Love is a strange thing, Jimmy Henley. It takes guts."

"What do you know about love?"

"I know what my daddy taught me."

"And what's that?"

"Love always perseveres, always hopes, always endures."

"Love never fails?"

She reached over and patted his hand. "I'm an old woman, and in all these years, I've learned something."

"Yeah?"

"Love makes heroes. And if you want to be a hero, if you want to be a prince, you have to know, deep down, that you're a son of the King."

Jimmy laughed, sad and hard, bitter. "Son of a king, huh? Just wait until I introduce you to my dad."

"You don't understand."

"We're here." He pointed to the big sign over Marnie's bookstore and coffee shop.

They pulled into the parking lot, up onto the sidewalk, and parked next to the bike rack. Thea slid out and locked the surrey to the rack. She looked back at Jimmy.

He hadn't moved from his seat. "How am I supposed to go in there looking like this?" He pointed to his shirt.

She grinned. "You look fine. It's the smell that's the problem."

"Thanks."

"They don't call me Aletheia for nothing."

Strange name, but he liked it. He didn't know what it meant, but it sounded cool.

"It means truth."

Suddenly, he didn't like it as much anymore.

Thea strode to the coffee shop door, opened it, and pointed inside. "Hurry up, while I'm in a good mood."

"This is a good mood?"

"Of course. Otherwise, I'd let Tulip come in for coffee and make you drink out of a bowl by the curb."

"I'd deserve it."

"Really?" She looked at him intently.

He passed her and stepped into the shop. Smells of coffee brewing and something baking in the oven tickled his senses. There were only a few people in the shop, a young couple, a single guy, and a woman tapping furiously on her computer. No one he knew. Thank goodness.

Thea pointed to a table. "Driftwood today."

Jimmy reached into his pocket and pulled out a couple bucks. "Here."

She shook her head and scowled at him. "You tempting me to sin? I said it was on me, and it'll be on me. Don't make a liar out of an older woman." She gave a curt nod, then walked up to the coffee bar. She chatted with Marnie a moment longer than it would have taken to order two coffees.

Marnie glanced at him from behind the bar and raised her eyebrows. Jimmy looked away. He heard her call out, but not to him.

"Hey, Joe, get one of the new shirts out for Mr. Henley, will you?"

Jimmy shot Marnie a look. *No, not Joe. Anyone but Joe.*

She waved at him and grinned. "The least I can do is get you a clean shirt before my customers start dropping change in a cup for you."

He nodded. "Thanks." Good gal, that Marnie. Never judged, just took care of people. Would she still be that way toward him if she really knew him?

He grimaced and sat at the driftwood table, Kinna's favorite. Why did everything remind him of Kinna? Especially today. Why couldn't that Thea woman have chosen the auto parts table instead? He glanced over. The woman with the computer was at that table. Driftwood it would have to be.

Joe appeared with a clean shirt in his hand, Marnie's Books and Brew embroidered in black on its front. He hobbled over and tossed the shirt on the table, then looked Jimmy over. "What happened to you? You smell like a polecat used you for a litter box."

"After all these years, that's all you got to say to me?"

"I call it like I smell it. So, you figured it out, huh?"

"When you ran off the other night. Didn't recognize you without all the long hippie hair."

Joe grunted. "And the scar don't help either. But at least I lost the beer gut, eh?" He patted his stomach. "Been meaning to say something for the last six months. Saw you come in and out, but never got up the nerve to come over and say, 'Remember me, boy?'"

"What good would that have done?"

Joe shrugged. "I don't know." He glanced away. "Maybe we could start over." He crossed his arms and refused to look in Jimmy's direction.

Heat flashed through Jimmy's chest. He knew what this old man was asking for. Forgiveness, pardon. To just pretend that none of that stuff from Jimmy's childhood had ever happened. Jimmy was good at pretending, but he wasn't that good.

"I don't have a father. Not anymore."

Joe sighed. "Reckon not."

"Just so you understand."

"And you need to too. Prison changes a man."

Jimmy stared at the tabletop. He didn't believe it. Nothing could change his father, and it wouldn't matter if it did. You couldn't erase the past. You couldn't run from it, alter it, or escape what you were. The last few days—the last few years—had taught him that.

"It changes him. Either makes him meaner or makes him smarter."

"And you're saying it made you smarter?"

"Showed me life's too short to be a fool idiot. Took a knife to my face and losing an eye for me to see it. Couldn't bully my way in there. Did no good to cast blame."

"So?"

"It showed me it ain't no good boo-hooing about the past. Gotta be thankful for what you got. Shoulda been thankful for the son I had. Should've let him know I loved him. Tim taught me that."

"Tim?"

"Cell mate. Talked to this fool picture of his son day and night. Jabbered away at a faded Polaroid, telling him everything from what we had for breakfast to how many birds landed on the jail yard fence. Talking about when he'd see him again. 'Not too long, now,' he kept saying."

"Was he right?"

"Turns out his boy died years before, hit by a stray bullet in a gang drive-by. Kid was ten years old. Tim would've done anything to see his son again, and here I was, my boy alive and well, and instead of treasuring him, I drove him away and got put away myself."

Jimmy didn't say a word.

"So I ain't asking you to forgive me. I'm just asking you not to be the same fool idiot I was. Don't throw it all away, Jimmy boy."

Jimmy looked up and caught his gaze. "It's too late, Dad."

"Never too late."

"It is for us."

"Maybe. But not for you and Kinna."

"Look at me and then say it's not too late."

"I've looked worse. Smelled worse too."

"I know."

"You do stink to high heaven, though." Joe's nose wrinkled. "Beer and "

"I know, I know. Stop rubbing it in." Jimmy grabbed the clean shirt and stood.

"So you're a drinker, huh?"

Jimmy turned hot. He pointed to the splatter on his shirt. "Gee, Dad, does it look like I'm a drinker? This was my first. Not a very good start, I'd guess."

Joe smiled and shook his head. "Booze is never the answer. Take it from me." He jabbed his thumb into his chest. "The—" He cleared his throat. "Sorry, almost let something slip. No cussing, no swearing, no taking the Lord's name in vain. Them's Marnie's rules. Now what was I saying? Oh yeah—take it from the voice of experience here."

Jimmy recalled all those hours he'd waited outside the bar, all those times his dad had ambled onto the beach with a bottle in his hand, all those nights when Jimmy had hidden under the covers and prayed his father would pass him by when he came home drunk. "You still drink?"

"Naw. Prison cured me of that. Twenty years in there did a longsight better job than twenty-eight days in the rehab center. And preacher-man had such high hopes."

"I remember."

"Tell me this, boy: why do you think preacher-man helped me like he did?"

"He was a pastor, I guess."

"He was also an alcoholic."

Jimmy paused. "What? I never saw him drink."

Joe coughed. "Course not. He was sober by then. Lost that big church in LA 'cause of his drinking. Never took another drink after that. Beat it, him and his God. But he understood the pull of it and tried to help me. Would have too, except I was hard-headed and got into drugs. Didn't know what a good thing I had." He sighed. "Long story short, I was an idiot."

Jimmy smiled. "Yeah, you were."

"Looks like you're being one now too, eh?"

"Looks like."

Joe sighed. "Come on, let's get you to the bathroom and clean you up before my shift's done. Least I can do after all these years."

Jimmy followed him into the bathroom and tossed the clean shirt over a stall door. The place was spotless. Joe opened a cabinet, pulled out a rag and some cleaner, and started to rub the counter around one of the sinks.

Jimmy took the other sink and turned on the water. Two clean hand towels appeared at his elbow. "Thanks."

Joe kept cleaning. "Just filled the soaps."

Jimmy took off his stinking shirt and dropped it into the trash bin. It was an old one anyway. One Kinna had bought for him. He dug it out again.

Joe cleaned the counters, then the mirror, then a spot on the floor. It was surreal, seeing him like that—an old man scrubbing the bathroom. An old man who was somehow also the same man who had ruined his life, the same one he'd never wanted to see again.

Yet here he was, and Jimmy couldn't think of a single thing to say to him except, "thanks for the towels." Maybe because today, Jimmy finally understood why his father had done what he'd done, been what he'd been. He finally understood what it felt like to lose the woman he loved.

Jimmy spread soap over his arms and hands, scoured them, then rinsed.

And still Joe cleaned.

"Plenty clean in here already."

"Sometimes a thing looks clean, but it ain't."

Jimmy opened his mouth to reply, then closed it again. Words of wisdom coming from the last place he'd have expected it. Sometimes everything seemed fine, but it wasn't. Far from it.

"So what drove you to drink?" Joe didn't look up as his rag swooshed over the paper towel dispenser.

Jimmy washed his face, dried it with a towel, and stared at himself in the mirror. "Wife kicked me out." He was getting lines around his eyes—from working in the sun, he supposed—and there was a bit of gray at his temples. He wasn't a kid anymore, with dreams and fairy tale plans. He was a man. And somehow the clean, safe life he'd built had fallen into rubble. Maybe it hadn't been so clean and safe after all.

Joe polished the faucet on the other sink. "Why'd she do that?"

A thousand answers flitted through Jimmy's mind. Because she was obsessed. Because she cared more about a baby than she did him. Because she wanted to be a mother more than she wanted to be a wife. But the truth was this was his fault. He'd failed her. "I made promises I couldn't keep."

"What did you promise?"

He chuckled softly, sadly. "Happily ever after." He looked at his reflection again. So ordinary, so unlike a prince. What was he thinking to promise a fairy tale? To promise everything? That's what he'd done. Not in so many words, maybe, but he'd done it all the same. In the things said and unsaid, in the way he looked at her, loved her, even way back then.

And even then he'd spoiled their paradise.

"You always did think too much of fairy tales."

"And you thought too little."

"Guess we're both wrong."

"Yep." *Just like we were then.*

He'd been so close, all those years ago, and then he'd blown it.

They'd come back to Monterey after Grandma died. A year passed and finally Dad was going to make things right—start over, pay the money he owed from years back. It hadn't worked out that way, but his dad had high hopes. After all, he'd made promises too. He'd promised his dying mother, Jimmy's grandmother, he'd get cleaned up and take that boy to church.

Kinna's church was the only one Dad had ever set foot in. Even Grandma's funeral was in the funeral home, with the preacher from her church and a dozen old lady friends from her Bible study. Dad wouldn't stay in her house after that. He was gonna honor his mama's last wish, so back they went to Monterey, to Kinna's church, to Kinna's daddy.

And a couple months later, they sat in Kinna's dad's kitchen, around Kinna's dad's table, eating Kinna's dad's food, and drinking Kinna's dad's decaf Sanka.

They talked about rehab for Jimmy's father. Twenty-eight days, that was all it was supposed to take. Twenty-eight days paid in full by Grandma's will, the only thing she had left her son. All that was needed was someone to look after "the boy" while his dad was gone.

Jimmy held his breath as the adults discussed the options. He stirred his Sanka, shuffled his feet, and tried not to breathe too loudly.

For once, his dad was sober, contrite. "He's an all right boy, won't be no trouble," he muttered.

Kinna's dad scowled. "I don't know anyone in the church who could take him in."

"My mama's last wish, you know, was for me to get some help."

Kinna's mom placed her hand quietly, gently, on her husband's arm. "There's the room over the garage."

It took a half hour more for Kinna's dad to agree, but in the end, he did. And even then, it took a year for Jimmy's dad to get up the nerve to go. But Jimmy didn't know that then. That night he thought he had never been happier. Everything would be right. All that was wrong would be fixed at last.

And then, as if to confirm all his hopes, he'd walked into that living room, saw her standing there, and known what had happened. He could tell by the way her shoulders stiffened, the way she held her arms tight over her chest. Steve always was a flake, but Jimmy was glad Steve hadn't shown, glad Kinna wouldn't be going anywhere with that loser.

Another perfect moment, and a promise of a perfect night.

He had come up behind her and put his arms around her. She felt so right there, as if he could hold her forever. He'd told her it was just pretend, make believe, but he'd meant every second, every breath. Especially when his mingled with hers in that one forbidden kiss.

He'd gone back to his apartment that night, packed his Boston and Billy Joel tapes, and waited for the day to come. And waited, and waited. For a whole year he waited with his tapes packed. And through it all, he believed, truly believed, that everything was going to be all right. Forever.

He was wrong.

He'd blown it all just one week after moving into the room above Kinna's garage, two days before the twenty-eight of rehab began. Blown it for a single dance in the moonlight. He couldn't stand to see her alone, couldn't bear to see the look on her face as she listened to the beat of the music from outside the door. So they'd danced. And it was worth it, worth every step of forbidden bliss. Just holding her in his arms, looking into her face, smelling the sweet scent of Bonne Bell.

That Monday he moved his stuff into the room above Kinna's garage, the room with a single bed, peeling wallpaper with faint lilacs all over it, a rag rug, and a trunk made from an old pine box. It was heaven. He unpacked his 501s and polo shirts, his books for civics and trig, gym socks, and his own leather basketball. He piled it all on the bed, then opened the old trunk.

That's when the knock came at the door and Kinna's dad walked in.

Jimmy knew what he was going to say before he said it. Saturday night wasn't forgotten, and it had changed everything.

He was right.

Her dad looked him in the eye and said, "Jimmy, it's time we went over the rules."

And they did, the whole long list of them, from where to put his dirty laundry to what time to show up for family devotions at night. After every one, he'd say, "Yes, Reverend Hollis," and nod his head. That is, every one except the last.

"And one more thing, Jimmy," her father said just before he left the room. "Stay away from Kinna. I don't want anything happening between you two while you're under my roof."

"But, Reverend—"

"No buts, Jim. You keep your distance. I would have never agreed to this arrangement if I'd suspected—" He broke off, and Jimmy knew he was thinking of the dance. That one, simple dance.

"But—"

"You make sure, Jim. I don't want to have to call your dad out of the rehab center after it took this long to get him in there. I'm watching you." He made a funny gesture, pointing to his eye and then at Jimmy's chest.

Jimmy understood. No matter how he felt, he and Kinna could only be friends. For his dad's sake.

Too bad it hadn't done any good.

Kinna's dad left the room. Jimmy watched him go down the steps and out the door. He moved to the window and followed his progress across the lawn to the house. The door slammed. He couldn't blame the man, but it still hurt.

He pushed the curtain-sheets back even further. They were mismatched, yellow and green, but the window was clean, the sill scrubbed. In the corner of the window sat that old, ugly doll Kinna had named

Sally. Jimmy smiled. Next to the doll, a small flower pot filled with violets sat on the sill. A tiny piece of paper stuck out from under it. He removed the paper, unfolded it, and saw Kinna's writing.

"Enjoy your stay, Jimmy," it read. "I'm glad you're here. I've left Sally to keep you company. She always liked your fairy tales. P.S. I've hidden some Oreos under the mattress on the bed. I hope they aren't all smashed."

Jimmy grinned, looked up, and saw her swinging back and forth in the tire swing they'd used as kids. Her hair blew in the breeze, shimmering like ribbons of warm caramel. He remembered the feel of it, the softness.

She glanced up and saw him. She smiled and waved, and it seemed, even from this distance, that her cheeks turned pinker.

Jimmy leaned forward until his nose was an inch from the glass and pressed his hand against the cool windowpane. A simple gesture, but in it, he hoped she could hear all he wanted to say. How he wanted to be with her, be more than friends, kiss her like he had that one night over a year ago. Only not pretend. He wanted to spend a lifetime kissing her and holding her in his arms.

But all he could do was whisper a promise through the glass, a promise so quiet that only he heard it. Him and God. "They won't keep us apart forever, Kinna. Someday we're going to be together. And then I won't ever let you go."

Except happily ever after hadn't turned out like he'd expected.

Joe shuffled over to the far sink and began wiping the rim. "One thing I learned, though, is you ain't God, son. I ain't either. We can't make happily ever after. Only He can do that." Quiet words, spoken to the rhythm of the rag, barely heard.

Jimmy shut off the water and turned from his reflection in the mirror. "I should have known that."

"And even God don't promise a fairy tale. Not in this life anyway."

"I hate you."

"I know. But it don't make no difference, does it?"

"No. But I'm used to it. I've spent my whole life trying not to be like you."

"Didn't work out so good, did it?"

"Nope." Jimmy slipped the clean shirt over his head. No fairy tales. No "ever after." No prince in shining armor. But Kinna deserved a fairy tale, deserved a better man. She deserved someone more like her father than his.

He should have listened to her dad all along.

And now, it was too late. For all of them.

21

A plastic grocery bag tumbled across the job site. A cat turned a circle and lay on the seat of a huge tractor. A fat gray spider lumbered over a stack of steel pipes.

And beyond that, workers crawled over the rising parking structure like a couple dozen black beetles. A cement pourer churned. Scaffolding glinted. Men in hard hats peered out from beneath a tier of forming steel.

Kinna stood at the site's perimeter, her shoes covered in dust, her eyes narrowed, and doubt tap-dancing in her gut. Her eyes searched the men again. Tall ones, short ones, thin, thick, grubby. Young guys who'd barely begun to shave, older men with gray hair beneath their hats. Men with dark skin, light skin, and somewhere in between—all turned the same gray-brown of the dust. But none of them was Jimmy. She would have known him anywhere.

She put her hand to her forehead to block the sun. She'd been so sure she'd find him at the Petersen job, up on the big Cat or calling out instructions in broken Spanish. How could he not be here? And if not here, where was he?

She turned away. It served her right. Didn't her mother teach her that girls should never go running after boys? Good girls waited. Boys did the chasing, the calling, the asking.

She never was good at waiting.

Not since that night at youth group so long ago. She'd broken the rules then, just as she was breaking them now. She thought if she could just find him, together they could make everything all right.

It had almost worked then. Maybe it would work now. Just find him and somehow, with the credit card money, get back into treatment and get that baby. They'd be a family, the perfect Christian family. No doubts, no questions, nothing but the assurance that God really was good and loving and kind. With that baby in her arms, she'd have such a wonderful testimony.

But she needed Jimmy. Needed to use that money. Needed to get past this place where everything always went wrong.

You can do anything you set your mind to.

Things had worked out before, even when they seemed impossible. And nothing was impossible. That's what Dad said.

All things are possible to him who believes…

That's what she'd once told Jimmy when they were young, back at that youth group meeting so many years ago.

Jimmy sat across from her in the large group circle. Behind him, a cassette of Keith Green turned in the boom box. Something about how God's love broke through. She wasn't listening; she was watching Jimmy.

His hair was mussed tonight, as if he'd hurried here after practice, and his collar was open, the sleeves of his plaid shirt rolled. He held an open Bible in his hand, but she could tell he wasn't reading, just staring.

The youth pastor stood up. Kinna glanced at the girl with the spiky hair and tube top, the guy in a pink alligator shirt, the two girls sneaking glances in Jimmy's direction and giggling. One had hair perfectly rolled back, like the captain's daughter on *The Love Boat*. Kinna wasn't allowed to watch *The Love Boat*, but she'd seen the commercials. The other girl's hair was teased and mushroomed above her headband like some kind of growth.

Kinna sighed. She shouldn't feel out of place at youth group at her dad's church, but in her simple skirt and her simple, straight, uncurled hair, she did. No tight *Flashdance* pants—not at church, anyway. No *Flashdance* hair—it had to be long and straight when she came to youth group. No shirt slipped over her shoulder with only a strap holding it up—inappropriate for the pastor's daughter on youth night. No curlers, no *Love Boat*, no friends. No *Fantasy Island*. No fantasies at all.

Except when she was with Jimmy. Jimmy still knew how to dream.

As if he could read her thoughts, he looked up, caught her gaze, and winked. At her, not at those silly girls with their TV hair.

She smiled back.

The youth pastor cleared his throat and ran his hand through his hair, still long and feathered like a guy from the seventies. He twitched the too-wide collar of his disco shirt, then grabbed his tattered Bible. "Please turn to First Samuel, chapter one."

No one turned to the page except Kinna.

"Who will read for us?"

Kinna raised her hand.

"Someone besides the pastor's daughter."

Kinna lowered her arm and stared down at her Bible, no longer seeing it.

Then Jimmy spoke, warm and confident. "I'll read, but Kinna would have done it better."

He read about a woman named Hannah who wanted a baby. About how God had mercy on her at last, and she gave her son to serve

God at the temple all his life. That boy grew into the great prophet Samuel.

Jimmy finished the story and slapped his Bible closed.

The youth pastor stood again and cleared his throat for the third time that night. "Hannah gave up what was most precious to her in order to serve God. What would you give up for God? What's most precious to you?"

"How 'bout you give up your tie-dye, man?" A guy's voice came from the far side of the circle, followed by scattered titters.

The youth pastor stiffened. "If you give up your Def Leppard."

"As if!"

A trio of low chuckles rumbled from the group of boys near the door, then subsided.

The youth pastor pulled at his collar again and cleared his throat—again. "So, I'll ask one more time. What's most precious to you?"

Kinna stared down at her Bible. What did she hold most dearly? Friends? Hardly. Church? Not really. School? No. She looked up. Jimmy was watching her. He glanced away.

And then she knew—her dreams. That's what was most precious to her, those hopes and plans she had for the future, as simple as they were. Get married, have kids, be a good Christian, and help people as a nurse.

She pictured it. A happy family, where the kids read their Bibles and watched *Fantasy Island*. Where they went for walks on the beach and wore shorts when it was hot. Where she could love someone, and they'd love her back because they wanted to, not because they had to. It'd be like her mom and dad, except with more children and no pastorate. And she'd be happy. Someday life would be just what she dreamed.

The voice of the youth pastor broke through her thoughts. "Okay, so what if God asked you to give up those things to Him?"

No. Kinna scowled. But God wouldn't ask that. He was the One who told Adam and Eve to be fruitful and multiply. He was the One who said, "Ask anything in my name…" And she wouldn't be asking much—just a nice family and a good job. That wasn't much at all.

"Would you give it up?"

Of course he wasn't talking about hopes and dreams. He was talking about things, like cars or nice clothes or cool stuff. He was talking about giving up your material possessions so you could be a missionary in Africa or something.

The youth pastor continued talking about Samuel and the temple and other children for Hannah, but Kinna wasn't listening. Instead, she reviewed names she liked for her children. *If it's a girl, I'll name her Lauren. Or maybe Brianne.*

The youth pastor had moved to the New Testament. He said something about Jesus washing the disciples' feet. He was talking about Judas, how Jesus washed Judas's feet too. And then, Jesus went to the cross.

The youth pastor lifted his Bible and pointed around the room. "So, what would you, and you, and you, give up to serve like Jesus did? Even for the Judases in your life?"

Kinna touched her fingers to the soft page of her Bible. *If it's a boy, I'll name him…* She glanced up again. *I'll name him James.*

Jimmy had closed his Bible and now gripped a pencil so hard she was sure he'd break it, which would be awfully awkward. She tried to motion to him discreetly.

The youth pastor stepped into the middle of the circle of chairs. "Who wants to be first?"

The girl with the mushroom hair popped her bubblegum and wiggled her fingers.

"Yes?"

"Diet Pepsi."

The girl with spiked hair laughed. "And I'll give up country music."

Everyone laughed at that.

Except Kinna, who scowled. "He means something real, like, I don't know, your curling iron or your night at the movies. Or—or your boyfriend."

The Def Leppard guy scoffed. "Yeah, no problem for you."

Jimmy rose and turned toward the guy. "Shut it, hoser." He stepped across the circle and sat next to Kinna. "Idiot." He swung his arm around the back of her chair.

The guy shook his head. "Cool it, Jim. All right?"

"All right." Jimmy took his arm from the back of her chair. His arm brushed hers. He still held the pencil in his other hand, still gripped it tightly.

The youth pastor once again cleared his throat. "So, um, what would you give up, Jimmy?"

Jimmy relaxed. He cocked his head at the pastor and shrugged. "Oh, I don't know...my dad?"

Everyone laughed again. Only Kinna knew he was serious. Only Kinna saw the tremor that ran through him. Only she knew his laugh was forced, his smile fake.

The youth pastor's voice rose. He clapped his hands. "Thank you. I'm glad you brought up parents, because that's my next point. The reason we can give up things to God is because He's our heavenly Father, and He loves us. Like your dad, He just wants what's best for you. That's why we can wash the feet of the Judases—"

The pencil in Jimmy's hand broke with a loud crack.

The pastor stopped. The girls giggled again. Jimmy stood and picked up pieces of pencil from the floor.

Kinna touched his pantleg. "Jimmy?"

"Guess I better get a stronger pencil." He shoved the pencil bits into his pocket and strode out the door.

Kinna went after him. She found him sitting in the dirt behind the hedges. He had a tulip in his hand.

She sat beside him.

He sighed. "I knew you'd find me."

"Can I stay?"

"When have I ever wanted you to go?"

She smiled and moved closer. A breeze ruffled the leaves of the tree above them and brought in the salty smell of the bay. "Thanks for what you did in there."

"What, killing a pencil?"

She chuckled. "No, calling that guy a hoser."

"Could have used a different word, but, you know, we were in church and all."

"I don't even know what that word means."

He grinned. "Me either."

"So what are we doing out here?"

"I just couldn't take it anymore."

"I figured."

They fell silent. A car rumbled by. Voices drifted from the youth room, indistinguishable mumblings against a background of cricket song.

Finally, Jimmy spoke. "What am I going to do, Kinna? Twenty-eight days ends tomorrow. What if nothing's changed? What if he's still the same mean, drunk dad he's always been?"

"He won't be."

"He will be."

"All things are possible…"

"Even Dad being cured?"

"Yes." She said it with more conviction than she felt.

"And if he's not?" He paused and made a fist. "If he's not, I'm not going to let him mess up my life again. I'll make him pay first."

Kinna put her hand on his arm. "Oh, Jimmy, you can't talk that way about your dad."

He scowled. She could see the expression even by the dim parking lot lights that filtered in through the hedge. He leaned away until the light shone off his eyes, once blue, now black in the night. "Why can't I say that? Because he's like God? Or God's like him? That's what the youth pastor said."

Kinna furrowed her brow. "God *is* like a father, Jimmy, just not *your* father. It means that God is what a father ought to be." She moved closer and put her head on his shoulder.

His arm snuck around her. "Life isn't always like it ought to be, is it?"

Her tone hardened. "You can do anything you set your mind to."

Jimmy's arm dropped away. "You don't know a thing, do you?"

She glanced at him. "Well, that's what my mom says."

He shook his head. "You aren't God, Kinna. And neither am I."

"But…but…"

He reached over and brushed her hair back behind her ear. His head moved closer, and for a moment, she thought he'd kiss her again. This time, for real. Or at least, she hoped it.

But he didn't. Instead, he moved away, and the distance between them became an ache within her.

"Jimmy?"

He took her hand. "I would never have known God if it weren't for you. Maybe He's enough."

It seemed simple then. They sat together in the dirt, his hand holding hers and hers holding his. The parking lot lights sputtered. Distant voices gave way to another indistinct Keith Green song.

Kinna spoke. "We'll figure something out. We'll get through this together."

Together.

The memory jolted to a stop.

Together…because God was enough.

What happened to the boy and girl holding hands behind the hedge? When did it stop being enough?

A long time ago.

She rubbed her temples. She just needed to find Jimmy. Find him, use that money, apologize for those stupid papers, and get a baby. A baby would fix everything. It would make them happy. A baby was enough.

"Love is patient…"

Stop!

She couldn't go back. Not to that night behind the hedge, not even to those early years of marriage, before everything went wrong.

"Love is kind…"

It was then, when love was new. Patient, kind, full of hope, just like the Bible described. But what was it now? Want, longing, manipulation. Doubt, fear, and faithlessness. G-I-V-E-M-E.

Stop it!

It's true.

I want a baby. Is that so wrong?

I want...I need... It's not enough.

The words echoed in her mind. She silenced them.

But she couldn't erase the image of Jimmy's eyes in the darkness. Quiet, sad, and touched with love.

22

Jimmy put his elbows on the table and gripped the coffee cup with two hands. Across from him, Thea sat fingering something in her pocket. She drew it out and placed it on the table between them.

Jimmy stared at it. The twined tulip design, the worn silver, the long chain. "Where did you get that?"

"Open it."

He did. Inside were the faded photos of two old people. Happy old people. "So?"

Thea sighed. "Don't those faces mean something to you?"

"No."

Thea grimaced and muttered something about "young fools" and "patience."

Jimmy closed the locket. "I got my wife a locket just like that. She doesn't wear it."

"Why not?"

"She's saving it for a picture of the baby."

"What baby?"

"Exactly."

Thea huffed.

Jimmy stared into his coffee.

Thea reached over and placed a tan, age-spotted hand on his.

"You're a good man, Jimmy Henley, only you don't know it. You can be as happy as my father in the locket."

He shook his head. "Yeah? How? By having a baby for Kinna?"

She squeezed his fingers. "No, by choosing to be. By daring to be." She let go. "Now, I have somewhere to be. You drink that coffee and think about what I've said. Then you go do what's right."

What's right. He didn't even know what that meant anymore.

Thea rose and called to Joe behind the counter. "You take care of him for me, will you? Maybe talk some sense into him."

Joe touched his forehead. "My pleasure, ma'am."

Thea chuckled. "And whatever you do, don't let him forget his dog." With that, she hurried out the coffee shop door.

Joe stalked over and threw his cleaning towel on the table in front of Jimmy. "Well, son, I ain't one to give you advice, but I'd say it's about time you made some plans."

Jimmy took a sip of black coffee. He hated black coffee. "Kinna makes all the plans."

"And you go along for the ride, eh?"

"Guess so."

"Well, the times are changing." He pulled out a chair, turned it backward, and sat with his arms resting on the chair's back. He peered at Jimmy over the latticework. "First, I say we get your job back. I done what you said and got me a second job over there at the Petersen site. Got signed up this morning. Pay's good. Work ain't, but that don't matter. I start this afternoon, when I'm done here. I'm just on clean up for now. But that'll change."

"They're back to work, huh? Didn't even miss a day." Jimmy set down his coffee cup.

"You surprised?"

He wasn't. Not really. He'd hoped George would slow down, play it safe after Alan's accident, but that was wishful thinking. For some people, nothing slowed them down or deterred them. Kinna was like that. And he just couldn't keep up, not with either of them.

"I ain't no expert, mind you, but things don't seem right out there. Folks in a big rush. They hired me right on the spot, didn't care about no background check. Didn't care about anything. Seems if they're hiring guys like me, they're doing other stuff that ain't so smart too. Could use someone out there who knew something. Could use you, son."

"The dad I remember didn't think I was any use to anybody."

"The dad you remember was an idiot."

Jimmy smiled. "I suppose so. You any better than he was?"

A ghost of a return smile touched Joe's mouth. "Couldn't say. A little, maybe."

"Well, nothing I can do over at the job. I was fired, remember?" It wasn't his problem if they were leaving out rebar, failing to compact the soil properly, not letting concrete cure—all things he'd seen George push for on previous jobs. This one was no different.

"Don't matter if you were fired. Time for you to take a risk. Things aren't like they should be out there, and you can say something. Do something. Don't matter if I say something. Old ex-con barely hired on? Nobody'd listen to me."

"They won't listen to me either." And they shouldn't. He didn't deserve it.

"You thinkin' some stupid thing?"

"No."

"You are. I see it written right there on yer face. Saw it often enough when you were little." Joe grabbed the rag and tossed it at Jimmy. It hit the coffee cup.

Coffee flew across the table onto Jimmy's lap. He snatched the cup and jumped out of the way as dark liquid spilled to the floor.

The old man smiled. "See? You know how to act when you need to. I knew you did. Now, let's talk about how you can avoid another spill in your life."

Jimmy scowled and slapped the towel onto the dripping coffee. "You're crazy, old man."

"Yep. And you're about to be a hero."

"No way."

"You always wanted to be a hero. That's all you ever cared about, swatting the air with some crooked stick and saying you were fighting the dragon. You haven't forgotten, have you?" The question, spoken softly, gently, pierced Jimmy like nothing else had.

"It's too late."

"It's never too late."

What if he was right? What if there was still a chance to do right? But he wasn't a hero. He found that out a long time ago, in a way that changed everything, stained everything. Showed him the monster he really was. Just like his dad.

"You just have to trust."

A tremor ran through Jimmy's arms. "Who, you?"

"Hardly. I ain't worth your trust. You of all people know that. No, you have to trust God."

"I do."

"Bull."

Jimmy pressed his palms into the tabletop and stared at his dad. "What are you doing here, Dad? Why did you come back?"

Joe sat back in his chair and stared at Jimmy. "That's the best question you've asked. Why do you think I came back? Why have I been watching you all these months, too scared to say anything, too cowardly to let you know it was me?"

Jimmy shrugged. "You wanted my forgiveness."

Joe chuckled without humor. "You'd think, but no. That's maybe what I told myself, but it weren't yer forgiveness I was after. I needed to convince myself you were all right, that I hadn't ruined your life for good." He paused and shook his head. "But it ain't no good. What I done to you can't be undone. I came back for absolution, but all I got was truth."

"It doesn't matter. I want to blame you—I've wanted to blame you all my life—but this isn't your fault. It's mine."

"I was no dad to you."

"No, you weren't."

"I should have been—"

"What? Better? Sober?"

Joe looked away. "Yeah."

Jimmy sighed. Didn't every guy want to be a better man? "It's hard to be the man you ought to be, isn't it?" His gaze bore into his father. "I've hated you for most of my life, blamed you…"

"For hitting you? Hurting you?"

Jimmy stared at him. "No. For making me a man like you."

"You ain't nothing like me, son. You don't drink. You don't fight. You go to church, say your prayers, read your Bible."

"And still, when it comes time to do right, when I have a chance to show the people I love that I love them, I don't. I'm not there for them any better than you were there for me."

"You always loved. I found that picture you made for me, crumpled by the trash can in your bedroom. And I know how you hoped and prayed for me when I was off at rehab. You were a good boy. It's just that I—"

"Things changed, Dad. Don't you remember?"

"What are you talking about?"

"The night that changed everything, that last night. Remember?"

Joe's gaze flicked down to the table and stayed there. His tone softened to a whisper. "I remember."

"That's the night I became the monster."

"It weren't your fault."

"Yes, it was."

It was supposed to be wonderful. Prom night. Him and Kinna, the prince and princess. A magical night when they'd ride off in their carriage, or at least in his old Rabbit, to happily ever after. He had it all planned out.

That was before he learned not to plan.

"You were just a kid."

"Not after that night."

Dad had come back from his twenty-eight days. Twenty-eight days during which Jimmy had promised to stay away from Kinna. But the wait was over, and he'd asked her to the prom. It was supposed to be a fairy tale night, and it had been. Until he came home after the dance.

The perfect night. Except for his dad and what Jimmy had done to him. Even now he couldn't face the memory, couldn't make himself live it again. He could only remember afterward, as he stood at the sink, his tux lying on the chair behind him, the water running and the radio shouting "I Don't Care Anymore" with the voice of Phil Collins. *I don't care. I don't care. I don't care.* The words pounded through Jimmy's head, blood wet on his hands.

That night, it had taken two and half minutes to wash the blood from his skin. Ninety-two seconds to stop shaking, forty-three to clean beneath his fingernails, fifteen for the water to turn from its sickly pink back to clear.

Two and a half minutes. An eternity. Because nothing could scrub away the shame.

All the while, Phil Collins growled about a man who wanted to be left alone.

He stared at the slim cuts on his knuckles. He clenched his fists and watched fresh blood, his precious "funny blood," well from the breaks in his flesh. Red drops fell from his fingers and dropped into the sink, joining blood that wasn't his own. Blood that belonged to his father.

He closed his eyes and refused to turn, refused to see. He knew what lay behind him in the doorway. A man. A beaten pulp that had been his father.

His hands trembled again. The images came, sickening him.

They washed over him, unrelenting. His own fists, hard and white, a blur through tears of fury. And the words from the radio reminding him of all the times he'd tried so hard, while his father laughed in his face. Words that gave fire to his fists until they were speckled with red as he punched and punched and punched, blind with a hundred memories of pain, deaf with the echo of all those years when he had taken the punches, when he had absorbed the lies.

Not anymore. Never again. He would see to that.

I don't care anymore!

He opened his eyes and gripped the edge of the sink. He dared not turn, dared not see the broken nose, the spatter over pale cheeks, the blood forming a small pool beneath his father's cheek.

Blood. His father's blood. The same blood that stained Jimmy's hands, that swirled pink in the sink and rolled away, mixed with his own. The blood of his own guilt, his own shame, staining him forever.

A sound came from behind him. Choking. Gagging.

Jimmy turned and saw too much. He spun back toward the sink and vomited into the basin.

He splashed his face with the cold water. Then he scrubbed his hands again. Scrubbed and scrubbed, as if by scouring his skin he could erase the images of what he had done.

But the images remained.

And the words that had driven him to this atrocity.

"You ain't no hero, boy. She ain't gonna want you."

The last words his father had spoken. The last Jimmy ever wanted to hear.

He'd been so determined to shut his father up. And he had, but the words echoed still, endlessly repeating, droning in the recesses of his mind and filling him with shame.

He'd thought he could silence them. He thought he could make it stop.

But it would never stop. He knew that now. He'd known it then, as he turned off the water and dried his hands on the towel.

Phil Collins finally gave way to strains of Air Supply's first album, mellow music drifting in from the living room. He shuddered. The music wasn't loud enough to drown out his father's words. Would it have mattered? Or had his whole life been building to that moment, his hands shaking beneath the flow of water, his father motionless behind him, and Russell Hitchcock's tenor voice crooning about being all out of love in the background?

All out of love. All out of luck. His father had finally turned him into a monster.

I don't care anymore.

Except he did. And always would.

Jimmy glanced at the clock. 10:57 p.m. He still had time to join the post-prom party and grab a sundae at Denny's with Kinna before he took her home.

10:58.

Time to drink a Mountain Dew and make jokes with his friends.

10:59.

Time to forget what he'd done and to pretend everything was all right.

He was good at pretending.

Jimmy grabbed his rented tux from the chair, his keys from the hook, and hurried out the back door.

11:00.

He left his books, his cassettes of Billy Joel and Boston. He left his clothes, his combs, his photos. He left the drawing of Prince Phillip fighting the dragon that Kinna had drawn for him when they were ten.

He left his father in a bloody pool on the kitchen floor.

He left and never went back inside that house again.

Except in some ways, he'd never left at all. He was still that boy, that trembling kid, sick at what he'd done, at what he'd become.

Joe's voice broke through his thoughts. "I had it coming, you know."

Jimmy stared at the remnants of coffee on the tabletop. "I beat you up. And then I just walked out."

Joe nodded. "And you've been walking out ever since?"

"Yep."

"I thought you were better off without me."

"And I figured I was done with you."

"But you weren't."

"No, I suppose not."

"Been carrying that night with you all these years. Been carrying me."

He had. He'd never realized it before today, but he had. That night changed everything. He had a basketball scholarship. It wasn't a great college, but it was college and basketball. He probably wouldn't have made it to the pros, but he'd never know for sure because he hadn't gone to college. He'd never tried. He stayed, got a job, and tried to forget.

But how could you forget the moment hope turned to shame? When the hero became a villain? When the prince turned to a dragon? When he had turned into the one thing he swore he'd never be? His father.

It had made him so afraid that someone would see the monster within and know it for what it was. Afraid that Kinna would see, would know, and he'd lose her.

But he'd lost her anyway, in the end.

Joe tapped the table with his fingers. "That's what kept you from being who you should have been? That's what's driven away that woman of yours?"

"Kinna wants a baby,"

"And you?"

Fury rose up in Jimmy, hot and blinding, filled with the frustration of too many years. "How am I going to be a good father to some kid? I don't know how to be a father. I don't know what a good father is."

He expected his dad to defend himself, to shout back, to tell him to be a man and forget the past. But he didn't.

Instead, Joe looked him straight in the eye and spoke as calmly as if he were settling a wild animal. "You got God, don't you, boy?"

Jimmy trembled. "Do I?"

Joe scooted closer until his nose was an inch from Jimmy's face. His voice lowered and became challenging and fierce, but so quiet Jimmy barely heard him. "You know what I think? It ain't that you don't get how to be a father. It's that you never learned to be a son." He hit the table with his hand.

The sound reverberated all the way to Jimmy's soul.

Kinna stepped back, away from the job site. Wind swept across the sidewalk behind her. She turned and watched the dirt swirl around the little flower stand at the side of the road.

Jimmy always thought everything could be fixed with flowers. A bouquet of tulips every spring. But that never changed anything. Never helped.

Kinna strode over to the beat-up van and stopped before a white bucket filled with pink and red carnations. She moved right, past a bucket of roses. The third held tulips. She stopped. She should have known. This was God's fault, rubbing her nose in her pain.

And yet, for that single breath, the sight brought her back to that evening beside the church when God was enough, when together was possible.

All things are possible...

She sighed. *Not anymore.*

A door opened and a wiry man with a dark mustache and a wide grin stepped from the van. "¡Hola, *señora!* You buy flowers today, sí? *Por su madre?* Mother? Or the *hombre* you love?"

She put up her hands. "No. Not today." She paused and spoke

more slowly. *"No hoy."*

The man frowned. "Special on tulips today. You want to buy tulips?"

Anything but tulips. She didn't want to see another tulip for the rest of her life.

"Half price."

"No."

He sighed. "Nobody want to buy tulips. They don't got worms or spiders, no? They nice flowers."

They were, but they hurt her. She turned away from the bucket and motioned toward the job site. "Do you know anything about this job here? Are any of the guys working somewhere else?"

The man shrugged. "No, all work here. Hurry hurry, rush rush. Big problem yesterday and everyone go home. Then come back *rápido*." His voice grew quiet. "No one come to flower stand now."

She glanced at him. "Did they before?" She couldn't imagine a bunch of rough construction workers buying flowers for their girl-friends.

The man rubbed his chin. "Only one. Good man. He want to buy tulips. He stand here for long time, but then he pay and no buy."

"What?"

"Give money and no take flowers."

That sounded like Jimmy. He never was good with money. "When did that happen?"

"Yesterday. Day of accident."

It had to have been Jimmy. But what stopped him from buying flowers?

You did. The words, quiet and accusing, rose up from within her.

She pushed them away.

"You got more questions, talk to that woman. She in there." He pointed to the administration trailer on the far side of the job site. "She keep close eye on workers. Very close."

Kinna glanced at the trailer. "Thank you."

"No buy tulips, huh?

"Not today."

"My wife get tulips again." He shook his head. "She learn to like tulips now."

Kinna threw him a quick smile, then started toward the construction trailer. Steps without rails led up to a small door on the side of the box-like building. It was a small thing, just ten feet by twelve if she guessed right, but inside, she hoped to find some answers.

She mounted the steps and tapped on the door.

"Since when does anybody knock around here? Come in." A woman's voice sounded from inside.

Kinna opened the door and halted. It was her. The other woman. Same long fingernails, same dyed hair. A different blouse, but low cut just the same.

The other woman glanced up from her computer. "I'm Karly. Can I help you?"

"Um, no. I..." Kinna took a deep breath and stepped inside the tiny room. The day was cool, but the room seemed hot, stifling. A fan stood silent in the corner. Stacks of papers lay against the walls, and a table sat crammed between two file cabinets. Dominating the room was the cheap particle board desk and the too-young woman behind it.

Kinna straightened and faced the enemy. She willed her voice steady. "I'm looking for Jimmy Henley. He's supposed to be working here." She closed the door and moved into the center of the room.

Karly's fingers paused on the computer keys and her face paled. Slowly, she rotated in her chair until she faced Kinna. "You're Mrs. Henley."

Not a question. An indictment.

"I am."

Karly's gaze slid away. Her voice lowered. "He didn't tell you, then."

A sick feeling rose in Kinna's stomach. She fought it down. "Tell me what?"

"Jimmy's been—"

The door slammed open. Papers flew off their stacks, and a long string of curse words filled the room. Kinna whirled toward the sound. Alan stood in the doorway, cast intact and midsection taut with tape, his face red and veins pulsing.

She caught her breath. "What are you doing here?"

Alan didn't even glance her way. He stalked toward Karly. "Did you know?"

Karly straightened in her chair. "You'd better behave yourself, mister. You've got no right to—"

Alan's voice rose to a shout. "Did you know or not?"

"I don't know what you're talking about!"

"You know why I'm not in the hospital?" He slammed his palms onto the top of Karly's desk, then winced. "Ouch. That hurt." He touched his side.

Karly glared at him. "Serves you right. Now, why aren't you at the hospital? Don't tell me, they couldn't stand you anymore."

Alan made a sound like a buzzer. "Wrong answer."

"So?"

"Try this on for size." His voice became high and whiny. "You should know, Mr. Miller, that the insurance information you gave us is out of date. That policy has been canceled." His voice returned to normal. "That's right. Canceled. I got no insurance. So you'd better get your pretty little behind up and start searching those files, 'cause I'd better be getting workers' comp."

"No insurance?" Karly's eyes widened, her face turning even paler than before. "What do you mean, no insurance?"

"You heard me, baby. We don't got no health insurance. Nothing."

"But, but…I need insurance. I can't be without insurance. Not now." Her hands slipped down to her lap.

Kinna's eyes narrowed and heat flared up her chest and neck. The room was more than warm now, it was hot. Unbearable. But she didn't move. She couldn't.

Nothing made sense. No insurance. How could she have not known that? But then, how would she? The insurance hadn't paid for infertility treatments or medications, and that's all she'd done for a long time. She couldn't have known, except…

She took a deep, shuddering breath. Jimmy's recent sperm tests were supposed to be covered. The new tests she'd insisted on because the others were over ten years old. He promised he'd get them done. But she'd never seen a bill for them. That meant, if there was no insurance, he'd never had those tests done at all.

She clenched her fists. *Liar!*

Kinna stumbled backward toward the wall. He lied to her about the tests, about checking the insurance again. *Jimmy, how could you? What else had he lied about?*

Alan turned. His gaze locked on Kinna. "You! You know about

this?"

Kinna shook her head.

"Jimmy, though. He knew, didn't he?"

Kinna's voice trembled. "I-I don't know."

Alan's face turned pale. "He knew. I bet a six-pack and two joints he's known all along. Going up to the big office, coming back, assuring us everything was okay. Making us work our hind ends off. And for what? Nothing, that's what." Alan made a fist with his good hand and slammed it into the wall. "He's gonna pay for this. And to think, I was starting to feel sorry for him. For both of you." He grunted. "What kind of man did you marry anyway?"

Kinna steadied herself against the wall. "I don't know."

"Well, guess you're finding out." Alan grabbed a pen from the desk and stabbed it toward Karly. "I wanna know about that workers' comp."

Karly nodded without looking at him. "Sure. Right away." The words were low and distant, her eyes unfocused. "Whatever you say."

Alan glanced at Kinna one last time, then hobbled out.

Karly raised her head. "Where are you going?"

Alan growled. "To see George up in that fancy, posh office of his. Living off us and sending his lap dog around to tell us everything's just fine. I'll show him 'fine.' And he'd better have paid that workers' comp." On the other side of the door, Alan paused and pointed his finger at Kinna. "Hope you got those papers ready, like we talked about. I'd say you'd better use 'em." The door slammed against the side of the trailer and stayed open.

Kinna moved toward the opening, then turned back toward Karly. If the woman was pale before, she was white now. "Are you okay?"

Karly shook her head. "I don't think so." She stood. "I think I'm going to be sick." She moved from around the desk, then raised her head until her eyes were level with Kinna's. She didn't speak—she just searched Kinna's face. Then she turned away. "You're a fool, Kinna Henley. Jimmy is a good man, and good men are hard to find. I should know." She pressed her hand to her lower stomach.

Kinna's eyes grew wide. She stepped back. The floorboards creaked. "No. You're not…not…" She couldn't be pregnant.

Kinna backed out the door and fell over the edge of the steps.

23

A son...

Joe stared at him so intently that Jimmy moved back in his chair.

"That's what I was supposed to teach you," the old man said, "and I didn't. That's where I failed you. Not that I was a bad father, but that I didn't let you learn to be a son."

To be a son.

The words called to him, beckoning.

Joe sat back. His gaze dropped.

What does it mean to be a son? Jimmy rolled the thought in his mind. His dad was right. Jimmy had no idea how to be a son. He only knew how to pretend, like he'd done that night so long ago when he'd walked out on his bleeding father, went to the party, went to Denny's, and pretended everything was all right.

But it wasn't. Nothing had ever been all right again. He lost something that night. His father, yes, but more important, he let go of what it should mean to be a son. To be God's son.

All these years, he'd always asked the other question: What was a good father? And how could he be one if he couldn't even imagine it? Maybe that was why he couldn't share Kinna's passion for having a baby. He was just afraid. Flat out scared he'd turn out like his dad and be an awful father.

But to be a son…

That changed everything. What if he didn't have to figure out what a good father was like? What if he only had to learn to be a son? Since he'd first met Kinna, he'd always tried to picture God as father, only conjuring a vague image he told himself to believe. He'd railed against his father's memory; he tried to forget, tried to pretend it didn't matter. But in the end, all he had was a flimsy faith built on make believe. He had the kind of faith that walked away.

That woman, Thea, had said he had to be a son of the King. Jimmy caught his breath. It made sense now—what she'd said then, what his father said now.

A son…

What was a son like? A son took his father's name. A son trusted, dared, fought for his father's honor. A son knew he was loved. That's how it was in all the fairy tales he'd ever read. The son of the king was a noble, dragon-fighting prince. There was no shame.

If he really, truly believed God was King, then he could be that son. He could be a prince after all, and not just make believe.

Before he had a child, he had to learn to be one. He had to let go of the past—no, not let go, but remember and embrace it, then move on and be the man Kinna once thought he could be. Not because he understood the concept of father, but because he was learning to be a son. A son of God Himself.

No more make believe.

Jimmy put his elbows on the table. Joe pushed down at the same time, and the table jarred. The coffee cup tipped and rolled, then fell and shattered on the hard floor.

Jimmy leaped up. "Oops. Sorry. My fault."

Joe paused with his rag halfway out of his pocket. His eyes narrowed and fixed on Jimmy. "No, it weren't."

Jimmy frowned. "What?"

Joe scooped up bits of broken ceramic and deposited them in a nearby trash can, then returned to his chair. His voice lowered and cracked. "I said it weren't your fault. You don't need to take the blame for something someone else done." He sniffed. "Taught you that, did I?" He threw a fierce glance at Jimmy, then bent down and finished wiping up drops of coffee from the floor.

Jimmy didn't answer. His dad had taught him he was to blame. For his mother's death, for the drunkenness, for everything. But maybe...a son wasn't to blame for everything. What if *that* was true?

Joe rose and stood before Jimmy, his rag brown with coffee. "You're seeing it now, ain't you, son? Seeing the truth."

Jimmy nodded.

"Sometimes things just happen. Accidents, troubles. Something tips, a mug falls and breaks. Life's like that. Ain't nobody to blame."

Maybe some mothers just died because life wasn't perfect. Maybe some fathers were just addicted to alcohol. Maybe... Jimmy's breath stopped in his throat. Maybe some couples couldn't have kids, and it wasn't always the man's fault.

Joe's voice dropped to a whisper as he moved closer. "If you take the blame when you shouldn't, you won't take it when you should."

Jimmy looked at the man. What was really his fault? Death? No. Alcoholism? No. Infertility? No. Walking away? Yeah. That one was on his shoulders. He'd let fear make his decisions for him. Fear and shame. Both were bad decision makers.

He pushed in his chair. "So what do I do?"

Joe shook his head. "Well, I ain't no expert on doing right, but I can tell you this: Doing right ain't the same as doing what's easy. And it ain't the same as doing what's safe."

"No fear, huh?"

Joe chuckled. "Life ain't a Nike commercial, son. You figure out what the right thing to do is, then do it, whether you're afraid or not. You don't let fear decide for you."

"Or shame?"

"Or shame. Or even money."

"You sound like Kinna, running up credit card debt so high that—"

"That's fear too."

"What do you mean?"

"Fear that she won't live up to her daddy's expectations, fear that life won't be what she'd hoped. Fear that God's plans for her life ain't as good as her own."

"What do you know about Kinna?"

Joe smiled. "Enough to know she needs a good man like you. Enough to know she didn't make a mistake when she married you."

"Wish that were so."

Joe stepped around the table and put his hand on Jimmy's shoulder. "Just love her, son. You love her, don't you? You always did."

"I do." Despite it all, he still did. He still wanted to be her prince charming. For real this time, not just make believe.

God, help me to love her, really love her. Like You do. For the first time in a long time, he didn't pray that God would make the troubles go away, that Kinna would lighten up, or that things would change. He just prayed that he could love her, even when it was hard, even when things went wrong. Nothing more. Once, that had been enough. It would be enough again.

Because this time, it wouldn't be a fairy tale. He wouldn't pretend everything was all right when it wasn't. Pretend infertility shouldn't matter, when it did. This time, he wouldn't walk away.

"God don't ask any more than you love your wife."

No, God didn't. Love wasn't just a feeling. It wasn't a kiss on a doorstep or a dance under the streetlights. It was a life lived together, facing the good and the bad. It was laying down your life for another. It was sacrifice. It was taking a risk. It meant doing right even when it was hard. It meant taking responsibility when he'd made mistakes.

It meant he had to get back to that Petersen job and make things right.

He turned to Joe. "Come on, we've got to go."

"All right, you go get your dog. Just keep it away from me."

Fifteen minutes later, Joe's rickety old Jeep pulled up to the Petersen job site. Jimmy jumped out of the passenger seat, let Tulip scramble out, then stared out over the job. Only Pedro's flower stand was the same. Buckets of yellow, red, orange, and pink dotted the sidewalk— carnations, roses, and tulips.

But behind them, much had changed in just one day. At the back of the site where there had been level earth, there was now the beginnings of a gaping hole. Where there had been clear sky, the rough concrete structure of phase one rose a story and a half higher than it had before. There were still men in hard hats, but they rushed about like ants over an anthill.

I knew it. George had done what Jimmy suspected. He'd pushed the job forward, not allowing enough time for the ground to be compacted properly, the concrete to have cured enough, or the rebar to have been set correctly.

Jimmy sighed and straightened his shoulders.

Joe came up beside him. "Progress, eh?"

Jimmy reached down and scratched Tulip behind the ears. "Too much."

Joe clapped him on the back. "Guess you want to start over there?" He pointed to the administration trailer on the far end of the site.

"Guess I'd better." Jimmy started toward the trailer. The dog trotted before him. He hadn't realized how much he'd hate coming back here, but he'd face it. And this time, he wouldn't walk away. He rubbed the back of his neck and quickened his pace. "It's like coming back to the scene of the crime."

Joe jogged beside him to keep up. "Yeah, what would you know about that?"

Jimmy grimaced. "More than I want to."

"What are you talking about, boy?"

"I told you already."

Joe slowed. "Don't tell me you're still talking about prom night. That weren't no crime."

Jimmy stopped. "Then why were there police cars outside the house when I came back that night?"

Joe grunted. "Thought you said you didn't go back."

"I, um…" He had gone back late that night, filled with shame and wanting to make things better. To figure things out. But then he saw those cop car lights and turned around. No way he was going back after that.

Joe stared at him.

It wasn't disgust in the old man's eyes. It was humor. Joe was laughing.

Jimmy scowled.

Joe wagged a finger at him. "Now don't tell me you thought they were there for you."

Jimmy shrugged and started toward the trailer again. "Assault's a felony."

They were almost to the trailer. Joe controlled his laughing. "Oh, son, you've got to be kiddin' me. They weren't there to arrest you. They were there for me. There's a reason you never saw me after that night. They put me away for drug dealing. You did 'em a favor, though. I was in such bad shape, I couldn't get away." He chuckled some more. "I cursed you up one side and down the other that night, but you did me a favor too. Would have never straightened out if not for my time in prison and that cell mate talking to the picture of his dead boy."

The trailer door banged against the wall.

Jimmy stopped, turned. From the corner of his vision, he saw someone fall from the landing above him.

Kinna plummeted toward the ground. Her heart slammed into her throat.

Then arms caught her, warm, strong, familiar.

"Jimmy?" She breathed his name, looked up into sapphire eyes. He had come to her, come for her. Rescued her.

His gaze softened. "Are you okay?"

She couldn't answer.

"What are you doing here?" His voice was so gentle, so caring. He held her, her pulse still racing, his heartbeat strong against her side.

For a moment, nothing else existed. No one else. Only them.

Then a voice broke the silence. *Her* voice. "Is that you, Jimmy? Good catch. About scared me out of my shorts." Karly giggled.

Jimmy set Kinna down. "What's going on here?"

A chill skittered into Kinna's stomach. "I…uh…" A dog came up beside her and rubbed against her leg, the same scraggly mutt she'd seen before. Jimmy's dog. She swallowed. "I need to talk to you."

The dog nudged her again and looked up, panting.

An old man stepped up, the man from the coffee shop. "I'd better get to work. I'll be in phase one, cleaning up on the bottom floor, should any of you need me."

Jimmy nodded without looking toward the man. "Okay."

The old man turned and hurried away.

Jimmy blew out a long breath and focused on Kinna. "Yes. We'll talk. But I've got business with Karly first."

Kinna stepped back. His words felt like a slap. *Karly?* He'd chosen Karly before her. "Jimmy?"

He didn't even notice, didn't care. Didn't even glance back at her as he mounted the stairs. "I'll be right back."

She watched him go, moving closer to the other woman and farther from her.

Karly held the door wide. "Come on in, Jim-boy." Her gaze slipped toward Kinna, then away again, and in that glance was Karly's victory. And Kinna's pain.

Kinna turned and ran away from the administration trailer, away from Karly. Away from Jimmy, who had left her.

Behind her, she heard the sounds from the job site: the grinding of machinery, the shouts of men, the ping of hammers on metal, and the rumble of a concrete mixer. She ran past the half-built parking garage, past the hole in the ground, past the empty lot she supposed would be the third phase of the project.

She ran past it all, toward the ocean, and eventually the sounds faded. But not the pain. Not the image of Jimmy ascending those stairs, of Karly's face, of that one horrible glance.

Kinna stopped. Below her, 17-Mile Drive wound along the ocean. A grassy hill sloped off to the north, and a bit of Pebble Beach was just visible to her left. A BMW crept along the road, passed, and then it was gone.

Kinna stood with nowhere to go. Not back, not forward. Nowhere.

Oh God, I don't know what to do. A strange prayer. She always knew what to do. What Jimmy should do. What God should do.

But not anymore.

Kinna sat in the grass and gazed out over the ocean. Surf crashed into the rocky shore and sent spray spitting along the crags, but the rocks stayed firm, unmoving.

"You're like those rocks, God. I've beat myself against You long enough." She wrapped her arms around her legs and watched another wave break along the shore. "I've crashed and slammed and pounded my fists against Your immovable chest. I've schemed and screamed. I've planned and prayed. And all I've done is break my life into a million little bits, a million little drops that change nothing. Do nothing. It's made no difference at all. I'm just as cold, just as empty, just as barren as the surf."

Footsteps sounded behind her. Kinna turned. "Jimmy?"

Thea stood behind her.

Kinna frowned. "Are you following me?"

Thea smiled. "The surf isn't dead, you know. It's teeming with life even as it casts itself on the rocks."

Kinna looked away, her eyes squinting into the light. "I guess it was a bad analogy, then."

Thea sat beside her. "No, it isn't. Look." She pointed to the rainbow of color the surf's spray made against the sky. "The waves aren't fighting the shore, they're meeting it. The water throws itself on the rocks not to change the rocks, but so the waves themselves are changed. See?" Another wave pounded against the shore and flew up in myriad colors. "Before it was green and murky. And now?"

Kinna watched a wave come in. "Now it's filled with light."

Thea moved closer and patted Kinna's knee. "Yes. Finally, you're seeing it. You understand."

"Maybe."

"Don't let the faces fade." Thea took Kinna's hand and pressed something small and cool into her palm, then stood.

Kinna opened her hand. The locket gleamed against her skin. "What are you doing?"

Thea bent down and closed Kinna's fingers over the locket. "It's yours now. Maybe it always has been."

"But…" She raised her hand toward Thea. "I can't take this."

Thea moved away and glanced over her shoulder. "You're almost there, Kinna. You just have to remember one more thing."

"What's that?"

"When love wasn't make believe."

24

Kinna was alone again in that barren place between land and sea. On the shore of tomorrow, with her feet dangling in the past.

The night love became real. Not make believe, not pretend, but true. As true as anything she'd ever known.

That was a long time ago. How could it matter anymore?

Kinna turned the locket over in her hand. The intricate tulip design was worn, the clasp was bent, the chain dull. She flipped it over. Tiny words were inscribed on the back: *Love believes all things. Genesis 1:31.*

Kinna frowned. That wasn't right. It should read 1 Corinthians 13:7. She'd memorized that verse often enough in Sunday school to know that "love…believes" was straight out of 1 Corinthians. One of the church ladies had read that same passage at Kinna and Jimmy's wedding.

So why did the locket say Genesis? What was Genesis 1:31, anyway?

Kinna searched through all those memory lessons she'd had as a kid. Genesis 1, the creation story. Verse 31, the sixth day. "God saw all that he had made, and it was very good."

Well, that was just weird.

Kinna opened the locket and stared at the faces. Those same happy faces. Two people in love, after all those years.

It should have been her and Jimmy. It could have been, except something had gone wrong.

They were in love once. Real love, not the kind that got fluttery because Jimmy was a basketball star. Not the kind that made her pulse race under the streetlights in a forbidden dance. It was the kind that believed all things. Patient and kind, it was the type of love that wasn't supposed to fail.

God's love, not just some kid's crush or high school infatuation. The kind of love a lifetime was built on.

She remembered when she knew it for certain, the very first time.

She remembered prom night.

It was going to be just another dance she wouldn't be allowed to go to, just another time to stand aside as others planned and laughed and had fun. Just another thing she'd have to endure to be holy.

But God had other plans, and so did Jimmy. Both had made promises.

Jimmy's was to her dad. No, Kinna wouldn't dance or drink. She didn't need to wear makeup or jewelry. Jimmy would keep her safe.

God's was to her heart. A promise of love.

She wore a pink dress with big ruffles, and he rented a cheap tux. The Disney prince and princess at last. The fairy tale they'd always dreamed of, magical and perfect.

When they reached the Hyatt, Jimmy lifted his elbow toward her, and she walked into that big room with her hand tucked against him. Music played from the stage. Dry ice made a cool fog along the floor. Whirring machines blew soap bubbles through the room, bubbles that caught the light and reflected it in a rainbow of shimmering color. They weaved through the flowered garlands, the tables with tiny rock fountains, their footsteps keeping time with the thrum of a Michael Jackson song in the background.

Halfway to the stage, someone touched Kinna's arm. She turned.

Tracy stood next to her, dressed in a daring off-the-shoulder gown with a string of pearls around her neck. Her dark hair was ratted into a poof around her head in a style straight out of *Tiger Beat* magazine.

Tracy leaned close and shouted to be heard. "I didn't think you were coming."

Kinna looked up at Jimmy and grinned.

Tracy squealed. "He asked you!"

"And Dad let me come." Because of Jimmy. Only because of Jimmy.

Tracy made a face. "I'm here with Steve." She stuck out her tongue.

Kinna laughed.

Tracy wiggled her fingers in a quick good-bye and scooted off toward the punch table.

Jimmy followed her. He paused and put on a bad Arnold Schwarzenegger accent. "I'll be back." His voice returned to normal. "With some punch. Find us a good seat."

Kinna turned toward a fountain laden table.

"Hey Preacher-Girl."

She froze.

"What are you doing here?"

She turned. Behind her were four large guys, all football players and popular. All with eyes red enough to tell her they'd had a few too many beers.

Mick Taylor, the quarterback on the field and off, spoke again. "Thought your daddy didn't let you dance."

Kinna tried to stand taller, it didn't help. "I…uh…"

Mick leaned in until she could smell the beer on his breath. "You wanna dance, Little Miss Priss?"

She cleared her throat, willed her voice steady. "Thank you for the invitation, but I can't."

The other guys laughed. A cold sound, unkind.

"Come on, Miss Prissy, let's see you dance." Mick stepped on her too-long hem.

She yanked her dress from underneath his foot. It tore. Her face flushed hot. "Stop it, you…you…"

Mick smirked. "Us what? Us big old bad boys? Such language. Shame on you. And from a Christian too."

"Yeah, well, the Bible says…it says…" What did the Bible say? Something about bad company. Something about… She didn't know. She couldn't remember a single thing the Bible said about anything. She stamped her foot. "You'd better just…because the Bible says… uh…"

Someone touched her shoulder, gentle yet strong. A voice came, calm but with an edge of steel. "The Bible says to pray for those who've got less brains than Boss Hogg."

She shivered. "It does not—" She glanced up. Jimmy had come at last.

He winked at her, then looked back at the other guys. "So, don't make me pray for you, Taylor. You'd better be just a good ole boy, never meaning no harm."

Mick scowled. "Shut up with the *Dukes of Hazzard* theme song. Besides, the Bible doesn't really say that, does it?"

"Sure it does. Maybe not in those exact words, but I wouldn't have to interpret for you if you'd come to youth group like I've been saying."

Mick waved his hand. "Yeah, yeah. Turn me into some prissy like her?" He pointed at Kinna.

Jimmy shrugged. "Well, someday you might be as good as her." He grinned. "Bible does talk about miracles after all."

Mick laughed. His tone turned light, joking as he gave Jimmy's arm a playful punch. "Dude, you're such a doofus."

"At least I know a good thing when I see it." He jerked his thumb toward Kinna.

Her chest swelled. The urge came to stick out her tongue at Mick, but she quelled it. Preacher's daughters shouldn't do that kind of thing. But that didn't keep her from thinking about it.

"If you say so." Mick shook his head.

Jimmy nodded. "Next thing you know, you'll be coming to youth group."

Mick chuckled. "You really do believe in miracles, don't you, Henley?"

Jimmy laughed. "Yeah, I do. I have to. Now, get out of here. I got a beautiful woman to woo."

Mick shoved the other guys in front of him. They ambled toward the snack table with only one backward glance.

Jimmy turned toward her. "Sorry 'bout that. Sometimes guys can be stupid."

Kinna sniffed. "Thank you."

"For what?"

"For what you said. Did."

"Well, sometimes a man just has to tell the truth." He touched her chin and lowered his voice. "Besides, I don't want anything spoiling our perfect night."

"Are you okay?"

He pulled her closer. "Yeah. I'm with you, aren't I?"

"I wish that hadn't happened."

He tipped her chin up. "Things don't have be what you planned to be good, Kinna." He turned and dropped his arm around her. "So, come on, m'lady. The night is young, and so are we." He backed up and held out his hand.

She looked at it, then up at him. "You meant what you said to those guys?"

"No."

"Huh?"

"I meant more."

Kinna placed her hand in his as they moved toward the stage. When they got close, Jimmy signaled to the DJ, and the man nodded. At the edge of the dance floor, Jimmy paused and turned to face her. New music swirled around them. Not Michael Jackson this time, but Boston.

Jimmy stepped closer, his voice rising over the strum of guitars. "I know we can't dance, but this is my favorite song." His eyes sparkled. He reached out and touched her hair.

"Dad won't know. Maybe we could."

He shook his head. "I promised." He moved closer still. His voice lowered until she could just hear it over the music. "But we can still pretend. Close your eyes, Kinna." He took her hands in his, warm and strong, his thumb brushing her skin.

She closed her eyes and imagined whirling across the dance floor like Cinderella with her prince, or maybe like Sleeping Beauty. After all, her eyes were shut and it did seem like a dream. She listened to the lyrics of the song playing from the stage. She let it flow through her, speak to her, a whisper of hope. A song about a guy who was going to say it like a man and make his girl understand that he loved her, a girl named Amanda. Asking if she'd walk away, knowing that he loved her.

She opened her eyes and gazed into Jimmy's sapphire ones. He touched her cheek, his lips mouthing the words to the song.

I don't think I can hide what I'm feelin' inside another day.

Was it real? Did he mean it?

The song grew louder. She listened, filled with the melody as the man offered a life together. Now or never, because, he said, tomorrow would be too late.

Beside the speakers at the prom, Jimmy drew her close, so near that she could hear his whisper in her ear. "There's one thing I want you to know, Kinna. This is not pretend."

Then he kissed her.

And she knew he loved her—for real, forever—and she loved him too. He'd shown her more clearly than anyone else what the love of God really was—not a love that restricted and held back, not a love that demanded she act a certain way, look a certain way, and be a certain way, but a love that defended, hoped, trusted, and believed. A love that endured all the hard things they had already faced and was supposed to endure all the days, good or bad, to come. For richer or poorer. In sickness and in health. With children…or without.

One thing had always been true—Jimmy's love. How could she think to throw that away? How could she believe she could love a child, when she wasn't even loving her husband? Not like she once did, anyway, not like that night. She'd been so worried about his love for her, but what about hers for him? Not *Give Me,* but something else. How did she spell love?

I don't wanna wait my whole life through to say I'm in love with you. The last line of Boston's song "Amanda." She'd sung it to him that night, and she'd meant it with all her heart. Did she mean it still? Could she?

Could it be like that night again, when there was no one in the world like Jimmy Henley? That night, when she could have kissed him forever, facing him, their lips touching, their hearts intertwined.

Like in the locket.

The thought broke over her, and finally she understood. That's what the locket was—two images facing each other, together, close. Inseparable. And that's what the inscription meant. *Love believes...* *Genesis 1:31.* Love believed that what God made was very good. Love believed that when it was just Adam and Eve and all the animals, it was good. Before Cain, before Abel, before any babies were born. Adam and Eve were happy, even without children. They were complete.

Love believed that. Once she had too.

A breeze came off the ocean and rustled the grass around her, cool, refreshing, and clear. It made sense now. She opened the locket and gazed at the faces of people who chose to be happy. They chose to love one another. Despite circumstances, despite failure, despite dreams and plans that never came true. That's what the vows meant. When hard times came, you chose to stand together. That's what the locket meant too. She closed it again so the faces were close together, locked together as one. Man and woman, together. Complete.

And God called it very good. He loved them, just like that.

She clenched the locket in her hand and closed her eyes. "Lord, knit me together with Jimmy the way the faces are together. Help me to see him as he is. Help me to let go of my dreams enough to embrace Yours, to embrace him. Help me to believe in 'very good.'"

A dog's bark split the air. Her eyes flew open.

A dog raced over the hill and plunged toward her. Jimmy's dog. Kinna jumped to her feet.

Thea appeared on the hill behind the dog. She motioned to Kinna. "Hurry! It's happened. We have to go."

The dog whipped around and raced back, up the hill, toward the job site.

Then the sounds came. A scream. Shouts. The loud grind of some machine. And next, a desperate call.

25

Jimmy pounded his fist on the desk and promised he'd get insurance reinstated for all of them, even if he had to camp out in front of George's office himself. He'd get his job back, do it right this time, run this Petersen job as it should have been done all along, and make sure George took care of his people. Even if Jimmy had to work for free.

His fist smarted. Karly stared at him with a hungry look, and he thought he might throw up, but he didn't walk away. Instead, he rubbed his hand on his thigh. "Look, Karly, set a meeting with George. I don't care how you do it, just get me in to see him. I've got to make this right."

"But Jim—"

Then came the crash, the awful sound of bending metal and collapsing concrete Jimmy had been dreading since he first set foot on the job site.

Next came an eerie silence, followed by feet running, voices shouting, and another whining shriek of twisting metal.

Jimmy sprinted out of the trailer and saw a cloud of gray dust settling over the remains of the half-built parking structure. Men ran everywhere. One stopped near the trailer steps and looked up.

"Jimmy, that you?"

"Bill, was anyone in there?"

The dust sifted down, framing a sight that made his stomach turn. Crumbled concrete, broken dirt, bits of rebar sticking out at odd angles, and it was still shifting. In a moment, the rest could come down.

This was all George's fault. No, it was Jimmy's fault too. He'd known, or at least suspected. He should have been a better man. But "should have been's" were gone. He only had now. Now he could be the man God called him to be. He could do what he could. He could dare.

Bill nodded at him, his face pale, chalky with dust. "There's a whole crew trapped under there. I'm going for the Cat."

Jimmy straightened his shoulders. "No, I'll do it." The words came out steady, sure.

"You certain, Jim? Last time…"

"I'll do it. You get over there and show me where to dig."

Bill nodded. "Good luck."

Jimmy bolted down the steps and ran toward the big yellow back-hoe. That's what they needed—not the Cat, the John Deere. But he'd need more than a good tractor and luck. From the look of that cave-in, he was going to need a miracle.

Another man leaped into the backhoe ahead of him, a man Jimmy didn't recognize.

Jimmy rushed up to the hatch. "I need this machine. Get out!"

The man looked at him with wild eyes. "Who are you?"

Another voice came, sharp and fierce. "Gus, that's Jimmy Henley, you idiot! Get off his backhoe."

Gus swallowed, glanced toward Jimmy, then climbed off.

Jimmy jumped in and turned the key. This was where he belonged. He glanced toward the fallen structure. A chunk of concrete came loose and tumbled down the front side, disappearing into the hole Bill and others stared into. He drew a steadying breath. He could do this. He was made to do this. *God be with me.*

Jimmy jammed the backhoe into gear. The machine lumbered over to the group of men. They parted, their skin sweaty, their faces dark with dirt. Two dozen eyes looked to him and waited. Jimmy stopped the backhoe. He leaned toward the mass of fallen parking structure and peered down the hole to the mess of rebar, concrete, and dirt.

Voices skittered up to him.

"We're all right."

"Get this stuff off us."

"Help!" The last voice sounded young. Some poor kid working part-time to pay for college, probably.

The parking structure shifted. Another concrete hunk rolled down into a small avalanche of gray.

Bill stepped up to the backhoe. "Tricky business, Jim. You gotta pick up the first layer, move it away. Then we can pull 'em out."

Jimmy nodded and set the stabilizer legs on the backhoe. Then carefully, skillfully, he lowered the bucket. He hooked it over the first slab of fallen concrete and slowly lifted it away. The structure shook but remained intact. He lowered the bucket again, gently, perfectly. Another load came free. He set it aside. And another. And another.

"Almost there, Jim."

Jimmy glanced at Bill as the man peered into the now-wider hole. Bill signaled Jimmy to put the bucket lower. "One more. I can see them."

Jimmy angled the bucket and removed another load.

"Somebody get a rope!" Gus shouted to nobody.

The structure creaked, shifted.

Bill shouted, "It's gonna fall in again."

Jimmy stuck his head out the window. "Get back. And forget the rope."

Bill moved back, along with a half dozen others. Gus held his ground.

Jimmy growled. "Get out of the way!" He extended the bucket and began to lower it.

Bill moved closer and shook his head. "I can't spot you, Jim. You'll have to do it blind."

Jimmy gave a curt nod. He could do this. He had to. He closed his eyes and focused on the bucket—the feel of it, the sound. He lowered it into the hole, trusting what he knew, trusting that God would help him. It tapped the concrete. He moved it in. The sound of scraping metal. It touched rebar. He moved it left, out, just a hair, then down some more. Act and believe. Turn, tilt. It wouldn't go down any farther.

He stopped and shouted out the window. "Can they reach it?"

Bill yelled down the hole. Indistinct voices answered him.

"You did it, Jim. They're getting in the bucket."

He could feel the weight.

Bill watched the hole. Then he gave Jimmy the thumbs-up. "You got 'em Jimmy. Pull up! Pull up!"

He raised the bucket, slow and precise.

Soon men's faces rose out of the hole, their hats dark with dust, their eyes peering out like a raccoon's from a mask of dirt. Two squatted in the bucket, and three more clung to the outside. One wore a torn CSU Monterey Bay sweatshirt. Poor kid.

Jimmy swiveled the bucket to solid ground, then lowered it.

The men let go. Another batch of concrete tumbled into the hole, but it didn't matter now. The guys were out, safe.

Jimmy rubbed his forehead. A face appeared at his window. A hand banged on the glass. Jimmy jumped.

The CSU kid jabbed a finger toward the hole. "Dude! There's one more down there, an old man."

One more?

"We couldn't get him out. Stuck under a beam." He motioned toward the middle of the fallen structure.

Bill jogged up to the window. "You gotta remove some of that rubble, then someone'll have to prop up that wall while someone else goes down and lifts the beam by hand. Can you do it, Jimmy?"

Jimmy studied the way the structure had fallen and understood. He nodded.

Bill and the kid backed off.

Jimmy stared again over the fallen structure. The beam was pinned down by rubble. The rubble would have to be removed before the beam could be shifted, and if it was done wrong, some old guy would die. Some...*oh no.*

His gaze shot around the job site. *Dad?* He hollered out the window again. "The old guy have a scar down his face?"

"Yeah. Big one."

His dad was pinned down there in the dark.

Jimmy knew what he had to do. He lifted the stabilizers and repositioned the backhoe. Then he began to dig. After seven buckets full, Bill gave him the sign to stop.

"Now push up that wall. That'll loosen the beam underneath." Bill stabbed his fingers toward the fallen wall.

Jimmy nodded, then hooked his bucket beneath a corner of the wall and pulled. Dust puffed up and made a gray cloud in front of the window. The wall lifted until it was upright, and Jimmy wedged the bucket against the wall. Now all he needed was the dozer and a couple expert operators.

He slammed open the other window in the backhoe's cab and yelled to the group of men watching. "Okay, this is what we need. Bill will get up here on the backhoe and hold it steady."

Bill moved to the opposite side of the backhoe and stepped close to the window.

Jimmy motioned to the men. "I need someone on the dozer to keep that wall up. After the dozer's in place, Bill, I need you to move the backhoe and lower me into the hole in the bucket, and stay alert in case things start caving in again. So, who can run the dozer?" He glanced over the men again.

Gus stepped forward.

Jimmy opened his mouth to call him, but before he could, he noticed the quick shake of Bill's head. Jimmy cleared his throat. Then he saw Alan. Still bandaged, still bruised, with a cast over one lower leg, but walking and moving. Alan was a great operator, at least when he wasn't smoking pot.

Jimmy motioned toward him. "Alan, can you run the dozer with that cast?"

For a moment Alan didn't answer. He just stared at Jimmy, his eyes narrowed.

"I could run that machine with both legs in casts. You know that."

"You sure?"

Alan hooked his thumb in the belt loop of his jeans. "Don't you trust me, Jim?"

"'Course I do."

Alan licked his lips. "You jumped on that backhoe mighty quick. Seems you can move when other people's lives are on the line."

"Look, Alan…"

He removed his thumb and waved his hand toward Jimmy. "Forget it. I'll do it. I ain't no coward."

"No, you aren't."

Alan nodded once, then turned and limped toward the dozer. Jimmy could see him muttering to himself but couldn't make out the words.

Five minutes later, Alan had the wall secure, Bill was seated in the backhoe, and Jimmy squatted in the bucket.

"Straight down, Bill." Jimmy leaned over the bucket and looked down the hole. It wasn't deep. Ten feet, maybe more. The jags of concrete cast shadows across the bottom, making the distance hard to judge. "Another five feet or so. I can jump down from there." It would be a tight squeeze, but he could do it.

The bucket lowered. The bottom still looked too far away. Jimmy grimaced.

The scoop halted.

He studied the darkness below him, then swung off the bucket, dangled there, and dropped. He fell another two feet. The hole was deeper than it looked.

He tipped his head up and shouted, "Bring it down another couple feet."

A face appeared at the opening, backlit by sunlight so he couldn't tell who it was. "What did you say?"

It was Gus. Great. "Have Bill lower the bucket two to three more feet."

"Lower it all the way, Bill!"

"No!" Jimmy cupped his hands to his mouth. "Two or three feet. That's it."

The bucket trembled then moved down the hole. It was coming too far. It would hit an outcropping of rebar.

"Stop! That's it."

"What?"

"Stop!"

"Oh."

The bucket stopped. Jimmy heard the backhoe's hydraulics whine.

"Now, have him wait."

"Wait?"

"Just hold on." Jimmy rubbed his hand over his forehead. "I'm going to get Joe. Tell Bill to keep the bucket right there until he can pull Joe out."

"Uhh…"

"Just do it."

"All right."

Jimmy waited to be sure Bill got the message, then glanced around. Only part of the parking structure had fallen in, leaving a gap like a small room near the opening, which narrowed into a slender corridor near the back. There, it appeared the structure had collapsed, leaving only a tiny bit unblocked.

Jimmy moved toward the corridor. Gray dust drifted through the air, illuminated only by slim shafts of light that sifted through the debris above. Chunks of concrete littered the ground, making a maze in the shadows.

Jimmy cupped his hands to his mouth. "Joe? Where are you?"

A gruff voice sounded from somewhere beyond the corridor. "Back here. But don't come. It ain't safe."

"I'm coming." He wound his way through the concrete and back to the corridor.

"Go back, I said!"

Jimmy followed the sound, inching through the debris, around a tipped post, to a narrow place where the rubble had fallen to make a passage only two to three feet from the ground. He dropped to his knees and crawled through. The passage widened enough that Jimmy could stand again.

He saw his dad. Joe's arm was pinned under a thick concrete beam. Bits of rubble lay scattered around him, and a drizzle of sunlight shone down from a small hole above. Jimmy rushed forward.

Joe scowled. "Never did listen. Not when you were a boy, not now."

"Well, you're in no position to give me a good lickin' now, are you?" Jimmy squatted down and put his hands under the beam.

Joe grunted. "Never worked then. Won't try it now."

Jimmy smiled and tried to lift the beam. It didn't budge. "I need leverage."

The columns shifted above him. Thick dust tumbled down, and a dozen concrete pebbles fell and shattered on the beam.

Jimmy glanced around. Half-hidden beneath a broken column was a two-by-six plank. Perfect. He edged over and grabbed the end, then moved it back and forth until some of the debris fell from its surface. "I think I can pull this free."

"Hold on. You're making that whole pile shiver like a long-tailed cat in a room full of rocking chairs."

Jimmy grimaced. "You always used to say that."

"One of my less colorful sayings, if I remember right." Joe's voice was rough, gravelly.

Jimmy stopped pulling on the board. "How are you doing?"

Joe grunted again. "A little cold, but fine. I'm fine. Been in worse places than this."

"Really?"

Joe coughed. "Been in prison, remember? This ain't much different than a stint in solitary." He cleared his throat. "'Course, the quarters are a bit tighter here."

Jimmy strengthened his grip on the board. "Well, let's see if we can do something about that." He worked the plank again. More dust filtered down from above.

"Easy there, son."

"You hold still, old man."

"I ain't the one moving."

Jimmy wedged a couple blocks of concrete under the rubble beside the board, then worked the board slowly back and forth until it started to come free. "This might take a few minutes."

The wall of rubble wobbled, then stilled again.

"Take your time. I ain't going anywhere."

"I'll get you out as fast as I can."

The old man sighed. "Look, son, you pull out that plank and this whole place'll come down, so how about you just get yourself back out of here? I ain't worth saving. You know that better than anyone."

"I know what I'm doing. And everyone's worth saving. Even you."

"You sure?"

Jimmy tugged at the board. More dirt sifted, plumed, and settled. Something creaked.

"Look at me."

Jimmy glanced over his shoulder and saw nothing but an old man, bald and pale, with a single shaft of light slashing across his eyes and face.

Joe shook his head. His voice softened. "Boy, remember what I done, then get outta here and save yourself."

Boy... There was something in the way he said it—the inflection, the way he lengthened the "oy"—something that made Jimmy's blood run cold. He dropped the board, turned, and stepped closer. He stared at his father, imagining him twenty years younger. Not bald, but with long, curly hair. Heavier, much heavier. And with blood-red eyes.

Joe nodded, his voice growing soft, quiet. "Would it help if I was holding a beer?"

Jimmy clenched his jaw. "Dad, I forgive you. And I forgive me too. And this time, I'm not walking away."

26

It's come to this, my dream that is not a dream. I won't fight it now. I'm here for a reason, that much I've figured out. Crazy or not, I know I won't wake up until I see this through.

We crest the hill and see it, a mass of concrete and metal, like a still shot of the ocean in a storm. Everyone is motionless, as if none dare even breathe. A man sits on a bulldozer, another on a backhoe. A group stands watching. No one moves.

And I know he's down there in the wreckage. I pray he comes out alive.

Kinna is beside me, her eyes wide, her breath coming fast. Good thing she's trained for this. She remembers to breathe.

She touches my arm. "Hurry. Someone may need me." Her features change, solidify, and I know she's telling herself to be calm, to maintain order. She's become Nurse Henley before my eyes. No longer afraid, no longer defeated. Now, at last, she reminds me of my mother. Tough old bird.

She looks at me. "Do you have your cell phone? Call 911."

Cell phone. I haven't had one of those in years.

She glances at me and frowns. "Mine's in the van, the one with the front smashed in. Get it and call for help." She grinds her teeth. "Men. Just standing around gawking. Probably no one's even thought to call the paramedics."

I hurry toward her car, whistling for the dog. We'll need her soon. I can sense it.

"Just do what's right," Mom constantly says. "There's always a way to do what's right."

The time is coming for me to do what's right. I can sense that too. The time to love, the time when God will show me why I have come.

So why am I so afraid?

———

Jimmy bent over and gripped the board again. He worked it back and forth, loosening it, focusing on the feel of wood against his palms, the shift of rubble, the sound of moving earth. This time, it would be different. This time, he would do what was right.

Joe coughed again. His voice grew quiet. "You stay down here, you're gonna die just like your mama did. I won't have that. I can't."

Jimmy paused. "Mom didn't die in a construction accident."

"No."

"Then how did she? I always thought it was my fault."

"Your fault? Naw. Weren't your fault she got hit in a crosswalk by some drunk. Weren't your fault she had that funny blood and nobody knew it. Might have lived except for her blood."

Jimmy caught his breath. Dust settled around them. "She was Lan negative."

"I suppose so. She lost so much blood. They just kept pumping more in, but they didn't know she'd reject it. Didn't know she had some strange rare blood."

Jimmy pulled. The plank came free. More dirt sifted down, but the structure remained steady. "I guess I could have saved her, then, since I'm Lan negative too."

"You could have saved her? You were five years old, all keyed up and crying for your mama. I didn't know how to tell you she was gone, so I didn't. Went for the bottle instead—first beer, then the harder stuff. All 'cause I couldn't tell a little boy his mama died."

"I'm sorry, Dad." He placed the end of the board under the beam and wedged it there.

"Well, what's done is done. And now that you know all the secrets of the universe, how 'bout you climb back out that hole and let me wait for the rescue workers."

Something creaked above them.

Jimmy shook his head. "This place isn't going to last till then. I'm going to lift this beam, and you're going to crawl out."

"Look, boy, only one of us is gonna get out of here alive, and I want it to be you."

"I told you I'm not walking away. Not this time."

"Son?"

Jimmy looked into his father's filthy face. He saw a streak of tears down the old man's cheeks and knew he was right. He knew what he had to do, no matter what. This time, he was going to be free. Free of the shame, free of the guilt, free of the fear. *"Perfect love drives out fear,"* the Bible said. And love wasn't a feeling, it was a sacrifice. It was what made men into heroes, what kept Jesus on the cross. The kind that knelt and washed Judas's feet.

That was love. That was faith. And that was what God asked of him now. Jimmy jabbed his finger toward the beam. "This is what we're going to do. I lift. You get out."

"No, son."

"This time we're going to do it my way, Dad. You have to see. This is the only way I can be the man God wants me to be. He allowed this"—he waved his hand toward the rubble above and around them— "and He's given me a second chance. I'm going to take it."

Joe didn't say a word.

"When you get out, signal Alan. He'll know how to stabilize this section long enough for me to get back to the hole."

"Come with me."

"I have to hold the beam until you get out. When you're safe and Alan's done what he needs to do, I'll get to the hole. Don't worry. I'm not dying down here today."

Not a chance. He had business to take care of, issues to resolve. A new life to live. One where he loved Kinna no matter what. He'd make things right there too, with God's help and strength.

He steadied his grip on the plank. "Ready?"

"You be careful."

"I'll be fine. I'm Prince Phillip, remember? I defeat the dragon."

The old man shook his head. "Never did understand the Disney thing."

Jimmy jammed the plank as far as possible beneath the beam. "Okay. On three. One, two, three."

The board groaned. Sweat broke out on Jimmy's brow. The beam moved a centimeter, then an inch. Two inches. He grunted. "Hurry."

Joe scooted out.

"Run! Run for the hole." Jimmy squeezed the words from between teeth clenched tight.

Joe hobbled toward the light. He glanced back only once. "You're gonna make it, boy?" A question that was meant to be a statement but failed.

"Go!"

Joe ducked and crawled under the low spot.

Jimmy lowered the beam slowly, praying the rubble above wouldn't shift. It did. He steadied the beam.

He could hear his father's feet, running toward the opening in the cavern beyond. Then came the sound of scraping metal and a banging, like a hand slapping the backhoe's bucket. The sound reverberated against the fallen concrete, echoing back to where Jimmy stood. Silence fell, and then came the squeal of the bucket rising. He'd have to get that thing oiled when he got out of here.

Someone shouted. He couldn't make out the words, but it could only mean one thing. Joe was safe. Now he only had to wait for Alan. He could hear the rumble of the dozer above.

His arms started to shake. He wouldn't be able to hold the beam up much longer. He loosened his grip on the plank, bit by bit. The ceiling of rubble trembled above him.

Come on, Alan. Hurry up.

The rumble of the dozer stopped.

Jimmy caught his breath. Alan?

The dozer didn't start up again. Alan had left him to die.

Jimmy dropped the beam and sprinted toward a corner just as the structure collapsed around him.

Kinna felt it before she saw it. The ground shifting, moving, the structure shuddering. The wall the dozer had held trembled. A large slab of concrete tipped and slid into another.

It happened in slow motion. The wall fell toward the dozer. Alan stumbled to safety. Concrete shattered against the dozer's side, tumbled, dropped, crashed into the rubble below. For a moment, only the dust moved.

Then came the second crash.

Jimmy! No! The denial screamed through her mind.

Kinna raced toward the fallen structure. Jimmy was in there. She had to get him out. She was a nurse. She could save him. She could make everything all right.

A hand grabbed her arm just as she reached the edge of the debris and pulled her back.

"Hold on there, missy. It ain't safe."

She turned. The old man from the coffee shop held her arm. What was he doing here? "My husband is in there. Help me!"

The man stared out over the wreckage. For ten long seconds, he said nothing. Then he pointed to a place newly caved in. "Better pray he moved. Where we was is gone."

"Jimmy!" she screamed, but no one answered. She stepped out onto the ruins.

The man pulled her back. She glanced at him and saw tears in his eyes.

He sniffed. "Can't go out there, girl. Not safe. You'll make the whole thing fall in, you with it."

A stone skittered away from her foot, down into the debris below. "But he might still be alive."

From the corner of her vision, she saw a man jump from the

backhoe and hurry toward the edge of the rubble. Other men came too, all shouting Jimmy's name, all with foreheads creased and voices sharp.

And still no one answered.

She ran toward the man from the backhoe. "Dig for him. Dig!" She jabbed her finger toward the backhoe. "Hurry!"

The man shook his head and shouted for Jimmy one more time.

Kinna reached him, grabbed his coat, and shook. "He's got to be okay. He's just got to be. Get him out."

He took her hands, unwound them from his coat, and held them steady. "We gotta know where to dig. Jimmy would have moved away from the unstable area. We just don't know where. If he's near the edge, we can dig him out, but he's got to give us a sign. Do you understand? We have to know where he is."

Half a dozen men shouted Jimmy's name again.

Then they paused, waited.

For nothing.

Kinna groaned, then shouted again. She shouted until her voice was hoarse, but it didn't matter. She was helpless. Hopeless, useless. She clenched her fists and screamed his name again. And then she broke down and sobbed.

Someone touched her arm, the old man again. He looked at her, his face still wet, his eyes red and familiar.

"There's nothing I can do," Kinna told him.

"Just pray."

Pray? All she'd done for the last dozen years was pray and hope. For nothing. Pray for a baby, pray this would be the cycle that answered her prayers. Pray and hope Someone was listening, even though month after month it seemed no one was.

The old man leaned closer and whispered in her ear, "Pray anyway."

Oh God...help.

She looked up and saw Thea coming toward her. God's answer, in the form of an old woman and a scraggly dog.

Kinna closed her eyes and let the tears come. In public for all to see.

It was dark, so dark. And hot. No, cold. Wet. Jimmy moved his fingers. They hurt. He hurt.

Something heavy lay on his back. He tasted dirt. His arm was free, but not his legs or his torso. Something held him in this dark, painful place. Face-down with dust up his nose, clogging his eyes, crawling down his throat.

He touched his forehead. Wet. Sticky. Hot. *I'm bleeding.* The thought came to him slowly, as if from a distance too far to hear.

Where am I?

Trapped. Held by something hard and unforgiving pressed into his back.

He blinked, but it didn't help. The darkness still settled around him, the choking smell of dirt, the heat of heavy concrete.

He heard voices calling, shouting. So very, very far away.

He tried to answer, but the pain in his chest wouldn't let him. It hurt to breathe, hurt to move. Impossible to talk, call out. There was only the pain and the blood. The blood on his hands.

Images formed in his consciousness, fuzzy, out of focus, but there all the same. Kinna sitting with him behind a row of tulips. A puppy named Dragon. The reflection of streetlights off the cold sidewalk, the sound of Air Supply playing behind. A princess in a pink dress. The way her eyes sparkled when he kissed her. The wonder of Kinna's hair against his skin.

His hands broken and bloody after beating his father. Hands stained with shame.

He never could get that blood off his hands.

The image blurred, then sharpened again, only this time they weren't his hands. They were different. Strange. New. These hands had holes…nail holes. He looked again, and his hands were clean. Perfect. Spotless. Someone had taken his shame.

Jesus?

27

That blessed, blessed dog. Kinna dashed away her tears and watched as the mutt trotted lightly over the rubble with its nose down, sniffing for Jimmy. It just had to be smelling for him. The dog zigzagged left, then came back toward her. It paused and whined, then took three more steps and stopped four feet from the edge of the rubble. It sniffed into the corner of the fallen structure.

Kinna held her breath.

The dog barked three wild yips and started to dig.

Thea whooped. "It's found him!"

"How do we know it ain't just barking at a buried bone?" A man called from the edge of the rubble.

Thea shook her head. "That's Jimmy's dog. Tulip knows what she's about, so somebody better start digging."

Another guy slammed the backhoe into gear. "Someone get that Bobcat over here."

A man jumped on the small Bobcat as Kinna raced toward the dog. She stopped at the edge of the debris. The Bobcat rumbled nearer.

Jimmy was down there. Kinna dropped to her knees and started to yank at a huge concrete block. Then, the men were beside her, ranged along the edge of the rubble. As one, they began to lift the outermost concrete pieces and toss them aside. Thea worked at a large block. The old man lifted another with his good arm. The others grunted, pulled, or directed the guy in the backhoe. And beside them, the little Bobcat plucked up heavier pieces in its scoop.

Chaos filled the air in the form of swirling gray dust. It choked her, spat into her eyes, her nose, filtered down her throat. Her eyes watered, blurring her vision. Around her, men grunted and swore, the sounds of their voices mixing with the thud of concrete and the hum of engines. Then came the shrill cry of a seagull, cutting across the rumble of moving concrete and the Bobcat's motor.

Kinna dug until her hands were raw, her fingers chewed by the rough concrete. Bits of blood smeared the rocks, but she didn't care. She kept digging. It didn't matter if her hands were scraped skinless or her breath came in ragged sobs. They had to find Jimmy. They had to.

Please…

Little by little, the pile of debris gave way. The corner became visible, two concrete walls pressed together, still unbroken. Below it, a fallen pillar and a mess of rough stones.

Kinna shouted to the men. "A little more. We're almost there."

The distant whir of a fire engine's siren and the hoot of an ambulance filled the air. Help was coming. But it wouldn't matter. Not unless they could get Jimmy out. Not unless they could reach him.

No one looked at her. They just pawed at the debris, their faces shiny with sweat, their jaws set, determined.

The sound of sirens came closer, then halted. Kinna glanced over her shoulder. The fire truck was here, the ambulance behind it. Men in rescue gear jumped from the vehicles and ran toward them.

The Bobcat grabbed another slab and moved it away.

"Look!" A man's voice came, sharp and fierce. Her head whipped around. Her gaze followed the sound of that shout through the rubble, down into the hole, and she saw it—a pale arm buried deep in the ruins. Jimmy's arm.

She shouted his name.

Nothing moved.

"He's there! I can see him."

Men pressed around her.

The old man signaled toward the backhoe. "Get that machine over here. We got a pillar to move."

The man in the backhoe stuck his head out its window. "What about another cave in?"

The old man shook his head. "The corner's steady."

"Somebody spot me."

A man in a yellow bandana stepped up and motioned to the man in the backhoe. "Over here, then bring the bucket down."

Kinna knelt at the edge of the hole. "Jimmy!"

The arm didn't move. She could see blood, dark against the gray concrete stones. Too much blood. Her stomach lodged in her throat. Someone knelt beside her, took her hand, and squeezed. She glanced up. Thea.

"I'm praying."

Kinna swallowed and nodded. There were no words. Not here, not now.

The bucket lowered, turned, caught, and pulled the pillar off her husband's still body. He lay face-down, his body twisted.

The backhoe pushed the pillar to the side before the bucket swung toward a group of men. The man inside shouted. "Someone get down there. Let's bring him up."

Two firemen grabbed the bucket as it lowered back into the hole. At the bottom, they let go and squatted beside Jimmy.

Kinna held her breath.

One looked up. "He's alive. Not conscious, but alive. Lost a lot of blood."

The two men pulled off the remaining stones, then lifted Jimmy carefully and put him in the backhoe's bucket. When Jimmy reached the surface, the paramedics rushed forward. So did Kinna.

He looked so pale, so broken. Her Jimmy. The one she'd danced with on the sidewalk, built sandcastles with on the beach, the one she'd thought to manipulate with divorce papers. She'd been such a fool.

The paramedics lifted Jimmy from the bucket and placed him on a stretcher, then took him to the ambulance. Kinna stayed with him, so close she could see the pulse in his neck. It beat so slowly, but it was there. It was still there.

Oh God, please don't let him die.

The paramedics slid him in the ambulance and hooked up the oxygen. Kinna crawled in with him. With quick, efficient movements, they worked to stop Jimmy's bleeding.

But there was so much blood. Gashes on his cheek, his arm, leg, pelvis. His jeans were dark with it, his shirt stained. And still he didn't move.

Kinna took his hand in hers. "Hang on, Jimmy."

A paramedic reached to shut the door. Before he could, a hand darted into the opening. Thea's face appeared in the doorway.

"Let me in."

The paramedic pulled at the door.

Thea's gaze caught Kinna's. "You have to trust me. I need to be here."

Kinna nodded. "Make room."

The paramedics stared at her.

"I'm a nurse. Make room."

The paramedics scooted closer to Jimmy. Thea pushed in.

Another hand appeared in the doorway. This time, it belonged to the old man. He didn't try to get into the ambulance. He just leaned in and grabbed Jimmy's stretcher.

The paramedic batted his hand away. "Let go, sir."

The old man scowled. "Don't give him the wrong blood."

"What?"

His gaze pierced Kinna's. "You listen to me, girl. He's got funny blood. Don't let them give him the regular stuff."

Kinna's grip loosened on Jimmy. "I know." Fear twisted in her gut and lodged there.

Thea touched the man's arm. "Don't worry."

He stared at her for a moment and nodded. He let go and backed away.

The paramedics shut the door, and the ambulance's engine roared to life. They cut through the top of Jimmy's pants and worked to stopped the bleeding near his pelvis.

Thea moved closer to Kinna. "He's going to be all right." The words came low but clear, confident. The same words Kinna herself had said a hundred times to patients' families. Sometimes she was right, sometimes not. How empty those words sounded now. How useless.

She pressed her hand over a gash on Jimmy's shoulder. Her teeth clenched as she willed the bleeding to stop. She spared a glance toward Thea. "All right? How can you know that?"

Thea rolled up her sleeve and pointed to the thick blood vessel that ran down the middle of her arm. "Because I know why I have come."

28

Kinna paced the hospital waiting room. If she hadn't been such a fool and stolen those vials, she could be in there now, making sure...

Jimmy was in good hands. Doctor Lim was a great doctor.

She reached the end of the waiting room and turned. Another lap, back and forth, counting steps, measuring breaths. Jimmy had been in there too long. She crossed her arms over her chest and stared at the light pink wall before her. Pink was supposed to be calming. It wasn't. Her gaze slid to the picture of the opening orchid hanging over the line of chairs. The orchid was supposed to bring peace. It didn't.

She kept walking.

Six steps later, she found herself at the other end of the room. She turned. If there was one thing the last three long, endless hours had taught her, it was that Mom was wrong. So very wrong. Not only could you *not* do anything you set your mind to, you shouldn't.

It wasn't about setting your mind at all. It was about setting your heart. She knew, because for three hours, hers had been breaking, crumbling, and what she'd discovered inside wasn't pretty.

When it came to setting your heart, you only had two choices. You could set your heart on God, on His plans, His dreams, His will. Or you could grasp after your own.

She'd been a grasper, so afraid her faith would fail if everything didn't turn out like she'd planned. She grasped and clung and filled her life with fear, and all that grasping hadn't saved her faith at all. It hadn't done a single thing except lead her here, with Jimmy's blood all over her shirt, and her shoes making squeaky sounds on the carpet.

She'd set her heart, all right, and become someone she didn't even recognize. And there was nothing she could do about it, nothing she could do to make things right. She could only wait. Just wait, just trust, just pray.

Jimmy's life was in God's hands. Just like the life of the baby she never had. Just like her life.

Kinna sat on a chair, drew up her knees, and wrapped her arms around them. She clenched her hands together.

Grasping.

She looked at her white-knuckled fists. She'd been clutching like that for a long time, so long that she didn't know how to let go. Not wholly, not completely. But all her work, her clutching, grabbing, planning, and fighting led only to this barrenness. To this empty place called a waiting room. Waiting, just waiting.

When being with Jimmy was where she belonged. Where she'd always belonged. How could she not have seen that? How could she not have seen that she was barren not because she was childless, but because she had emptied her soul of love? Real love, the kind that sacrificed, served, cared, put others first. That was true barrenness, when a heart forgot how to love.

And now, she could lose Jimmy too.

There had to be something she could do.

"How do you spell love, Kinna?"

I don't know.

Not G-I-V-E-M-E, but G-I-V-E-U-P.

Give up?

Let go.

No.

Die.

I don't know how. The Bible said that whoever wanted to save his life would lose it, but whoever lost his life because of Jesus would save it. Because how did it profit a man, a woman, if she gained the whole world, everything she wanted, but lost herself, lost her soul, lost love?

And what was her life but her dreams, her plans—those things she'd always clung to?

That's what it meant to die. It meant giving up her dreams in order to live His. It meant doing what was right and good. It meant believing that God loved her even when it didn't feel like it. It meant facing doubts, living them, and choosing to believe in love anyway. God's love. It meant living the life God gave her, even when it was not the life she'd dreamed.

It meant she had to trust God's love enough to surrender.

Lord, help me…

A door swung open at the far side of the room. Kinna stood. A doctor entered, still in his scrubs, his mask pulled down to his neck. Kinna's heart leaped to her throat.

"Sit down, Kinna."

No. Oh God, no. She slid into the chair. "Jeff, don't tell me…"

The doctor came closer. "He's stable."

"And?"

"He'll have more stitches than I care to count, but he's going to make it."

Kinna let out her breath, then frowned. "But? I hear a 'but' coming. Be straight with me, Jeff. What's wrong?"

The doctor sat in the chair beside her. "It's his back. Crushed vertebrae and I don't know what else, not unless I get in there."

"So get in there!"

"I'd like to, but…" He paused. His voice lowered. "But it's not *critical.*"

Kinna gripped the arms of the chair. "I get it. He has no insurance, so you're not authorized to proceed."

The doctor shook his head. "Not without a prepayment. You know the rules."

She certainly did. Knew them too well, and the price for breaking them. "How much?"

He sighed. "Well, you should talk to billing, but I can tell you it'll be about fifteen thousand." He stood. "I want to do that surgery now, Kinna. I don't think we should wait. But I know you don't have fifteen grand lying around either." He fiddled with the mask at his neck, then rubbed his hand over his face. "I don't know what to tell you."

"Do the surgery."

"You heard me. I can't."

"I have the money." Fifteen thousand dollars on her brand new credit card account—the one she'd gotten as a last ditch grasp at having a baby, the one she had planned to use for the in vitro procedure that would finally secure her dreams. Fifteen thousand dollars acquired through a desperate call to Visa. *Zero percent for six months.*

A chill raced up her spine. That was no coincidence. That was God. He was helping her let go, helping her give up the credit card money for Jimmy, give up her dreams and take up His. He was helping her love.

She didn't know how she'd pay back the money with her job gone and Jimmy hurt, but she knew God intended it for this. Intended her to lay it down—not just the money, but the dream of a baby that money represented.

"I can pay."

"Thank God."

"Yes. I do." She rose and placed her hand on Dr. Lim's arm. "Just take good care of him for me, will you? I'm going down to the administration office. You'll have your approval to proceed by the time you rescrub."

Dr. Lim nodded. "Your husband is a strong man. He's going to make it through all this just fine."

Kinna smiled. Yes, Jimmy was strong. But God was stronger. He would save Jimmy. He would save them both.

They've brought me to this little room and placed me on a vinyl bed. A needle sticks into my arm and dark red blood flows.

I stare at the white ceiling and remember Kinna's face as I walked away. She didn't understand, and I didn't know how to explain. Lan negative. A rare blood type. They won't have enough to replace what he's lost.

But I do. I have the same rare blood.

Send away the cats, because I'm not a crazy old woman after all. I finally understand why I'm here. Why I've come. This isn't a dream.

Jesus says to save my life, I must lose it. I must give it away. I know what I have to do.

I watch the blood flowing out of me and filling the clear container.

A nurse comes closer. "Are you all right, ma'am?"

I'm not, but I don't tell her that. I don't tell her I feel as cold as ice, as cold as the ocean in April. I don't tell her I feel my breath slipping away. I don't tell her I feel as if I am drowning again.

Because Jimmy will live. He has to.

I touch the birthmark behind my ear, the small spot shaped like a flat seashell. I can't see it, but I know it's there. When I was little, Mom called it her special kissing spot. Then she'd give me a dozen loud, exaggerated kisses and tickle my tummy until I squealed with laughter.

But that was a long time ago. Or maybe not so long. It seems like just yesterday. Today. Tomorrow. I can't tell anymore.

My breath becomes shallow, and still the blood drips. I close my eyes, and a memory comes to me. A scene from the past, from the future. I watch it like a movie across the screen of my mind. A man, a woman, and a little girl on the beach. The little girl is me. Years ago, when cars still ran on gasoline, letters were sent with stamps, and the mysteries of infertility were mostly unsolved.

That day, the sun shimmered on the sandy beach and capped the water with blinding brightness. The little girl ran along the water's edge with a scraggly mutt at her side. Light danced off her caramel-colored hair as she turned and waved behind her.

"Hurry up, Mom. Hurry, Daddy! The pirate ships are coming in."

"We're coming, Aletheia." The woman smiled and moved closer to her husband.

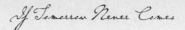

He grinned down at her, a sparkle of mischief gleaming in his eyes. "She has the patience of her mother."

The woman laughed. "And the imagination of her dad."

A flock of gulls flew overhead, filling the sky with the sound of their chatter.

The child paused, then picked up something from the sand. She rushed back toward them. "Look, Mommy, a pink shell." She held it up in her small hands. Her face glowed.

Her father took the shell between his fingers and held it up to the light. "This is no shell. This is the bed of a tiny mermaid princess, fashioned from a perfect pearl."

Aletheia's eyes grew wide. "Like Ariel?"

He chuckled. "Just like Ariel."

Aletheia snatched the shell back and clutched it to her chest. Then she turned and pointed. "There's our rock. Let's go play. Come on, Tulip." She patted her leg and ran toward the dog, calling over her shoulder. "I wanna build in the sand. Okay?"

She and the dog bounded toward the big rock tucked in their special little cove, and she dropped to her knees beside the boulder. Tulip lay down beside her.

Her parents joined her. Her father released her mother's hand and squatted next to her. "All right, Thea. What should we build today?"

She scooped up a handful of sand and tossed it in the air. "A big castle, just like the one Ariel lived in with Prince Eric." She sat back on her legs and looked up at her dad with big, blue eyes. "I'll be Ariel, okay?"

He ruffled her hair. "And I'm Prince Eric?"

Her mother put her hands on her hips. "There's no way I'm going to be that ugly octopus, Ursula."

Aletheia giggled. "You be the beautiful mermaid queen." She pushed sand into a pile. "You sit right there on the rock throne."

Her mother settled onto the big boulder. "Your daddy builds the best sandcastles in the world."

"Really, Daddy? Show me how."

He placed his big hands around her small ones. "The trick to castle building is to get just the right amount of sand and water."

Her mother reached out and brushed her fingers over a bit of sand on the child's cheek. "You know, Thea, they say there's something magical about this spot."

Aletheia glanced up at her.

"They say there's a little piece of heaven on earth hidden behind this big stone on the beach. Sometimes you can find princes and princesses here. Sons and daughters of the Great King."

Aletheia caught her breath. "I thought this place felt like heaven." She flipped back her hair to reveal a small red birthmark behind her left ear. A birthmark in the shape of a perfect seashell.

I open my eyes now. Little Aletheia is safe. They're all safe. My children, grandchildren. All the lives that will come from the two people in the locket.

Tomorrow. Today. Yesterday. They mix and merge, and I sense myself stepping into that strange, gray place where time has no meaning, where today touches tomorrow and reaches back to yesterday. Where only the fog is real. Only God. Only the knowledge that tomorrow starts today. It starts now.

I have finished what I came to do. I helped them remember.

I helped them to live. My pictures in the locket, my parents. Kinna and Jimmy Henley.

Someday, they will know it was their own faces that looked back at them from the silver. Someday, they will remember that we met before.

And now I can let the ocean, the fog, the draining away of my blood, take me back, take me forward, to where I belong.

Jimmy opened his eyes to a white ceiling reflecting dim yellow light. He moved his head and saw a pastel curtain held by thin chains, a TV attached to the ceiling, and a plastic pitcher in dull mauve. He pressed his head back into the pillow. He'd done it, then. Done what he had to do and lived.

This place was too ugly to be heaven, and it certainly wasn't hell. He took a deep breath and felt the dryness in his throat, the scratchiness of air through his windpipe. *So this is what it feels like to be a man. A real man.*

He tried to move his arm. *It feels stiff.* He almost smiled.

He focused on his feet, wiggling his toes. They moved. He'd be all right, then. He had a lot to do, so much that he wanted to try, to experience, to dare. Infertility treatments with Kinna, maybe a day out kayaking with his dad. Dancing on the beach with his beautiful wife, taking that old dog out for a run. And they'd need him on the Petersen job. Especially now.

He peeked under the sheet and frowned. From the looks of things, it would take a while to get back to dancing shape, but he would do it, do it all. God had made him new. He was clean, healed, whole. Maybe not physically, but for the first time in his life, he was right on the inside, in his soul. He'd believed in Jesus since he was kid, since Kinna had told him about a Father who loved him and his grandma had taken him to that little church on the corner, but he never really understood. Never grasped that the hands marked by the nail holes made by his sin also had taken his shame. There was no more blood on Jimmy's hands. None at all.

He wanted to tell Kinna he could be the man God wanted him to be. Because with God, all things were possible, and finally, he believed it. All things…because that's what love did, it made the impossible true.

A knock sounded at the door.

Jimmy reached for the bed controls and tilted the bed up so he could see an edge of the door through the curtain. "Come in."

Light splashed through the opening as the door swung open. Someone glanced in. "He's awake." Jimmy recognized Mai's voice. "And you no worry. Our collection went well. Construction site, hospital, down at the coffee shop. You have friends."

"Friends?" That was Kinna's voice, soft now, gentle. The way he remembered it used to be.

"You think life is barren, but it is not. Many people care about you and Jimmy. Life is full."

"I know." He could hear the smile in Kinna's tone. "I know that now." Her voice became louder as she moved past Mai and through the doorway. "Do you think he wants to see me?"

"No stupid talk. Go see your husband."

A couple tentative footsteps squeaked against the floor, and the curtain pulled back. Kinna peeked around it. "Jimmy?"

He looked at her, his Kinna, his wife. She was beautiful with her shirt mussed and bloody and a funny dirt splotch on her nose. She hadn't bothered to change or wash. His careful, determined wife, still in her grubby clothes with dirt on her face. For him. All for him.

He grinned. "So, Kinna Ann Henley, you gonna just stand there blocking the sun, or you wanna play?"

A smile touched her lips and spread to her eyes. "You remember."

"Of course, I do. But that wasn't the first time we met."

"Sure it was."

"Nope. Let me tell you about the first time." And he did, every detail, every moment, every color, including the bright splash of tulips.

She stood at the foot of his bed, and as he told it, her eyes misted. "Oh, Jimmy…"

"A man remembers the first time he fell in love."

She smiled. "They say you're going to be okay."

"I am now."

She looked at him. He looked at her. And in her eyes, he saw pride, respect, and love. She didn't have to say a word, because he could read it. She hadn't looked at him that way in a long, long time, but she was looking now, with her heart in her eyes.

"Come here, Kinna."

She came toward him, her hands outstretched. She took his hand in hers and kissed it. "I've been such a fool, Jimmy."

He reached up with his other arm—slowly and painfully—and touched her lips. "Shh. We've got a second chance now. This time, we'll do it right. I love you, Kinna Henley."

"I know. And I don't deserve it."

He brushed back a bit of her hair, felt it in his fingers. "None of us does."

She reached into her pocket and pulled out a locket. The locket. She laid it on the bed beside him. "But we can choose to love. We can choose to be happy."

He put his hand over hers. So she'd met the old woman too. And she'd seen the faces in the locket, just as he had. That seemed right somehow, fitting. He squeezed her fingers. "We'll choose to be the people in the locket."

She leaned over and kissed him, and suddenly, he was the fairy tale prince after all.

Epilogue

The sun is shining. I sense it on my face, warming my weathered skin. I open my eyes to see light splashing across the floor in front of me. My chair creaks. Or is it my bones? I've fallen asleep in the chair again, watching Mom as she naps.

Only she's not napping. She's watching me and smiling. Her face wrinkles until I can barely see her eyes, but I can tell they're sparkling.

I blink and glance through the curtains to the sky outside. Clear and sunny, the ocean a bright blue in the distance.

It was a dream. Only a dream after all.

Then I hear my grandchildren playing in the backyard. The swing set squeaks. Little Ellie laughs. The twins are playing ring around the rosie, and Caleb is shooting his water pistol. I can tell by his yells of, "Gotcha!" followed by a squeal and the fast patter of small feet. The youngest calls out for Grammie, and I grin.

I want to rise, to go to them. I want to sing with them, dance, play. And I will soon. For now, I settle for the sounds of their joy. I listen and know I am home. At last.

My mother's voice, soft and wheezy, floats toward me like soap bubbles blown by the wind. "You've left it behind." Her smile widens as she says it, and she chuckles.

I touch my neck. The locket is gone. I stand and peer under my chair, searching.

"You won't find it."

I glance around the room, but there are no cats, not a single one. There's only my boxer, Cisco, lying on the mat and little Ellie's goldfish in its bowl in the corner.

Thank You, God, for dogs.

A happy scream rises from outside. The dog gets up, shakes himself, and ambles toward the front door. Then I hear the door slam.

Dad appears at the bedroom door. He's bent now, his back bowed, his head tilted on his shoulders, but he can still drive the big Caterpillar. At least that's what he tells us. Mom won't let him, of course, so he settles for the riding lawnmower once a week, and he's happy.

Today, though, I see he's been to the store. A bouquet of bright flowers peeks from behind his back. Tulips.

He totters toward Mom and pulls out the flowers.

As always, she feigns surprise. "A year passed already?"

"And you're looking just as beautiful."

They say that every year.

Mom gestures toward me with her head. "It's happened."

He nods. "Finally." He turns to me and winks. "Did you enjoy the Rollerblades?"

I take a step back. "But...but it was only a dream."

Dad wobbles over to the dresser and pulls something from the top drawer. He opens his hand, and I see a locket gleaming against his palm. An old locket, more worn than I remember mine. He opens it.

And there are the faces, unfaded, as sharp as they were when my dream began.

I walk toward him.

His arm trembles. Bits of sand trickle from the locket, and I catch the tiny grains in my hand, brown and gray against my skin. Tiny testimonies to what I can't believe. "But, but...it's impossible."

Mom speaks, quietly, slowly. "Thea Jean, with God..."

I finish the sentence. "...all things are possible."

And then I understand. He loves us that much, loved them, loved me so much that He made the impossible true. To save us all.

Because of that, because of Him, tomorrow has come at last.

Acknowledgments

Bringing a story from a nebulous concept to a printed book is always a team effort. And I thank God for the fabulous team He has given me. Here, I'd like to thank just a few of the team members who helped so much in the process of developing *If Tomorrow Never Comes*.

First, to my husband, Bryan. Thank you for your constant support and the sacrifices you make to give me the time to write the stories God gives me.

To Janelle Schneider, my first reader (besides Bryan), for great tips and for giving me the courage to send the thing in.

To Lisa Bergren. Thanks for your excellent comments and suggestions on how to make this story stronger, better, and closer to the vision God had for it.

To Julee Schwarzburg. It is always such a pleasure to work with you in all the moments of the editing process. Thanks for all you do!

To the rest of the fine team at WaterBrook Multnomah who took this story from words in a file to a finished book on the shelves. What a blessing it is to partner with you!

And finally, thanks to you, readers. Thanks for giving me a reason to write, for your notes of encouragement, and for sharing the journey with me. May God fill your lives with wonder and your hands with great books!

Dear Reader,

Thank you for traveling with me through Kinna and Jimmy's adventure to discover the extent of God's wondrous love, even when circumstances make it seem as if that love is distant. Their story has particular significance to me since I've personally dealt with infertility for most of my adult years. Through the infertility journey God has taught me some of the most profound lessons of my life. One of those lessons is that when God says, "For my thoughts are not your thoughts, neither are your ways my ways" (Isaiah 55:8), He really means it!

While I was writing *If Tomorrow Never Comes,* I was also undergoing some final infertility treatments. Those treatments did not result in a much-hoped-for baby, but rather in four miscarriages.

The miscarriages were particularly difficult because before we began our last round of treatments, I'd asked God for one thing: "Please, God, just no more miscarriages. They're too awful, too painful. Spare me that."

But God didn't answer my prayer the way I'd hoped. Hardly! Instead He made me face the pain, live the nightmare, and in it find a glimmer of breathtaking wonder.

And yet, in living through that pain, I also found that I'm not the first mother to stand by, helpless, as her nightmare came true, as her prayers fell unanswered.

Mary, Jesus's mom, lived her nightmare too. Can you imagine watching your firstborn son arrested, beaten, spat upon, and then nailed to a cross to die? That was never a part of Mary's plans. I know because she prayed too, a beautiful prayer from Luke 1:46–55 that often gets read at Christmastime. She prayed about how God brings down rulers, helps the humble, brings food to the hungry, and brings renewed glory to Israel. That was her vision for what it meant for Jesus to come into the world.

She would have never thought that prayer would end with her son dying while she stood at the foot of a Roman cross. Right there, so close, as the blood dripped, and her son's anguished cries echoed in her ears. Her son. The son she loved. What could be more gut-wrenching and horrendous? Even the sky turned black.

Yet, it is in that horrific moment—the one that encapsulates the very epitome of what it means for plans and hopes to go awry, to die— that we find the most incredible, wondrous, breathtaking act of God of all time. It is the moment of redemption, of glory, of splendor, of the answer to all the prayers and hopes from the beginning of time until now. It is where we find the salvation of the world, when all our dreams came true.

Yes, the precise instant when all Mary's hopes died, when all her plans came to nothing, became the moment of answer, when truly the poor were provided for, a ruler of evil was overthrown, and mercy was given, just as she prayed all those years before. It was a glimpse of ultimate glory.

I think it may always be that way. That there, at the very place where our dreams don't come true, where our expectations are shattered—that is where God is standing in the greatest power. Those are the times, the places that change the world, where we find a depth and wonder deeper than we ever dared to dream.

So my hope for you, my friend, is that you will see the God of glory when life doesn't go as you planned. That you'll discover His riches in the bare fields of life. That you'll glimpse His wonder and be caught breathless at the depths of His love for you.

If you were touched by Jimmy and Kinna's journey in *If Tomorrow Never Comes,* I hope you'll send me a note and tell me about it! You can e-mail me at marlo@marloschalesky.com, or send a note to me via my publisher at:

Marlo Schalesky

c/o WaterBrook Multnomah Publishing Group

12265 Oracle Boulevard, Suite 200

Colorado Springs, CO 80921

And to find out more about me and my books, as well as tips on surviving the infertility journey, please visit my Web site at www.marloschalesky.com, and my "Tales of Wonder" blog at www.marloschalesky.blogspot.com. I'd be delighted to hear from you!

1. In Chapter 1, Kinna believes she can bury her guilt by burying the Perganol vials. Does it work? What's a better way to deal with guilt?

2. Kinna believes God can prove His love by answering her prayers in the way she wants them to be answered. Do you think "answered prayer" is an appropriate way to determine God's love? How do you measure God's love in your life?

3. Consider this Bible verse from Jeremiah 29:11: "'For I know the plans I have for you,' declares the LORD, 'plans to prosper you and not to harm you, plans to give you hope and a future.'" Now, reread this verse with the emphasis on "I." How does this change your understanding of the verse?

4. When faced with situations that seem out of their control, Jimmy and Kinna react in opposite ways—Jimmy walks away, Kinna digs in to try to make things turn out the way she wants. How do both these responses exemplify a lack of trust in God? What would be a better way for each of them to respond? Do you relate more with Jimmy's reaction or with Kinna's?

5. Kinna's mother taught her that you can do anything you set your mind to. That's a common saying in today's culture,

but is it true? And should we do anything and everything to try to make our own dreams come true?

6. Given Thea's true identity, what would have happened if Jimmy and Kinna had called it quits on their marriage? What would have been the long-term consequences of that decision, not just for themselves but for others? If you're married, consider your own marriage. How will the choices you make today affect future generations?

7. Early in the story, Thea says that her mother taught her that sometimes not getting what you want is the best thing for you. Do you agree? Why or why not? How did Kinna learn this lesson through the story? Looking back over your life, can you think of things you once wanted but it turned out that it was good that you didn't get them? How do you think God was involved in those times of failure and disappointment?

8. Near the end of the story, Kinna discovers that she is very much like the surf, beating herself against the Rock. She also realizes that it's only when she casts herself onto that Rock (God) that she can be filled with light, life, and color. Have there been times in your life when you felt as if you were beating yourself against God? Can you see how He was shaping and changing you during those times of brokenness?

9. In the end, Kinna finds that letting go of her dreams to embrace God's plan cannot be accomplished by a pure act of her will. She needs help releasing her goals and plans. What help does God give her to allow her to finally let go? Is there something that you want very badly that God is

not giving you? How might He work in your life to help you to release your dreams to Him?

10. The Bible tells us that with God all things are possible. Do you think that verse applies to the story's surprise ending? In light of how God became man and died on the cross for us, does it surprise you how far He went in this story to rescue Jimmy and Kinna and save their marriage? What does God's commitment to them tell you about His love for you?

HERE'S A SNEAK PEEK AT MARLO SCHALESKY'S NEXT NOVEL, *SHADES OF MORNING.* COMING SPRING 2010!

Snow fell like fat angels fluttering to earth. Emmit sat on the snowbank, his eyes closed, his head tipped back. He was a snowflake too, drifting on the breeze. Cold nibbled at his wings. Ice kissed his lashes. He stuck out his tongue and caught a flake. It melted. Why did the snow always go away just when he thought he'd finally got some? He reached up and scratched his too-small ears with a too-small hand. Then he adjusted his thick, coke-bottle glasses.

Today, he was fifteen years old. That was a big number. They all said so. He was a big boy now. All grown up.

The snow fell in heavier clumps. He opened his eyes and waited.

The pretty light would be coming soon. The big whirring one on top of the truck that picked up the garbage from the cans on the street. He liked the light. Round and round. Round and round. It would come.

A screen door slammed. He looked back, over his shoulder. A puffy white coat stood on the doorstep with a matching hat perched atop wisps of brown hair. The coat waved.

Emmit waved back. That's how a mom should look. White coat and a pink smile peeking from between collar and hat.

"Mighty cold out here." She motioned toward the snow as she spoke.

Emmit grinned. "I wait for pretty light."

She nodded and trudged to the mailbox by the street. The box creaked when she opened it.

Then the pretty light came with a chug, a squeal, and the grinding of gears. The light turned and turned, made its way around the corner and up the street.

"Pretty light! Pretty light!" Emmit called out to her, but she didn't turn.

Instead, she stood there, hunched over a stack of white envelopes in her gloved hand.

The wind gusted.

The whirring light rumbled closer. Closer.

Then it happened. So slowly, yet too fast for him to move to stop it. An envelope skittered from her hand and blew into the street. She went after it.

He could see the moment when her boot hit ice, when it slipped from under her. Envelopes mixed with the angels in the air. Fluttering, flying, drifting on the breeze.

Then a terrible squeal. A dull thud.

The light stopped.

And next came a moment of pure silence.

Later other lights came. Red and blue and more yellow. Lights on a black and white car. Lights on a big red fire engine. Lights on a white van with the letters A-M-B-U-L-A-N-C-E printed in big letters on the side.

They weren't pretty lights. Emmit didn't like them at all.

He was cold now. But no one noticed him. They just buzzed around the new lights like bugs. Buzzed, and shouted, and flew away.

He laid back in the snow, moved his arms and legs up and down, up and down. Three times to make the image of an angel in the bank.

A perfect angel. A snow angel. Just for her. Because she had been what a mom should be. And she was going home soon.

The new lights left.

And then, the snow stopped falling.

Marnie Helen Wittier hated baby showers. She also hated her middle name, but that was another story. What mattered now was that despite her intense dislike of powder pink balloons, little crocheted socks, and cheap plastic baby bottles, she was now weaving in and out of hand-made tables at her own coffee shop offering flowered-dressed women fresh cookies and specialty lattes.

The only thing worse would have been if she had to wear one of those foo-foo dresses. But a gal had to draw the line somewhere. If not at pink balloons and pastel teacups, then at least at swaying dresses and, gasp, high heels. She wouldn't be caught dead in heels.

But she could put up with pretty tulips on the tables, the pink and white streamers, and that ridiculous It's a Girl! papier-mâché sign, because after all, this shower was for Kinna Henley. And if anyone deserved the perfect baby shower, it was that woman. After all last year's troubles piled onto years of infertility, Kinna had earned the best shower Marnie could think of. That's the only reason she'd smiled and said "of course" when those ladies from the church asked to hold the event here.

Still, that didn't stop Marnie from snatching a pink napkin, scrawling the words "hosting a baby shower…what was I thinking???" on it, and stuffing it in her pocket. The napkin would go into her box of regrets later. A reminder to never, ever to do anything this stupid again.

Marnie delivered her last latte to a woman dressed in a particularly agonizing shade of fuchsia, then hurried back to her spot behind the coffee bar. Her reflection shot back at her from the mirror behind the bar—short, spiked hair, dyed jet black, and dark plum eyeshadow to match. The look would have worked perfectly with a nose ring, except she couldn't stand to get one. How on earth did people blow their noses with that thing sticking in there? So she'd settled for an extra sterling silver stud in her ear and called it good. She supposed she ought to try out a more conservative look, now that she was turning thirty-five, but so far she hadn't got up the nerve. Besides, it was too fun shocking the old ladies at church.

She grinned, then stuck her tongue out at the image in the mirror. There, that was more like it. Marnie Wittier was not going to let one baby shower get her down.

She put her hands on her hips and turned back toward the room. Half was a coffee shop, the other half a small bookstore. Her favorite things: books and coffee. And people enjoying both. Right now the crowd of pink-cheeked church women were gathered on one side of the coffee shop while a few customers lingered on the other.

Kinna was opening gifts. A hundred little pink packages with little pink outfits and little pink blankets and little pink ribbons and bows. At least the baby was a girl. Marnie could handle a shower full of pinks and yellows. But not blue. Lord knew she'd never be able to face blue.

On her right, Marcus wandered the aisles of the book section, straightening and shelving the latest box of Christian fiction she'd ordered. He had an earring, in his eyebrow, not his nose, and his hair stood out in all directions. Good kid. Honest. Even if his head looked like the wrong end of a mop. He grinned at her, and she smiled back.

Old Joe cleaned the table they would use for a book signing that evening. And just coming through the door was the new girl from Oklahoma. Poor thing, mother named her Daisy. Daisy from Oklahoma, with corn cob colored hair and cornflower blue eyes. She'd be lucky if she survived two weeks in California. But everyone deserved a chance. Even a girl named Daisy.

Marnie sighed and gathered up some cookies from the tray on the counter. She glanced toward her employees and customers. They were her friends, her family. What a family should have been. Not that she knew anything about that. Foster homes didn't teach her a whole fat lot about family. But she was great at packing a suitcase in forty-five seconds flat. So the whole foster home thing wasn't a total waste.

Laughter drifted from the group of women. Marnie smiled. She couldn't help it. Yeah, this was a baby shower. And yeah, that woman with the unnaturally pitched voice was wearing heels that looked like they could kill a rhino. And there was entirely too much pink and pastel in her usually-hip coffee shop. But it was worth it to see the change in Kinna Henley. And not just in the size of the woman's belly, but in her eyes. In her soul. Something had happened last year. A miracle, she said. Well, Marnie didn't know much about miracles. Mistakes maybe. And disasters. And huge, monstrous mess-ups. But miracles? Those were for other people. Good people. Like Kinna and Jimmy. Not for single, coffee shop owners who had run away from home a long time ago.

Don't worry, God, I'm not looking for any miracles. Her gaze shot up to the ceiling, and she winked.

Half a second later, the floor rolled. The walls shook. Glasses jiggled, and one stack of paper cups tipped and fell. Marnie widened her stance and allowed the ground to rumble beneath her.

Conversation stopped, and in the jingling quiet came a sharp squeal. Daisy. The floor stilled. Voices took up where they'd left off. And life rolled on, just as before. Except for the cornflower girl huddled beneath the table.

Marnie suppressed her grin as she sauntered toward Daisy and helped the girl up from beneath the shiny table. You could always tell the out-of-staters. Poor kid.

The girl's eyes were as big as pumpkins. "Th-that was a big one, wasn't it?"

Marnie patted her arm, then cocked her head toward the church women. "Listen."

Then the numbers came.

"Four point three." That guess came from Kinna.

"Naw, that was at least a five point six."

"Five point zero even, mark my words."

A Vietnamese woman named Mai stood up, though you could barely tell she was standing. "What earthquake?" She shook her head. "I no feel a thing. You white girls are such pansies."

They all laughed.

Then a single, old, trembling hand rose from amid the group. Josephina.

Marnie leaned closer to Daisy. "Are you listening? Here it comes."

Josephina's quavering voice silenced the others. "Four point eight." She stuck her gray head out from the group of women. "Turn on the radio, *mija*."

Marnie clicked on the news. After a few minutes, it came. A deep-timbered voice saying, "Reports of a four point eight earthquake centered outside Castroville," not too far from Marnie's in Pacific Grove.

Everyone clapped, including the customers on the far side of the room.

Marnie put a finger under Daisy's chin and closed the girl's mouth.

Daisy's tone dropped to a whisper. "How does she do that?"

Marnie chuckled. "She's lived in Monterey County since her *familia* came over the border in the early thirties. Rumor has it Josephina was three years old. And she hasn't set foot out of the county since. Been here for every last earthquake that's shook the coast. The woman's a phenomenon." She slapped her hands together and raised her voice over the dwindling applause. "Okay, Josephina's special tea for everyone, on the house."

They all cheered.

It had taken Marnie eight tries to get the tea just right. "You have to make it just like *mi madre* used to make it," Josephina kept saying, and ever since it had been a customer favorite. Marnie's special mix.

The bell jingled from the front door. Marnie looked up. A purple-shirted man pushed through the opening. He turned. No, not a man, just a kid. A pimply-faced boy with a silly purple hat to match his plum purple shirt, with an electronic clipboard balanced on his arm.

He waved at her. "Hey, Marnie."

She lifted her eyebrows. "Scott? You got a new job?"

He grinned and pointed at some tiny lettering on his shirt. "We do it faster."

Marnie stepped toward him. "Who are you looking for?"

"You."

Marnie blew her bangs off her forehead with a quick puff of air. Thank goodness. She'd been waiting and waiting for that new bean grinder from Italy. She rubbed her hands together. "Well, where is it?"

Scott pulled a slim envelope from beneath the clipboard and held it out to her. "Here ya go."

"That's not a bean grinder."

"Huh?"

Figured. "That it? Just an envelope?"

"Yep. Sign here."

Marnie took the plastic pen, signed, and watched as Scott tucked the clipboard back under his arm and strode toward the door. He threw another jaunty wave over his shoulder.

"Got a new toffee nut," she called after him. "Come back later and try it out."

"New books too?"

"A whole shipment came in just this morning."

"It's a date." The door thudded shut as Scott left.

A series of ooo's and ahh's rose from the women. Marnie glanced toward them. Kinna was holding up a complete set of pink onesies. Striped pink, flowered pink, pink polka dots, and even one with little pink monkeys. Good grief. Call out the pink police.

She turned away and reached for the letter. It was in a beige linen envelope, heavy, official. Expensive. Who would be sending her something like that? She flipped it over.

The air escaped the room. Time sucked in an empty breath. And Marnie sensed her world tipping around her. *No…* Slowly she extended her finger and touched the fancy attorney's logo on the envelope's upper left corner. Her arm moved as she traced the names beneath. His name. But it couldn't be. Shouldn't be. Must not be. And yet…

Marnie blew out a long breath. The earthquake had come. The real one, more real than any earth tremor, than any tipping cups, than walls that shuddered and stopped. A single logo, a single name. They rocked her world. And if she were to measure, she'd call it an eight point zero.

She closed her eyes. *It's not real. It can't be.* Her life was good now. Finally. She was surrounded by people who cared. They cared because they didn't know, didn't suspect. People who just knew her as Marnie, the friendly Books and Brew owner. That's all they needed to know. But the man whose name would be inside that envelope knew something else. He knew the truth. He knew everything. Including the fact that she'd once loved him.

Marnie stuffed the letter into her pocket. It burned there like hot espresso. But she couldn't open it. Not here. Not now. Seeing that logo was enough. After all these years, it had happened.

He found me.

They say love is *blind.*

This time they're right…

A woman lies unconscious in a hospital bed. A man sits beside her…between them lies an ocean of fear and the tenuous grip of memories long past. Daylight flees. Darkness deepens. And mystery awaits…beyond the night. A captivating story that will renew your wonder at what God has promised to those who love Him.